### THE OMEGA COMMAND

A conspiracy so sinister it cuts across government, big business, outer space, and beyond . . .

### THE OMEGA COMMAND

A vicious plot cleverly conceived and sure to succeed—unless one man can stop it . . .

### THE OMEGA COMMAND

The heart-stopping new thriller by a writer whose talent for sheer suspense and adventure is . . . incredible!

Fawcett Gold Medal Books
by Jon Land:

LABYRINTH

THE OMEGA COMMAND

# THE OMEGA COMMAND

## Jon Land

FAWCETT GOLD MEDAL • NEW YORK

A Fawcett Gold Medal Book
Published by Ballantine Books
Copyright © 1986 by Jon Land

Library of Congress Catalog Card Number: 86-91184

ISBN 0-449-12955-1

Manufactured in the United States of America

First Edition: November 1986

For Professors Elmer Blistein and George Monteiro, and the English Department of Brown University. Thanks for taking a chance.

# ACKNOWLEDGMENTS

For technical assistance along the way I am greatly indebted to Alfred Souza, John Signore, and Bill Krieger.

Thanks to Richard Levy for assistance with the selection and capabilities of various armaments, and to Shihan John Saviano for help with the choreography of numerous fight scenes.

For creative support well beyond the call of duty, my heartfelt appreciation to Ann Maurer and the miraculous Toni Mendez, and, of course, Dr. Morton Korn, who makes his fifth consecutive appearance on this page of my books.

I am also blessed with a brilliant editor, Daniel Zitin, and a truly supportive team at Fawcett.

Mention must be made as well of a superb article by Lee Dembart* and an excellent book by Richard S. Lewis**, both of which provided invaluable information.

And last my deepest thanks to Emery Pineo who gives of himself so generously to his students and has also been generous enough to share his brilliance with me.

*Discover*, November 1984, pp. 90–92.
**The Voyages of Columbia*, Columbia University Press, 1984.

# PROLOGUE

"**H**OUSTON, this is *Adventurer*."

"Come in, *Adventurer*."

Astronaut Marjorie Rait tightened her grip on the joysticks that controlled the space shuttle's mechanical robot arm. "Ready to begin satellite retrieval procedures again."

"Roger, Marge. Here's to sticky fingers."

Rait smiled and pushed the right-hand joystick up and to the right, eyes locked on a small television monitor above her; its image was also broadcasted back to the Johnson Space Center in Houston. This was the fourth time she had attempted to use the robot arm to bring in the rogue communications satellite for minor repairs; the previous three having failed due to a combination of mechanical breakdown and bad luck. Rait pressed her lips together as she watched her efforts on the screen—the steel arm extended slowly toward the satellite. Since the tragic loss of *Challenger*, failure had become a nonexistent term in the NASA vocabulary. Too many people were watching, waiting for something else to go wrong. *Adventurer* had been constructed with precisely that in mind, and its previous two missions had come off without a hitch.

The robot arm was in line with the satellite now. Rait cursed the sweat forming on her brow.

"Looking good, Marge," came the voice of the Capsule Communicator, better known as Cap-Com.

"Just a little farther," noted astronaut Gordon Caswell from his post in the shuttle's open cargo bay. The plan was for the robot arm to deliver the satellite down into it so he could effect repairs. "Easy does it."

Marjorie Rait manipulated the left-hand joystick to maneuver the arm's huge pincers, easing them forward. She squeezed her fingers together gently. The pincers closed over the satellite's lower left pod.

"I've got it!" she said.

"Bring her down slow, Marge," advised the Cap-Com, following the arm's descent toward the cargo bay on the main Houston television monitor.

"Houston, this is Caswell. Think you boys'll ever be able to build one of those arms small enough to give a horny astronaut a hand job?"

"Oh, Christ," came the muffled voice of mission commander Nathan Jamrock in Houston, as he reached into his pocket for a fresh package of Rolaids.

"We're on an open line here, Gordon," warned the Cap-Com.

"Musta slipped my mind," said Caswell.

The satellite was right over him now, coming down directly in line with its slot in the repair bay. Marjorie Rait followed its progress on the monitor, drawing the right-hand joystick straight back now. At 180 miles above Earth's surface, there would be no comforting sound of metal clicking against metal, not even an echo from the cargo bay to tell her she had been successful. She kept easing the joystick back.

"Bingo," said Caswell, and Rait allowed herself two deep breaths as her grip loosened on the joystick. Her eyes stayed locked on the monitor, which now pictured Caswell coolly fastening the satellite down so he could begin repairs.

Marge didn't see the red light flashing on the warning panel directly above her.

"Houston, this is Caswell. I've got my toolbox out. Looks like you guys forgot to pack a Phillips head screwdriver."

"Guess you'll have to improvise, Gordon."

"That's a roger."

The television monitor now showed Caswell working on the lower right portion of the damaged satellite with what looked like an ordinary socket wrench. After a few seconds he returned this tool to his box and extracted another. All the tools snapped snugly into slots tailored specifically for them to prevent them from rising into the zero gravity of space. The box itself was magnetically sealed to the bay floor and could be moved about in a variety of directions thanks to rollers. Caswell's motions looked slow and drawn out, due not only to the absence of gravity but also to the need to be precise to the millimeter.

In the cockpit a repeating beep found the ears of Marjorie Rait.

"Oh, my God," she muttered, looking up finally at the red light flashing on her upper warning panel. "Houston, this is Rait. Sensors have picked something up. Repeat, sensors have picked something up."

In Houston dozens of technicians turned to panels which were large, virtual replicas of those inside *Adventurer*. Some of them had been on duty for *Challenger*, and their boards, albeit less sophisticated, had provided no warning then either.

"Marge," came the Cap-Com's calm voice, "we show nothing down here. Probably equipment malfunction. Check your circuits."

"Negative," Marge shot back. "Circuits all operative. Something's coming at us from behind, in line with our orbit."

Rait felt the icy grip of panic through her space suit. Why didn't the instruments in Houston show what hers did?

Another warning chime went off on her instrument panel.

"Object closing, Houston. Repeat, object closing!"

"We still read nothing, *Adventurer*."

"What the hell's going on?" Caswell asked, a wrench slipping from his hand and sliding into space. "You guys are starting to make me nervous."

The voice of mission commander Nathan Jamrock found his ears. "Gordon, look around you. Is there anything out there, an asteroid chunk, a wandering satellite, anything?"

"Nothing out here but us spacemen. All I see is black and— Hey, wait a minute. There *is* something coming in from the rear. Still a ways off but definitely closing."

"Can you tell what it is?"

"Negative, Houston. All I caught was what seemed to be a reflector, maybe something blinking. . . . There it is again."

"Metallic?"

"Must be."

There was a brief pause and then Nathan Jamrock's voice returned. "Gordon, can you reach the television camera?"

"Affirmative."

"Then raise it in line with whatever's out there. Let us have a look at it."

"That's a roger."

Jamrock stripped the headset from around his ears and turned to his executive assistant. "Signal a red alert."

An instant later an alarm began wailing throughout mission control. Personnel rushed to different stations. Satellite tracking procedures were activated all over the world. NORAD, the air defense command in Colorado, was put on line and would now be monitoring all subsequent communications. A call was made to the President. Jamrock chewed another Rolaid.

One hundred eighty miles above Jamrock, Gordon Caswell shuffled toward the television camera mounted at the front of the bay. He had been an all-American running back in college, but speed meant nothing in space. Covering ten yards felt like a thousand, and the harder Caswell pushed, the slower he seemed to move.

In the cockpit Marjorie Rait followed Caswell's agonizingly deliberate walk as she pressed buttons to ready *Adventurer* for emergency maneuvers. She had begun to strap herself into the pilot's seat when the monitor showed Caswell stop in his tracks. She had been an astronaut long enough to know there were no sounds in space. Which made it all the stranger that it seemed to be a sound that made him turn. And then gasp.

"Oh my Christ . . ."

"*Adventurer*, this is Houston Cap-Com. What do you see? Repeat, what do you see?" Mission control at the Johnson Space Center had turned silent as a tomb.

Caswell watched the thing in the black air unfold before him as it drew closer.

"Damn, it's going to attack," he muttered.

"*Adventurer*, did you say 'attack'?"

"It's coming closer now. I can see that—"

The transmission became garbled.

"You're breaking up, *Adventurer*."

"Goddamn . . . closing . . . bigger than . . ."

"The television camera," said Jamrock, headset back on, "adjust it so we can see, Gordon. Do you copy?"

"Affirma—"

For an instant the television monitors in mission control were filled with Caswell's gloved hand reaching toward the lens to aim it at whatever was approaching the shuttle.

"Adjustment complete," Jamrock made out through the static.

Caswell's hand moved away. Mission control personnel held a collective breath, then released it.

Because the transmission fizzled, broke up, scrambled.

"Get back inside the shuttle!" Jamrock ordered. "Marge, fire the main engines. Marge, do you read me? Marge, this is Houston, do you read me?"

Static.

"*Adventurer*, this is Houston, please come in."

"You're . . . garbled," responded Rait finally, voice ruffled and weak. "Systems blowing, shorting out. Mayday! MAY—"

More static.

"*Adventurer*, this is Houston, do you copy?" from the Cap-Com this time.

Nothing.

*"Adventurer*, this is Houston, please acknowledge. . . ."

In mission control nervous glances were exchanged.

*"It's right on top of us!"*

Gordon Caswell's desperate words were the last thing mission control heard before all shuttle monitoring lights flashed red and then died out altogether. Men scrambled to press new buttons, try different switches, but their efforts had the same hopeless desperation of an operating team fighting to revive a clearly dead patient.

"*Adventurer*, this is Houston, can you hear us?" asked the Cap-Com one last time.

Gordon Caswell couldn't hear a thing. He continued describing the monstrous thing that seemed ready to swallow him as its vast bulk covered the shuttle. There was a bright flash which sent bolts of heat through Caswell's suit, and he was dimly conscious of his visor cracking, melting, exposing him to the emptiness of space. He was turning in the brightness now, seeming to float.

And then there was nothing.

In his private office Nathan Jamrock squeezed the receiver tighter to his ear. For the last ten minutes he had been filling the President in on what little NASA had been able to conclude about the fate of *Adventurer*. He had taken over the space shuttle program in the wake of damning hearings which had forced a total restructuring at NASA. Never in his wildest nightmares had he imagined such a report would ever be called for again. Too many precautions had been taken. He had made sure of it.

"You're sure there's no mistake?" the President asked.

Jamrock peeled away the foil from another package of Rolaids. "It's on tape, sir. Caswell clearly indicated something was about to attack. What happened was no accident this time."

"You think the press will see it that way?"

"I don't much care at this point. We've got more important things to concern ourselves with." He paused. "I recommend calling a Space-Stat alert."

"That would be a first, Nate," the President said hesitantly.

Jamrock raised two of the tablets toward his mouth. "Today seems to be full of them."

# PART ONE

# Madame Rosa's

Monday Afternoon to Wednesday Afternoon

# CHAPTER 1

*God rest ye merry, gentlemen*
*Let nothing you dismay*

The carolers dominated the corner, flanking a smiling Santa Claus, who was ringing his bell over a noticeably empty urn. Perhaps Santa's smile had shrunk since the day had begun. Perhaps not. All that could be said for sure was that his beard was dirtier, grayer, and thinner from the children pulling at it and coming away with polyester strands.

The New York City streets were icy and slick. The storm that had battered the New England coast had spared the city its brunt, touching it only with a graze. The light snow that had been falling steadily for hours now added to the difficulties of the cars struggling to negotiate over it. With only eight shopping days left until Christmas, New Yorkers were not likely to let the weather beat them.

*Oh, tidings of comfort and joy*
*Comfort and joy*

A red Porsche snailed down the street, grinding to a stop before Santa and the carolers. The driver beeped the horn, slid down the passenger window. Santa came over and the man handed him a ten.

"Merry Christmas, sir!" said Santa.

Easton simply smiled. He was in the mood to be generous. His channels had come through with an early Christmas present. Three months of grueling, tedious, and sometimes dangerous work had paid off beautifully.

The Santa Claus thanked him again, backing away from the Porsche. Easton hit a button and the window glided back into place. The Porsche started forward again. Easton shuddered from the new cold and flipped the heater switch up a notch. He down-shifted well in advance of a red light, realizing his hand was trembling slightly over the shift knob. He had stowed the microfiche within it, and just thinking of its contents brought his breathing up a notch with the heater. The windshield began to fog. Easton swiped at it with his sleeve. The light turned green and the Porsche fishtailed through the intersection. He was almost to his destination.

The right thing, of course, would be to deliver the microfiche immediately. But his superiors would have to wait, for Easton had his therapy to consider. On the road for nearly twelve weeks, he had been forced to miss four of his sessions. He could see the brownstone now and the doorman standing before it. His stomach fluttered with anticipation. Already he felt more relaxed.

Traffic snarled and the Porsche skidded briefly before finding pavement. Snow was collecting on the windshield again and Easton switched the wipers back on. Traffic started forward in front of him, and Easton eased the Porsche to the right, sliding to the curb where the doorman stood waiting. The brownstone stood beside several others like it, an ordinary sight from the outside.

The doorman opened his door for him. "Mr. Easton, how good to see you back," he said, signaling for a parking attendant.

Easton tipped the doorman with the usual amount, not at all uncomfortable with the use of his real name. Names meant nothing at the brownstone, professions even less. Everything was done with maximum discretion. Senators, mayors, businessmen—the brownstone was a place where they could leave their professions at the front door.

Easton watched his Porsche pull away toward the parking garage and then stepped through the door the doorman was holding for him. An impeccably attired woman was waiting inside.

"Ah, Mr. Easton, it's been too long."

"I've been traveling. Work, you understand."

"Of course." The woman smiled graciously. She was striking for her age, which was at least sixty. Her face showed barely a wrinkle, and her dull blond hair fell easily just below her ears. She was a walking testament to modern cosmetics and surgery. Madame Rosa had a role to play and she had to look the part. "I've reserved your usual room."

"And the . . . subjects?" Easton asked eagerly.

Madame Rosa smiled again. "I'm sure you'll be pleased." She took his coat and led him toward the stairs. "Are any refreshments in order?"

"No."

"Hashish, marijuana, cocaine?"

"Never."

Madame Rosa scolded herself. "Ah, yes, how silly of me. Dulls the reflexes, of course. We can't have that, can we?"

Easton just looked at her.

Madame Rosa stopped halfway up the first staircase. "Stop and see me on your way out. I'd appreciate your evaluation of our new subjects."

Easton nodded and continued on alone. No mention had been made of price. There was simply an account to be settled at regular intervals, always in cash and never with argument. Easton reached the third floor, turned right, and entered the second room down.

The smell of sweet incense flooded his nostrils. The room was dimly lit, but Easton made out the two figures lying naked on the bed. A boy and a girl—twins. Just as he had ordered. Madame Rosa had outdone herself this time. Easton began stripping off his clothes. He was trembling, already aroused.

The girl moved from the bed and helped him with his pants, unzipping his leather boots and caressing his legs. She was thirteen or thereabouts, a dark-haired beauty with tiny mounds where her breasts would soon be. Her small nipples stood erect.

Her male twin was just as beautiful, dark hair cut not as long but smothering his ears and falling easily to his shoulders. He lay on the bed, legs spread, fondling himself, dark eyes glowing in the soft light.

Easton let himself be led by the girl onto the huge bed, careful to toss his shoulder holster to the side so it would be easily within reach. He fell backward on the sheets and settled next to the naked boy. The boy rolled on top of him, first hugging, then licking, then sliding down till his mouth neared Easton's groin.

Easton felt the boy take him inside at the same time the girl parted his lips with hers. He groped for her thin buttocks and squeezed them to him, vaguely conscious of the boy's head rising and falling, taking more of him in with each thrust. He wanted both of them, he wanted *all* of them. There was no time limit, would be no rude interruptions. They were his for as long as he wanted them. Madame Rosa's never failed to satisfy.

Easton's right hand wandered toward the girl's small, hairless vagina, his left finding the boy's long hair and caressing it as his head rose and fell . . . rose and fell . . . rose and fell. Easton felt the pleasure mounting everywhere, surging, yet he still had the sensation of something terribly wrong an instant before the door shattered inward.

At that same instant Easton's metamorphosis back to himself was complete. He pushed the girl from him and went for his gun. But two figures had already stormed into the room with weapons blasting. The boy's naked body absorbed the first barrage, red punctures dotting his flesh. The girl's head exploded next to him, and Easton felt a volley of bullets pierce his abdomen as his hand closed on his pistol.

He might have lifted it from the holster had not the boy's bloodied corpse collapsed atop him, pinning his arms. The boy's sightless eyes locked on his, and Easton felt the bursts of pain everywhere the pleasure had been only seconds before. He was still trying for his gun, finding it just wasn't there anymore, as his breath rushed out and all that remained was the boy's dead stare before oblivion took him.

"I've already been briefed on this mess," the President said, striding grimly into the Oval Office. "I want to know what's being done to clean it up."

The two men seated before his desk rose as he approached it. CIA director Barton McCall was the more nervous looking of the two. But McCall always looked that way, just as Andrew Stimson, head of the ultra-secret Gap, always appeared calm.

"New York is cooperating brilliantly," Barton McCall reported. "Under the circumstances we couldn't ask for more. Fortunately the woman called us first."

The President stopped halfway into his chair. "What woman?"

"Madame Rosa," answered McCall. "Owner of the . . . house where Easton was killed."

"She knew his identity?"

"Apparently."

"Terrific." The President's eyes flared toward Andrew Stimson. "Helluva ship you got running there, Andy."

Stimson seemed unfazed by the comment. "Madame Rosa's has enjoyed an exclusive clientele for fifteen years. Easton never told her a damn thing. She knew he was intelligence and therefore knew approximately whom to call this afternoon. She's got a feel for such things."

"And apparently Easton had a feel for something I don't exactly remember seeing in his file."

Stimson shrugged. "An agent's private life is his own business."

"Not when it gets him killed."

Stimson nodded with grim acceptance. Years before, when the CIA had come under increasing scrutiny and the methods of the NSA under fire, a gap resulted between what the intelligence community needed to bring off and what it could effectively get away with. So a new organization was created to take up the slack, appropriately labeled the Gap. Stimson was its first and so far its only director.

"Just remember, sir," he said to the President, "that the pressure men like Easton are under sometimes forces them into undesirable pastimes."

"The mess at Madame Rosa's can hardly be referred to as a pastime, Andy."

"I think we'll be surprised when we find out the identities of the customers in the other rooms at the time."

The President cleared his throat. "The real question, gentlemen, is whether Easton's murder was random, perhaps the result of someone else's kinky fantasy, or whether it was carefully orchestrated."

"Evidence seems to indicate the latter," reported CIA chief McCall. "The men behind it were pros all the way. No one saw them go in and we're not even sure anyone saw them go out. We got a report that two black men were seen leaving the area immediately after the murders, but even that's sketchy. The weapons used were Mac-10s, a pair of thirty-round clips totally emptied."

"Jesus . . ."

"Easton took fourteen slugs alone, the kids about the same."

The President raised his eyebrows. "We going to have any problems from the relatives of those kids?"

McCall shook his head. "Madame Rosa was their legal guardian. She'll take care of everything."

The President didn't bother pursuing the matter further. "Someone must have wanted Easton dead awfully bad. He was due in soon, wasn't he?"

"Tonight," answered Stimson. "That's when the briefing was scheduled, by him I might add."

"So he had completed his current assignment."

"At least enough to bring it to the next level."

"Okay, Andy, refresh my memory of what he was on to."

"Internal subversion," Stimson replied. "Terrorist groups, revolutionaries, that sort of thing."

"Specifically?"

"Something big. Easton felt he was on to a group whose size and resources went way beyond anything we've faced before. His reports were vague, but he was closing in on the top. He believed there was a time factor involved."

"Which this afternoon's incident has apparently confirmed," the President noted. "Now all we have to do is find out who was counting the minutes. Terrorists?"

"That's the assumption," Stimson acknowledged. "But the Gap's dealt with plenty of terrorist groups here at home without losing agents to such brutal assassinations. Like I said before, whatever Easton uncovered was a helluva lot bigger than a run-of-the-mill bombing or hostage situation."

"And since we have no idea what," said the President, "I hope you gentlemen have devised a contingency plan to find the missing pieces."

"He might have left some bit of evidence for us somewhere," McCall suggested.

"We're checking that possibility now," Stimson responded. "Safe deposit and mail drops, hotel rooms, safe houses—all that sort of thing. Easton's car, too . . . once we find it."

"Find it?" said the President.

"I'm afraid it was conveniently stolen around the same time Easton was killed," Stimson reported.

"Then the logical question is what does that leave us with? What in hell do we do?"

"Replacing Easton is our first step," came McCall's swift reply. "Send someone out to pick up where he left off."

"All well and good if we knew where that was," Stimson countered. "We haven't got a clue, and if we did, sending a man out now would be tantamount to having him walk a greased tightrope."

"I believe, sir," McCall said, turning toward the President, "that my people are more than capable of picking up the pieces as soon as you authorize this as a Company operation."

"It started with the Gap and that's where it will end," Stimson said staunchly.

"Stow the bullshit, gentlemen," the President said. "I asked you here for answers, not boundary squabbles. Andy, you sound pretty adamant about keeping this within Gap jurisdiction. I assume you've thought out our next step."

Stimson nodded, stealing a quick glance at his counterpart in the CIA. "What Barton said before about a replacement for Easton has to be the first priority. But there is no one present in our active files who fills the necessary criteria and who we can afford to label expendable."

"That puts us back at square one," muttered the President, his voice laced with frustration.

"Not exactly." Stimson paused. "I suggest recalling someone from the inactive list."

"Recalling who?" McCall asked suspiciously.

Stimson didn't hesitate. "Blaine McCracken."

"Now, hold on just a min—"

"I've thought this thing out." Stimson's voice prevailed over McCall's. "McCracken's not only the perfect man for the job, he's also . . . expendable."

"With good reason," McCall snapped.

"McCracken," said the President. "Don't think I've ever heard of him."

"Consider yourself fortunate," McCall went on. "McCracken's a rogue, a rebel, a deviant son of a bitch who—"

"Has always had a knack for successfully completing missions," Stimson broke in.

"Always on his own terms and always with complications."

"I would suggest that in this case the terms and complications are meaningless," Stimson followed with barely a pause. "Results are all that matter."

"At what cost?" McCall challenged. "McCrackenballs

doesn't obey orders and has proved an embarrassment to this government every time we've sent him into the field.''

The President leaned forward. ''McCracken*what*?''

McCall cleared his throat.

''It's a long story,'' Stimson replied.

''We've got loads of time. Easton's funeral isn't for two days,'' the President said bitingly.

''I'll sum up the man we're dealing with here as succinctly as I can,'' Stimson continued as if he had memorized the words. ''The early stages of McCracken's career were routine enough. Two decorated tours in 'Nam with the Special Forces. Lots of medals. After the war the Company put him to use in Africa and later South America. Deep cover. McCracken's specialty was infiltration.''

''Along with teaching schoolchildren how to make Molotov cocktails,'' McCall added.

''His orders were to promote resistance against the rebels.''

''And there was hell to pay for his little escapades with the kiddies once the papers got hold of them. If we hadn't covered our tracks in time, the whole episode would have made the Nicaraguan training manual business look like back-page news.''

''He was following orders,'' Stimson reiterated.

''No, Andy, he was interpreting them in his own unique manner.'' McCall shook his head as if in pain, turning toward the President. ''We sent him to London to train with the SAS.''

''Buried him there, you mean,'' Stimson snapped.

''But he dug himself up quite nicely, didn't he?'' McCall shot back. ''There was an unfortunate episode where an Arab group nabbed a plane and threatened to shoot a passenger every minute the authorities exceeded their demands deadline. The British were convinced they were bluffing. McCracken was certain they weren't. In the end, by the time the SAS stormed the plane, four passengers were dead.''

''Oh, Christ . . .''

"McCracken screamed at British officials on national television, shouted that they had no . . . balls."

"*His* word?" the President asked.

"His *exact* word," nodded McCall. "Then to reinforce his point, he went to Parliament Square and blew the balls right off Churchill's statue with a machine gun, at least the general anatomical area under the statue's greatcoat."

The President looked dumbfounded.

Stimson leaned forward. "Because innocent people died at Heathrow. McCracken can't stand civilian casualties."

"And he's convinced he's the *only* man who can avoid them," McCall countered. He swung back to the President. "McCracken's a goddamn lone ranger who won't even let Tonto play. Dismissal at his level was, of course, out of the question. So we started moving him around from one petty post to another to avoid further embarrassments. He finally settled as a cipher operator in Paris."

"And he's stuck it out, hasn't he?" Stimson challenged. "Does everything he's told to from confirming scrambled communications to sorting paper clips even though it's probably busting him up inside."

"An agent could do a lot worse."

"Not an agent like McCracken. It's a waste."

"More a necessity, Andy. He's brought all this on himself."

"Fine. Then I'll take the responsibility for lifting it off." Stimson's eyes found the President's. "Sir, I would like McCracken reassigned from the Company to the Gap to take the place of Easton."

"Out of the question!" McCall roared.

"Which," the President began with strange evenness, "would have been my exact reaction if you told me yesterday that one of our agents was going to be gunned down at a bordello in the company of two pubescents. Andy, if you want to use McCracken to clean up this mess we've got, then use him. Just get it done."

McCall's face reddened. "Sir, I must protest—"

"The matter is closed, Barton." The President sighed. "In the past twenty-four hours, we've had a deep-cover agent murdered and a space shuttle blown right out of the sky. Nathan Jamrock will probably be here tomorrow with a report indicating that little green men destroyed *Adventurer* and, who knows, maybe the same little green men visited Madame Rosa's this afternoon carrying Mac-10s instead of ray guns. Wonder where they'll strike next?''

A heavy knock came on the Oval Office door. Before the President could respond, his chief aide stepped swiftly into the room.

"Sorry to intrude, sir," said the wiry, bespectacled man, "but we've just got word a jet has been seized by terrorists in Paris with over a hundred Americans on board."

The President's empty stare passed from McCall to Stimson, then to neither. "Well, boys, it looks like my question's been answered."

# CHAPTER 2

"**S**o what are they asking for?" Tom Daniels, chief of CIA operations in France, asked Pierre Marchaut, Sureté agent in charge of the seizure at Orly Airport.

Marchaut regarded the American patiently as he moved away from the telephone and consulted his notes. "The usual things, *mon ami*. Release of political prisoners being held in French jails, safe passage to the country of their choice, a message to be read over the networks this evening."

Daniels strode abruptly to the window and looked out over the 767 in question, apart from other aircraft on one of Orly's main runways.

"The deadline?" he asked Marchaut.

"The first batch of prisoners must be delivered here within two hours."

"Delivered *here*? Great, just great. And if we refuse?"

"They will blow up the plane." The burly Marchaut, whose face was dominated by a pair of thick black sideburns, shrugged. "Did you expect anything different? The terrorists also requested fresh meals for their hostages."

"How compassionate . . ."

"My thoughts exactly."

A thin man walked quickly into the operations room with a manila folder open in his hands. He spoke so rapidly in French that Daniels was barely able to keep up with him.

"We have just received positive identifications of the two male and one female terrorist involved. They are known professionals wanted in a combined total of seventeen countries. They have all killed before, especially the bearded leader, an Arab named Yachmar Bote. The woman has been linked to a number of brutal assassinations as well."

"So now we know they are capable of doing everything they say," Marchaut concluded grimly.

"If they're caught, it means the death sentence," said his assistant. "They have nothing to lose."

"Wonderful," Daniels moaned, starting for the phones. "I'd better call Washington."

"What about the explosives?" Marchaut asked.

His assistant shrugged. "Inspection of pictures snapped through windows reveal heavy wiring and what appears to be plastique. But without visual inspection there is no way to be sure."

"And the positions of the hijackers?"

"The bastards are clever. One is always seated among the passengers, presumably holding the trigger for the explosives."

"Then a raid is out of the question," Marchaut said with his eyes on Daniels, who had hesitated before lifting up the phone. "And so, I'm afraid, is acceding to their demands."

Daniels stepped forward, closer to Marchaut. The others in the room, French police and airport officials, surrounded them in a ring.

"Then our only alternative is to play a waiting game," the American said. "That would have been my suggestion anyway. It's worked before and I don't buy the explosives bit at all."

"Yes," Marchaut added, "once the deadline passes, the advantage shifts to us. Perhaps there is a way to use this request for food to our advantage. . . ."

"The hijackers won't eat it," came an American voice from outside the circle. "The passengers are their biggest worry, not you clowns. You know, feed the prey before you slaughter them. Keep them full and happy.''

The fifteen or so men and women gathered in the emergency operations center turned toward a tall athletic-looking man with dark hair and perfectly groomed black beard highlighted by a slight speckling of gray. His skin was tanned and rough, that of a man accustomed to the outdoors and quite comfortable in it. A bent nose and a scar running through his right eyebrow marred an otherwise ruggedly handsome face. His piercing eyes were almost black.

"Oh, no," muttered Daniels.

"You know this man?" Marchaut asked, taken aback.

"Unfortunately." Then, to the stranger, "McCracken, what in hell are you doing here?"

"All the movies were sold out, so I had to seek my entertainment elsewhere," Blaine McCracken said. "I'm not disappointed. You people really know how to put on a show. Really give a guy his money's worth."

"Get out of here this instant!" Marchaut ordered.

"Intermission already?"

Marchaut started forward. McCracken's eyes froze him.

"Do as he says, Blaine," Daniels advised.

"And miss the finale? Not on your life, Tommy my boy." He moved forward just a step. "You guys should really listen to yourselves. It's a scream, let me tell you."

"Who is this man?" a now uncertain Marchaut asked Daniels.

"He works in the CIA equivalent of the mail room over here."

"Then what—"

"I'll tell you what, Marchaut," McCracken said abruptly, and the Frenchman reeled at mention of his name. "You assholes are talking about waiting the terrorists out, going beyond the deadline, and all you're going to get for it is a planeload of hamburger. And in case you guys didn't know it, there are forty seats in tourist being taken up by kids from a junior high in Fort Lee, New Jersey. Tell you what else, Marchaut, take a good look at the leader Bote's file. He's a walking psycho ward. He's been trying to get himself killed in a blaze of glory for years. This is right up his alley, always was, right back to the time I met up with him in Chad.''

Confused, Marchaut swung toward Daniels. ''I thought you said he worked in the . . . mail room.''

''I'm a man of many hats,'' Blaine told him. ''And the one I've got on right now tells me these terrorists *want* to blow the plane up. Allah must be running a special on martyrdom this week. Their demands can't possibly be met. If *you* know that, don't you think they do?''

Daniels stormed forward, eye to eye with McCracken. ''You're finished, Blaine. No more second chances, no more token appointments. Maybe they'll send you home in a box.''

''Get this man out of here!'' Marchaut screamed in French to a pair of uniformed policemen who grasped McCracken at the elbows.

''As long as you're ordering boxes,'' Blaine said, allowing himself to be led backward, ''see if you can get a group rate, Tommy my boy. You're gonna need plenty of them before this day is done.''

The police forced Blaine from the room and closed the door behind them. Agitated, Marchaut stepped nervously to the window, looking out over the captured 767.

''You must learn to keep your subordinates on a tighter leash, *mon ami*,'' he said to Daniels.

''McCracken's not just an underling,'' the American replied. ''He's a damn pariah, the scourge of American intelligence.''

''Knowing your country's methods, I am surprised this man has remained on the active list so long.''

Daniels simply shrugged. The elimination of McCracken had been discussed many times. But how could he explain to the Frenchman that no intelligence overlord wanted to be the one to approve the sanction for fear that failure would cost him his life? McCracken had many enemies, but his capacity for survival and, more, his instinct for revenge, kept them from contemplating true action.

Minutes passed in the operations center. Words were

exchanged with nothing said or decided. The decision was thus made. The deadline was now only an hour away, and it would pass with none of the terrorists' demands met.

The emergency phone linking Marchaut to various positions around the 767 beeped twice. The Frenchman picked it up.

*"Oui?"* His mouth dropped, face paling. "Someone's *what*? No, I didn't order it. No, I don't want— Hold for a second."

Marchaut dropped the receiver and moved to the window with a dozen officials right in his tracks. They all saw a man driving a front-end loader, the kind used to transport meals from airport kitchen to plane galley, behind the 767 toward its loading bay. The driver passed out of sight quickly but not before Daniels glimpsed enough of his face through a pair of binoculars.

"Oh shit," he muttered.

McCracken took a heavy swallow of air as the loader neared the red and white jet. He had come to Orly Airport as soon as word of the seizure had reached his small office cubicle—over AM radio, not cipher. Officials had no reason to involve him in such pursuits any longer. And, in fact, Blaine had driven to Orly determined to remain merely an observer, until examination of the runway area and obvious procrastination on the part of officials involved convinced him that asses were being dragged, as usual, and that other asses were going to become chopped meat as a result.

Didn't they understand what they were dealing with? Didn't they realize you couldn't keep playing with terrorists and expect to win? Not these anyway, not Bote and whatever stooges he had brought along this time.

A raid on the plane was the only chance the passengers had to survive. And since the French were too busy picking their nails, McCracken would take it upon himself to do the dirty work. A one-man operation. Much better that way. The terrorists' request for food had provided his cover.

He might have been able to walk away from the whole

episode if it weren't so clear history was about to repeat itself and innocent lives were going to be lost again. Five years ago in London, authorities had twiddled their fingers while terrorists squeezed triggers with theirs. Mc-Cracken wasn't about to let that happen again. His mistake in London had been to go after a statue's balls after it was over. He should have gone after the testicles of the damned officials who couldn't make up their minds in time. Flesh and blood would have made his point better than ceramics.

The galley door opened and Blaine backed the loader into position, then climbed on top of the bay next to the steel casing which held 150 microwave-warmed stuffed-chicken dinners. He pressed a button and the lift began to rise, stopping when it was even with the open galley door. He had started to wheel the cart inside when a hand grasped his hair and yanked him viciously backward. Blaine tumbled to the galley floor and found his eyes locked on the barrel of Bote's machine gun. The terrorist's wild hair and beard seemed all one piece. He was grinning malevolently.

*Dinner is served, sir,* Blaine wanted to say but stopped himself because being too cute would get him thrown off the plane or shot, and either way his plan would be ruined. So he just gazed up, trying to look helpless.

"Ari, search this bastard!" Bote ordered.

A dark-skinned, black-haired boy little more than sixteen loomed overhead and shoved Blaine onto his stomach. Thin hands ruffled his person up and down, satisfied finally he wasn't carrying a gun.

"He's clean," the boy named Ari said, and Bote grabbed Blaine by the collar and yanked him back to his feet.

"You a cop?" Bote asked.

"Yes," McCracken answered, because that was the way something like this would be done.

"They send you to check us out?"

"No," Blaine replied. "They've already got a hundred

pictures of the plane's inside. I'm here just to fill your request for the food.''

Bote seemed impressed with McCracken's apparent honesty. "An unfortunate assignment all the same."

"I volunteered."

"You know I can't let you leave the plane."

Blaine nodded. "I figured as much, but it would be a good gesture on your part if you released a few passengers in my place."

Bote raised his rifle as if to strike him, features flaring. "I am not interested in gestures. In forty minutes, when your people fail to give in to our demands, I will blow up this plane and everyone in it." A pause. "That means you, too, now, asshole."

Blaine stood his ground. "They plan to meet your demands," he told Bote, again because that was what the man he was pretending to be would have said.

Bote snickered and slammed him against the galley wall, a hand full of sweater tight under his chin. The terrorist was bigger than McCracken had remembered. His body stank of perspiration and his breath reeked.

"You will pay for your lies," Bote said softly. "You will all pay for your lies. But first you are going to distribute the dinners to our nervous passengers in need of reassurance. Ari will guide you the whole way, and if you make one move that doesn't look right, he will kill you." Bote nodded to the boy, who nodded back.

McCracken pulled the food cart inside the jet and then, obeying Bote's orders, latched the heavy door behind him. He maneuvered the cart forward and swung it gingerly so it was facing the rows and rows of terrified passengers, many of them children. Blaine gazed out and seemed to meet all their stares at once. With Ari holding an Uzi a yard behind the cart, he started to pull it down the right-hand aisle.

Bote remained in the front of the cabin, poised before the movie screen, which was still in position.

Blaine knew that the third terrorist, a woman, was seated somewhere among the passengers, finger ready to press a button that would trigger the explosives. He could see the wires looped across the ceiling and peeking out from the overhead baggage compartments, where the plastique must be stored. The wires strung the explosives together, but the detonator would be transistor-powered; no wires to give the female terrorist's position away. Determining her location was the centerpiece of McCracken's plan, though. That a second terrorist would be so close when he acted was a godsend, but nothing mattered if he could not find the woman.

Blaine stopped the cart a bit down the aisle and continued distributing the chicken dinners that had been kept warm within the heated slots. Most of the passengers weren't hungry but took a plate anyway just to have something to do. McCracken's eyes strayed always a row or two ahead, seeking out the eyes of all women, in search of the pair belonging to the one holding the detonator. Most of the front rows were occupied by the children from New Jersey, which gave his eyes plenty of opportunity to roam, but the high seat backs blocked him from seeing too far ahead.

In the tenth row a woman smiled and accepted the dinner gratefully. Their eyes met and Blaine felt a gnawing in his stomach. There was something wrong about her. He broke the stare and handed a tray to the man seated next to her. The man's eyes darted sideways toward the woman, a nervous signal—inadvertent perhaps but nonetheless confirming Blaine's suspicions. This woman had to be the one he sought.

"Hurry up," the boy terrorist urged, poking at the steel cart with his rifle. The boy never should have let McCracken position the cart between them, of course, but in this case fortune proved more useful than design.

Blaine reached inside the cart for another tray and let his hand wander deep into the back, where he had taped the Browning pistol. It came free easily and he moved it under a tray he was already maneuvering out with his left hand. The result was to make it appear as if he were holding the tray sandwichlike, with both hands. No reason for either of the terrorists to be suspicious.

He pulled the tray from the cart and started to lower it toward a man sitting two seats away from the female terrorist on the aisle.

As the man waved off the dinner, Blaine fired the Browning twice. The woman's head snapped back, rupturing, and showered passengers with blood and brains.

A small black transmitter slipped from her lap onto the floor.

The boy terrorist let the shock consume him for just an instant, but an instant was all it took for McCracken to turn the gun on him, the tray that had been covering it flying to the side. He placed two bullets in the young chest before the boy could squeeze the trigger of his Uzi.

He grasped it as he fell and the bullets stitched a jagged design in the jet's ceiling. Passengers screamed, jostled, collapsed against one another.

"Stay down!" Blaine screamed, but the last part of his warning was drowned out by Bote's machine gun.

The bullets blasted into the food cart which had become his cover, and Blaine fired a volley back high. From this angle he didn't want to risk hitting a passenger instead of Bote.

The terrorist was still firing in a wide arc, when McCracken rose and pumped off four rounds in his general direction, his bullets digging chasms into the thick aircraft walls. Bote kept firing the machine gun behind him as he disappeared around the corner.

*Another detonator*, Blaine realized with a clap of fear in his stomach, *he's going for another detonator*!

McCracken vaulted over the food tray and tucked into a roll to the chorus of people still screaming. He was back on his feet almost immediately, rushing down the aisle toward the galley where Bote had taken cover. A hail of machine-gun fire forced him into a dive as he neared it. The dive carried him to the front of the galley, where Bote was grasping for something in a black bag. His free hand came around with the machine gun.

Blaine fired first.

His initial shot tore into the terrorist's chest, pitching him backward. The next two bored into his head, obliterating it in explosions of blood and bone. Bote slipped to the floor with the black detonator gripped in his hand.

Blaine was still lying prone on the floor amid the continued screams of the passengers, when a pair of the 767's doors shattered outward and a troop of French security police tumbled in, nearly falling over themselves.

"Smoking or nonsmoking?" he asked them, rising carefully with arms in the air.

"You're finished this time. You know that, McCracken?" Daniels shot out accusingly in the backseat of the Peugeot heading back to the American Embassy.

"No, Tommy my boy. Why don't you tell me about it?"

Daniels shook his head. "You're a walking embarrassment, McCracken. I thought I'd heard it all with that Parliament Square incident five years ago, but today beats everything. Now you run a rogue operation on foreign soil. Do you have any idea what that means?"

"Not off the top of my head."

Daniels's driver made a hard right.

"Well, you just might lose the top of your head, McCracken. This is a diplomatic disaster. Washington will have to hold your head up on a stake just to get the French to talk civil to us again." Daniels's stare grew incredulous. "None of this really matters to you, does it?"

"What matters to me is that none of the passengers died."

"That's not the point."

"Then what is?"

Daniels's emergency phone rang and he grabbed it from its rest on the back of the seat before him.

"Daniels." A pause. His eyes found Blaine. "Yes, I've got him with me now . . . What? That wasn't the original plan. I'm more than capable of—" Another pause. Daniels's face reddened. His teeth ground together. "Yes, sir, I understand . . . Yes, sir, immediately." He replaced the receiver and looked back at McCracken. "I've been ordered to send you back to Washington. Pronto. Looks like the President wants to fry your ass personally."

"I'll make sure he saves some grease for you, Tommy my boy. There's plenty to go around."

# CHAPTER 3

FIRST thing Tuesday morning Sandy Lister walked down a third floor corridor in the network's New York headquarters and popped her head into the fourth doorway down.

"You ready?" she asked her assistant.

T. J. Brown nodded nervously. "The research is all finished, if that's what you mean. But am I ready for a meeting with Shay? No way, boss."

"Good," said Lister. "You'll do just fine."

And seconds later she was hustling T.J. toward the elevator that would take them up to the fifteenth floor and the office of Stephen Shay, executive producer of the newsmagazine *Overview*.

Sandy had been through scenes like the one coming dozens of times before, but this one had her more nervous than usual. It was a story she really wanted, one that hadn't come through network channels and was arguably somewhat out of her league. The network had hired her away from her previous position as anchor of a rival's morning news program to become one of five reporters on a new television magazine slotted to compete with the flagging *60 Minutes. Overview* would be more people-oriented and promised to deal with issues crucial to the American public as determined by up-to-the-minute polling. It would be fresher, more spontaneous than its counterparts. Or at least that was what the network had told Sandy and the public. Thus far four episodes had aired with another two in the can and the results had been something neither fresher nor more spontaneous than any other television newsmagazine.

The ratings, though, were at least as good as expected, especially during Sandy's segments, mostly because the lighter, profile segments she hosted were more to the public's liking than hard news. When you came right down to it, who wanted to hear about chemical waste anyway? Plenty of viewers had enough troubles paying the bills to make sure their toilets kept flushing, never mind worrying about someone else's unsanitary landfill.

The fact that she wasn't a hard journalist didn't bother Sandy and probably never would. She took pride in her interviewing technique, glad not to be likened to the coarse, falsely intimate style of Barbara Walters or the puffy, prepackaged smiles of the *Entertainment Tonight* staff. On those occasions where research was required, she headed the process every step of the way, refusing to just step before the camera on call and read what someone else had written. Nor would she permit redubbing of her questions and shamelessly superficial reaction shots. The result was a far more spontaneous, unaltered interview and this as much as anything accounted for the fact that Sandy's popularity rating was the highest of any woman in broadcasting.

Accordingly, Sandy felt a growing confidence in herself. She had no desire to expand her reach into hard journalism per se, but felt ready to take a more active role in story selection and follow-through.

Starting today.

Her contract in these areas was vague. Her meeting with Stephen Shay this morning would not be. She knew what she wanted and, more, how to present it in terms he would understand. She would ask for the one specific story she wanted most. From there everything would take care of itself.

She was aware of T. J. Brown hovering close behind her as they stepped into Shay's private office together. Sandy nodded at the secretary, who smiled and picked up the phone immediately.

"Sandy's here, Mr. Shay." Then, looking at Sandy, "You can go right in."

T.J. seemed frozen in his tracks.

"Piece of cake," Sandy whispered. "Just picture him naked."

"Huh?"

"I had a public speaking teacher once who said to avoid nervousness when giving an important speech, just picture your audience naked."

That made T.J. smile as they moved toward the inner office door. "Shay naked? I'll give it a try."

T.J. had graduated from the Columbia School of Journalism three years before, fourth in his class and just as black as when he went in. Broadcast spots for minorities were still limited, so T.J. wallowed around for a while with newspapers and radio stations before applying for a research assistant's position at the then infantile *Overview*. The five anchors had screened the over four hundred applicants personally and Sandy Lister had come away especially impressed with T.J. He was actually overqualified for the job, but nonetheless seemed eager to be considered. Hiring him became Sandy's first completed business with her new network, a decision she had not regretted for one moment, even when T.J. urged her to go harder on her subjects and dangled plenty of research to help her do so.

She stepped into Stephen Shay's spacious office as smoothly as she stepped into the living rooms of millions of Americans on Thursday nights.

Shay rose from behind his desk and moved away from it, grasping Sandy's hands and kissing her lightly on the cheek.

"Perfect timing, San," he told her. "I just got the nationals from last week. Up four share points."

Shay was a dapper, elegant man with perfectly groomed silver hair waved over his ears and a measure of his forehead. He preferred three-piece suits to all other forms of clothing, and not one person at network headquarters could ever recall seeing him without his jacket on during business hours. His face looked as soft as a baby's, his Lagerfeld aftershave applied in just the right quantity to last the entire day without being too strong.

"That's great," Sandy said honestly. "Steve, I'd like you to meet my assistant T. J. Brown."

Shay took T.J.'s extended hand. "Thomas James, isn't it?"

"Er, yes. But how did you know?"

"You're in my department, son. I make it my business to know. Heard good things about you, damn good things."

"Thank you, sir."

"Don't thank me. Just keep it up." Shay's eyes moved back to Sandy. "Since you brought your assistant up with you, I gather you want to discuss a story."

"On the money, Steve."

"Coming to me direct for any special reason?"

"Do I need one?"

Shay smiled. "Not at all." He extended his hand toward a leather couch and set of matching chairs surrounding a table, drenched with sunlight from a nearby window. "Let's sit over here."

A pair of phones was perched in the table's center. Men like Shay seldom strayed far from the Touchtone.

"Coffee?" he offered when they had sat down. Sandy and T.J. both declined. "I suppose you want to get right to the point. What are you on to, Sandy?"

"Nothing earth-shattering. I'd just like to do a piece on Randall Krayman."

"Billionaire and recluse?"

"That's the one."

"Tough to interview a man who hasn't been seen in public in five years. Got an in with somebody?"

"No."

"Any of our rivals got the story on their dockets?"

"*60 Minutes* started to put one together, then abandoned it."

Shay nodded. "As I remember, we tossed a Krayman piece around here as well and rejected it, probably for the same reasons. Interviews without a subject are tough, San, even for you.''

"That's why I brought my case direct to the fifteenth floor, Steve. I think we can put a damn good piece together on Krayman without the usual interview. Make a conceptual picture of him based on interviews with others and background material.''

Shay looked away skeptically. "That kind of story isn't your specialty, San.''

"You mean, that kind of story isn't why you're paying me two million a year.''

"No," Shay said defensively, "that's not what I mean. One on one with a subject, you're fantastic, the best I've ever seen. I don't care how Joe or Joan Hollywood reconcile their personal life with their professional life, but you make *even me* care. You bring these people to life and you do it in a way that doesn't demean you. There's no way anyone can put a price tag on that kind of gift.''

"Don't tell that to my agent.''

"I'm serious, San. Conceptual stories are great when they work, but they're boring as hell when they don't. Stick to the media, San. That's your beat.''

"But Randall Krayman *is* the media," Sandy insisted. "Just hear me out. T.J.'s been doing some research, and his findings have got me thinking Krayman falls right into my beat.''

"I'm listening," said Shay reluctantly.

"T.J.," Sandy cued.

Brown cleared his throat and opened the manila folder he'd been fondling since the conversation began. "I'd better start at the beginning. Krayman was born in Boothbay Harbor, Maine, in 1940. His father was a moderately successful businessman who got in on the ground floor of plastics and made a fortune during the war. It looked like he had taken the business as far as it could go when he died in 1957. On paper the company was taken over by old man Krayman's wife, but in reality all the decisions were made and the managing done by Randall, who had just turned eighteen. Randall gave up his plans to go to college and

ended up quadrupling the company's profits in only two
years, turning it into perhaps the largest plastics producer
in the country. Not one to rest on his laurels, Randall Krayman invested every cent of the profits he was responsible
for in millions of acres of land across Wyoming, Montana,
and thereabouts. Scientists knew there was oil under it
somewhere, but back then, this is fifty-nine remember, no
one could envision the technology needed to bring it up.''

T.J. flipped to the next page. "Except Krayman. Within
ten years his wells were spouting as much crude as the best
Texas had to offer and he owned every ounce of it lock,
stock, and literally barrel. He made another fortune, this
one too large to even contemplate. But once again he didn't
sit still. He took all his profits and launched massive in-
vestments into a new and mysterious field, something called
the integrated circuit.''

"Computers," muttered Shay.

"The beginning of the explosion thereof," T.J. continued. "The integrated circuit laid the foundation for the
computer chip, the microchip, micro-circuitry—the whole
shooting match. Krayman made another incredible fortune.
Some called him the first landlord in Silicon Valley.''

"Hell of a crystal ball he must have," Shay noted. "First
plastics, then oil, then computers. You can't do much better than that.''

"And Krayman didn't stop there either. About ten years
ago his computer researchers came up with something
called the Krayman Chip, an advanced ultra-density memory chip with unheard-of storage, tailor-made for computers used to control television and radio signal switching,
telephone routing, radar screens—anything that qualifies
as data transmissions. And most incredibly this new chip
was produced through a process so cheap that Krayman
was able to undercut the entire industry.''

"Yet another fortune," concluded Shay, his interest
growing with each flip of T.J.'s notes.

"That's what I meant about Krayman being such a great
part of the media," Sandy interjected. "People should

kneel and bow twice to the Krayman Tower in Houston every time they turn their televisions on.''

"That doesn't mean they'll turn them on to watch a story about it," Shay said softly.

Sandy kept her calm. "Howard Hughes's death sent the networks scrambling to scoop each other. People ended up fascinated by him because they're fascinated generally by power and wealth, the more immeasurable the better. Well, Krayman makes Hughes look like a business school dropout. They'll watch. Believe me.''

Shay weakened. "Any chance of getting in to see the man himself?''

Sandy shrugged. "There's always a chance, but I doubt it. I've set up an interview with Francis Dolorman for a week from today. Dolorman's the man who's been running Krayman Industries since his boss's extended vacation began five years ago. If anyone can set up a meet, it's him.''

Shay's eyebrows flickered. He hesitated. "I can spare you for a week, San. No more. And no cameras either, just the preliminary stuff. We'll put everything you come up with together at the next staff meeting and see if there's a story here or not.''

"Fair enough," said Sandy.


"You were great in there, T.J.," Sandy said, as the elevator headed down. "Thanks.''

"Like you said, boss, nothing to it. I didn't even have to picture him naked.'' T.J.'s face grew somber. The elevator came to a halt. "Now that you've got the go-ahead for the story, maybe you'd like to see the rest of my research.''

"*Rest* of your research?''

They stepped slowly from the elevator. T.J. nodded. "Into Krayman Industries. Everything's not kosher there, if you know what I mean.''

Sandy stiffened and walked on ahead. "Sure. How about this afternoon?''

"What's wrong with now?''

Sandy kept walking down the corridor. T.J. hurried in front of her.

"You don't want to hear it, do you?" he charged.

Sandy looked away.

"What happened to getting to the bottom of Krayman Industries, boss?"

"*Randall Krayman*, T.J. That's the story Shay approved upstairs."

"And that sounds like Shay talking now; his distinction, not yours." He paused and looked at Sandy as a few people walked by. "Randall Krayman *is* Krayman Industries. You can't separate one from the other."

"You can't interview a corporation, T.J."

"You can't interview Krayman either, but that's not stopping you from doing the story. I've got some material for you that might help it."

Sandy's features tensed. "This isn't Columbia, T.J., it's network headquarters. Things function differently here. I want this story, but it's got to be on Shay's terms. You know what those terms are. He made them plain."

T.J. nodded blankly and started to walk away.

"This afternoon," Sandy called after him. "I'll look at what you've got then."

"Sure," T.J. said, too soft for her to hear.

The rest of the morning dragged for Sandy. She couldn't get the confrontation with T.J. out of her mind. Surely what he had uncovered about Krayman Industries would be laced with suppositions in desperate need of substantiation. These were distractions she plainly couldn't afford. They would cloud the true essence of her story and make pursuit of it even harder than it promised to be already.

But who was she kidding? She didn't want to learn what T.J. had discovered because she couldn't stand complications. She had gotten what she wanted from Shay, so her inclination was to leave well enough alone. Her field was people and with people selectivity could be maintained. The parts of their lives that didn't figure into the story could simply be left out. It was up to her. Years disregarded in favor of the latest love affair or big budget film. Things were simpler that way. She felt more in control, even of Randall Krayman, a man she would have to profile without meeting. That was a challenge she could handle. But dragging Krayman Industries into it? No, she didn't need that.

Sandy was still struggling with these issues when the elevator reached the lobby. It was almost noon and she had an early luncheon appointment to keep. As usual, she couldn't exit the building without signing countless autographs. The people came in droves, and the circle around her seemed to engulf those walking past it. Sandy signed as many as she could but tried to keep moving. How she longed for those cold winter days when, wearing hat and scarf, she could walk about unrecognized. The people wanted to talk to her, discuss whatever was on their minds. Their voices rose above one another's, competing, some reaching the level of screams as Sandy passed through the revolving door into the bright December day.

She was still signing autographs, hands beginning to stiffen, when the man shoved his way through the crowd to reach her. Sandy was only vaguely conscious of him until he was right before her, and then she felt a tremor of fear because his hand was reaching out, probing for her with something dark between its fingers.

At that instant Sandy knew all the fear celebrities live with in public, the vulnerability of fame and all its risks. John Lennon had been shot because he wouldn't give an autograph, a bullet for every two letters.

The man grasped her with his left hand and Sandy felt a scream forming behind her lips. But it didn't emerge until her eyes followed the man's hand as it slid across her white jacket, leaving a trail of blood behind.

Then he was collapsing and pulling her down, and Sandy saw he was bleeding everywhere, his overcoat open now to reveal splotches of scarlet. His voice, dry and rasping, reached her as they fell together to the sidewalk, his words barely discernible through lips pressed against her ear.

*"Stop them! You've got to stop them!"*

Sandy was screaming again, feeling the man's dying hands clutch at her.

*"No time left! No—"*

The man died with a rush of breath right then, but not before pushing the thin dark object into Sandy's pocketbook.

# CHAPTER 4

M<small>C</small>C<small>RACKEN</small> reclined tensely as the 747 streaked beneath the clouds toward Dulles International Airport. The pilot's voice announced that the temperature in Washington was thirty degrees with overcast skies and a good chance of snow. Dull and dreary to say the least, which fitted Blaine's mood perfectly.

They had given him little time to settle his affairs in Paris and then pack. Take everything, his orders said, you won't be coming back. Three men escorted him to Orly late Tuesday morning, but none of them accompanied him on the plane. Why should they bother? McCracken had no place to go but home. Running was not an option. Sure he could do it, quite effortlessly in fact. But they would catch up with him before too long. There was no place he could hide if they wanted him bad enough. All that crap about being too good to go after was the stuff of fiction, not reality. No matter how good you were, there were always enough of them to get you.

Blaine wondered what they would do if he didn't show up at the airport. What if he just boarded another jet and headed for South America? No, they couldn't let him go. If he cooperated, they'd let him live, but total freedom was out of the question. They'd bury him somewhere deep where he couldn't scratch his balls without an eye down his shorts.

43

The jet landed and McCracken moved slowly through Dulles en route to the baggage claim area. The whole of his life filled two suitcases and a packer bag, and he was not surprised to see a burly well-dressed man waiting to help him tote the stuff and escort him from the airport. The big man recognized him immediately, and his eyes avoided Blaine's as he hefted one of the suitcases.

"This way," the man said, and those were the only words exchanged between them. There was no reason to say more.

The man led him toward a Cadillac limousine with its engine purring. Blaine opened the back door for himself as the big man climbed behind the wheel.

"Good afternoon, Mr. McCracken. I trust your flight was comfortable."

The voice surprised Blaine because he had expected to ride alone. A reception party seemed uncalled for.

"There was enough turbulence to make me feel right at home," he told the gray-haired man in a tan overcoat. Blaine sat down and closed the door behind him. The driver pulled away. The opaque glass divider slid up between the seats.

"The name's Stimson, Blaine, Andrew Stimson. I run the Gap."

More surprise flashed in McCracken's eyes. "The name was sufficient." He hesitated. "I was expecting the standard Company escort, a couple of twin goons like your driver up there. I guess I should feel honored."

"The Company doesn't even know you're back in the States."

"What?"

"I brought you in on my own," Stimson explained. "It was all arranged up front until that business at Orly yesterday soured the President on you real fast. Your file was put on hold. The Company, and everyone else for that matter, think you're still under detention in Paris. I've arranged it so everyone thinks someone else has the key."

"What about Daniels?" Blaine asked.

"Don't worry about that. I'm sure Daniels won't question an order he thinks came from this high up."

"Thinks?"

"Don't push it. The point is, since no one talks to anybody else anyway, the ruse could go on indefinitely."

"Then it looks like you've sprung a jailbird, Mr. Stimson."

"Call me Andy. With what I'm about to tell you, we might as well be on a first-name basis."

"So what is it?" Sandy Lister asked T.J. after handing over the thin round object she had found in her purse an hour after spending nearly three at the police station.

"You mean the stiff planted this on you and you didn't give it to the cops?" T.J. asked, flustered.

"The man died giving it to me. I'd like to know what it is first."

"That doesn't sound like the girl who gave me the lecture on professional ethics this morning." T.J. held the object out before him. "Never had much use for computers, have you, boss?"

"As a matter of fact, no. Why?"

"Because this is a floppy disk used for storing programs."

"Can you find out what's on it?"

"Just as soon as I switch on my terminal." T.J. lowered the disk to his desk. "What about the stiff?"

"The first job for your terminal. His name was Benjamin Kelno, but that's all I know."

"Just let my magic fingers get to work, boss."

"I'll be in my office. Call when you've got something."

A half hour later, after several reroutings and overrides on T.J.'s part, a capsule biography of Benjamin Kelno flashed up on the screen. He read quickly, stopping halfway through, when his lips began to quiver.

"Jesus fuckin' Christ . . ."

The limousine turned onto the George Washington Memorial Parkway.

"I guess you had a good reason for springing me," Blaine said, breaking the silence.

"I understand you have a reputation for getting things done."

"Sure. Just ask the French for a reference."

"I wasn't talking about methods. I was talking about results, and you're as good at getting them as any operative I've ever heard of."

McCracken just looked at him.

"Ever heard of Tom Easton, Blaine?"

"A Gap man, isn't he?"

"Was. Somebody killed him in New York yesterday. It wasn't pretty. He was working on something big and now that work has died with him. We haven't a clue as to what he was on to."

"How was he killed?"

Stimson settled back. It didn't surprise him that a man like McCracken would want to know that first. "There's a . . . house in New York called Madame Rosa's. . . ."

"I've heard of it."

"Well, Easton was a regular customer," Stimson said, and went on to relate all the lurid details of the assassination.

"Professional," was McCracken's only comment.

"Brutally so," Stimson added. "Apparently, whoever we're dealing with isn't fond of subtle methods. Or the stakes of what Easton uncovered ruled them out."

"You want me to pick up where he left off," Blaine concluded.

"And retrace his steps."

"As long as I can skip Madame Rosa's. Little boys and girls have never been my style."

"They knew he was headed there," Stimson said. "Everything was planned out."

"You said Easton was a regular customer. It fits."

"Security at Madame Rosa's is tighter than anyone's in the capital, and that includes the Oval Office. If it was breached, you can bet somebody big was behind it, someone who stood to lose a lot if Easton made it in."

"When was he due?"

"Last night."

"That's cutting it pretty close."

Stimson nodded. "The opposition waited for him to expose himself."

"Literally," Blaine added. "Easton's field was internal subversion, right?"

"His specialty. Terrorist groups, revolutionaries—that sort of thing."

"Then the implication is one of those paid the visit to Madame Rosa's."

"But which? The execution was utterly clean, more worthy of a KGB hit squad than a domestic terrorist group made up of unhappy college students."

Blaine's eyebrows flickered. "You're underestimating them just as Easton did."

"I've been through the Gap files a dozen times. No one listed there could possibly have pulled this off."

"So we're dealing with someone new . . . or someone your files haven't done justice to."

"How do we find out who?"

McCracken smiled at Stimson's use of *we*. Obviously, the Gap director had already assumed he would cooperate, since the alternative was probably a return to detention in Paris. Blaine thought briefly.

"Easton's car, did you find it?"

Stimson nodded without enthusiasm. "Stripped clean and partially burned."

"You go over it?"

"There wasn't much to go over. But yes, we did." Stimson shook his head. "Nothing."

"The car's been brought here to Washington, I assume."

"Of course."

"I'd like to have a look at it."

"Why?"

"Because whoever visited Madame Rosa's must have known Easton left a bit of security in his car. Otherwise they wouldn't have bothered to steal it. I'm hoping they didn't find what they were looking for.''

"In which case, our people would have."

McCracken smiled knowingly. "It meant more to the killers. If they had found it, they wouldn't have bothered to torch the car. Obviously, they didn't want anyone else picking up where they left off and maybe getting luckier.''

Stimson nodded. "Interesting.''

"I'll check it out first thing tomorrow after a steak dinner and a good night's sleep.''

"I've arranged accommodations.''

"Safe house?''

"The Four Seasons Hotel under an assumed name. Remember, no one else knows I've brought you in, and we've got to keep it that way.''

"That could provide some complications.''

"I don't think so. You'll report to me and only to me.''

"No channel cover or access code? No backup?''

Stimson shook his head. "There isn't time. And even if there were . . .'' He seemed to be groping for words. "The thing of it is, Blaine, I know all about you. A rogue, a renegade, 'McCrackenballs'—all that shit. And shit's just what it is, because when everything's said and done, you succeed. I'm not holding a leash on you, but also I can't accept responsibility if this thing blows up and one of my counterparts at a three-letter agency grabs hold of you.'' Stimson's stare held Blaine's. "Look, I don't care whose nuts you have to bust to get to the bottom of this, just do it. You've got all the resources of the Gap behind you, and when all this is over, I can promise you a position on any terms you dictate.''

Blaine eyed him closely. "You've assumed I'd go along with this all along.''

Stimson nodded. "Like I said, I know all about you. They've had you stashed in purgatory for five years now. I'm offering a way out.''

"To heaven or hell, Andy?''

"That remains to be seen.''

* * *

The President's meeting with Nathan Jamrock, who in addition to heading the shuttle program served as chief of the controversial Special Space Projects section devoted to the deployment of weapons in space, didn't begin until six P.M. The militarization of space was considered by most in Washington to be inevitable as well as the one area where America held a distinct strategic advantage over the Soviet Union. If the next war was not fought above Earth, many thought, it would at least begin there. The present Space-Stat alert system had been developed with precisely that in mind.

"Then you're telling me you're no further along now than you were two days ago," the President said dejectedly, after Jamrock had finished his latest report.

"I'm afraid not, sir."

"What about the tapes?"

Jamrock shook his head and reached into his jacket pocket for a package of Rolaids. This was going to be a six-tablet meeting, he figured. "Computer magnifications and enhancements have yielded nothing new. By the time Caswell had gotten the camera up in the direction of . . . whatever was coming, the transmission had been jammed."

"Jammed by what, Nate?"

Jamrock's teeth sliced into his first pair of Rolaids. "The same sophisticated apparatus we suspect that's keeping our ground-based radar from tracking the damn thing. It's nothing our current technology can definitively account for any more than we can account for the means by which the shuttle was destroyed. Of course that doesn't mean the Russians haven't come up with something we're not yet aware of."

"I've already spoken with the Soviets and I'm satisfied that they had nothing to do with what happened. They claimed and I've already confirmed that two of their unmanned crafts were destroyed under similar circumstances. Somebody obviously wants control of space for themselves. That still doesn't tell us what that somebody is up to." The President paused. "But I'll tell you this much, whoever it is has got something big up there, and destroying our shuttle was an outright act of war. Why? And what was Caswell trying to describe?''

Jamrock fidgeted impatiently in his chair. ''Our only means of learning that will be to send something else up.'' He swallowed the grit from his Rolaids. ''Mr. President, I can have *Pegasus* ready for launch in nine days.''

The President tapped his fingers on his desk, considering the implications of Jamrock's suggestion. *Pegasus* was the prototype for what was envisioned as a fleet of laser-armed shuttles that could knock out of the sky anything that strayed too far into American air space. Short of a Star Wars shield, such a fleet would provide the ultimate security from enemy attack, along with being the controversial first step in the militarization of space. *Pegasus* had been tested and deemed ready for deployment. Technologically, all lights were green. Politically, red ones flashed everywhere.

''There's plenty of demand from the press and on the Hill for another series of hearings, Nate.''

''NASA couldn't survive them, sir. And even if we could, it probably wouldn't matter much. Whatever was responsible for *Adventurer*'s destruction is still up there, and I'm betting whoever's controlling it isn't finished yet. Forget questionable O-rings and frozen SRBs. What happened up there this time was an act of war.''

The President turned his gaze out the window at the night sky. ''How many days to get *Pegasus* airborne?''

''Nine.''

''Make it eight, Nate.''


''I still can't believe it,'' Sandy Lister said, rising uneasily from her office chair.

''You'd better, boss,'' T. J. Brown told her. ''Benjamin Kelno worked for Krayman Industries. Makes you think, doesn't it?''

''T.J.—''

He stood up and looked at her across the desk. ''Just hear me out. He showed up with the computer disk the very day you got approval for the Krayman story, pouring blood all over the sidewalk, but he still made it here because he wanted you to have that disk. Not anybody, just you. What was it he whispered?''

''That time was running out, that I had to stop them.''

''Stop *who*, boss?''

''You want me to say Krayman Industries, but I won't.''

''But it fits!''

''What fits? You're grasping, T.J. We don't even know what's on the disk yet, do we?''

T.J. shrugged. 'It's some sort of predetermined flight program. For what I don't know. But that air force friend of mine just might be able to help. I'm having lunch with him tomorrow.''

''Look, Krayman Industries is a major multinational corporation, a Dow Jones blue chip. It's crazy to think they'd be implicated in anything like this.''

''There's lots about them you don't know. Like I told you this morning.''

Sandy sat back down. ''Then maybe it's time I learned.''

# CHAPTER 5

Eᴀꜱᴛᴏɴ's car had been taken to the CIA's forensic laboratory, located not in Langley but on spacious grounds overlooking Rock Creek Park near the Walter Reed Army Medical Center in Northwest D.C. That was to be McCracken's first stop Wednesday morning thanks to a pass secured for him by Andrew Stimson. The pass was made out in a false name, Stimson's signature being the sole important feature. Clearly, no one could be allowed to learn Blaine was in Washington. Word spread fast in the capital, and if it reached the wrong people, the operation would be blown.

The CIA's private lab was better known as the "Toy Factory" since its primary task over the years had been to develop new weapons for use in the field. McCracken bypassed these sections, which made up the bulk of the Toy Factory, and moved toward an area reserved for forensic work of a more mundane nature, where Easton's Porsche was being stored. The car sat in a separate garage bay and McCracken was escorted to it by a man in a white lab coat who seemed intent on charting Blaine's every move on his clipboard.

"This may take a while," McCracken said when they reached the bay.

"My orders are to remain with you," the man said. "But I'll stay out of your way."

He unlocked the bay door and slid it up, revealing the formerly flaming red Porsche, now charred black and marred by cracked and bubbled paint. The scent of burnt metal was still in the air. The handles had been stripped and Blaine had to use the inside latch to get the door open.

The car was a shell. Its seats had been ripped out along with just about everything mechanical. The steering column was bent at an impossible angle, as if someone had tried for the wheel as well but then gave up.

Blaine spent the next two hours going over every inch of the Porsche, oblivious to his escort's claims that it had all been done already. His hands and clothes were grimy from the effort and his enthusiasm waned with each chunk of flesh lost on the spiny underside of the dash. He looked at the escort before starting on the two remaining tires and decided that CIA personnel were more than capable of inspecting the innards of burnt rubber.

It didn't make any sense, Blaine thought. Burning the car indicated they hadn't found what Easton had hidden. That meant it was still in the Porsche somewhere, unless the fire had claimed it. But Easton's hiding place would be a spot impervious to flames.

McCracken climbed back through the door and settled himself where the front seat used to be. The hiding place would be convenient, within arm's reach, so as not to attract attention when Easton used it. It would not have to be big but would be reinforced, protected with padding perhaps.

His fingers wrapped around the shift knob, which was leaning off to the side. With nothing better to do, he stripped it off even though it had already obviously been checked by both Easton's killers and the CIA. He unscrewed the lower portion, squeezing with all his strength. It came off, exposing the knob's hollow interior, a perfect hiding place for something small. He stuck his index finger through the opening and felt around the inside. Nothing but dust. He rolled the knob around in his hand, then wedged his finger back inside and held it up to the light as if it were a mystical crystal ball that might show him the answer.

The knob remained black and charred. No magic today. . . .

Blaine was about to discard it when something occurred to him. The knob was an inch in height but only three-quarters of an inch of his finger was inside. That left another quarter-inch within the knob unaccounted for. Another compartment. There had to be another compartment.

Blaine removed his finger and wiped the black grime from the top of the knob. Shifting instructions for the famed Porsche five-speed appeared. Neutral was in the middle, represented by a red $N$. Blaine pushed the $N$.

The charred top of the shift knob popped up.

Unseen by his escort, McCracken lowered the knob to his lap and peered inside.

There was a section of microfiche, thin and blackened around the edges. He lifted it carefully out and eased it between layers of his clean white handkerchief.

"I give up," Blaine said, tossing the shift knob aside.

"About time," responded his escort gratefully.


McCracken met Andrew Stimson thirty minutes later on a park bench on Pennsylvania Avenue.

"We'll let the computers have a go at this," Stimson said, fitting the microfiche into a clear plastic envelope. "Fiche is composed almost totally of a plastic, highly flammable material. There's probably enough information on this one to fill a dozen magazine pages, but I don't know how much even the computers will be able to salvage after the heat it's been exposed to."

"A name, a location, anything," Blaine said.

"We'll do the best we can. If we get lucky, there'll be repetition of certain words and phrases the computer can lock on to."

"Could take a while."

"Probably."

"Then I think I'll catch the shuttle to New York and pay Madame Rosa a visit."

* * *

The taxi slid down East Eighty-sixth Street, taking the ice ruts as they came.

"Early snow's a bad sign for the winter," the cabbie told Blaine. "A bad sign."

They passed a corner where a Santa Claus was surrounded by singing carolers, their breath misting in perfect rhythm in the bright air. Blaine hadn't been in the States for Christmas since his banishment five years before. Lots of mistletoe and roasted chestnuts had come and gone. Christmas in America was like Christmas nowhere else, but he found himself strangely unmoved by the joyous atmosphere of people rushing around and not seeming to mind it much.

Truth was, he disliked the holiday season because it left him empty. Holidays were for sharing, but Blaine had nothing to share and no one to share it with. He was an only child of parents dead for several years, with a splattering of aunts and uncles across the country whose names he could barely remember. There had been many women in his life, but the affairs had never lasted long enough to be labeled relationships.

This rarely bothered Blaine, but Christmas was an exception. His work had been his life and that work allowed no attachments. Enemies could get to you through people who were close, and anyone who thought that to be a violation of the rules of the game didn't really know the game. You flew alone, ate alone, lived alone, and mostly slept alone. Some operatives chanced marriage but seldom children because children were the most vulnerable of all, too easy to make disappear.

Worst of all, Blaine reckoned, was that the fear of attachments came not only out of regard for the opposition but for your own people as well. Your superiors liked leverage. They always treated family men better because if they misbehaved there were always those buttons that could be pushed.

"This it?" the cabbie asked him.

They had come to a halt in front of a brownstone with

a doorman blowing breath onto his gloves before the entrance.

"Yeah, this is it," Blaine told the driver, flipping him a twenty with instructions to keep the change.

Blaine stepped out of the cab and approached the entrance to Madame Rosa's to find his path blocked by the rather burly doorman.

"Do you have an appointment, sir?"

Blaine fingered his beard. "A trim will do for today. I'll take the manicure next week."

The doorman was not amused. "This is a private club, sir."

"Club? Is that what they're calling these places today? My, my, leave the country for a few years and the whole damn dictionary changes."

The doorman's eyes swept around him, obviously unsure. Avoiding a scene was foremost on his mind. Making one was foremost on McCracken's.

"Tell Madame Rosa a friend of Tom Easton's is here to see her."

"I know no woman by that name, sir."

Blaine moved a little closer, leery of the bigger man's feet and hands. "Let me spell it out for you. Either I go by you or through you. Your choice."

The doorman moved toward a phone suspended in a box to the right of the windowless entrance. "Who should I say is here?" he asked McCracken.

"Rudolph R. Reindeer . . ."

Blaine knew the name didn't matter because the doorman was already going for his gun. The man's bulky jacket precluded a quick draw, which allowed McCracken the instant he needed to close the gap between them and to lock his hand on the doorman's drawing wrist. Blaine pounded his face once with a fist and then slammed his groin with a knee rocketed from the pavement in a blur of motion. The doorman gasped, eyes dimming, and started to slump. McCracken grabbed him, providing support, and pounded rapidly on the door.

"Hey, you inside! Help! Open the door! This guy's sick!"

McCracken could feel himself and the doorman being observed through the peephole.

"Come on!" he urged, striking the door harder.

It finally opened and a short, slender Oriental man stepped out.

"I don't know what happened," Blaine explained, as he helped drag the doorman in. "He just collapsed."

The door closed behind them.

"Excellent performance," came the voice of a woman through thin raps of solitary applause. And then Blaine saw the gun in the Oriental's hand. "Now, if you would be good enough to put your hands in the air . . ."

T. J. Brown met his air force contact for lunch five hours after depositing the computer disk on his desk. The captain's name was Alan Coglan and T.J. had become friendly with him during research for a story he had done a few months back on the new breed of test pilots.

Coglan arrived at the restaurant late and approached the table nervously, face as stiff as his air force uniform.

"Where did you get this?" he asked, holding the disk in his hand and making no move to sit down.

"Does it matter?"

"I'll say it does." Now Coglan seated himself but kept his legs outside the table. He had left his overcoat on. T.J. watched him smother the disk with a napkin and slide it across the table. "I'm giving this back to you because I want nothing to do with it. You never met me, understand? And if you won't tell me how you got this disk, go to the FBI and tell them—right now before it's too late."

T.J.'s eyes showed fear. "Al, you're scaring the shit out of me. That ain't no way to treat a friend. All this over a goddamn flight plan?"

"A goddamn flight plan," Coglan parodied. "Sure, the goddamn orbital flight plan of the space shuttle *Adventurer*."

\* \* \*

McCracken raised his hands and let the small Oriental push him against the wall in order to search him. The man found his Browning but kept right on jostling him up and down until he was satisfied that was all Blaine had been carrying.

He turned slowly and faced an elegant woman dressed in a blue sequined gown.

"Your errand boy here didn't take my wallet, Madame Rosa," Blaine told her.

The woman smiled comfortably. "I thought I'd give you the pleasure of telling me who you are and what you're doing here yourself." Her eyes moved to the Oriental. "Chen, show him to my study."

The Oriental led Blaine down a lavishly appointed hallway lined with original artwork and antique sculptures displayed on pedestals. They stopped at the last door down, and Chen waited inside with him until Madame Rosa made her appearance.

"Stay by the door," she instructed him.

Chen bowed slightly and took his leave.

Madame Rosa closed the door behind him.

McCracken glanced around the room. It contained a strange mix of colonial furniture and modern technology. A row of video screens was built into the wall above a rolltop desk. A board with either red or green lights flashing for each of the brownstone's rooms rested on an ancient cherry carpenter's table.

"So that's why my ruse didn't work," Blaine said, eyes back on the monitors, specifically one that showed the brownstone's front. Five others provided different views of the building's exterior.

"It was quite a performance," said Madame Rosa.

"I aim to please."

"Just so long as you're not contemplating any encores in here. Chen is quite adept at dealing with intruders. He would be most pleased if I turned you over to him."

"Can he buy his clothes in men's sizes yet?"

Madame Rosa cracked a smile which held no trace of amusement. "All others who underestimated him were buried soon after. I brought Chen over from China. His reputation preceded him.''

McCracken walked about the room, inspecting it. "In which case he must fit in perfectly at this glorified whorehouse. Tell me, did you ever consider putting a red light over the front door?''

Madame Rosa's face grew taut with impatience. "You mentioned Mr. Easton to the doorman outside.''

"Yes, I suppose I did.''

"If you're here to threaten closing me down, forget it. I'm protected . . . all the way to Washington.''

Blaine's dark eyes dug deep into the madam's. "Lady, you piss me off and I won't close you down, I'll blow you up.''

"You worked with Easton?''

"Let's say we fished in the same stream and I'm taking over his boat. We have a code in our business that lives on after death. I'm here to find out who killed him.''

Madame Rosa's sequined gown seemed to blink. "I told everything I know to the others.''

"I like hearing things firsthand.''

"And just who are you?''

"The name's Blaine McCracken if it matters.''

"It doesn't.''

"We were talking about Easton. A regular customer, I presume.''

The woman nodded. "Twice a month when he could fit it into his schedule.''

"Same days?''

She shook her head. "Never. His work and security factors made that impossible. Sometimes he would book his appointments only hours in advance, sometimes days. Monday was different.''

"How so?''

"We had filled a . . . special order for him. He had been waiting for some time.''

The twins, McCracken realized. What kind of world had he entered here?

"That distresses you, Mr. McCracken?''

"Treating people like they were something out of a Sears catalogue has never rubbed me the right way."

"Then consider yourself in a minority. People need relief, refuge, a place where their wildest dreams can be made a reality. A house like mine releases people's pent-up inhibitions in a way that hurts no one."

"Tell that to Easton . . . and his twins."

Madame Rosa hesitated. "That was an entirely different situation."

"And quite puzzling, if you ask me." Blaine walked over to the bank of six video monitors. "I assume there's another of these at your security station."

"Of course."

Blaine nodded. "So two men were able to bypass all this surveillance to get in and out of the building and murder three people in between. Something smells."

"They were professionals."

"So am I."

"Maybe the killers were just better."

"More likely they had inside help."

Madame Rosa's features flared. "I will not stand here and—"

"I'm not finished yet. Not only did they get in and out without being seen, they also knew exactly what room Easton would be found in. No need for trial and error, right?"

"He used the same room all the time," she replied defensively.

"But someone would have had to tell the killers that, wouldn't they? And maybe this same person, or persons, looked the other way, perhaps pulled the plug on your million-dollar surveillance for five minutes or so Monday afternoon." Blaine paused. "You're still standing there, madame."

"Your conclusions are unfounded. Discretion has always been a primary concern here. My people go through more security checks than the President's staff."

"What about beyond your people?" he challenged her. "Someone might have known something. Enough."

"No," the woman replied after a pause long enough to convince Blaine she was holding something back.

"Madame Rosa," he began more compassionately, forming a lie, "I'm here on no one else's authority but my own. This is purely personal. The killers of Tom Easton cannot be allowed to go unpunished. Otherwise, none of our kind are safe."

"There is nothing I know that can help, I assure you." Her eyes softened and she seemed to feel less threatened. "But if there's anything else I can do . . ."

Blaine nodded. "I'm retracing all of Easton's steps up to the time he died. I'd like to see the room where he was killed."

# CHAPTER 6

"I'LL have Chen show you upstairs," Madame Rosa said. "But the authorities have been over the room a dozen times. You won't find anything they haven't already."

"Won't know that till I try, madame."

Madame Rosa accompanied Chen and Blaine to the stairs and left them to go up on their own. Following behind the Oriental, Blaine drastically altered his estimation of the man, or perhaps just conceded it. He had known Chen's kind many times over the years, mostly in 'Nam. Quick, silent killers who could move with the air and vanish into the wind. They were nimble and lithe, capable of killing efficiently with their bare hands. McCracken had heard of several large and powerful men like himself who had fallen prey to their misjudgments of killers like Chen. He would have to make sure he didn't follow them.

Blaine kept his distance as Chen led him to the third floor and unlocked a door no different from the others.

The inside of the room was something else again.

Obviously, Washington or Langley or both had decreed that it be left as it was, and no amount of days since the killing could stop Blaine's stomach from pitching. The blood was everywhere, dried and blotchy, splattered against the walls and floor, soaked into the sheets. The scent of incense was thick in the air, but nothing could erase the lingering smells of death or the feeling of it. McCracken felt certain that even blindfolded he would have been able to pick this room as the one where violent death had occurred. A bit queasy, he stepped farther inside. Chen remained in the corridor and pulled the door three quarters closed.

Blaine could see it all happening in his mind. The children rolling atop Easton, young faces mechanical and uncertain, innocence adding to their fear and thus the perversity of the scene. Then the doors bursting open and two men rushing through, hot bullets tearing from their guns barrels, separating blood and bone from body and spilling them about. Thoughts of the confused, dying children made Blaine tremble, and suddenly the room felt ice cold.

He had to get out. Of course Madame Rosa had been right about there being nothing up here for him to find. But still he'd had to see and feel it all for himself. That much accomplished, he moved for the door.

In the corridor Chen was gone.

That did not fit. His orders would have been to stick close to this intruder into the private world of Madame Rosa. Then where was he?

Blaine pushed the question aside. He just wanted to be rid of this place. There was nothing that could be of any help to him here. He descended the stairs on his own, leery now, senses sharp as an animal's at a killing field. He reached the ground floor. The brownstone felt deserted.

There was a noise down the hallway in the direction of Madame Rosa's study, too brief to be identified but sharp enough to be out of place. Blaine moved toward it. Halfway down the corridor he drew the Browning pistol Madame Rosa had returned to him before permitting him to go upstairs.

He neared the woman's office, uncomfortable with the silence. The door was ajar, and Blaine saw that the room was dark inside save for the light stolen from a window and the dull haze cast by the video monitoring screens. He was operating on instinct now, and it was instinct that led him through the door gun-first.

And instinct that made him pull his wrist back fast so the swirling object struck his gun instead of his hand. The Browning went flying.

Chen came at Blaine with his *nunchuku*, swinging them hard and fast in a blur of motion. Blaine ducked and a china lamp shattered into a thousand pieces. Blaine backpedaled, steadying himself. The effectiveness of "nunchuks," twin foot-long wooden blocks connected by wire or cord, was due mostly to myth. The Americans had made them into a flashy weapon when in truth they were the least effective and glamorous of any weapon from feudal Japan. McCracken had never had much faith in or fear of the nunchuks. You just had to keep your calm and seize the advantage when it came.

Chen charged at him again, snapping the nunchuks in a straight overhead angle, using one as a fulcrum to whip the other out from the cord. Blaine felt the hard wood whistle by his ear twice, dodging at the last instant both times. Chen now seemed like a cobra frustrated by the mongoose, his moves rushed and less certain, sweat forming on his brow. The advantage became Blaine's until he tripped over something in the dim light and went sprawling. He found himself almost eye to eye with a dying Madame Rosa, whose head lay in the blood pouring from the narrow slit in her throat. So it must be wire, not cord, that strung the twin sections of the nunchuks together, and the wire was what Chen had used to do the job.

Chen swooped at him with a throaty scream and swung the nunchuks in a roundhouse fashion. McCracken managed to get to the side and raise his arm fast enough to keep the weapon from a killing blow, taking the full force on the fatty part of his forearm. The pain exploded horribly, but there was no time to be slowed by it. Blaine grasped the wooden section hard and pulled, only Chen went with his action instead of resisting it, coming straight in and lashing a kick under his chin as McCracken struggled to rise.

Blaine felt himself drifting backward, drifting altogether. His head banged against a table and he managed to move it in time to avoid Chen's next strike, which split the table in two, showering both of them with splinters. Chen was off-balance now and Blaine came in hard against his legs, using his superior size and strength to its best advantage. He shoved Chen backward, but again the Oriental flowed with the move, using McCracken's own momentum to smash him headlong into the wall. The nunchuks came down hard on his muscular back and Blaine felt his whole spine go numb.

Somehow he found the strength to rise and this time it was Chen who did the underestimating, coming in with a wide strike to finish him. The wood whistled through the air in a long arc, too long, giving Blaine the time to dart inside Chen's center and grab his flailing arm when the nunchuk strike was well past its impact point. Blaine threw his right hip across the Oriental's small body and circled his thin neck hard with his free arm with enough force to throw Chen up and over his hip. The Oriental's back and head smashed onto the floor.

As he struggled to rise, Blaine slipped behind him, manipulating the nunchuks to his advantage now. Holding on to one section with his left hand, Blaine grasped the other with his right and drew the sections back fast and hard, yanking them apart. Whatever grip Chen retained on them was relinquished.

Blaine's knee found Chen's back at the same time the wire dug deep into his throat, slicing the flesh as smoothly as cheese. Blood sprayed forward. The Oriental's head snapped backward and then slumped over obscenely to his chest, nearly severed from his neck. McCracken pushed the writhing corpse to the floor and stepped over it on the way to Madame Rosa's body.

Incredibly, he found she was still alive. Just barely, but alive. Her dying eyes sought him out. He thought he saw her mouth move, trying to form the shadow of a syllable. Her face was ghastly pale and the blood was still oozing from the tear in her throat.

"Se . . . bas . . . tian," she rasped, and the disjointed

word seemed to come more from the slit in her neck than her mouth. "Se—"

She started the word again, but this time a gurgle swallowed it and her eyes locked forever on the six monitors broadcasting black and white pictures of what had been her world.

McCracken was back on his feet immediately. He had to get out of there before Chen's people arrived. The front door was the only way out he knew. He found his Browning and held it before him as he rushed back up the corridor.

Still there was no one. What had happened? Where were Madame Rosa's customers, her security guards?

He was almost to the door when a closet caught his eye. He threw it open and grabbed the first coat he saw, black cashmere and perfect for hiding his bloodied clothes. Shoving his arms through the too short sleeves, McCracken rushed out the heavy door into the street.

No doorman either. Madame Rosa's seemed utterly deserted.

The cold air struck him and with it the pain. Blaine instinctively catalogued his injuries. His forearm was swollen thick and numb but nothing was broken. His back ached and made movement painful; again, though, nothing serious. Beyond that there was a throbbing through his entire body. He blocked out the pain, glad for the frigid air because it braced him.

Blaine didn't run because that would draw too much attention. At a fast walk he passed several pay phones and debated using one to call Stimson at the Gap. No, his first priority was to escape the area. A cab would do; he needed a cab. Hailing one would mean staying in the same spot, perhaps for several minutes. Blaine decided to chance it.

Luckily, one pulled over in seconds. McCracken was in the backseat almost before the driver came to a halt.

"Take it easy, Mac," the driver said. "You in a rush?"

"Yeah."

"Where to?"

"Just drive."

It was the icy stare in Blaine's black eyes that made the cabbie turn back around, gulping air. McCracken needed time to think, to regroup and find a safe place from which to call Stimson.

*And tell him what?*

Madame Rosa had been murdered because she knew something, something she might have told Blaine if given time.

*Sebastian . . .*

Her last word. But who or what was Sebastian and why would she send Blaine to him or it? Another connection perhaps, a link in a chain being severed one piece at a time.

He could tell that much to Stimson. It was all he knew. The people behind Easton's murder were not going to leave a trail. All tracks had to be covered. Stimson would run Sebastian through his computers, Chen, too, and perhaps some of those tracks would be revealed. There was the microfiche to consider as well. If they had been able to decipher it at the Gap, Blaine's job would be that much easier.

The cab reeled over the ice ruts like a roller-coaster car, until it stopped in traffic across from a group of merry carolers and Santa Claus ringing his bell. Santa shoved a copper cup toward passersby who tried to avoid making a donation.

Santa saw the snarl in traffic and moved into the street to take advantage of it. Blaine wondered if he got a percentage of the take for his trouble. He leaned back and squeezed his eyes closed, the cold air streaming through the window, keeping him alert. Horns honked, blared.

A bell disturbed him and forced his eyes open.

"Merry Christmas! Merry Christmas!"

Santa was coming toward the driver's side of the cab, aiming for the open window. Blaine slid over to roll it up, but the fake-bearded man got there too fast.

"Merry Christmas! Something for the poor and needy, sir?"

Blaine shrugged. Paying the man would be the quickest

way to get rid of him. He reached into his pocket, groping for some change.

Santa thrust his copper cup farther into the car. There was something peculiar about the angle at which he held it . . .

Blaine's hand emerged with a pair of quarters.

. . . and something even more peculiar about the way he held his eyes.

It was the eyes that moved McCracken to action more than anything. Just as Santa started his cup forward, Blaine lurched to the side and watched its liquid contents spray by him, splattering the upholstery. Hot steam began to rise as the vinyl and cloth beneath it melted.

Acid! McCracken realized, the Browning already in his hand.

Santa had his gun out, too, but Blaine sent two shots into him high and hard before he could fire it, staining his lapels the scarlet color of his suit. Santa pitched backward, slammed into another traffic-wedged car, and then slumped to the cement.

"Jesus fuckin' Christ!" screamed the cabbie, and his hand groped desperately for the door handle.

A number of bystanders chuckled because it looked like Santa had finally gone for one dollar too much. A few even applauded.

There was no mistaking the actions of the carolers, though.

In unison, as if rehearsed, they pulled weapons from inside their overcoats. The first out was a sawed-off shotgun and its wielder fired both barrels as Blaine hugged the taxi's floor. The pellets turned the car's frame into a pincushion and the cabbie's head into splinters of bone. The shock of death forced his foot down, and the cab shot off to the right, colliding with one car, another, then pushing a third with it onto the sidewalk before coming to a stop.

Blaine was tossed violently one way and then the other. His hand grasped for the door handle and yanked it hard. The door sprung open and the movement threw his body onto the sidewalk. The cab itself provided cover.

The carolers fanned out in military fashion, oblivious to the screams and panic of those around them. A series of sprays from the machine pistol of one tore into the cab's engine block and rocketed flames outward.

McCracken rolled away, exposing himself long enough for a pair of carolers to empty clips at him, chewing cement and spitting glass everywhere. He rolled again and found cover behind a truck.

He crawled under it and locked his Browning on two carolers gliding across the street with heavy rifles in hand before them. Only seven shots remained in the Browning, and his spare clip was still in the overcoat he had left at Madame Rosa's. He had to make each shot count.

He squeezed off a pair at the two approaching carolers, taking both in the head and dropping them there. Before their bodies had even struck pavement, a hail of fire coughed up fresh tar before him, coming from two directions at once. The impact stunned him briefly, and he was only vaguely conscious of figures darting across the street to better their positions.

*Christ, how many carolers had there been? Six? Eight? Ten maybe? . . . A fucking army!*

Blaine could tell they were trying to encircle him. They would keep him pinned where he was with heavy fire while they readied a simultaneous offensive he could not possibly survive. He could hear the distant wail of sirens now, but traffic and icy roads considered, the police could not possibly arrive in time to be of any help to him. He would have to beat the carolers on his own.

*How, though?*

Blaine pushed himself backward and felt his foot dip into an opened manhole at the rear of the truck. He had a vision of plunging downward to his death and saving the carolers the bother. Wait! Plunge, yes, but not to his death!

McCracken dragged his frame backward so that his legs passed into the manhole, beneath which lay the labyrinth of tunneled storm drains the DPW was currently servicing. A perfect escape route.

But he needed more.

With his legs dangling down the manhole, Blaine waited for the next hail of fire from the approaching carolers before firing two of the Browning's shells into the truck's fuel tank. Gas began to spill immediately, some spraying him.

He could feel the carolers' footsteps almost on top of the truck now. Sirens wailed closer but not close enough. Then he saw feet, lots of them, everywhere around the truck. That was his cue. He pushed the rest of his body into the manhole and plunged into the bowels of New York City.

Upon landing, Blaine yanked a wad of cash from one pant pocket and his lighter from another, flicking it to life. The dried bills caught on contact and he hurled the flaming packet through the manhole opening into the spill of gasoline.

The explosion came almost instantly. McCracken felt the intense heat of the blast surge into him as he ducked and covered his head. He feared for a moment that the flames might follow the heat and consume him. They descended as if shot from a flamethrower, then gave way to coarse black smoke. There were more explosions, smaller secondary ones, mixed with agonized screams from above.

The screams didn't last long, though. All of the carolers had been too close to the truck to avoid the blast. Most of them were probably in pieces by now.

Blaine rose to his feet, finding that his head just cleared the ceiling of the storm drain. His plunge through the manhole had brought the pain to his back again, but he moved quickly in spite of it. The drain, lit by sporadically placed lamps, was growing dank and putrid by the time he was a hundred yards in.

Finding a spot to climb out proved harder than he had hoped. The many manhole covers he passed were impossible to push off from below. He had to keep walking until he found another DPW crew performing similar service.

It took a good half mile before he came upon one.

"Mayor's office," he said, straight-faced, to the men gawking disbelievingly at him as he climbed a ladder back to the street. "Just wanted to make sure you boys weren't tanking on the job."

Blaine was no longer concerned about being spotted by potential assailants. He was predominantly conscious instead of his grubby, damp clothes and the attention they might attract. He would have to make arrangements to wash and change somehow, but first he would have to call Stimson. He had plenty to tell him.

He reached an available public phone at the corner of Fifty-sixth and Madison and pulled the Gap director's private number from his memory. The call went through unhindered by operator assistance or anything as mundane as regular charges. The access code punched prior to the number overruled the need for that.

"Yes?" The phone was answered by a male voice, but not Stimson's.

"I need Stimson."

"He is unavailable."

"Get him."

"He is—"

"Get him, you ass! Now!"

"I'll send out a page," the voice said after a brief pause.

Blaine wished he could have reached through the phone to tear the damn bureaucrat's throat out. It was another minute before Stimson came on the line.

"This is Stimson."

"We've got problems."

"Blaine, is that you? What's happened?"

"Long story. You'll be hearing about much of it before too long, I suspect."

"Complications?"

"Violent ones. There are lots of people dead up here, Andy, and I was lucky not to be among them."

Stimson paused. "Were you blown?"

"My investigation of Madame Rosa's didn't include the fringe benefits."

"Blaine, *please*!"

"No, Andy, I wasn't blown. They were waiting for

somebody, that much I can tell you, and they must have
had a pretty good idea it was me.''

"I need details, Blaine, details!''

"Madame Rosa's dead. Her whole place is deserted.
Somebody pulled a lot of strings and they waited until I
got there to pull them. Outside I was made by Santa Claus
and a bunch of elves who carried sawed-offs instead of
Christmas presents. And you might be getting a bill from
the city for one truck.''

"When I told you to crack all the balls you wanted, you
took me at my word, didn't you?''

"Only because I didn't want mine cracked, Andy. This
thing must be even bigger than we thought. And if you ask
me, the Santa Claus I blew away has connections in places
other than the North Pole.'' Blaine paused. "What about
the microfiche? Anything?''

"Nothing concrete, but we're making progress.''

"If your computers can handle a little more work, I need
a few checks made.''

"I've got pen in hand.''

"First, I need everything you can get me on someone
or something called Sebastian.''

"That's it, just Sebastian?''

"He or it was involved somehow with Madame Rosa,
if that helps any.''

"It might. What else?''

"An Oriental named Chen, probably of Chinese extrac-
tion. Very small but very deadly. Alas, now very dead.''

"Somehow I'm not surprised. . . .''

"He's probably a hired gun. Free-lance. I'd like to know
who he's been working for lately.''

"Why?''

"Because somebody placed him with Madame Rosa,
somebody with a lot of time, patience, and reasons. The
Easton thing was set up for quite a while. Either Madame
Rosa's was infiltrated through and through, or Easton's
killers were invisible.''

"Do you need to be brought in?'' Stimson asked grimly.

"The way I look right now, Andy, I'd have to travel in

the baggage compartment. No, I'll get cleaned up and hole up here for a few hours while you dig up that information for me. When should I call?''

"It's almost two now. Say anytime after four.''

"Perfect.'' Blaine was about to say good-bye when one final thought occurred to him. "Oh, and, Andy, that Santa Claus who's seen his last chimney?''

"Yes?''

"He was black.''

## PART TWO

# The *Narcissus*

**Wednesday Afternoon to Saturday Afternoon**

# CHAPTER 7

"THE space shuttle *Adventurer*?"

Sandy Lister couldn't believe what a nervous T.J. had just told her. She had spent the balance of the morning reviewing the information he had gathered and passed on the previous day concerning Krayman Industries. Little of his research would stand up in court, but it was accurate with one point irrefutable: Krayman Industries had channeled vast energies and resources into gaining control of different segments of the media and all spheres of telecommunication in general. The corporation was the controlling force behind twenty-seven local television stations nationwide, skirting FCC ownership regulations by forming new companies to control subgroups of stations in different regions. Holding all of them together and serving as an umbrella unit for Krayman's vast holdings in the media, electronics, transportation, and computers was Communications Technology International. Tens of billions of dollars were involved. COM-U-TECH had become the ultimate consortium in the telecommunications field. But why? Men like Krayman did not move randomly. So what was he after?

"It's something called an orbital flight plan," T.J. continued, fidgeting nervously in the chair before Sandy's desk.

"That's all your air force friend was able to tell you?"

"We ain't friends anymore, boss."

"Lunch wasn't pleasant?"

"Lunch never happened. Coglan just dropped the disk off like it was burning his fingers and pointed me in the FBI's direction."

"Obviously, he had a good reason for wanting you to get rid of it."

"Sure. How does high treason grab you?"

Sandy started to laugh but quickly stopped when she saw T.J.'s sullen expression. "You're not kidding, are you?"

"Not unless Captain Coglan was, and he didn't seem to be in a joking mood." T.J. sighed. "After the *Challenger* explosion, it was the Defense Department that saved the shuttle program and now furnishes virtually all of its funding. In typical Defense Department fashion, everything's very hush-hush, and even if it weren't, possessing a computer program made up of the last flight of a shuttle lost in space wouldn't be looked at too kindly by the authorities. To put it bluntly, they might crucify us. So if you're ready to go to the FBI, I'll drive."

"What happened to the gung-ho journalistic bravado from yesterday?"

"Deep down, I'm a coward."

"Is that why you haven't bothered speculating on why a murdered Krayman Industries employee would have an orbital flight plan disk in his possession?"

"Look who's making the connections now. . . ."

"It would be hard for even a celebrity interviewer to miss them. Kelno worked for Krayman, he had the disk, I'm about to start a story on the man himself when a dying Kelno slips it into my purse. Sounds like a progression to me."

"You gonna take this to Shay?"

Sandy hedged. "Not yet."

"Because you want it to be your story?"

"Because I haven't got enough to take to him yet. Right now we've got two leads: Kelno and the disk. Your job is to dig up everything you can on Kelno while I find out exactly what good an orbital flight plan would be to anyone other than NASA."

"How?"

"Your friend Captain Coglan. If lunch didn't work, I'll try dinner."

McCracken began stripping off his dirty clothes as soon as the door to his room in the St. Regis on Fifty-fifth Street was chained behind him. It felt good to be out of them and he called down immediately to the hotel valet service to have his sport jacket and slacks cleaned and pressed. Yes, they assured him, the job could be done within an hour. An extra fee would be required, though. So what else is new? Blaine thought.

He took a long hot shower, steaming the grime away, ordered up a turkey club from room service, and after finishing it dialed Andrew Stimson's private number at exactly four o'clock.

"Stimson," came the Gap director's voice.

"It's Blaine, Andy."

Silence filled the other end.

"Andy?"

"Hell of a mess you made outside Madame Rosa's," Stimson said sharply.

"Thought I'd warned you."

"You damn near blew up the whole street. It's a can of worms, Blaine, and if the truth comes out about your involvement, it's gonna get spilled all over my lap. Every agency in the book is up there trying to piece together what happened . . . and I mean literally. There isn't much left standing."

"What about innocent bystanders?" Blaine asked reluctantly.

"Some hospitalized, none critical. Relax, your record's intact. The essential point now is that it won't take the Company and Bureau boys long to put together that a pro was responsible up there and that might lead them to my doorstep. They won't like what they find inside. Remember, this whole assignment exists only between you and me."

"I know."

Stimson sighed. "I won't tell you to go easy because I know I gave you a job to do. I would suggest that under the circumstances you leave New York."

"Not until I find out where Sebastian fits in. Any luck finding him or it on your software?"

"It's a he and he's somebody else's property."

"Meaning?"

"Meaning the FBI's been on to Sebastian—alias Don Louis Rose, alias J. D. Sabatini, alias Dominque Derobo—for some time. He's a trafficker."

"Drugs?"

"Some," Stimson said. "But he specializes in people."

"Ah, an old-fashioned white slaver . . ."

"Except Sebastian's as black as they come and he deals in meeting orders for men and women, boys and girls of all makes and models. Most of his business comes from high-fashion whorehouses like Madame Rosa's, but he has quite a few private clients as well."

"The twins," Blaine muttered.

"What?"

"The twins. Madame Rosa told me Easton ordered them special. She must have put me on to Sebastian because she knew he was the only other person who knew the twins' delivery date, and not from the stork either. Where can I find Sebastian, Andy?"

Stimson hesitated. "I think you better steer clear of him."

"Uh-uh. There are too many loose ends he can tie up. He had to tell somebody about the twins and that somebody set up the hit on Easton."

"Blaine, the FBI's got Sebastian eyeballed twenty-four hours a day. You walk in and they'll have you eyeballed as well."

"I'll be subtle."

"Sure."

"Look, Andy, whoever infiltrated Madame Rosa's would have known everything except the date of delivery for Easton's twins. Only Madame Rosa and Sebastian would have known that and since the madame maintained the ultimate in discretion, that leaves us with Sebastian. Where is he?''

Stimson didn't hesitate this time. "FBI reports indicate he moved out of his Manhattan penthouse two days ago. Since then he's been holed up in a freighter he owns. It's docked in New York harbor.''

"Two days ago. . . . Interesting.''

"I thought you'd like that. And there's more. Sebastian's got an army guarding his ship, almost like he's expecting a siege.''

"The question is by whom?''

"If you're set on looking for the answer," Stimson cautioned, "make sure you do it without attracting attention from the FBI. If they ID you . . ." The Gap director let his voice trail off at the end to illustrate his meaning.

"Don't worry, Andy, I've already got a few ideas.''

"And no repeat performances of Eighty-sixth Street.''

"One a day's my limit. Anything on the carolers or Santa Claus?''

"Free-lance muscle, as near as we can tell. Pros, for sure, as you suspected, but all without links to any major group. Looks like they were hired for this one job.''

"Or two," McCracken corrected him. "Lest we forget Easton.''

"The two who nailed him were black.''

"As was the Santa Claus.''

"A pretty thin connection.''

"I don't think so, Andy. How many black Santa Clauses have you seen ringing money bells in posh sections of Manhattan?''

"None with acid in their cups, if that's what you mean.''

"It goes deeper. I can feel it. I assume there's nothing new with the microfiche.''

"The computer's working overtime, but the fiche was burned worse than we thought originally. My people assure me we're still close to something.''

"Which brings us to Chen, Andy. What'd your people turn up on him?''

Stimson cleared his throat before answering. "Our records are inconclusive."

"What do they show, Andy?"

"Blaine—"

"What do they show, Andy?"

"CIA. They show Chen's on the Company's payroll."

Sebastian's freighter, McCracken learned, was called the *Narcissus* and was docked at West Twenty-Third Street on the Hudson River. Blaine decided to make his appearance after dark, ruling out commando tactics since Sebastian's private army would significantly reduce the chances they would succeed. Something more subtle was called for, something that would keep the FBI off his back at the same time. The answer came to Blaine quickly and might even allow him to have some fun in the process.

What wasn't fun was considering Chen's link to the CIA. It was certain that he had infiltrated Madame Rosa's for the express purpose of executing her if she became a threat. But why would *the Company* want her dead and, more, want Easton dead? It made no sense any way he looked at it. Sure, there was competition between the various intelligence groups, some of it heated. Never, though, did one agency go around murdering the operatives of another. More likely, Chen had been doubling during a lag in his Company duties. Doubling for whom, though?

Around sunset McCracken changed back into the sport jacket and slacks returned by the hotel valet service and hired a limousine to pick him up outside at seven o'clock sharp. Then he walked two blocks to a men's store and purchased an expensive camel's hair overcoat to complement the modest deception he was planning.

He was really running up an expense account on this assignment, but it didn't matter much. Since Gap and Company agents seldom maintained permanent addresses, bills for credit cards and the like all ended up at a central location to be dealt with in-house. Personal expenses were deducted directly from salaries. It was simpler that way.

The limousine arrived right on schedule. McCracken paid the driver in advance and gave him the address.

"You sure you got that right, pal?" the driver asked him in a gravel voice.

Blaine said he was.

"Usually people go down there, they do it in fast cars to make fast exits, not in tanks like this." The driver shook his head. His face was creased with scars and his nose was permanently swollen. He looked like a boxer who'd fought on well past his time. Blaine noticed his knuckles were callused as he gripped the wheel hard after restarting the car. "You ask me, the goddamn Port Authority should build an electrified fence around the whole fuckin' complex, keep the damn foreigners from shitting up the city. Know what I mean?"

Blaine just shrugged.

"I live in the city all my life," the gravel voice continued, pulling into traffic now. "Fought Carlos Monzon twice and he busted my nose both times. But he didn't bust it good enough I can't smell the stink rising from where you're headed. I got a piece stashed at my place. You want for a few extra bucks we'll stop over and I'll watch your back."

"Just watch the road."

"Suit yourself, pal. But if I hear shots from inside that boat, don't expect me to stick around and find out who caught the lead. Name's Sal Belamo by the way."

"Pleased to meet you," said McCracken.


The *Narcissus* had the look of a ship long out of love with its own reflection. The freighter was a giant, long and wide, a whale of a ship whose flesh was rotting with death and decay. Barnacles hugged her hull, which was rife with fresh repair patches and plenty more spots in need of the same. The letters proclaiming her name were cracked and peeling, the dot of the *i* missing and the final *s* with only a lower half. She held on to the dock the way elderly people dying alone and unwanted grip the handrails of their cold beds.

Blaine saw the first of Sebastian's guards when the limousine was thirty yards away from the *Narcissus*'s darkened slot on the pier. Four of them stood in a spread before the wooden planking leading onto the ship. They showcased their automatic weapons openly, as if a different set of laws applied down here on the docks, and Blaine supposed to a great extent it did.

"Holy Christ," moaned Sal Belamo. "You ask me, we shoulda stopped and grabbed my piece. What the hell's going on?"

"Pull up slow," McCracken instructed him. "Act like their presence here doesn't bother or surprise you."

"Their fuckin' presence has me shittin' in my pants, pal."

"I'll spring for a new pair of undies, Sal. Just do what I tell you."

Belamo obliged, but his hands tightened hard around the steering wheel.

Blaine knew he was in the FBI's sights right now and had to hope visits to the mysterious man on board the *Narcissus* were not unheard of. He hoped his modest disguise would eliminate the need for further investigation on the Bureau's part. A well-dressed man arriving in a limousine should appear to be just another of Sebastian's exclusive customers.

Belamo pulled the limousine to a halt just before the dock. McCracken could see the guards at the head of the walkway stiffen, hands starting to slide toward their rifles.

With a deep breath Blaine started to open the door.

"You ask me, pal, you're makin' a big mistake. Lots of people come down here end up as fish food and nobody gives a shit. Know what I mean?"

"Thanks for the comfort, Sal. Just keep the engine warm."

"Blazing, pal, blazing."

Blaine stepped out and closed the door behind him. He moved slowly and calmly forward, then stopped in front of the four guards. They watched him with cold intensity, eyes as black as their flesh, all layered with muscle thick as shoulder pads.

"I'd like to see Sebastian."

"He ain't here," said one of the men, and Blaine was honestly not sure which.

McCracken fingered his beard, edged a little closer so that the top of the plywood walkway complete with rope handrails was visible. More guards were up there standing watch over the gunwale.

"He'll be here for me," he said calmly.

"Write what you want to tell him in a letter. I'll make sure he gets it," said the shortest black with a chest the size of a beer keg. The man showed his rifle.

"Look, boys, I got business with the man. If he doesn't want to see me, I'll climb back in my car and beat it out of this rat hole, but I want to hear it from him first."

"You might lose your balls in this rat hole, shit for brains," the shortest guard charged, and his gun came up farther. An M-16, Blaine noted. The guard had the look of a man who had used one plenty of times before.

"You want to play with guns, friend, do it after you tell Sebastian that Madame Rosa bought it today and there's a spot on the farm waiting for him unless he sees me."

"Sebastian knows what happened to the old bitch."

The voice came from the top of the walkway and Mc-Cracken turned toward it along with the guards.

"Sebastian knows everything," the voice continued.

Blaine couldn't make out the speaker's features clearly in the misty darkness but did see him rest his hands on the rail.

"It's all right, Henry," said Sebastian, "send him up. But search him first and make sure he's clean inside and out."

Blaine submitted to the shortest guard's rough, calloused hands without complaint, all the time wishing he had his Browning or even Sal Belamo's piece to poke down his throat like a tongue depressor. Finding no weapon, Henry led him up the plank walkway, where Sebastian was waiting at the top in the center of a half-dozen more guards.

"Let's take our business inside," he said. "I been out long enough for one night."

The dapper Sebastian looked clearly out of place among his butcherous legion. His Afro was finely sculptured and rode just over the tips of his ears in slight ringlets. His skin was coppery light; his eyes were caramel brown and definitely scared. He was wearing a silk shirt and a pair of obviously expensive trousers. Chains, bracelets, and rings chimed and glowed everywhere about him. His fingernails were neatly manicured.

"This way." Sebastian beckoned, and Blaine followed him down a narrow staircase into the bowels of the ship with three guards and their guns shadowing his every step. Two more stood in front of a doorway and the larger held the door open when Sebastian approached. Blaine followed him inside, ducking his head a little under the low frame.

The light stung his eyes and then the setting itself made them widen. Sebastian's private quarters on board the *Narcissus* had been converted into a luxury apartment done in colonial woods and rich brown fabrics with a touch of nautical styling tossed in for good measure. A couch was bordered on both sides by end tables layered with coarse seaman's rope. Sets of leather-bound books were held up in three large wall units by various gauges that might once have occupied positions on some captain's bridge.

The door closed behind them and Blaine was surprised none of the guards had entered. Sebastian seemed to read his mind.

"If you try anything," he warned, "you'll be dead before you finish it."

"Your men that fast, Sebastian?"

"This is," the black man said, revealing a derringer he had been palming the whole time. "Two bullets loaded with hollow-point grains. Especially effective at close range. Please excuse me for holding it on you while we speak."

"Be my guest."

"Pull up a chair. Or would you prefer the couch?"

"A chair will do fine."

Blaine pulled one up. Sebastian crossed his legs on the couch.

"You're a well-protected man, Sebastian," Blaine opened, not worrying about the gun pointed at him.

"So was Madame Rosa and they got her."

"But you let me up."

"Because you're not black. When they try for me, the man will be black. Besides, I'm heading for Europe tomorrow at dawn. The ocean's got lots of hiding places."

"And, of course, you'll be filling more special orders once you reach land again." McCracken could not disguise the sarcasm in his voice.

Sebastian leaned forward. "I don't know who you are, but if you're aware of what happened to Madame Rosa, I figure you're as marked as I am and maybe you know something that might be able to help me. Now I'm realizing there's nothing that can help me so long as I remain in the States."

"Then you don't plan on returning. A lot of kinky assholes will just have to go wanting, I guess."

Sebastian squeezed his features together. "Mister, things are gonna start changing pretty fast in this country before long, and I don't want to be around for it."

Blaine felt a stirring in his stomach. Sebastian was scared, all right, but of more than just the threat to his own life.

"Who are you anyway?" he demanded. "What's your connection with all this?"

"I'm going to tell you the truth, Sebastian, because I see no reason to hold anything back. My name's Blaine McCracken and I've been called in to replace Tom Easton on his current mission. You remember Easton, don't you? He got sliced up by a couple of machine-gun clips along with a pair of twins you got special for him."

The last lines seemed not to reach Sebastian. "If you're replacing Easton, then you'd be smart to head for the oceans too."

"Sure, let's head out together. This could be the beginning of a beautiful friendship."

The humor was lost on Sebastian, but he smiled anyway. "You don't know what you're on to yet, do you?"

"I was hoping you might be able to help me there. You fingered Easton for the hit team, didn't you?"

"I had no choice," Sebastian said, suddenly defensive.

McCracken glanced around him, locking finally on the door. "For a guy who's got a goddamn army of chaperons, that sounds pretty strange."

"I got the army after they came the first time." Sebastian's stare grew distant, his grip slackening on his derringer. "They knew Easton was a patron of Madame Rosa's and that he required special orders to be filled from time to time. Since I was Madame Rosa's exclusive supplier, they came to me. I told them about the twins, when they were due in. The men seemed satisfied."

"You set those kids up along with Easton," Blaine charged. "You're as guilty as the men with the Mac-10s."

Sebastian stood up, trembling with rage. "Spare me your moralizing, McCracken. When I found those children, they were living in the streets of Athens and picked fruit to earn a penny or two a day."

"So you rescued them. And I always thought Jerry Lewis knew no equal. . . ."

"I provide a service, McCracken. I supply products to people who would otherwise be unable to obtain them. And ninety percent of the time everything is respectable, everybody comes out ahead, and nobody gets hurt."

"But then there are those other ten percent, right? And I'm not talking about just Easton either. You've probably gotten lots of innocent kids killed, Sebastian. But they're better off being tortured in some weirdo's bedroom than picking fruit, I suppose."

Sebastian's lips squeezed briefly together. "I don't plan to argue ethics with a hired killer, which is all you are. You're no match for who's behind all this. My advice is to run before they find you like they found Easton."

"Before *who* finds me?"

Sebastian hesitated. "The PVR."

"Never heard of them."

"Where have you been, out of the country or something?"

"As a matter of fact, yes. Tell me about this PVR. Why have they got you so scared that you've got an army protecting you above the water and divers protecting you below it?"

Sebastian's eyes flashed fear. "What divers?"

"I saw air bubbles rising on my way up to the deck."

Sebastian was shaking horribly now. "I don't have any divers!"

McCracken rose to his feet. "Then who . . ."

As if both men had realized the answer simultaneously, they rushed toward the door together, linked by the terrible certainty that they were going to be too late. They bolted up the stairs with a set of befuddled guards right behind them and had reached the deck when the explosion came, shattering the stillness of the night. Heat singed the air and buckled Blaine's flesh an instant before the world was yanked from under him. He reached out to grab something, anything, but it was all floating away.

Blackness came mercifully before impact, so it seemed he was still floating into a tunnel up ahead, and he tumbled into it falling, falling . . .

# CHAPTER 8

WHEN Captain Alan Coglan first saw Sandy Lister enter the restaurant, he couldn't take his eyes off her. It came as quite a surprise when she approached his table.

"Captain Coglan, I'm Sandy Lister."

Coglan rose to greet her. "Yes, I know," he said, starting to feel suspicious now.

"Please sit down, Captain. I'll try not to take up too much of your time and I'm sorry if I interrupted your dinner."

T. J. Brown had learned that Coglan ate dinner regularly at this small Italian restaurant near his station post, and Sandy had come with the intention of prying more information from him. Rarely did she take advantage of her celebrity status. It was great for avoiding long waits in restaurants or airports, but generally it was a burden to be shrugged off. Often during interviews her mere presence made people eager to please and under those circumstances they often revealed more than they intended. She was hoping for similar results tonight.

Coglan hadn't quite settled himself back in his chair when Sandy spoke again.

"T. J. Brown works for me, Captain."

Coglan's face stiffened. "I'm not sure it's a good idea that we speak, Miss Lister."

"What's an orbital flight plan, Captain?"

Coglan leaned across the table. "Miss Lister, please. By all rights I should have reported that T.J. had the disk in his possession, but for some reason I didn't. Your questions might force me to change my mind."

"I don't think so, Captain, because then you would have to explain why you waited so long. Your people might also somehow learn that you had dinner here with me, a television reporter. I doubt very much they'd appreciate the timing of that," Sandy warned, her threat spoken gently.

"Miss Lister, the information you're asking for is top secret."

"Not anymore, Captain. The disk was passed on to me by a civilian who died for the effort. Murdered, more specifically."

Coglan hesitated. "Everything I say will be considered off the record?"

"Absolutely."

"And you'll forget about this meeting ever taking place?"

"It never happened."

Coglan pulled his chair farther under the table and lowered his voice to a whisper. "The shuttle program is not my field, but I do know some basics. To begin with, the on-board crew under normal conditions has little control over the shuttle once it attains orbit. Everything is controlled and monitored by computers in Houston talking to computers one hundred and eighty miles above Earth. Through disks, Miss Lister. The disk T.J. brought me was one of the most important of all because it contained the preprogrammed space orbit *Adventurer* was to follow: when and where the shuttle would be at every instant of its orbit, barring malfunction, of course."

"And did any malfunction occur on the flight?"

Coglan shook his head. "No. Everything was running green."

"Just like *Challenger* . . ."

"No," Coglan said defensively, "not like *Challenger* at all. The final transmission . . ." His voice trailed off.

Sandy's eyebrows rose. No final transmission had been released to the press. "What transmission?"

Coglan backed off. "Miss Lister—"

"The shuttle was deliberately destroyed by someone, wasn't it?"

Coglan hedged, then nodded slowly. "Or something. It's been sealed tight under something called a Space-Stat alert, the space equivalent to a situation of war."

"What happened up there, Captain?"

"All investigations have been sealed, as I said."

"But there must be talk. There's always talk."

"Just rumors."

"I'd like to hear them."

"Off the record, right?" Coglan asked, needing the reassurance.

Sandy's nod left no doubt.

Coglan sighed. "Drone satellites have just returned with pieces of the wreckage. It's like nothing anyone's seen before. The shuttle wasn't just blown up, parts of it were totally vaporized."

"Jesus . . ."

"The real anomaly lies in the fact that Houston's radar board showed green the whole time *Adventurer*'s sensors were screaming bloody murder. Even when . . . whatever it was came into view of the astronauts, there was no evidence of it on any board back on Earth."

"That doesn't seem possible."

"There are plenty of scientists with million-dollar salaries claiming the same thing. A few are actually theorizing the attack came from outer space, as if we finally had strayed too far into someone else's territory."

"You believe that, Captain?"

"Absolutely not. I'm a military man, Miss Lister, and I don't buy passing off every unexplainable occurrence to some empire's death star. A human finger pushed the button that destroyed *Adventurer*, and I've got a feeling whoever owns that finger isn't finished yet."

\* \* \*

"A mess!" the President raged. "A goddamn raging, stinking mess!" He turned from the window of the Oval Office and faced Andrew Stimson. "Permission for you to use McCracken was revoked after the Paris incident. What in hell gave you the right to call him in on your own?"

Stimson found himself wishing fewer lights were on in the Oval Office so the fury on the President's face wouldn't be so obvious.

"Tom Easton gave me the right, sir," he said plainly. "He was my man and somebody sliced him to bits. McCracken was my best bet, my only bet, to find out who did it and why. I felt his skills were the ones that were needed."

"Skills that have brought the French to the verge of breaking off intelligence relations with us after his little escapade in Paris," Barton McCall snapped.

"What about the three dead terrorists? Or doesn't that count for anything?"

"Oh, it counts for plenty when the shooting was done on foreign soil by an agent who hasn't had kill clearance for five years." McCall paused, then raised his voice. "Plenty of embarrassment! And if that weren't enough, he pulls a repeat performance on the streets of New York this afternoon. *The streets of New York*, Andy! If only that explosion had killed him once and for all . . ."

"What was McCracken doing on that boat in the first place?" the President asked.

"I explained that. Sebastian was connected with Madame Rosa. He set up Easton."

"Then you knowingly let McCracken intrude on a Bureau operation?"

"I had to. There was no choice." Stimson's eyes flashed between the President and McCall, finding no support from either.

"The Bureau doesn't share your view," the President told him. "They're steaming over this. Six months of surveillance and investigative work went down the drain."

"Thanks to the bomb, not McCracken."

McCall lit his pipe. "And what about this famous microfiche McCrackenballs miraculously discovered? Has it yielded anything yet?"

"It will," Stimson said, not sounding as sure as he had tried to.

McCall puffed away. "You know, Andy, we could have avoided all this if you had kept closer tabs on the personal . . . tastes of your agents. Twins, Andy? I mean, really."

"And what about Chen, Barton? Or is it routine for you to station your men in whorehouses to murder madams?"

McCall yanked the pipe from his mouth and held it out like a gun. "I had no knowledge concerning this man Chen until you informed me of his involvement this afternoon."

"Maybe it's *you* who should keep closer tabs on your agents."

"Chen was freelance. On retainer with the Company but he filled plenty of other orders as well."

"Enough, gentlemen!" the President broke in. "I'll accept what's happened because I have to. The question now is, how do we pick up the pieces? What's McCracken's condition, Andy?"

"He's been slipping in and out of consciousness since the explosion. Moderate concussion and numerous bruises and lacerations. Nothing broken though. He'll be duty-fit within a few days."

"Then he'll also be fit enough to be pulled out," the President said flatly. "He's become too much of a liability. As soon as he's ready to travel, Andy, I want him brought down here to face a proper board of inquiry on the fiasco over in Paris so a determination can be made about his future."

"Retirement, sir?" Stimson asked, his meaning clear.

"*Normal* retirement. I want him buried so deep he'll never become a thorn in our side again."

"In a desk job, sir, or a casket?"

Sandy Lister met with T. J. Brown in his office first thing Thursday morning. She began stripping off her coat as he looked up from his computer terminal.

"Benjamin Kelno is clean as driven snow, boss," he

reported, punching up the results of his labors on the monitor screen.

Disappointed, Sandy sat down before it. She had hoped something in Kelno's background would offer some clue as to where he came into possession of the orbital flight plan he died planting on her.

"He spent the last twelve years of his life with the COM-U-TECH division of Krayman Industries," T.J. began, highlighting the information displayed on the monitor, "in the research and development areas. He was instrumental in creating The Krayman Chip, but as so often is the case in these matters, he received no credit."

"Disgruntled?"

"Not openly. His salary was six figures, he was promoted four times, and he left a loving wife and family. As near as I can tell, he turned down numerous offers from Krayman competitors in Silicon Valley, but there's no evidence he ever even interviewed with any of them." T.J. stopped and leaned back. "Now it's your turn. How'd it go with Coglan?"

Sandy moved away from the monitor screen. "*Adventurer*'s destruction was no accident, that much is for sure. And whoever blew it out of the sky would have needed to know its orbital flight plan."

"Kelno's disk," T.J. muttered. "Krayman Industries . . ."

"I'm not ready to make that connection yet."

"Sure, boss. But if it's true, and they killed Kelno because he tried to bring the story to you, it's not hard to figure who they'll be going after next."

"Calm down. Your own research doesn't show a damn thing that supports that conclusion. Krayman Industries is after control of the media. Destroying space shuttles doesn't fit there anywhere I can see. Who knows what Kelno might have been up to in his spare time?"

"We going to Shay with this yet?"

"Give me a couple more days."

"For what?"

"You're the one who said Krayman Industries and Randall Krayman were one and the same. My first interview is scheduled for tomorrow with a man who's got good reason to drag mud through the Krayman Tower. If something's going on there, he just might know what it is.''

# CHAPTER 9

Francis Dolorman looked nothing like the stereotype of the chief executive officer of a multi-billion-dollar consortium. As the man who succeeded the great Krayman upon his withdrawal five years before, he craved little attention and received even less. Anyone passing his small, thin figure on the street would never give him a second look and barely even a first.

Though Francis Dolorman was powerful and prominent, he did not throw lavish parties. He did not wine and dine political officials. He did not dream of his picture on the cover of *Time*, *Newsweek*, or *People*, and would have refused such a request if it were ever made of him. He preferred to lurk in relative obscurity. Public invisibility was a godsend because it permitted movement.

Dolorman had lived by that credo for the five years he had managed Krayman Industries and for many years previously. That such a seemingly meek, almost shy man could have risen to such a position would have been impossible if not for the calculating soul that lurked within. For as long as he could remember, Dolorman had thrived on others' underestimation of him. To be able to surpass a rival before he even considers you a threat is a great gift, especially in the world of business. Dolorman took tremendous pride in that advantage and saw no reason to change things at so late a stage in his life and career.

Similarly, he took pleasure in the fact that he could enter
the Krayman Tower in Houston and move to his private
elevator without drawing so much as a glance from his own
employees. Only those who saw him arrive in his limousine, the one luxury he allowed himself, might gawk briefly
or stammer out a greeting. Dolorman would smile back but
never stop for a hello or, God forbid, a conversation. The
less people knew about him, the better.

The limousine pulled to a halt before the main entrance
of the Krayman Tower Thursday morning and Dolorman
eased himself gingerly out. He had been on a destroyer
sunk by a Japanese kamikaze in World War II and his back
had suffered the brunt of the damage. The pain seldom let
up, and like everything else in life, it was just something
you got used to.

Because Dolorman could swallow his emotions as deftly
as his pain, the anxiety he felt this morning showed not the
slightest trace on his features. His skin was conspicuously
pale, as usual, and his white hair cropped close enough to
resemble a solid sheath. He made a straight, solitary path
toward his private elevator and rode it to his office on the
fifty-third and top floor. His mind recited the various man-
agement facilities of Krayman holdings as he passed them
floor by floor with the flashing of different numbered lights.

His secretary eyed him subserviently as he moved lightly
from the elevator. The pain in his back made Dolorman's
steps seem a glide rather than a walk.

"Mr. Wells and Mr. Verasco are waiting in your office
as instructed, sir."

"Thank you."

Dolorman entered and closed the door behind him. Wells
and Verasco rose out of respect, a study in contrasts. Verasco was a short, squat, olive-skinned man who chain-
smoked cigars everywhere except within Dolorman's
chambers; he knew Dolorman couldn't tolerate smoke of
any kind. His roles with Krayman Industries were many,
but none more important than overall coordinator of Omega; he had nursed the project almost since its inception.
Verasco's appearance, like Dolorman's, was deceiving. At

first glance he looked sluggish, even dim-witted. But his mind was quick and agile.

Wells was something else again. He was chief of Krayman Industries' Special Operations Force, a title which could not be found on any door but nevertheless gave Wells responsibility for preventing covert activities on the part of rivals and orchestrating these same activities against rivals when necessary. He was a front-line security man for the consortium, and Dolorman felt the job couldn't be in better hands. Wells stood a half-foot over six and continued to wear his hair in a stubbly crew cut long after his tenure with the army had come to an abrupt end. His considerable bulk more than filled out his frame and his neck was so layered with knotty muscle that it seemed a mere extension of his head.

Dolorman's glance toward Wells was typically short this morning; lingering looks were only for the strong of stomach. Wells's left eye was sealed tight by scar tissue that covered the better portion of that side of his face. An eye patch would have covered the bulk of the damage, but Wells disdained it in favor of maintaining an appearance that intimidated his enemies and sometimes his own men. His disfigurement extended up to a hairless patch on the left half of his scalp and down to his lip, so that side looked always to be cracked in a sinister grin. The only bothersome factor to Wells was the missing sight from his closed eye because it made him vulnerable from the left.

Luck had never been much on Wells's side. He had been bounced out of the Special Forces in 'Nam after a fellow officer ratted on him. They sent him home to a wife he didn't miss and a post as a drill instructor for elite recruits at Fort Bragg. A year into his tenure he caught his wife sleeping with a captain. He tore the man's throat out with his bare hands and was heading for the front door when his wife tossed a pot of boiling oil into his face. Wells turned away in time to save one half, but not the other. The pain was indescribable, but he fought it down and tore out her throat as well.

He was ripping at her chest, trying for the heart, when

the MPs arrived. It took a whole squad of them with black-jacks to subdue and then hospitalize him.

The case of the mutilated war hero received little atten-tion nationwide but a brief newsclip reached Francis Dolor-man, who saw a rare opportunity. In Dolorman's world there was often need for a man with Wells's . . . temper-ament. The problem was finding one trustworthy and loyal enough. Dolorman pulled every string he could to win Wells's release, and then hired him. Wells had been en-raged that night in the bungalow but his madness was far from permanent. He wanted very much to live and as a dedicated soldier swore lifetime allegiance to the man who had saved him from certain execution. Actually, it was far more than allegiance.

Over the years Dolorman had made considerable use of Wells's cruder skills, as well as his planning abilities. Wells was a master of shrewd commando tactics and, from train-ing and instinct, was able to organize carefully planned strikes on rivals when they suited the needs of Krayman Industries.

Of course, if Dolorman had sent Wells to handle the incident in New York, he would be faced now with one less pressing problem to occupy his immediate attention. He eased himself into the chair behind his desk and rotated his gaze to Verasco and then briefly to Wells.

"There are three issues we must deal with today," he began, systematic as always, "so let us take them in order of occurrence for progress reports. Wells, what is the latest on Kelno?"

"Our people in the New York police department have been especially cooperative," Wells replied. The left side of his mouth lagged a bit behind his right, leading to a slight slur of his speech, as if he spoke always with a small mouthful of food. "Unfortunately, their efforts have not produced the missing disk. It was not on his person and subsequent checks of his office and home have turned up nothing."

"Could he have mailed it or used a safe deposit box?"

Wells shook his massive head. "Impossible. Our people insist he had it on him when they made their move."

"Failure is not becoming to you, Wells."

Wells took the criticism without emotion. "Public executions are often interrupted by the unexpected. Such was the case in New York. Kelno was able to disappear into the subway before our men could finish him."

"With the disk, of course."

"Apparently. They caught up with him at the headquarters of the television network."

"Where Sandy Lister enters the scene. Problem number two. . ."

Wells made the semblance of a nod. "We know he whispered something to her, and it is quite possible he somehow slipped her the data. As of yet, though, we have no evidence that she has reported its presence or that it is in her possession."

"She's a reporter, Wells. She wouldn't part with it easily or advertise its existence."

"I've considered that and I've also considered this story she's proposed for her newsmagazine *Overview*. I don't think you should keep that interview with her next week."

"If I cancel it at this stage, Wells, it will serve only to raise her suspicions, and we must avoid that under the circumstances. Your own reports indicate we've been keeping tabs on her movements and that there's nothing to indicate Kelno said anything that links us directly to what he uncovered." Dolorman shifted uncomfortably in his chair and faced Verasco, who seemed a dwarf next to Wells. "And that, of course, brings us to the disk itself. What damage can its contents do us in Sandy Lister's or someone else's hands?"

"Next to none," Verasco reported surely. "Even if they've managed to learn what's on the disk, there's nothing that can possibly produce any link to us."

"Except in Lister's case," Wells reminded him. "Kelno worked for us and that is connection enough—too much. I suggest allowing me to set the wheels in motion for her elimination."

"I find that hardly the safest strategy to pursue at this time," Dolorman countered. "Her story on Randall Krayman is in the most preliminary stages and her investigation of the disk, if she has it, will not even reach that level. Besides, she is an interviewer, not a reporter. Investigative prying is not her specialty. But if she dies mysteriously, people she works with who do specialize in it might ask questions that will eventually lead to us. We can't have that."

"Agreed," Wells said just loud enough to hear. "For now."

"I am more concerned," Verasco started, "over our inability to learn the means by which Kelno obtained the disk and who he was working with."

"The disk was replaced with a dummy at COM-U-TECH here in Houston and relayed to Kelno in New York," Wells reported.

"For delivery to Lister?" Dolorman asked.

"If so, she wasn't expecting it. Kelno sought her out only after learning of her coming story on Randall Krayman. The real issue is who else Kelno was working with within our own organization."

"I've suspected a sub-layer of resistance for some time," Verasco advanced. "A group that has latched on to the essence of our Omega operation and has committed itself to disrupting it. They sought out Lister in an attempt to gain access to the media through which to expose the operation."

Dolorman nodded, his tight features squeezed even farther together. "Yes, if Kelno had lived long enough to tell Lister everything he knew, Omega would have been compromised."

"The point is he didn't," Wells said.

"You miss *my* point. Kelno is out of the way, but the people behind him, this layer lurking directly beneath us, is still active. They might seek out Lister again, guide her, help her."

"All the more reason for her elimination."

"I would prefer cutting the cancer out at its source,

Wells. We must learn more about our enemy within. We must destroy them.''

''They have withdrawn,'' Wells told him, ''gone even further underground. They know we are watching for them. That probably explains why they have yet to make contact with Miss Lister again.''

''Then we must keep the pressure on,'' Dolorman told him, ''increase it. Time is on our side. Activation of Omega is barely a week away. The sub-layer will begin taking risks before much longer. That will enable us to destroy them.''

''I don't think they're very large in number,'' Verasco theorized. ''But their potential to do us harm must still be respected.''

''We are in the process of retracing all of Kelno's movements for the past two months,'' Wells reported. ''The process is long but necessary. Eventually it will lead us to the other conspirators.''

Dolorman nodded and felt the stiffening along his spine. ''I am satisfied that everything possible is being done in both these regards, but there is also problem number three to consider.''

Wells nodded, sliding an eight-by-ten black and white photo from an envelope on the edge of Dolorman's desk. ''We now have positive confirmation that this man was the one outside Madame Rosa's as well as on board Sebastian's ship.'' Wells handed the picture across the desk to Dolorman. ''His name is Blaine McCracken.''

''Yes,'' said Dolorman, inspecting it. ''And he survived both the attack outside the brownstone and the boat explosion?''

''Yes. Details on the latter are sketchy, but apparently he was the only survivor of those who were on board at the time.''

''That doesn't seem to surprise you. Do you know this man, Wells?''

Wells stared blankly forward. ''I know him. From Vietnam. He and that Indian . . .'' Wells's voice trailed off, as if he were lost in a memory. Then he stiffened. ''I know where McCracken is now: Roosevelt Hospital in New York. His condition was just upgraded from serious to fair. I'm afraid we can't rely on God to get him out of the way for us.''

"Then perhaps we should ignore him," Verasco suggested. "After all, one man . . ."

"McCracken is not just one man," Wells snapped suddenly. "He must be killed and fast while we hold the advantage. More than anything else we've discussed, he poses a threat to Omega.''

"A hospital," Dolorman muttered. "We have someone we've used in similar situations before, I believe. Scola, wasn't it?"

Wells nodded halfheartedly.

"Then make the proper calls, Wells.''

"Scola's not the right choice for this job.''

"You have a better suggestion?"

"Me.''

"We can't spare you on such routine matters.''

"McCracken's anything but routine, and Scola's no match for him. Only someone who exists on his level can deal with him.''

"We'll use Scola, Wells," Dolorman said firmly. "Clear?"

Wells grunted his acceptance.

Dolorman started to rise painfully. "Then if you'll excuse me, gentlemen, these new developments must be reported. I've got a phone call to make.''


"Where are my flowers?" Blaine McCracken asked as Andrew Stimson walked into his hospital room Thursday afternoon. "You could have at least brought a box of candy.''

"Dipped in poison, if Washington had its way.''

"I take it our little ruse has been blown.''

"Exploded would be a better way of putting it.''

"But of course you're not considering pulling me off.''

"Damn right," said Stimson. "All I have to do is figure

out a way to keep the CIA and all other interested parties off my back.''

"Give me one more day's rest and I'll handle them myself. The wounds aren't as serious as they look. A few bruises, a concussion, and a rocky stomach from being fed through the arm.''

McCracken shifted about uneasily in his bed. Just about his entire body hurt, and negotiating around the IV setup was no easy chore to begin with. Outside the window a light snow had started up, draping a peaceful shroud over the grinding of tires struggling to stop and start.

"Do they know you came up here personally?" Blaine asked.

"I doubt they care very much. Too busy planning your funeral.''

"The reports of my death are soon to be greatly exaggerated.'' McCracken paused. "Someone saved my life at the docks, you know. Someone pulled me out of the water. I'd be singing with the angels now if it weren't for him.''

Stimson checked his watch and moved to the foot of the bed. "I haven't got much time, Blaine. I've got to get back to Washington before I'm missed by the wrong people. Did you learn anything from Sebastian?''

"Bits and pieces. He was scared shitless, I can tell you that much. Said he was gonna head his freighter into the open waters come dawn.''

"Apparently someone didn't want him getting away.''

"Somebody called the PVR. That mean anything to you, Andy.''

Stimson's face paled. His hands circled the bed railing and grasped it tightly. "The People's Voice of Revolution, a subversive group the Gap's been watching for some time.''

"A subversive *black* group?''

"Yes. Still making something of that?''

"It's already made, Andy. Think for a minute. Two blacks hit Easton, that Santa Claus with the acidic coffee was black, and Sebastian said the only reason he let me up was because I was white. The PVR is the clincher. Seems we've got a pattern here. Sebastian also said he was leaving the country because things were going to start changing very fast and he didn't want to be around for it. That fit the PVR pattern?''

"Not up till now. Their methods have always been non-violent, or at least nonconfrontational. But the potential's there for sure.''

"Membership?''

"Big and getting bigger. The People's Voice of Revolution is blessed with true charismatic leadership in the person of a fanatic named Mohammed Sahhan. Remember him from that election a few years back?''

"Vaguely. I was overseas at the time. French papers weren't always loaded with news from the home front.''

"Anyway, Sahhan rose to prominence by openly insisting that a national conspiracy was committed to keeping blacks the doormat of American society. Ninety-nine percent of the population, blacks included, figured he was crazy and just tuned him out. But, as they say, there's always that one percent. Sahhan developed quite a fanatical following, dedicated to rebuilding society from the ground up.''

"Doesn't sound very nonviolent to me,'' Blaine noted.

"The connection's there, Andy. The PVR got what they needed from Sebastian and then paid a visit to Madame Rosa's at the right time to ice Easton because he was on to their true nature. Everything fits. All we need now is for that microfiche to confirm it.''

Stimson sighed. "For the time being, the confirmation will have to come from somewhere else. We've pulled everything we can off the fiche, and besides lots of blank spaces, this is what we've got.'' Stimson groped in his jacket pocket and came out with a piece of paper. "See what you make of it.''

He handed it over to Blaine, who inspected it eagerly:

CHRISTMAS EVE DINNER FOR 15,000

Listed below that heading was a dozen or so foods—tomatoes, turkeys, bread loaves—all with numbers preceding them.

"It looks like a shopping list," McCracken offered. "Maybe Sahhan's planning a big bash on Christmas Eve."

Stimson was not amused. "Our top cryptographers are running it through the computers over and over again. We figure it's got to be a number/letter sequence combination, but we may have lost too much of the fiche to find the proper keys. There's a message in here somewhere, but we don't know how to put it together."

"Easton use anything like it before?"

"Not that we've been able to find."

"Maybe I shouldn't have killed that Santa Claus," McCracken muttered. "After all, he's the expert on Christmas Eve. Maybe the PVR's got a plot afoot to murder elves or kidnap Rudolph."

"If they do, only one man can tell us why," said Stimson.

"Mohammed Sahhan," said Blaine, while outside on the street below, a PA mounted atop an ancient Chevy repeated its taped message over and over: *Get your shopping done! Only seven days left until Christmas!*

# CHAPTER 10

"**L**ADIES and gentlemen, in preparation for our landing in Billings, the captain has turned on the no-smoking sign. . . ."

For Sandy Lister, following the trail of the elusive Randall Krayman began late Friday morning with a journey to Billings, Montana, to interview Alex "Spud" Hollins. Hollins had lived on top of the business world for a brief period after his company developed a new ultra-density microchip that effectively antiquated all similar products of the competition. The chip made life far easier in electronic switching stations used in telecommunications. Sandy did not pretend to understand the specifics of what she was dealing with here. What interested her more was the fact that it was Hollins's company that Krayman had first bankrupted and then bought out when the invention of the famed Krayman Chip by COM-U-TECH rendered the Hollins version obsolete. Hollins hadn't gone down without a fight, though. His battles with Randall Krayman made front-page news in *The Wall Street Journal* for weeks on end, battles he was destined to lose since the Krayman Chip would be manufactured at a cost one-third that of his own.

Still, there was no reason to shed tears over the fate of Spud Hollins. Already a rich man, Krayman's buy-out of his company had made him a multimillionaire and allowed him to pursue his true dream of raising horses on a vast

Montana ranch. He had achieved that dream now, and it surprised Sandy somewhat that after so many years out of the public eye he would consent to an interview on a subject as touchy as Randall Krayman. Perhaps, she thought, it was because Krayman could do no more to hurt him than he had already. Perhaps, too, Hollins was motivated by a desire for revenge, in which case Sandy would have to sift through his words carefully.

She hoped that Hollins might be able to shed light on Krayman Industries as well as on Krayman the man. She came to Billings more excited about a story than she had been in years. The incidents in New York had her wondering what really went on within the Krayman Tower. Surely she should have gone to Shay with the new developments, but she had stubbornly resisted because he would have taken the story away from her. Randall Krayman was hers, which meant Krayman Industries was too. She had never tired of personality journalism, but here was a story that called upon her mind as well as her smile. The change was refreshing, the challenge welcome. She felt like she was reliving the early years of her career, when she had to scratch and claw for every interview. The rewards had been fewer but the satisfaction greater.

Sandy descended the jet's steps into the frigid air of Billings, and her flesh seemed to freeze on contact. She had forgotten to put on gloves, and her fingers were already numb when she raised them to shield her face. She had known eastern winters for all thirty-three of her years, but nothing she had ever felt prepared her for such sub-zero cold. She stuffed her hands into her overcoat pockets and tucked her carry-on bag under one arm. Besides that there was only one other suitcase she had to retrieve inside the terminal.

At the baggage claim area several passengers asked her for autographs but most kept to themselves. Finally seeing her suitcase rolling toward her on the conveyor belt gave her an excuse to beg off. She was reaching for it as it passed, when a large hand cut in front of hers and grasped the handle.

"I'll take that for ya, Miss Lister," a voice drawled.

"Excuse me?"

"Mr. Hollins sent me out here to fetch ya, ma'am. Didn't mean to startle ya none."

"You didn't. It's just that I wasn't expecting anyone to pick me up."

The man, who was big and broad, in his fifties, with a wind-carved face, yanked off his cowboy hat. "Yeah, well, a storm blew in last night and dumped more 'an a foot on the roads. Plows don't always make it up to our spread and Mr. Hollins didn't want you drivin' some rented Ford into a gully." He smoothed his hair, replaced his cowboy hat, and led her toward the airport lobby, suitcase in hand. "Mr. Hollins also told me to issue ya an invitation to stay over at the ranch if you'd like."

"I have a reservation at the—"

"Nothin' beats good ol' Hollins hospitality, ma'am." They were almost to the exit doors. "Come on, ma'am, got your limo parked right this way. Name's Buck, by the by."

The "limo" as it turned out was a four-wheel drive Chevy Blazer with the license plate SPUD 6. Buck had left the engine running to make sure the inside remained warm for her, a gesture which was not lost on a city girl who knew anyone doing the same at Kennedy or LaGuardia would end up one car poorer for the effort.

Buck hoisted her suitcase through the open tailgate as Sandy settled herself on the front seat. It was quite a climb from ground level, and one of her high heels almost didn't make it. Obviously she was not dressed appropriately for Billings weather. A gush of frigid air smacked her as Buck slammed the tailgate closed. A few seconds later he pulled himself up behind the wheel.

"Where's all the cameras, ma'am?"

"What? Oh, you mean for when we film the interview. I'll come back with those after we put the story together, after it's approved. First I've got to learn what Mr. Hollins has to say."

"Sorta like an au-dition, right?"

"Not far from it, I suppose."

"Kinda gives ya a jump on the guy you're puttin' the story together on, don't it?"

Buck pulled the Blazer out into the road that circled the airport. Sandy could see the snow piled high along the sides, pushed there by powerful plows.

"That's the nature of the business, Buck," Sandy said.

"Yeah, well, I been hear'n 'bout news media types slantin' stories and rearrangin' them to say what they want 'em to say. Can't say I take a fancy to that."

"Neither do I."

"See, the way it is, ma'am, there's lots of us work for Mr. Hollins hate to see him hurt. Know what I mean?"

"I think I do."

They drove north on I-87, heading toward the outskirts of Roundup and Spud Hollins's ranch. Buck's frankness had Sandy wondering what kind of man it took to inspire such loyalty. She looked forward to meeting him all the more.

"That there's the Musselshell River, ma'am," Buck announced, thrusting a finger across her toward the right. "That's where we get the water from for our ranch. Damn thing's frozen solid by this time of year. Been a bad winter so far and winter ain't even shot its biggest load yet. Could be the worst since sixty-two, when . . ."

Buck droned on for five more minutes until they came to the entrance of the Hollins ranch, a simple gate with one word burned in wood over it:

SPUD'S

"Here we are, ma'am," Buck said, spinning the wheel. "Five thousand acres of the prettiest land you ever did see."

Buck followed the winding road for what might have been a mile over snow that seemed more packed down than plowed. It didn't seem to faze him. And he was right about the land; it was postcard perfect, especially with the snow-

covered mountains standing watch over it all beneath the
crystal blue sky.

Finally the Blazer reached the semi-circular driveway that
fronted the two-story mansion built of dark-stained natural
wood, its roof covered with a coat of snow. Buck hurried
around the Blazer to help Sandy down and then set about
collecting her tote bag and suitcase. The heavy double doors
at the front of the house opened as she approached them,
and a striking middle-aged man stood smiling before her
with his hand outstretched.

"Spud Hollins, Miss Lister. Pleasure to meet ya."

Sandy said that the pleasure was all hers and she meant
it. Her research put Hollins's age at fifty-nine, but he
looked a good dozen years younger. His straight, silvery
hair, showing no sign of thinning, hung over his ears and
forehead. He wore faded jeans, a denim shirt open at the
collar to reveal a bandanna, and scuffed cowboy boots. His
flesh was wizened and creased, coppery from the mountain
air and the winter sun. Hollins's deep eyes, the same color
as the Montana sky, watched Buck tote her bags inside.

"She accepted your invitation, Spud," he said.

"Ain't that nice," said Hollins, and Sandy smiled
tightly, not recalling that she had actually accepted at all.

Hollins closed the double doors. "Wanna talk first or
get freshened up?"

"Talk," Sandy said eagerly. "I've been traveling too
long for freshening up to do any good."

"A pretty lady like you don't have much call for that
anyway, I reckon. Let's go in the den. Coffee?"

"Please."

"Buck," Spud said, "have the kitchen mix us up a couple cups."

Then the two of them moved down a short hallway into
a large room with a fire crackling in a central hearth.

"Wow," was all Sandy could say.

"Yup, it's my favorite room too."

"It's beautiful," she added lamely, enchanted by the
natural wooden decor and the view provided by the large
expanse of glass on one wall.

Hollins's gaze grew distant. "Sometimes, well, I just sit here and wonder what took me so long to get out of the real world and into this one. I guess it was just stuck in me like a drug. I wanted to get out, but I didn't have the guts to do it. Guess I owe Randy Krayman a debt more than anythin'."

Sandy's eyes danced at that. Interviews came much easier when the subject broached the issue at hand first. Sandy now determined she would not use tape and take no notes while they spoke, intent on doing nothing that might disrupt the natural flow of Spud Hollins's thoughts. She found herself captivated, enthralled by this man. He was like one of those politicians you can't take your eyes off when they come into town. Perhaps he had missed his true calling. No, more likely Spud Hollins was just a man who could stand tall because he had escaped the constant pressures that weigh on so many in the business world. He looked like a character out of a Ralph Lauren aftershave commercial. In fact, he looked like a crusty, country version of Ralph himself.

"Let's sit on the couch, Miss Lister," he offered, and as they did, Sandy noted a mantel lined with pictures of his various children and grandchildren. His wife, she knew, had died some years before, when the Krayman battle was reaching its head.

"I think maybe I'm doing a story on the wrong man, Mr. Hollins."

Hollins laughed. "Call me Spud. I left all that kind of stuff behind me 'long with my seat on the stock exchange. Your ass, if you'll excuse my word choice, takes on a funny shape when you sit in business too long. Nope, Krayman's a much better choice for a story than me. He probably ain't got much of an ass left by now."

A maid entered and put two steaming cups of coffee along with generous helpings of cream and sugar on the table in front of the couch.

"Not many people are willing to talk about him on the record, Spud," she said, adding two spoonfuls of sugar and a dash of cream.

"Can't say I blame them, Sandy. People are scared of old Randy Krayman because he's been known to chew a few up over the years."

"Like you?"

Hollins smiled but didn't laugh. "Well, most of the chewin' in my case was done by me. Krayman added a couple bites here and there."

Sandy sipped her coffee. It burned her tongue but tasted wonderful.

"Bites is an interesting choice of words, Spud, considering it was over the computer kind that the two of you went to war."

"Business ain't war, Sandy. In war you take prisoners. In business you take shit. I got out 'cause I didn't have the stomach for the shit anymore."

"And you sold out to Krayman."

"If I had kept fighting him, I would have been selling out period. Like I said before, old Randy did me a favor. Made me a damn good offer. Had good reason to also." Hollins crossed his legs and reached for his coffee. "How much do you know about what went on between us back then?"

Sandy wished she had her notes to consult. "Most of it concerned an ultra-density memory chip. Your company got one into production first, then COM-U-TECH developed a better one and undercut the price by two thirds."

"Yup." Hollins nodded. "They did at that. You know what this ultra-density microchip did, Sandy?"

"Not specifically."

"Way it was, see, all computer chips used to be placed side by side. The ultra-density chip could be stacked one on top of the other so you'd end up with a job done in a fraction of time since the information had lots less space to travel. The discovery revolutionized lots of industries, mostly oriented 'round communications. What with cable startin' to boom and the explosion of live satellite feeds, there was need for new micro-switching equipment capable of doing things quicker and cheaper than ever. Radio was the same way, telephone, too, maybe most of all. Way I hear it, the chip revolutionized the whole airline industry as well. Whole damn telecommunications industry had to rethink and retool almost from scratch.''

''All because of one chip?''

Hollins smiled faintly. ''Hold up your hand, Sandy. See your thumbnail? That's the size of the chip we're talking about.''

''And you had it first, didn't you?''

Hollins's smile became even more faint. ''I suppose you could say that.''

''But it was Krayman who made millions on the chip, a fortune.''

''That's what you've heard, ain't it?''

''That's what everybody's been hearing for a decade.''

''It ain't true.''

''What isn't?''

''Krayman didn't make no fortune off his famous chip. Matter of fact he lost money. Sold the buggers at less than half his cost.''

''How can you know that?''

Hollins returned his coffee to the table and almost spilled it. '' 'Cause there never was no such thing as the Krayman Chip. He stole it from me.''

It took a few seconds for Hollins's words to settle in.

''Wait a minute,'' she managed, ''are you saying that the famous Krayman Chip was just a version of yours?''

''Nope, not a version. It was mine lock, stock, and barrel with a few cosmetic changes thrown in for good measure. Sort of like retyping *Gone with the Wind* and publishing it under a new title.''

''But how—''

''Believe me, Sandy, there haven't been many days over the years when I haven't asked myself that same question.'' Hollins glanced around him. ''Least until I got here. Anyway, computer espionage makes what goes on between the Russians and our boys look like playschool. The real cold war is a circuit war and it's bein' fought right here in the U.S. of A. Always has been. I don't know how Krayman got hold of my design. Guess I never will. Fact is he did, though, and brought it out into the market 'bout a year after I did with a new name . . . and different price.''

"But if what you're saying is true, he must have lost the same fortune he was reputed to have made.''

"And don't ask me why neither. First I thought he had some vendetta against me in particular. Maybe he didn't like somebody 'sides IBM diggin' in the same yard as he was. Maybe it was worth all that money to him to get me out of the way. Lord knows he could afford it. Then I figured it was a pretty expensive proposition to carry out just for pride. 'Sides, if that was what was on his mind, why'd he buy me out for sixty mill when my stock was about to hit rock bottom anyway? Nope, it made no sense then. Still don't.''

"Some part of a larger picture perhaps?''

"Way I figure it, the whole deal ended up costing him a hundred, maybe a hundred and fifty million dollars and the loss sheet ain't been balanced yet. Pretty expensive picture.''

"Did you tell anybody this when it was happening?''

"Sure, lots of people. Nobody wanted to hear about it. And them that did, well, something made them change their minds pretty quick and a few seemed to just vanish. Most gave me the courtesy of listening and said they'd check things out.'' Hollins snickered. "Maybe they're still checkin'.'' His face grew somber. "Can't say I blame 'em, though. It's like you said before 'bout nobody wantin' to talk on the record about Krayman now even though he ain't been seen in five years. Imagine what it was like then when he was makin' newspaper headlines every day.''

"You could have sued.''

"I did. Case stayed in the courts long enough for me to realize I was fighting for something I didn't want anymore. I'd spent too much time up here raising horses in God's country to go back to all that. I figure I made out pretty good on the deal. Got everything I ever wanted. There are days up here where the phone don't ring at all and I like that just fine. Yup, if you ask me, Sandy, I made out lots better on the deal than old Randy. A just Lord gave him his due. He pulled up stakes and ran like I did, 'cept the difference is he's hidin' and I'd wager he ain't got half the space I got even if he's got ten times the land.''

Sandy found herself totally transfixed by a man who had openly come to love his life. Through all his words, all the painful rehashing of his hardest times, his voice had not so much as wavered. Emotion was absent, contented acceptance clear, as if the past had happened to someone else. And maybe it had. Alex Hollins had become simply Spud.

''What about the effects of the Krayman Chip on the rest of the computer industry?'' she asked him.

''Well, Sandy, now we come to the real fun part of the story. See, the ultra-density chip makes computers work so fast that they can talk only to computers that are wired the same way. So I guess you could say it revolutionized the entire production industry, too, and Randy's got himself a monopoly on the ultra-density market. It's too damn specialized for anyone to challenge him, 'specially after what he done to me. The whole goddamn telecommunications industry is probably wired by now with chips that oughta have a little *S* for 'Spud' tattooed in their corner. Why, you can't turn on a TV, fly in an airplane, use one of them automatic teller machines, or even make a phone call without bein' affected by Randall Krayman.''

''So maybe a one-hundred-fifty-million-dollar loss was worth it, after all.''

Spud Hollins's expression stayed chiseled in stone. ''Depends on your perspective, ma'am.''

After the interview was complete, Sandy used the need to freshen up as an excuse to dash upstairs and try to capture all of the salient points of Hollins's comments on her notepad. It wasn't easy. She wanted to remember each and every word he said, each colorful expression, and ended up confusing things and having to reconstruct the conversation in her mind from the very beginning. When she had finished, twelve pages were full of scribbling and almost two hours had passed. Dinner would be coming up shortly and she didn't want to burden Hollins's hospitality by being late.

Still, she had to check in with T.J. He would be expecting a call and she wanted to learn if anything new had turned up regarding the computer disk. He answered his phone on the second ring.

"It's me, T.J. How's—"

"I'm scared, boss. Oh, God, I'm scared." His voice sounded frantic.

"Slow down. What's wrong?"

"The orbital flight plan. It's . . . gone."

# CHAPTER 11

$F$RIDAY night Scola moved stealthily down the corridors of Roosevelt Hospital, hiding her face as well as she could behind the cart she was pushing. Amazing how busy the place was during the daylight hours, but once night fell, a shroud of somber silence seemed to enclose it. So far no one had said a single word to her. They seldom did when she donned her nurse's disguise to carry out a mission.

Being a woman was a great aid to her in her work as an assassin. She was able to get into dozens of places men couldn't and the possible disguises were endless. Somehow targets didn't feel threatened by women. They let them get too close and often that was when Scola struck. The nurse's guise had always been one of her most effective. So often over the years when others had failed to carry out their assignments, wounding the target instead of killing him, Scola was called in. She wasn't sure of the precise circumstances surrounding her target in room 434, nor did they concern her. All that mattered now was that she was totally prepared, her instrument of death stored openly on her nurse's cart.

Scola had worked for a time with the CIA, quite effectively in fact. Then, though, drugs had entered in. This was hardly unusual in the case of active field agents, especially assassins, so the Company was well equipped to deal with it; that is, so long as the subject could be con-

sidered a soft case rather than a hard one. Five months
after her cocaine habit began, Scola found her file upgraded
from soft to hard and she was out of a job. The Company
wanted no part of an addict. The odds of a slipup were
simply too great. Scola fumed briefly, then plunged into
the free-lance market, where the pay was exorbitant, the
hours better, and no issue was made of her habit.

The wheels of her cart squeaked a bit as she headed
toward the elevator. The sound soothed her. Yes, returning
to a hospital for a mission was like coming home. These
buildings were all the same, and she had never failed in
one yet.

The elevator doors opened and Scola shoved her cart in
ahead of her.

Blaine McCracken accepted the pain-killers only at night
to help him sleep. He knew he needed his rest if he wanted
to make a quick return to duty. He'd leave it to Stimson to
sort out the political complications. He was concerned only
with healing his own body or at least making it functional.
For this he needed sleep but for sleep he needed the pain-
killers.

Blaine had always hated them. He'd seen lots of young
boys in 'Nam become addicts after only a few injections
of morphine in the field and since then had avoided any
drugs at virtually all costs. But this was different. More
than twenty-four hours had passed since his meeting with
Stimson and the inactivity had begun to gnaw at him. He
was restless and sleep was virtually impossible without
chemical help. The two pills he had taken an hour before
were just starting to reach their full effect. He felt himself
starting to float into the darkness of the room.

In the final moments before consciousness left him,
Blaine focused on what information the fiche had yielded:
*Christmas Eve dinner for 15,000* and the list of foods with
numbers preceding them beneath it.

Stimson's computers had gotten nowhere in their quest
to break the code. Nor would they ever be able to if too
many alphabetical and numerical components were miss-

ing. Without the complete text, no patterns could be found, and without patterns Easton's cipher would continue to elude them.

But what if such alphabetical and numerical patterns weren't important? There was something Blaine wasn't considering, something the computers *couldn't*. In his half-sleep he could almost reach out and touch it.

*It looks like a shopping list. . . .*

McCracken's mind had locked on that thought, when sleep overcame him.

Francis Dolorman held the receiver to his ear as he punched out a private number. His line was "swept" daily to insure no tap or recording devices were in place, nothing that might betray the frequent discussions that were so crucial to the success of Omega.

"Yes," responded the man on the other end.

"There are further complications, sir."

"I'm listening, Francis."

"We confirmed that Kelno delivered the disk to Sandy Lister and now we have it back in our possession."

"Then what's the problem?"

"Miss Lister, sir. This development makes her a grave risk to us at this stage."

"But with Omega only five days from activation, eliminating her remains even more risky. Without the disk she has no proof and you've already assured me there was nothing on it that could in any way lead back to us."

"Unless more of Kelno's accomplices link up with her. Wells is making no inroads toward learning their identities. If they reach Lister, it could be disastrous."

"Except, Francis, to do so they'll have to surface, which is just what we want. Make sure Wells is ready at that time. They'll show themselves before long. The pressure's on them, not us. Now, what about the McCracken business?"

"It's being handled this evening, sir. I expect no complications."

"With men like McCracken there are always complications. Get back to me when it's finished."

Scola eased her cart around the sharp corner and headed toward the bank of private rooms on the fourth floor. She could already tell that no guard was stationed outside room 434. This would make her job even easier than she had been led to expect it would be.

The nurses on duty at the central station were chatting and giggling, so Scola was able to move smoothly by without having to announce herself. An orderly eyed her as he passed, but Scola smiled routinely and kept going. Room 434 was just up ahead.

Scola could feel her heart beating hard now. This was partially due to the cocaine she had ingested only an hour before. The drug sharpened her senses and made her feel as though she could accomplish anything. Failure was out of the question.

Scola opened the door to room 434 and dragged the cart in after her. The door closed softly.

She stepped into the darkness.

McCracken felt himself come drowsily awake. He wasn't sure what had stirred him from his rest, and his mind was too slowed to utilize its normal reasoning powers. There had been a sound and something else, something that had come to him in his sleep.

*Christmas Eve dinner for 15,000 . . .*

He had found the answer in his sleep! His body must have stirred for fear he might lose his grip on it during the long hours of the night. Blaine fought with his dulled mind, fought with it to yield the answer sleep had revealed.

*So simple, so damn simple . . .*

It was this slight sharpening of his senses that allowed him to feel the presence of another person in the room. He could feel the intruder closing on him. No, not feel—hear. There was a squeaking sound that suddenly stopped.

For an instant Blaine drifted toward sleep again, then struggled back.

By that time in the darkness Scola had removed her target's IV pouch from its hook and replaced it with one from her cart, the contents of which would lead to a quick, mysterious death. All she had to do now was reinsert the needle in her pouch.

Blaine felt the slight tugging on his arm and shifted his eyes lazily to the side. They were slow to respond to the near total blackness of the room, broken only by a slight spill of light sneaking through a crack in the venetian blinds.

The spill caught something white moving at his side.

Blaine knew it was a nurse, knew her presence here was all wrong. Adrenaline surged through his veins, reviving him, providing the thrust he needed to regain motor capacities.

Scola's needle dug deep into the IV pouch and a clear liquid began flowing out immediately, heading straight for her target's veins.

The suddenness of his movement shocked her, but she thought it was more a spasm than an action until she saw he was clearly reaching out for her. Scola recoiled and slammed into her cart.

Blaine had almost made it from the bed when the numbness grasped him. It seemed to start in all his limbs at once, leaving his brain frustrated and confused. The white figure was hovering back over him now and it should have been so easy to reach up and choke the daylights out of her. But when he tried to reach, there seemed to be nothing to reach with, as if his mind and body had become two separate entities.

He tried for a scream, but all that emerged was a muffled rasp. Then, as if to preclude further effort on his part, the white figure threw something down upon him—a hand, that was it, a hand over his mouth, and Blaine felt his head rocking helplessly back and forth. With an incredible effort he shook the hand from his mouth and, using the last reserves of his strength, twisted the arm bearing the needle that was killing him violently enough to strip it from his flesh.

The white figure groped for it while Blaine flailed with a heavy arm for the nurse's call button. He had almost reached it when the white figure snatched his arm and pinned it to the bed. He tried to roll free, tried for anything, but his motions came one frame at a time, which was how he saw the white figure grasp the pillow and lower it toward him.

*Help, somebody, help!!!!!!!!!!!!!*

Blaine had screamed the plea only in his mind. The pillow was over his face and it took a few seconds before his dulled brain registered that he couldn't breathe. He tried to use his arms, but they were heavy and slow. Consciousness skipped and darted but strangely he felt no pain, just emptiness.

There was a sudden smack in his ears, followed rapidly by two more, a pause, and then a last. The pressure eased up on the pillow and Blaine realized he could breathe again. Then the pillow was yanked from his face, exposing his eyes to sudden stinging light. They closed reflexively, then opened slowly again to find a familiar face looming over him wearing a half-smile.

"That makes it two you owe me, pal."

And Blaine caught the wink of Sal Belamo.


It was two hours later before he came fully around and faced the chauffeur who had driven him to Sebastian's boat in the harbor.

"It was you who pulled me out of the water," Blaine said in what had started out as a question.

Sal Belamo nodded, the light emphasizing that bent nose. "You ask me, this whole assignment was weird from the start."

"You were almost too late tonight."

Sal's eyes tilted toward the bloodstained floor, where earlier the fake nurse's body had been. "Fucking bitch locked the damn door. I had to run back and grab a key. Her name was Scola. Used to work for the Company."

"Stimson set this whole thing up?"

Sal Belamo got up from his chair and stretched. "He

didn't send Florence Nightingale with the poison bedpan, if that's what you mean.''

"I mean you."

Belamo nodded. "He had a watch put on your phone line at the hotel two days back. When you called for a limo, he figured he might as well take the opportunity to provide some backup.''

"Why not tell me?"

Sal shrugged. "You got me on that one, pal. I was just followin' orders. Maybe he didn't want you behavin' any different 'cause I was around. Tonight he figured someone would try to whack you, and I had orders to keep you safe and sound. 'Course, that brings us to the next stage of the plan. You ask me, it's a little much, but orders again.''

"What?"

"Boss wants to make sure you're dead."

"You mean, it's supposed to look like Scola was successful," Blaine realized after a few breathless seconds.

"And got offed herself in the act," Belamo acknowledged. "Should give you room to move around, stretch your legs a little.''

"I gotta hand it to Stimson."

"Yeah, like I said, he knew somebody'd be coming to finish the job the explosion started. The thing was, I had to let them make the attempt. You ask me, it got a little close. I mean, if there's no one with keys at the nurse's station . . .''

McCracken sat up a little more in bed. Twin sledgehammers went off in his head.

"We gotta head down to Washington, pal. You okay to travel?''

"Give me till sunrise and I'll be fine. Right now I want you to get Stimson's private number for me.''

Belamo's cold eyes showed he didn't approve. "You're supposed to be dead, remember? Hospital lines are open, pal, and corpses don't talk much.''

"Stimson will understand. I'll take the responsibility."

"Damn right you will." Belamo moved reluctantly to

the phone on Blaine's nightstand. "I just do what I'm told. You ask me, life's a lot simpler that way." He pressed out the proper series of numbers and handed the receiver over to Blaine. "It's your neck, pal. Be a shame if he chops it off after I just saved it."

"Stimson," came the Gap chief's groggy voice after four rings. Obviously the call had reached him at home. It must have been later than Blaine thought.

"This is your wake-up call, Andy. Coming straight from the Pearly Gates."

"Blaine! I left orders with Belamo not—"

"Pipe down and get your pants on, Andy. You're gonna want to get right down to the office after you hear what I've got to tell you. The computers couldn't figure out the fiche because you sent them in the wrong direction. It's so simple we almost missed it. I had it right from the beginning and I didn't even know it."

"Am I dreaming all this?"

"Yup, and it's a nightmare." Blaine paused. "Christmas Eve dinner for 15,000—the fiche *is* a goddamn shopping list. But not for food, Andy. The list is for *weapons*. Each food represents a different armament. I'll give you the specifics later, but according to the menu, Sahhan's got enough to outfit an army of, you guessed it, fifteen thousand or so."

# CHAPTER 12

SAL Belamo drove McCracken to LaGuardia an hour past dawn on Saturday. At the hospital they made use of service elevators and exits, so that no one would see Blaine leave. Meanwhile, a John Doe that had shown up the night before was being given Blaine's name, chart, and fake death certificate. The apparent hospital murder would be sealed tight, but Belamo would make sure enough leaked out to reassure Scola's employers that Blaine McCracken had indeed perished. Belamo, in fact, had set up the whole ruse in the last hours of darkness before they left. He was far more clever than his beaten-up exterior and gravel voice suggested. Blaine should have figured Stimson would never have left him to visit Sebastian on his own, let alone leave him vulnerable at the hospital.

"Be seeing ya, Sal," he told Belamo at the airport, where he'd be taking a private Learjet to Washington.

"First let me get over the cold I got from jumping in that water."

"Deal."

The flight to Washington was smooth and short and, as arranged, McCracken climbed into a cab with the designated license plate outside Washington National Airport. Andrew Stimson was waiting for him in the backseat.

" 'Morning, Andy."

Stimson's face was pale and his eyes were sagging.

"This is everything we've got on Mohammed Sahhan and the People's Voice of Revolution," he said gruffly, flopping three stuffed manila dockets onto the seat between them. "Go over it carefully. There may be something in there that can help you."

"Was I right about his army?"

Stimson sighed. "Not that we can prove, but that doesn't mean a thing. You're right. Everything fits together this way, and for now we proceed on that premise." A grim nod. "In which case, a fanatic radical has fifteen thousand troops at his command. . . ."

"And plenty of weapons," Blaine added.

"We don't know he has them now," Stimson said hopefully. "He may not have taken delivery yet."

"Maybe not total delivery, but the amount of armaments we're talking about here would have to be smuggled in and distributed gradually, over a period of months even. And don't forget that Easton's menu was for Christmas Eve. That's only four days from today."

Stimson's features whitened still more. His head slipped backward a bit. "My God, a Christmas Eve strike . . ."

"Like it or not, that's the indication. It's a little crazy if you ask me. Where'd he get all those men? Fifteen thousand's an awful lot of people to inspire to take up arms."

"Not when you consider there'd still be twenty-five million blacks on the same side of the fence as us," Stimson explained. "Not a surprising ratio, is it? There've probably been plenty on the other side all along. It just took someone like Sahhan to motivate and organize them."

The cab negotiated through the early morning rush hour traffic.

"That's where this mess breaks down, Andy: with organization. Armies need lots more than motivation to make their guns work."

"This isn't an army in the traditional sense. Most of what they need to know could have been taught to them in small groups, or even privately."

"But sooner or later they'd have to link up."

Stimson shook his head. "Not really if Sahhan's done

his homework. The Gap, Company, and Bureau have several recent studies on how many organized terrorists it
would take to throw the entire civil order of the country
into utter chaos if the timing was right. The numbers we
considered were all substantially lower than fifteen thousand.''

"Then you must have considered possible tactics and
strategies as well.''

"And all of them are right up Sahhan's alley. Terrorists
wouldn't have to knock out the whole country, just the
major urban centers—say the top thirty. That would mean
five hundred per city—organized, well armed, and acting
totally with the element of surprise on their side.''

"And striking on Christmas Eve, when all police and
reserve units operate on skeleton crews.'' Blaine suddenly
felt chilled. "With the firepower Sahhan's got, based on
that shopping list, we could have martial law by Christmas
morning.''

"Precisely why I've already contacted an old friend of
mine, Pard Peacher, commander of the Delta Force anti-
terrorist commandoes. He's sending small crack squads undercover into all major cities to locate the individual
terrorist cells, a kind of search and destroy mission.''

"So long as word doesn't get around about their presence,'' Blaine pointed out. "Sahhan's men would only retreat further underground. We'd never find them.''

"Peacher's a pro and his men are the best, all trained
by the Israelis. They know what they're doing.''

Blaine's mind had returned to another track "But the key
is still weapons, Andy, not men. Assuming Sahhan's taken
delivery of his arsenal, chances are distribution of that kind
of firepower is being held to the last minute. So if we can
latch on to his supply channels and trace the chain to his
storage dumps, we could prevent distribution and stop the
bastard in his tracks. No guns—no revolution.''

Stimson's eyebrows flickered. "I like your thinking. And
there'll be no need for a firing squad now because for all
intents and purposes you're already dead.''

"Does Washington know about your contacting Peacher?"

"No, it's just between us. I explained the situation to Pard and he agrees. The element of trust doesn't exist anymore, if it ever did. They did us a favor by trying to take you out in New York. Now we'll have Washington off your back, as well as Sahhan."

Blaine hesitated. "Assuming he was the one who hired Scola."

"Who else would have?"

"I don't know. But something stinks here and all the smells don't lead back to Sahhan. Take Scola for example. She doesn't impress me as the kind of assassin he'd hire or even have access to. But there's more. I can't put my finger on the reasons, but I know there's someone else involved here, Andy. Sahhan's just a part of what's going on, connected to something even bigger."

"We're talking about a goddamn civil war in five days, Blaine. How much bigger can you get?"

"Plenty. Let's backtrack. Let's assume that Easton uncovered what Sahhan was up to, that and nothing else. We know it was Sahhan's people who set him up through Sebastian and two blacks did carry out the hit. But that's where the PVR connection breaks down. Chen wasn't theirs, the carolers weren't theirs, and neither was Scola."

"You're saying that Sahhan has got some sort of silent partner."

"Someone who also has something to gain from civil unrest. But who? And why?"

Stimson pointed to the date displayed on his watch. "Today's the twentieth, Blaine. Christmas Eve's Wednesday. That doesn't give us a whole lot of time to find the answers." Stimson pulled an envelope from his pocket and handed it to McCracken. "Sahhan is giving a speech at George Washington University this afternoon. Here's a ticket to it along with an invitation to the reception following. Might give you some insight into the man we're dealing with here."

"I can't wait."

* * *

Sandy Lister had been over it a dozen times with T. J. Brown, so once more couldn't hurt.

"You say you left the disk on your desk?" she asked.

"No!" T.J. shouted into the phone. "I put it into my top drawer and locked it. I'm sure I did. I put the disk back in its storage case and locked it away."

"Did anyone see you do it?"

"For the last time, I didn't notice. How could I? My office isn't exactly isolated. Anyone who wanted to could have seen me. Look, I didn't sleep at my apartment last night. I didn't even go back there. I'm scared. I think someone's . . . watching me. I've got this awful feeling that the people Kelno stole the disk from have it back now. That means they know we had it—*I* had it. And they killed Kelno for the same reason. They killed him!"

Sandy knew there was no sense trying to calm T.J. down. "What do you want me to do?" she asked.

"Call Shay," he snapped back. "This is all way over my head, yours too. Get him to help us."

"All right," Sandy said. "I'm leaving for Texas in a few hours. I'll call him from there. Just let me get straight what I'm going to tell him. Now, what have you got for me on Simon Terrell?"

"The address in Texas you asked for. Got a pen?"

When Sandy descended the stairs for a late breakfast in the Hollins kitchen, she found her packed bags waiting for her.

"Where you headed next, ma'am?" Spud Hollins asked her as they moved into the kitchen.

"Texas, on the trail of Simon Terrell."

"Krayman's assistant until old Randy elected to pull up stakes?"

"The very same."

"Well, you come back and see us again real soon." Hollins winked at her. "And don't forget to bring your camera."

Sandy stopped just before they reached the table. "Can I ask you one last question, Spud?"

"Fire away."

"Why are you willing to go on camera about all this after so many years? You've got everything any man could ever want, and by your own admission Randall Krayman did you a favor. Yet you're willing to go public again, risk recrimination, follow-up interviews, even lawsuits. Why, Spud?"

Hollins smiled, but Sandy could tell the gesture was turned inward. " 'Cause what Krayman's done ain't right and I got me a feeling he ain't finished yet."

Mohammed Sahhan's lecture was scheduled for two o'clock in the afternoon in the Lisner Auditorium on the George Washington campus. McCracken had been on the advance security team for countless heads of state over the years and the precautions taken by Sahhan rivaled most. The only feature his thirty or so bodyguards lacked was the tiny earphones that characterized the Secret Service.

Blaine was able to snare a seat in the VIP section with the help of Stimson's pass. He had a clear view of the podium, and if he had come here to assassinate the radical, he couldn't have hoped for a better angle.

He had spent the better part of the morning going over the vast files Stimson had provided on Sahhan. The PVR leader was taking fanaticism and making it almost respectable. He was seen pictured with diplomats, congressmen, foreign leaders, important businessmen. One press clipping reported in depth the story of a predominantly black work crew walking off the job in an Alabama factory. Things got violent in a hurry. Sahhan made peace and kept it long enough for him to work out a new contract with the company which was substantially better than anything the striking workers had reason to hope for. In another instance, when a major urban electric company up north shut off power to poor families in the ghetto who couldn't pay their bills, Sahhan not only paid the bills for them, he did it by personally delivering an individual check directly to each affected family.

Sporadic clapping began in the front rows as the leader

of the People's Voice of Revolution strode out onto the stage without benefit of introduction. The applause picked up as soon as the remainder of the audience saw him. Sahhan smiled and raised his hand to the crowd as he approached the podium. The spotlights' glare bounced off his dark sunglasses.

Blaine was not at all impressed with his physical appearance, utterly unlike the prepossessing stature of a Malcolm X or Louis Farrakhan. Sahhan was small and thin. His hair was worn in a tight Afro over skin of a dark copper shade. He wore a medium gray, finely tailored and obviously expensive suit. His hands had barely grasped the microphone and torn it from its stand, when his thick voice filled the auditorium.

"Brothers," he began, and paused immediately. "That's right, I address you all as brothers. I wear these glasses so I won't be able to tell the exact color of your skin and expression on your faces. I assume because you've come here today that there is something in your hearts that cries out for justice. Brothers and sisters, I hear those cries and have heard those cries. I've traveled this country and seen the pain and the hardship of so many blacks and whites too. I've shed tears, but the tears wash away. I've changed from a man of prayer to a man of action. I'm a general, brothers and sisters, and I come here today hoping you will find it in your souls to join my army."

McCracken felt a chill at Sahhan's fateful metaphor. How many in this auditorium suspected the truth? What thought was the PVR leader trying to plant in their heads?

Sahhan moved slowly to the front of the stage and then moved around it as he continued.

"Brothers and sisters, there is a conspiracy in this nation, a conspiracy so large in scope that it threatens to choke off the life blood of an entire people. I am speaking of us, brothers and sisters, the blacks of America. Those in the audience whose flesh is not black, search your hearts for pain and injustice. You are here because you, too, have been hurt and cheated, unrighteously stripped of something precious that belongs to you. You may stand against my words and my cause, but beware someday that you are not a victim of the same offenses I have come here to speak of today. For these offenses and cruelties and injustices are not limited to race or culture. They are spreading and soon, very soon, color will no longer divide us.''

Sahhan raised his free hand, as if to God. ''Yes, there is a conspiracy and my people have fallen victim to it. Those who have walked these roads before me, men like Malcolm X and Martin Luther King, were all struck down for their words and deeds, for speaking the truth. They were men of peace and they offered a hand of friendship to the society that scorned them only to be destroyed.'' He pulled his hand from the air and balled it into a fist. ''I will make no such offer. The time for extending unilateral friendship is past. We must make a stand and refuse to accept the awful conditions under which we have been forced to live.''

Sahhan moved back toward the podium and slammed his fist down upon it. The room shook from the pressure of the echo coming through the speakers.

''Do not listen to their lies!'' he screamed into the microphone. ''Do not think for one moment that urban renewal or affirmative action have made a difference. They are merely screens put in place by the conspirators to distract your attention from the truth. And the truth is that there never was any such plan as the Great Society. I was there those many years ago when all the papers were signed and promises made. But the promises wilted and the papers gathered dust and the Great Society became just another screen.'' He lowered his voice and seemed to relax a little. ''So where does that leave us, brothers and sisters?'' Sahhan asked from behind his dark glasses, hesitating, as if he expected someone to answer. ''It leaves us living on the outskirts of society with no hope of ever being allowed in. The roadblocks will be in place permanently, always impeding our way, denying our hope. The roadblocks will remain forever . . . unless we take steps to move them ourselves.''

Applause splintered the end of Sahhan's words. Blaine

heard a few screams and whistles of support, but also noticed more than a few members of the audience rising to leave. He realized for the first time that Sahhan was speaking without benefit of notes or prepared text, which added all the more fire to his presentation.

"And so who do we count among the guilty, brothers and sisters? Who do we take as the enemies we must strike down? Look at the Shylocks who own the heatless buildings we share with rats. We pay them rents we can't afford and they return the favor by selling their roach-infested buildings and sending us out into the street when it serves them better financially. They own the banks, and the newspapers, and the television stations. They carry politicians in their back pockets and those politicians insure that the roadblocks remain in place. They . . ."

Blaine was beginning to understand how truly dangerous Sahhan was. For the audience he was a mirror of their deepest frustrations. For most the feeling would not linger. For others these radical preachings would be hard to shrug off. For a few, by far the smallest segment of all, action would be demanded.

These were the ones Sahhan had come here to reach.

"So, my brothers and sisters," he went on, "we remain a people without a home of our own. In this world of the few over the many, we must draw our line and stand firm. It is not just the landlords and bankers who stand on the other side, of course, but countless others who think and act against us. All of them, too, are our enemies. All of them, too, must be shown that we will take no more pain and injustice. . . ."

Sahhan continued to spout off his rapid-fire teachings at a machine-gun pace. To Blaine he seemed to be repeating himself now, rehashing old ideas. McCracken let his eyes wander along with his mind. He wasn't expecting to find anything in particular and was thus quite surprised when he caught a glimpse of a fat black man standing just in front of the backstage area Sahhan had first emerged from.

The man's name was Luther Krell.

And he was an arms broker.

# CHAPTER 13

**B**LAINE had known Luther Krell during his tenure in Africa in his last days of good standing with the Company. Krell had brokered deals for various revolutionary groups, arranging shipments, transfers, and all the rest for an exorbitant fee. Krell played no favorites, and politics mattered to him only so far as it could fill his pockets. Liberal or conservative, reactionary or radical, it mattered not at all.

A growing reputation as a double-crosser had forced Krell to flee Africa for South America. Then he dropped out of sight. But rumor had it he had always remained available to the right party at the right price to broker arms deals. Mohammed Sahhan was certainly the right party, and the random violence promised by the PVR was right up Krell's alley. If he was in with Sahhan, he should know where the guns and armaments were. Seize them and Christmas Eve would stay peaceful.

The problem was how to confront Krell while he was alone and vulnerable. Blaine was considering the best way to make his move when Sahhan's speech abruptly ended after forty-five minutes. In the course of it, Blaine estimated, a good third of the audience had lost interest. The remaining 400 or so applauded Sahhan as he exited slowly, some with levels of enthusiasm so high that their hands threatened to snap from the effort.

Sahhan's bodyguards immediately fronted the stage to keep everyone back. That ruled out this moment for approaching Krell and left Blaine with only the reception as an option.

George Washington University was located in the heart of the capital, bordered by Pennsylvania Avenue on one side and Virginia Avenue on another. The entrance to Alumni House was just down from the Lisner Auditorium on Twenty-first Street. Blaine waited outside, watching people enter, before being satisfied there was a sufficient number to hide himself among. He climbed the steps and displayed his invitation to the uniformed guard, who eyed him warily.

The reception was being held in a suite of rooms usually reserved for the most exclusive alumni functions. The furniture and decor were surprisingly extravagant. For the moment Blaine could spot neither Sahhan nor the fat arms broker. Women in black and white outfits walked around balancing trays bearing champagne glasses and various hors d'oeuvres. For those guests who preferred something other than champagne, a pair of bars had been set up at the end of the spacious room.

There was a stirring in the rear and McCracken didn't have to see him to know that Sahhan had arrived. The white guests, campus and local officials probably, lingered noticeably back while others flocked to congratulate Sahhan on the success of his speech and catch any further words he might utter.

Still no Krell. This kind of gathering had never been the fat man's cup of tea. Blaine would have to draw him out, and that meant taking the offensive. Ordinarily such a move in such an atmosphere would have been out of the question, the risk of exposure to the enemy hardly worth the bother. But Christmas Eve was too fast approaching to save anything for tomorrow, so Blaine started across the room toward Sahhan with no real idea yet of what he was going to do when he got there.

He managed to down a pair of champagnes on the way to the group surrounding the PRV leader as he politely

answered questions. A pair of monstrous bodyguards
flanked him. The sunglasses, of course, were still on, and
he was holding a glass of what looked like soda water in
his hand. Sahhan made a weak joke and the group laughed
almost on cue. Blaine was the only white among them, and
when the black leader rotated his concealed eyes around,
they locked on him long enough to provide the opening
Blaine needed.

He stepped forward. "I enjoyed your speech very much,
Mr. Sahhan, but I do have one question."

Sahhan looked surprised. His head tilted a bit to the side.
"Please."

Blaine didn't hesitate. "Do you honestly believe that
crap about a conspiracy of landlords and bankers, or do
you just use it as propaganda to give your followers a concrete enemy?"

With that there was dead silence broken only by a single
champagne glass sliding to the carpet. The huge bodyguards looked first at each other and then at Sahhan uncer-
tainly. Other guards, sensing trouble, approached from the
doorways.

Sahhan held them off with a wave of his hand and
cracked a slight smile which broke the tension. "An in-
solent question, sir, but one I suppose I am obliged to
answer. Who asks it, though?"

Blaine edged a bit more forward. "Sam Goldstein of the
Associated Press."

Sahhan's smile vanished at that. He eyed Blaine like a
boxer sizing up his opponent before the opening bell.

"Yes, Mr. Goldstein," he said smoothly, "I believe
everything I said to be based in truth."

" 'Based in truth' or true? There's a difference, Mr.
Sahhan."

"None that I can see."

"Then you must not be looking too hard."

Silence spread through the rest of the room. Other guests
approached slowly, forming a circle around the two verbal
combatants the way kids do for a schoolyard fight. Blaine
knew the crowd was against him and didn't care. He needed

to keep the conversation going until Krell made his appearance among the rest.

Sahhan closed the gap between them to barely a yard, with his two bodyguards riding every step. "Let me tell you what I see, Mr. Goldstein. I see black unemployment standing at nearly twenty percent, more than three times that of whites. I see continually successful attempts by Congress and the judicial branch to take back what little we gained in the sixties. I see civil rights cases now decided before a trial ever takes place. Tax exemptions are granted to schools that discriminate and we have lost ground with the Voting Rights Act instead of gaining it."

"All true and all unjust," Blaine agreed, "but hardly conspiratorial."

"But I'm not finished, Mr. Goldstein." Sahhan knew he had the crowd now and worked it. "Look out the window and I'll tell you what *you'll* see. The proportion of black families headed by women has increased to almost fifty percent. One out of four black babies today is born to a woman nineteen or younger and nearly ninety percent of these mothers are unmarried. Hundreds of thousands of blacks every year are cut off from food stamps, and the school lunch program is dwindling to nothing. People like you are filled with questions and challenges, but would you pose them after witnessing a baby die from rat bites? Or a family of eight bundled up in moth-eaten blankets in front of a kitchen stove in the middle of winter? I could list more examples, hundreds more, but I know you wouldn't hear them because you're still not listening. No one ever listens . . . until they are made to." Then, to his bodyguards, "Remove him from here. He reeks of everything we despise, everything that has caused our desperation." Sahhan thrust a skeletal finger in McCracken's direction and returned his attention to the crowd. "It is his kind who will soon know a day when we will fight them on their own terms. Their chances have been exhausted. Their fate is sealed. *Remove him!*"

Blaine felt the powerful hands of the two giant bodyguards grasp him at the shoulders and begin shoving backward. He was able to hold his ground against them long enough to utter one last sentence.

"Merry Christmas, Sahhan."

Their eyes met through the dark sunglasses, and Blaine could feel Sahhan's panic. The fanatic had grasped his meaning. His mouth dropped, but before he could respond, if he had meant to, the huge bodyguards had yanked Blaine toward the rear exit. McCracken guessed there would be a beating in store for him outside and had to decide how much of it to take before putting the two men down.

Not much, he decided after they had tossed him down a set of steps in the back of Alumni House. He was rising slowly from the cement, when a familiar voice froze him.

"I got orders to take over from here."

The bodyguards held their ground. A fat man passed down the steps between them, followed by a pair of men who seemed smaller but just as deadly. He stopped on the second step, so as McCracken stood up their heights were equal, and Blaine found himself staring into the yellow eyes of Luther Krell.

"Hello, Krell. Long time no see."

Krell motioned Sahhan's bodyguards back inside. They retreated subserviently. "I knew I'd get my shot at you if I was patient, McCracken."

"You're still waiting, Krell. Today's not your day."

The fat man smiled. The men behind him on the steps showed their guns. The area was surrounded by large buildings deserted for the Christmas break, so passersby were not a concern.

"Today *is* my day, McCracken."

As if on cue, a black Cadillac sedan pulled around the corner of Alumni House and stopped just before them.

"We're going for a ride," Krell said. "You're on your way to hell."

"What are they wearing there this time of year?"

"Try something tropical."

Then Krell's men were upon him, shoving him against

the car and searching him thoroughly. When they found nothing, the fat man seemed disappointed.

"Not carrying today?" he teased.

"I was expecting metal detectors at every door. Didn't want to go and cause a scene. . . ."

Blaine had barely finished the sentence, when he was pushed into the backseat between Krell's two men. The fat man climbed into the front along with the driver, who started the big car around the other side of Alumni House and then swung right onto Twenty-first Street.

"I hear you've fallen on bad times, McCracken," Krell said. "You've become a joke in the field. I'm surprised they let you back in the States."

Blaine fixed his eyes on Krell's. "I've got friends in low places."

"Someone sent you to assassinate Sahhan, didn't they?"

"Not at all. It's you I was after, and I'm going to do you a favor. Have these clowns pocket their pistols right now and talk to me and I'll let you live. Otherwise, you'll be leaving me no choice."

Krell swung enough of his hefty frame over the seat to lash a backhand across McCracken's face.

"Why, you cocky son of a bitch!" he snarled, eyes glowing.

Blaine felt the blood dribbling from his mouth. The Cadillac turned right onto G Street. "Using big words and everything, fat man. Wouldn't be going respectable now, would you?"

"You're in no position to ask questions, McCracken. I've been waiting for this day for a long time."

"Last chance, fat man . . ."

"It's going to hurt, McCracken. I'm going to make it hurt."

Blaine swept his tongue over his back teeth and freed a crown-size capsule that had been lodged in a molar.

"Just promise you won't sit on me, all right?"

Krell had leaned forward to strike him again, when Blaine bit down on the capsule and fired its contents for-

ward. To the two guards it looked as if he were simply
spitting at the fat man and, in fact, the capsule's contents
were projected in saliva. Once they reached air, though,
the contents turned into a gas similar in effect to the mus-
tard variety outlawed in World War I. The gas struck the
fat man's face and he howled in pain, clawing for his eyes
and mouth. The agony forced his head to slam back, and
he smacked solidly into the driver.

The Cadillac careened out of control down G Street.
Other cars spun to avoid it as it skidded sideways, tires
screeching.

The guard on Blaine's left was struggling to steady his
pistol, when McCracken grabbed his wrist and slammed
the steel barrel into his face. He felt the cartilage and bone
give at the same moment his other hand shot out and forced
the second guard's gun up as it fired. The bullet cut through
the heavy steel roof, filling the small compartment with the
sharp smell of sulphur.

The second guard was going for another shot when the
Caddy crashed into a row of parked cars on G Street, pitching all of its occupants forward. The driver struggled to
regain control, but it was much too late. The Caddy shoved
a whole line of cars up onto the sidewalk and then came
to a rubber-ripping halt against them.

Blaine saw the first guard's gun on the floor and grabbed
it just as the second guard was recovering his bearings.
Blaine pumped two bullets into his head. Blood splattered
against the windows. Krell was still screaming. The driver
started to reach into his jacket for something, and Mc-
Cracken didn't wait to find out what. One bullet tore out
the back of his skull and slammed him up against the windshield.

Then Blaine lunged through what remained of the rear
door of the passenger side and yanked Krell out after
him through the front. He dragged him down the G Street
sidewalk until they reached a collection of dormitories
off to the right. He pulled Krell onto a narrow cement
walk running between two dorms and thrust him to the
ground. The fat man was writhing, puking, still clawing

for his face. Blaine made sure he saw the gun in his hand.

"Anything," Krell begged between rasping breaths. "I'll tell you anything." Spittle and drying vomit caked the corners of his mouth.

Blaine pressed the pistol against his temple. "What do you know about Sahhan's army?"

"Nothing!"

Blaine dug the gun's barrel home until he broke flesh. "Christmas Eve, Krell, tell me about Christmas Eve."

"I don't know. I'm just a middleman. I relay orders, arrange shipments."

"Of arms?"

"Yes."

"Through who?"

"Deveraux," Krell rasped. "In France."

"Deveraux?" Blaine said, more to himself than to Krell. Deveraux was the most successful, respected arms dealer in the world. Why would he be mixed up in something like this? "You'll have to do better than that."

"It's the truth! Nine major shipments so far. One left to go. I coordinate all the activity between Deveraux and Sahhan so there's no direct link between them."

"Did Sahhan set all this up?"

"Not at first. . . . You've got to let me live! *I'm telling you everything I know!*"

"Just answer my questions. Who put you on to Sahhan?"

"I don't know their names. They sent me to him and handled all the financial arrangements. I was just a middleman, I tell you!"

"Were they black or white?"

"What?"

"The men who approached you, were they black or white?"

"White. All of them. They stressed that Sahhan was never to be implicated in the dealings. I was told to get the best from the best. Price didn't matter. I went to Deveraux."

"And Deveraux handled the shipments. . . ."

"But he didn't realize to who. I had dealt with him before. He thought the weapons and explosives were bound for South America."

"How was payment handled?" Blaine realized his hand was going stiff from the pressure of holding the gun against the fat man's temple.

"Cash, always cash. Delivered in leather attaché cases. Sums too impossible to believe . . . *I'm telling you everything!*"

"Where were the weapons shipped?"

"I don't know."

Blaine shoved the barrel harder against him and Krell tumbled to the side. McCracken kept him pinned there, one side of the fat head squeezed against the cement.

"I swear I don't know. I'd tell you if I did. Deveraux handled all that. The weapons were gathered in central warehouses, where Sahhan's men distributed them. The process has been going on for months. Armories have been set up in every major city, all well hidden."

"Where are these armories? Which cities?"

"They never told me. I never asked. That wasn't my department. You've got to believe me!"

Blaine did believe him. He glanced around. No one was near. The sirens were still blaring. He had little time left before the police would be everywhere.

Krell swallowed hard. "I've told you everything I know. You've got to let me go."

Blaine said nothing, just started to tighten his finger on the trigger. Krell had to die.

*"You promised!"*

And in that moment of hesitation, Blaine knew he couldn't pull the trigger. Not now, not like this. Krell was a dead man anyway. He had talked and that meant someone else would be along to do the job.

McCracken pulled the gun back and lifted Krell up with one powerful arm.

"Get out of here, fat man! Disappear! They'll be taking numbers to burn your ass before long."

Krell looked back just once, shocked but grateful, then stumbled around the corner and was gone.

Andrew Stimson met McCracken in the backseat of another cab ninety minutes later, accepting the details of McCracken's report with grim reserve.

"You've certainly lived up to your reputation, Blaine."

"You get what you pay for, Andy. There's no time to fuck with these people. This is the only way I know to get the job done."

"I wasn't criticizing. I know what we're dealing with here." Stimson hesitated. "But I can't say I approve of your exposing yourself to Sahhan."

"It got me to Krell, and that made it worthwhile. I'm not worried."

"I gather your impression of Sahhan wasn't favorable."

"He's a fanatic, Andy, and all fanatics with a following as large as his are dangerous. When it comes to organizing this Christmas Eve business, though, he's had lots of help. Somebody's using him and that same somebody set up Krell as a middleman for the arms deals with Deveraux."

"Our friends who hired Chen and Scola?"

Blaine nodded. "The very same. The one thing out of place is Deveraux. He sets the standard for respectable arms dealers, the ones who don't operate out of a garage. A couple of yachts, a villa in the south of France. Definitely the good life. He's sold lots of bullets."

"Know where to find him?"

"He conducts all his business from Paris. I've got contacts who can bring me the specifics."

A look of concern crossed Stimson's face. "Be careful who you talk to, Blaine. This is a one-man game you're playing."

"Right. What's the latest from General Peachtree?"

"It's Peacher. His teams are starting to move into the

cities. It'll take some time before he has anything to report."

"Then I guess I'd better get to Paris fast."

"Just try not to leave too many bodies in the streets," Stimson warned. "I won't be able to cover for you with my people over there. You're totally on your own."

"Wouldn't have it any other way."

# PART THREE

# San Melas

### Saturday Afternoon to Tuesday Morning

# CHAPTER 14

THE past day had been an exercise in total frustration for Sandy Lister. The only bright spot had been the call to Stephen Shay she had promised T. J. Brown. Shay listened attentively to her story, from the moment she received the computer disk to its disappearance after her interview with Hollins in Billings. Somehow Shay's silence made Sandy feel all the more tense. During the course of her story, her mouth got drier and drier, and by the end a thin taste of blood coated her tongue.

"You should have filled me in on this at the beginning," Shay said when she had finished. "You broke procedure."

"I know."

"You jeopardized a police and possibly a federal investigation by withholding evidence, and then you breached national security by talking to that man Coglan. Not to mention the fact that you pursued a story totally out of your jurisdiction without prior network approval and—"

"Say no more, Steve. I'm on my way home. If you want my head on a platter, you've got it."

"Wait a minute, you didn't let me finish. I'm not applauding your methods, but the fact remains you're on to a hot story here and I was a journalist a long time before I became a producer."

"All I've ever been is an interviewer, remember? Smile

at the right times and dig out fresh responses from basically boring people.''

"No, San, the connection to Krayman makes this your piece, so I want you to stay with it. And as for the disk, well, possession is nine tenths of the law, and we haven't got a damn thing anymore.''

"But who stole it, Steve?''

"That's what I expect you to be able to tell me by Christmas.''

"It had to be someone from inside the network. And T.J. thinks he's being watched.''

"Probably his imagination. But I'll put our security people on it to be on the safe side. You've got to stay in touch with me on this from now on, San. Call in regularly. I want to know every move you make. I want to know where you're going before you get there.''

Sandy breathed a sigh of relief and barely managed to hold back tears of gratitude. "I'm on my way to Texas now,'' she told Shay, "on the trail of Simon Terrell, Randall Krayman's chief assistant until a few years before he pulled out.''

"Terrell . . . Never heard of him. Why bother pursuing the Krayman angle anyway now that you've got the space shuttle bit?''

"Because they're connected. I just don't know how yet. That interview with Hollins raised a lot more questions than answers. Randall Krayman wanted very badly to have total control of that ultra-density memory chip used in telecommunications. He's got his hand in every television, telephone, and radio in the country and there's something very wrong about that.''

The line went silent briefly.

"That's quite a mouthful, San.''

"You should have heard Hollins.''

"I will . . . when you return to tape the interview.''

"Thanks, Steve.''

"Just make sure I don't regret this.''

As it turned out, Sandy might have felt better if Shay had pulled her off the story. Her flight from Billings was

airborne only forty minutes Saturday afternoon when a
snowstorm forced it to land in Wyoming. She spent four
miserable hours in a miniature airport eating prepackaged
vending machine food with smudged expiration dates.

She finally made it to Dallas early Saturday night only
to find that Simon Terrell was no longer at the address T.J.
had given her. His new one meant a drive up Route 35
toward Denton in a rented car which overheated twenty
miles down the highway. It was replaced by the rental
company quickly enough with a sub-compact that changed
lanes based on the whims of the wind.

Things got no better in Denton. Simon Terrell had va-
cated his apartment there nearly six months before and had
left yet another forwarding address, this time hundreds of
miles away in Seminole, Oklahoma.

Sandy spent the night in a roadside motel and left for
Seminole early Sunday morning. She stopped for breakfast
at a diner and bought a road map of Oklahoma at the gas
station where she filled up the car. It was already blistering
hot as she headed north. The air conditioner was a blessing
for a while, but then the car's temperature needle climbed
dangerously toward the red and forced Sandy to use the
windows instead. The hot breeze gave her a headache,
drowned out the weak radio, and drenched her back with
sweat to the point where she felt herself sticking to the
vinyl upholstery.

Incredibly, though, she found Seminole with little trouble and quickly located Simon Terrell's latest forwarding
address.

"You're sure this is the address you're looking for?"

"Absolutely," Sandy told the caretaker of the Green-
leaves Cemetery.

A wry smile crossed the man's face. "Then you're gonna
find it mighty tough to get yourself an interview. Most of
our tenants don't have much to say." And he laughed.

With that lead behind her, Sandy would have to find
Terrell, if he was among the 7,500 people of Seminole,
through good old-fashioned legwork.

The heat had evaporated as she drew farther into Okla-

homa, and Seminole was comfortably cool. The radio pre-
dicted a chance of showers. Sandy stopped first at a bar
and grill and started asking questions. The people inside
seemed suspicious of her, their answers abrupt and terse.
None of them had ever heard of Simon Terrell.

"You that woman on TV, ain't ya?" one of them asked
her.

"Yes," Sandy replied, glad for once at the recognition.

"Oh," was all the man said before he went back to his
beer.

Sandy went through three cups of coffee trying to figure
out her next step. If Simon Terrell had come to Seminole,
he would have used a different name. She moved from her
booth and settled down at the bar next to the man who had
recognized her. His hair was graying, his eyes tired, and
he wore a patched-up down vest.

"Has any man moved into town in the last few months,
say a man about forty?"

"Lots of people pass through," the man told her, looking up from his beer.

"I mean somebody who settled down."

The man churned his mug until suds formed on the top.
"You lookin' for a husband?"

"Just a story."

The man raised his bushy eyebrows. "This guy you're
after, he do somethin' wrong?"

"No, he's connected to someone else I'm doing a story
on. I need his help."

"Any chance of me gettin' on your show if I help ya
too?"

"Nope," Sandy said frankly, and they both smiled.

The man downed his beer and signaled for another.
"Only one man I seen 'round here fits your boy, but his
name ain't Terrell. I deliver stuff to all the Indian reser-
vations in these parts and he showed up at one a few months
back. A teacher or somethin'."

"Around forty?"

"I ain't too good judgin' ages, but I'd say yeah, give or
take a few years. Got long hair, though."

"You remember the man's name?" Sandy asked, flipping the bartender a bill for the beer before the man could get his hand into his worn-out pants.

"Trask, I think," he told her. "Steve Trask."

The man's directions to the Indian reservation were easy to follow, the roads straight, and the turns well marked. Sandy knew she had finally found Terrell. Men on the run often changed their names but kept the same initials to avoid questions about labels on luggage, books, towels, and other possessions. Simon Terrell was running, all right. Denton hadn't been right for him, nor had Greenville, so he was trying Seminole with the same initials but a different name.

The reservation was located out on the plains, free of power lines, cables, even telephone poles. If Terrell had wanted to hide, he had certainly come to the right place. But why in Seminole? Why among Indians?

Sandy's certainty that Trask was Terrell dwindled as she drew closer to the reservation. There were no identifying signs on the fence enclosing rows of small, well-constructed homes. There were larger buildings as well, none of which were identified in any way. She pulled her compact between a pair of pickups and climbed out.

There were few people around, and no one paid much attention to her. In all probability few of the reservation's inhabitants would recognize her. She moved through the dusty grounds, longing for a pair of boots, and outside the parking lot she approached a plump, middle-aged Indian man.

"Can I help you?" he asked politely.

"I'm looking for Steven Trask."

"You'll find him somewhere around the school." The Indian aimed a callused finger to the left. "About fifty yards that way. He'll probably be with the kids behind the building."

Sandy followed the Indian's directions and found herself walking through a different age. Beneath the clearing sky women sewed and stirred the contents of tall pots over open flames. She didn't see many men and guessed they were at work in the surrounding fields.

The schoolhouse was not hard to find, and as she drew closer to it, Sandy could hear the giggling of children not far away. She followed a path around to the rear of the building. A group of twenty or so kids was engaged in various games, and another ten sat in a circle around an elaborate arrangement of small stones. The head of a single adult dominated the scene, his back to Sandy. She moved closer and took a deep breath.

"Mr. Trask?"

The man turned around slowly and stood up.

"Hello, Miss Lister, I've been expecting you," said Simon Terrell.

# CHAPTER 15

"**H**ow did you know—"

"That you were coming?" Terrell asked, his arms on the shoulders of a young boy and a young girl who flanked him. "I have a friend at your network who told me you were on my trail. I knew you'd track me down sooner or later, though I expected you'd have a camera crew along for the ride."

"Would you have talked before a camera?"

"I'm not sure I have anything to say to you even without one. And you can forget all about that off-the-record crap because with the people you're looking into, there's no such thing."

The wind whipped up and ruffled Terrell's overlong hair. He looked pretty much like the picture Sandy had of him, except a bit more ragged and less polished. His curly hair fell naturally around his face, styled by the wind. He had a two- or three-day growth of beard and sunburned skin that made his light blue eyes look even icier. His boots clip-clopped on the pebble ground as he moved toward Sandy, the two children still clinging tight to his forearms.

"Go play with the others," he told them softly. They resisted for a second, then took off with jealous eyes on Sandy.

"This is quite a departure from Krayman Industries, Mr. Terrell," she said, taking his extended hand.

Terrell glanced around him. "I should have done it years ago. Call me Simon, by the way."

"How did your contact at my network know how to reach you?"

"I'm not a total recluse, Miss Lister."

"Sandy."

"Sandy. There are a few people who know how to reach me in an emergency."

They walked toward the schoolhouse, until they reached the shade of a big tree.

"This is as good a place as any," Terrell told her. "As long as you don't mind getting your pants dirty. I should keep my eye on the kids."

"This is fine," Sandy said, and they both sat down on the ground. Her eyes swept over the young children playing. "Are you their teacher?"

"Weekdays, yes. On weekends I become a baby-sitter. The older kids are working with their parents, mostly in the fields. Some are out hunting. I volunteered for this duty."

"Doing penance for past sins?"

Terrell smiled briefly at that. "No, just trying to forget about them. My whole life had been based on technology for so long that I almost forgot what people were all about. Finally it got to be too much. I felt more like one of the machines I was tending than a man. I had to get out, so I ran away."

"But you're still running, aren't you?" Sandy prodded. "Is someone after you?"

Sandy expected Terrell to hesitate, but his response came immediately. "No one's after me and I think the running has stopped. For a dozen years I worked for the most powerful man in the world. I saw things I'd rather forget and did things I'd love to blame on somebody else. You could say I've been running from myself more than anything. Withdrawing, I guess."

Sandy thought of Spud Hollins living at his ranch in the hills of Montana. "Randall Krayman seems to have that effect on people. You left Krayman Industries a few years before he dropped out of sight, correct?''

"It was about four," Terrell said. "A new wave was taking over the company, led by a man named Francis Dolorman. They got Randy's ear and twisted his thoughts around. He wouldn't listen to me anymore.''

"You were on a first-name basis with Krayman?''

"We were friends, Sandy, and that made leaving him all the harder. It became one long guilt trip, especially when he dropped out of sight.''

"Have you spoken to him at all in the last five years?''

"I've tried to reach him, but either he doesn't want to hear from me or someone else doesn't want him to. I think he's in trouble.'' Terrell paused and began toying with the grass near his knees. "I think maybe Dolorman and his cronies 'arranged' Randy's disappearance so they could run his companies as they saw fit.''

Sandy felt her pulse quicken, surprise mixing with excitement. "You're saying they *kidnapped* him.''

"At the very least.''

"My God . . . but why? What could they hope to gain?''

"Plenty. I'll have to backtrack a little for you to understand. I knew Randy Krayman better than anyone. I knew what made him tick, what he loved and what he loathed. And what he loved most of all was America. I know that sounds trite, but it's true. This guy loved his country obsessively and would literally lose sleep over his fears that it was being mismanaged and mishandled into oblivion. People just didn't understand what was going on, he thought; they had to be educated, informed, even controlled, if that's what it took.'' Terrell found Sandy's eyes. "Controlled through the media. This goes back almost twenty years. Krayman started buying television stations, and when cable came along, he got in on the ground floor. He figured if he owned a major affiliate in every state, maybe even a network, he could go a long way toward influencing public opinion and with the help of cable, eventually *create* public opinion.

"It didn't work, Sandy. Sure, he swayed a few elections

his way. Probably won himself a lot of support, too, in addition to making a shitload of money. But what he really wanted was to have his voice be the only one America listened to, sort of an omniscient Paul Harvey telling people to stand by for lots more than just news. When his plan to control television stations and networks didn't go far enough toward accomplishing this, he began to look elsewhere for the means. We're going back ten years now, not long before I left.''

''What he ended up finding has something to do with the Krayman Chip, doesn't it?''

''Everything.''

''And he sold the chip for a fraction of its production costs.''

Terrell looked surprised. ''How'd you learn that?''

''Spud Hollins. Remember him?''

Terrell nodded. ''Poor bastard. One of the many Krayman Industries chewed up and spit out when Dolorman and his gang first began to assert themselves.''

''Your former boss paid him sixty million for a bankrupt business. Why feel so bad for Hollins?''

''Randy paid him because he felt guilty, because he knew what he had done was wrong but that didn't make it any less necessary to accomplish what he wanted.''

''Then you're confirming that COM-U-TECH plagiarized Hollins's discovery and marketed it as the Krayman Chip.''

''If that's the scoop you're looking for, Sandy, your vision is too narrow. It's old news. Nobody cares anymore.''

''But the chip was part of a bigger plan, wasn't it, Simon? Krayman wanted his chip in every piece of telecommunications equipment. Why?''

Terrell shrugged. ''I wish I could tell you for sure, Sandy, but I can't. It was around that time that Dolorman grabbed hold of Randy's ear and convinced him to shut me out. Randy was more obsessed than ever at that point, willing to stop at nothing to have the country running the way he wanted it to. His intentions were good, really they were.''

"You know what they say about the road to hell, Simon."

"Sure, but it wasn't Randy who was walking it, it was Dolorman and his cronies. They were pulling the strings and Randy was letting them." A pained look crossed Terrell's face. "I saw less and less of Randy in those days. Eventually I was reassigned, but I stuck it out in the hope I could save him from the people around him as well as from himself. I was his friend. I had to try. But Dolorman turned him against me. He caught Randy at his weakest moment and exploited it to the fullest. We didn't talk much those last few months, and when we did, the things Randy said truly scared me."

"What kind of things?"

"All vague. I don't remember any of them clearly. The common theme was that it seemed he had finally found a way to get what he wanted."

"Control of American public opinion?"

"More like control of the entire country. Dolorman and his gang had put him on to something, and all I know for sure is that its origins were connected somehow to the Krayman Chip."

"When was the last time you spoke to Krayman?"

"About six months before he dropped out of sight, I managed to make contact. He was talking crazy. They were getting close, he said, but it was wrong. All wrong. That's his phrase, not mine. He said he was going to stop them before it was too late . . . and then he conveniently disappeared."

"You're saying Dolorman and his people killed Krayman?"

"Or kidnapped him and kept him prisoner."

"But you never told anybody about that or your fears concerning the Krayman Chip."

"Who was I going to tell, Sandy?" Terrell challenged, frustration mixing with fear in his voice. "Dolorman was running Krayman Industries and he'd inherited all the power that goes with it. There are lots of folks on the Krayman payroll who don't draw a regular paycheck, if you know

what I mean. Randy kept key officials and politicians in
his pocket and you can bet Dolorman switched them into
his five years ago. The list keeps growing all the time. The
little guys they picked up early have grown into big guys
by now. With the kind of power Krayman Industries wields,
it wouldn't be beyond them to own a president someday. I
didn't like the odds of going up against that kind of power,
not without Randy to back me up."

"But that didn't stop you from speculating on what they
were up to, did it?"

"I spent lots of sleepless nights. Still do. Coming here
didn't erase the past, it just dulled it a little. Computer
electronics have always been my thing, Sandy. That's what
brought Randy and me together in the first place and in the
end it was probably what split us apart. The implications
of the Krayman Chip were all pretty frightening, but some
of them stand out."

"I'm listening."

"It gets a little complicated and technical. And the key
comes down to changes in society itself. The computer is
now the axis around which everything else spins. We've
become an information-oriented society instead of an industrial one. It would be too trite to call what's going on
now the information revolution, but the ramifications of the
changes taking place are not unlike the ones suffered during
the industrial revolution."

"*Suffered* implies pain, Simon."

"A poor choice of words on my part. The computer has
far more good points than bad. It certainly has simplified
a lot of lives and a lot of businesses. Like I said, though,
times are changing. It's not so much a question of data
processing anymore as data transmissions. The whole national power grid is controlled by computers talking to other
computers."

"Hollins mentioned something like that," Sandy told
him. "He said the Krayman Chip allowed them to do it
faster."

"A lot more than just faster, a hell of a lot more. If you
wanted to control the country, telecommunications would

be the best way to go about it. Stop the computers from talking to one another or make them say what you want.''

''Through the Krayman Chip?''

''Well,'' said Terrell, ''if there was a way to shut all of them down at once, the whole nation would be brought to a standstill.''

Sandy's hair ruffled in the breeze. A number of children were sitting just out of earshot now, watching them.

''But what about all the communications satellites orbiting thousands of miles above ground?'' she asked him. ''I've heard they may make land-based forms of communications obsolete someday.''

''An insightful observation, but not an altogether accurate one. To begin with, yes, com-sats do play an increasing role. Before their signal can be beamed to various sub-stations, though, it first has to be relayed up to them, and that switching process relies predominantly on—''

''The Krayman Chip again,'' Sandy completed.

Terrell nodded. ''And just for the record, Krayman Industries has four com-sats of their own in orbit as we speak.''

''And maybe something else . . .''

''What do you mean?''

Sandy spoke softly. ''What would you say if I told you I had evidence linking Krayman Industries to the destruction of *Adventurer* last week?''

''What kind of evidence?'' Terrell asked, leaning forward.

''A copy of the shuttle's orbital flight plan delivered to me by a dying Krayman employee.''

''Did you say *dying*?''

''Murdered, more specifically.''

''Oh, God,'' Terrell muttered. ''It doesn't make any sense. Destroying a space shuttle; no, that doesn't fit.'' He looked down, then up again. ''Unless *Adventurer* saw something or was about to see something it wasn't supposed to. That would explain why Krayman would be in possession of the orbital flight plan in the first place. If they put something in the sky, they'd want to know if the shuttle's path would eventually intersect with it.''

"Wait a minute, how would Krayman get whatever it is *up* in the sky?"

"The same way they got their com-sats up, by contracting for a launch.''

"Through NASA?"

"In this case, more likely overseas, through France probably. They'd want a minimum of questions and the French ask none so long as all accounts are paid on time.''

"But what have they got up there that could destroy a space shuttle?''

Terrell's face paled, his thoughts elsewhere. "Christ, this explains it. . . .''

"Explains what?"

"The *Pegasus* launching.''

"Simon, what are you talking about?"

He looked at her intensely. "An armed shuttle scheduled to be launched the day after Christmas.''

"Armed? That program was outlawed by Congress.''

"No program the military wants badly enough is ever outlawed. The funds are just redirected. In *Pegasus* they have a whole new generation shuttle complete with deflector shields, advanced radar technology, and a pair of laser cannons that can cut through steel two yards thick.'' Terrell's stare tilted to the sky. "And it's being sent up there after whatever destroyed *Adventurer*.''

"How do you know all this?"

Terrell sighed. "I can't leave all my old life behind me, Sandy. I still care about emerging technology. I know the proper numbers to dial, and just yesterday one of those numbers yielded me the information about *Pegasus*.''

"But you have no idea what it'll be facing up there.''

"Or what the thing was launched for in the first place. Com-sats orbit at around twenty thousand miles, but *Adventurer*'s orbit would have placed it at only one eighty. From that altitude there's not a hell of a lot you can do.''

"Apparently there's enough," Sandy said. "I don't suppose you've got any ideas where I might fill in the missing pieces.''

"Just one—Houston."

"NASA?"

"And Krayman Industries' corporate headquarters."

"How convenient," Sandy managed halfheartedly.


Dolorman leaned painfully forward, his eyes wide with disbelief. "Will you repeat that, Wells?"

"The man posing as a reporter at Sahhan's reception was Blaine McCracken."

"McCracken's dead. We received positive confirmation of that."

"I wasn't convinced then, and now I'm certain he's alive. There was an incident following the reception that fits McCracken's style."

"What sort of incident?"

"The middleman Krell disappeared and his bodyguards were killed."

"Even so, a certain 'style' is hardly the basis for such a conclusion on your part," noted Dolorman.

"I'm also going by descriptions from the scene of the reception," Wells told him. "I said from the beginning that Scola wasn't capable of dealing with McCracken, and I stick to my claim."

"What is it between the two of you, Wells?" Dolorman asked. "What happened back there in Vietnam?"

"I've got a debt I owe him," was all the big man said.

Dolorman's expression wavered. "If you're right, Wells, all of Omega might be in danger. With only seventy-two hours until activation, we can't have that."

"We're going about this in the wrong way, I think," Verasco interjected. "If McCracken is still alive, we must assume he is still working for Andrew Stimson and the Gap. It would seem a much simpler matter to get rid of Stimson."

Dolorman turned the scarred man's way. "Wells?"

Wells's one working eyebrow rose. "Leave it to me."

"I have already left to you the elimination of security leaks, and little has been accomplished in that regard."

"My people are closing on the source now. A breakthrough should come at any time."

"See that it does. The fewer complications we face in the coming days, the better."

"I assume, then, that the order to leave Sandy Lister alive remains in force."

Dolorman nodded. "We are better off letting her follow a path that can ultimately lead nowhere." He turned gingerly toward Verasco. "I'm more concerned about Sahhan. Did that unpleasant business at the reception unsettle him?"

"If anything," said Verasco, "he is more charged than ever. Our people close to him say he is working himself into a frenzy. He can barely sleep at night. Apparently Christmas Eve can't come fast enough for him."

"Or us," added Dolorman.

# CHAPTER 16

MCCRACKEN reached Paris late Saturday and immediately set the wheels in motion for locating the world's most celebrated arms dealer, François Deveraux. Deveraux held the unique distinction of being the only arms dealer ever profiled by a major American television newsmagazine that had set out to break the stereotype of the dark-eyed man selling stolen rifles out of a warehouse. Indeed, most of what Deveraux did was both respectable and totally legal. The great majority of his business arrangements were made with legitimate military or paramilitary groups who wanted American- or Russian-made arms and, who, for whatever reason, chose not to deal direct. His equipment was often surplus and frequently secondhand. Deveraux made no secret of his profession and chose his clients with as much caution and discretion as he could afford.

Blaine knew the arms dealer quite well, in fact had saved his life once a decade or so back when a group of fanatical Arab terrorists were upset after Deveraux backed out of a deal with them. Blaine had stepped in and handled the hit team personally. The credit went to the Israelis.

So Deveraux owed him and that should make the situation infinitely simpler, though that didn't make Blaine any fonder of the prospect of returning to Paris. He had spent by far the worst five years of his career stationed there, frustration simmering until it had boiled over at the airport

barely a week before. The smell of Orly Airport itself
brought back all the bitterness of those years, all the anger
over the fact that his own people had buried him.

Blaine checked into a hotel, made a series of phone calls,
and then waited in the darkness flirting with sleep. It was
morning before he learned that not only was François Deveraux in town, he would be attending a special performance
at the famed Paris opera house that very evening. Deveraux
would be sitting in his private box and Blaine would let
him enjoy the first act before making his appearance. It
was a tremendous stroke of luck actually, for if Deveraux
had been out of town or otherwise indisposed, precious
time would have been lost getting to see him.

The opera setup presented McCracken with only one
problem—dress was strictly formal, at least if he wanted to
move comfortably in Deveraux's circles and not stand out.
Blaine rang up the hotel concièrge, who sent up a tailor to
take his measurements. A rented tuxedo in the proper size
would be delivered to his door by six that evening, no
small accomplishment on a Sunday.

The worst thing about life in the field was the waiting.
And the worst thing about waiting was that it gave you
time to think. All of Blaine's thoughts as he lingered in his
hotel room throughout the day centered around Luther
Krell. He should have killed him. Plain and simple. It was
the expected thing to do and the right thing, too, since
Krell could have blown his dead man's cover. Sure he could
tell himself that after talking, the fat man would never dare
return to Sahhan, that he was as good as dead anyway. But
it didn't wash. McCracken couldn't do the job because he
didn't have the stomach for such execution-style killings
anymore. Killing in self-defense or the defense of others
was one thing; putting a bullet in a whimpering lump of
flesh, something else again. It implied vulnerability. Five
years ago there would have been no doubt, no hesitation,
and Blaine trembled at the thought of where that hesitation
might show up next.

His tuxedo was delivered thirty minutes late, at half past
six, which left him just enough time to dress and make it

to the opera house prior to the start of the first act. Most disquieting was that he lacked a firearm. Smuggling in or obtaining a gun had proven impossible; there was too much risk involved. Blaine felt naked as a result. He took a cab to the opera house. His ticket was being held at the box office, so there was really no reason for him to rush except that he needed time to spot Deveraux's private box.

The Paris opera house was a huge building constructed nearly two hundred years before. Though remodeled numerous times in the interim, it nonetheless retained the elegant decor of its birth. The lobby of the building was huge, with a swirling staircase rising through the various levels. People in formal attire clustered in small groups to chat and sip champagne. Blaine hoped he might find Deveraux mingling among them, in which case he could finish their rendezvous early and spare himself sitting through the opera's first act.

No such luck. The arms dealer was nowhere to be found and Blaine found his own seat five minutes before the lights were dimmed. His eyes swept the rows of private boxes above him, some set back so far that their occupants were hidden. He borrowed a pair of opera glasses from a hefty woman seated next to him and intensified his sweep, aware that once the house lights were turned down, he would have to break the search off. The orchestra had finished tuning their instruments. He had only seconds left.

He was studying the middle boxes on the left side of the hall when a man rose to greet a pair of female guests. Blaine smiled. François Deveraux hadn't changed a bit. His toupee seemed to fit better than the last time they had met, but other than that he looked exactly the same. His flesh was baked bronze by the sun, the absence of lines and wrinkles due not so much to nature as to a plastic surgeon's skilled knife. His smile flashed white and full, and he kissed the ladies politely.

The lights dimmed and a drumbeat pounded the air. The opera was about to begin. Blaine returned the glasses and slumped back in his chair, making himself applaud until the people next to him stopped.

The next hour was as long as any he could remember. He did not know the opera's title, nor could he follow its plot as it unfolded onstage. The high notes and orchestral reverberations stung his ears, and he found himself stealing as many glances as he could up at Deveraux's box, wondering what he might do if the arms dealer was similarly unenthused about the performance and made an early exit.

At last the first act came to an end and Blaine pushed by the others in his row and made his way up the aisle. It was already crowded, and he felt the nag of frustration in the pit of his stomach, eyes cheating up toward Deveraux's box. He needed the arms dealer alone up there. If Deveraux had opted for a trip to the bar, Blaine might have to stomach another act, and he wasn't sure if he was up to that.

He moved with the crowd back into the lobby and then against the traffic up one of the circular stairways closest to Deveraux's box. He had tried to pin down its location from its proximity to others, a needless task as it turned out, since two guards were stationed before its private entrance. Deveraux's guards were there more for show than anything else, since the private boxes were connected, split only by a thin dividing wall and a curtain. Blaine passed Deveraux's and entered the one two down from it.

"Excuse me," he said, pushing by two exasperated couples and sliding behind the curtain.

He repeated the same process at the next box and then stuck his face out from behind the curtain at Deveraux's.

"*Bonsoir*, Monsieur Deveraux."

The two women gasped. Deveraux swung around quickly.

"*Mon dieu*," he muttered, face suddenly pale.

"Take it easy, François, you look like you've seen a ghost," Blaine said, and stepped out from behind the curtain.

"I believe I have, *mon ami*, or perhaps the champagne was too strong."

"Mind if I join you?"

"*Oui, oui*. Come in, please."

Blaine moved forward and smoothed the curtain back into place. Deveraux told the two women to bring back another bottle of champagne and inform the guards to make sure he wasn't disturbed.

"I heard you had been killed in the States, *mon ami*," Deveraux said softly when they were alone.

"Couldn't kick off until the debt was square between us, now, could I?"

Deveraux slid a small table holding a golden spittoon closer to him. In spite of his rich, urbane life-style, he had never abandoned the habit of chewing tobacco. The only concession he made was to buy the most expensive supply around, packaged in gold foil pouches that looked quite respectable. He packed a small measure in his mouth.

"We need to talk, François."

"Are you in trouble? If so, my house is yours. No one in France would dare touch you under my protection."

"It's not like that. No one in France knows I'm here besides you." A pause. "I'm working again."

"For your own people? I would have thought your days with them were over."

"They are formally. This is strictly undercover and unofficial. No accountability and all that."

Deveraux expelled a wad of tobacco juice into the spittoon as gracefully as he did everything else.

"Which branch?"

"The Gap."

"Ah, the most secretive of them all. . . ."

"Also the most desperate. They lost an agent a while back and I'm taking his place. The agent was on to a plot by some black fanatics planning to try the civil war all over again starting Christmas Eve."

"And where do I come in?"

"You've been shipping them the weapons to do it."

Deveraux almost missed the spittoon. He tried to hold his calm. "Because we are friends, Blaine, I will try to forget you said that. You know me too well to suspect me of doing business with such a cause."

"Not knowingly, perhaps. And in this case the cause

has lots of help. Let me put it this way. You have made nine almost identical weapons shipments to different regions of the U.S. in the past six months, haven't you?''

Deveraux's eyes flashed unsurely. "Yes, quite large shipments, to various new American mercenary units destined for Latin America.''

"That's what they wanted you to think.''

"They had proper authorization.''

"Anything Luther Krell's involved in is never what it seems. You should know that better than anyone.''

"The fat *bastard* . . .''

"I've taken him out of circulation for a while.''

"Yet another debt I owe you, *mon ami*.''

"You can pay both of them up by answering a few questions.''

"*D'accord*. I am at your service.''

"Where were the shipments sent to, François?''

Deveraux spit again and thought briefly. "Major cities. New York, Los Angeles, Houston, Philadelphia, Chicago. The others I cannot recall off the top of my head.''

"The weapons were divided equally by region?''

"More or less. There was no reason for me to question it.'' Deveraux hesitated. "Tell me more about what is going on.''

"It gets complicated, but it's centered around a man named Mohammed Sahhan.''

"I've heard of him, *mon ami*. Very dangerous.''

"And now very armed.''

"I did not know,'' Deveraux said apologetically. He raised the spittoon to his mouth, as if not trusting his aim anymore.

"No one's accusing you. Sahhan had help. Someone set Krell up with him and Krell set you up.''

"Who?''

"That's what I don't know. But it's somebody with power, connections, and resources. Attaché cases don't normally come packed with cash.''

This time Deveraux missed the spittoon though he still

held it under his chin. His lips trembled. "Leather attaché cases," he muttered.

"The way Krell told me he arranged payment to you."

"Yes, but there is another client who's been paying me the same way, also shadowy. They have purchased even more arms than Krell arranged for. But all shipments have gone to one place."

"Where?"

"An island in the Caribbean called San Melas. Small. Remote."

"Which tells us nothing."

"Wait, I haven't finished yet. The island is privately owned by that American billionaire." Deveraux hesitated to be sure of the name. "Randall Krayman."

For a long moment McCracken just sat there looking at Deveraux. Krayman, whose fortune was estimated to be four times that amassed by Howard Hughes, certainly possessed the resources to be the mysterious party backing Sahhan. And the connection between them was now unavoidable. But what would Randall Krayman have to gain from an association with a radical fanatic and his plans for a Christmas Eve revolution?

"Blaine?"

Deveraux's voice lifted him from his trance.

"I'm sorry, François."

"The second act is about to start, *mon ami*. We should conclude our business before then," Deveraux said, eyes looking away.

"You're scared."

"Krayman is a powerful man, not someone to cross."

"You're not crossing him, François. You're just providing information that may be the only thing that can save thousands of lives Christmas Eve."

"You really suspect Krayman is the force behind Sahhan?"

"I've got to proceed on that assumption. What I don't know is why."

"That I cannot tell you, *mon ami*. Where does the island come in? Why does he need so many arms?"

McCracken shrugged. "Training probably. He must be using San Melas to prepare Sahhan's troops for the assault. It makes sense. A few hundred at a time every few weeks would be more than sufficient. No one would even raise an eyebrow." Blaine found the Frenchman's stare and bore into it. "I've got to get onto that island, François."

"*Impossible!* Reports from my supply planes stress that it is heavily guarded and that the waters are mined. Several innocent fishermen who have strayed too close to the shore have conveniently disappeared." Deveraux seemed to think of something. "Wait, there might be a way, but it is so risky. . ." His eyes sharpened. "One final shipment is due to leave for the island from one of my airfields late tomorrow morning."

"Then it's simple—I'll just have to be on board."

Deveraux shook his head. "Not so simple." He yanked the wad of tobacco from his mouth and dropped it into the golden spittoon. "The people representing Krayman have insisted that the same crew make the drop each time. For you to replace one of them would arouse suspicion and would not help you accomplish your task in any case."

"Why not?"

"Because my men are watched constantly from the time they land on San Melas until the time they depart. They are never out of sight of guards the whole time the shipments are unloaded onto trucks on the airfield."

"Then I'll have to stow away and make my escape while the shipment is being unloaded."

Deveraux shook his head more resolvedly. "*Non, mon ami.* The airstrip is quite a distance from what must be the training grounds, and it is out in the open. You are talking suicide. I owe you too much to let you take such a risk."

Blaine smiled. "Then I guess we'll just have to think of something else. . . ."

When he had finished detailing his plan, the orchestra was tuning up for the second act.

"It is still risky, very risky," Deveraux said, unconvinced.

"I've got to get onto that island, François, and you haven't come up with a better way."

The Frenchman nodded reluctantly. "Be at my airfield in Gournay by eleven o'clock tomorrow morning."

"You mean I actually get some time to sleep?"

Deveraux winked. "You can even stay for the rest of the show now, *mon ami.*"


"What do you know about Randall Krayman, Andy?" McCracken asked from his hotel room later that evening. The call had been routed through a sterile emergency exchange to make tracing or eavesdropping impossible.

"Why?" Stimson asked.

"Because I think he's the missing piece we've been looking for in all this." And Blaine proceeded to relate his conclusions based on the information passed on by François Deveraux.

"Let me get this straight," Stimson said at the end. "A billionaire recluse is financing Sahhan's Christmas Eve strike and training the principals on his private island in the Caribbean."

"That's right," Blaine confirmed. "An island called San Melas, where I'll be headed tomorrow morning."

"And what might Krayman have to gain from all this?"

"Won't know that until I get there, Andy. Maybe your computers can provide us with a head start. There's got to be something on them that will give us an idea what Krayman, or his people, are up to. Every damn move of this thing has been carefully planned, from Chen to Krell. Any word from Peachfuzz?"

"His men are making progress, but it's slow. Too slow. The game's still yours."

"I've got a feeling the fun's just beginning."

# CHAPTER 17

D EVERAUX's landing field in Gournay was hardly an official strip. In fact, no one outside of a necessary few even knew it was still in limited operation. It had been constructed by French Resistance troops at the peak of World War II as a means of smuggling people out of and weapons into France. It had served brilliantly back then and continued to serve Deveraux as one of ten airfields he kept active in continental France.

McCracken arrived by rental car in the bright chill of ten-thirty A.M. to find the transport plane already warming its engines.

"Mr. McCracken?" a man with a French submachine gun said, approaching him.

"Greetings from Paris."

"Mr. Deveraux contacted us. You are expected. I will make arrangements to have your car driven back to your hotel. Mr. Deveraux insists that no evidence exist of your being here."

Blaine closed the car door behind him.

"My name is André," the man, who looked to be still in his twenties, told him. "Mr. Deveraux has requested that I be at your service. Everything is arranged as your instructions indicated. We had to improvise, but I think you'll find the results most satisfactory. Follow me."

The whirl of the propellers stung Blaine's ears as he

followed André in a trot toward the large plane's cargo bay. They climbed up a ramp into a damp, dark world broken by the half-light cast by irregularly placed work lamps.

"Over here, Mr. McCracken."

André led him toward a wooden crate in the far left corner, approximately the same size and shape as all the others.

"A pair of heavy machine guns are inside here," André explained, "with a compartment constructed between them for you to conceal yourself in upon reaching the island. A section of the crate has been cut out and loosely refitted, so moderate pressure applied by you from the inside will pop it out to secure your freedom." André's eyes became cautious. "If the crate is dropped or rammed, your escape hatch might be prematurely discovered. It was the best we could come up with on such short notice."

"I understand."

"In any event, it will not be necessary for you to take refuge in the crate until the crew informs you they are beginning their descent. At that point they will help you lift one of the heavy machine guns aside temporarily and remove one of the false separators so you can slip inside. Any questions so far?"

"Is this crate first class or tourist?"

André smiled. "Whatever you prefer. Just don't expect any pretty stewardesses. Will you be needing a handgun?"

Blaine nodded. "Something small and reliable. Heckler and Koch, if you can manage it."

With a thin smile André produced a sleek pistol from his pocket. "Mr. Deveraux anticipated your request," he said, handing over a Heckler and Koch P-9.

"Perfect," Blaine said as he took it.

"The flight will last approximately nine hours if winds are favorable. The crew will do its utmost to keep you as comfortable as possible."

Blaine stowed the pistol in the pocket of his jacket and thanked André. He had dressed casually for the trip in sport shirt, slacks, and windbreaker, a wardrobe right for the

Caribbean but not for France in December. His flesh stung with cold. The rest of his baggage was being forwarded to a Gap depot in the States, where he would retrieve it once he returned.

His return from San Melas was something he hadn't considered yet. He had looked far enough into the future only to hope that his crate was placed somewhere he might manage an unobstructed entry from into Krayman's base. There was always a way to escape, he told himself, and he had never failed to find it before. Improvisation was the key, the ability to create something out of nothing.

Even though he had managed six uninterrupted hours of slumber the night before, Blaine drifted off to sleep soon after takeoff and the surprisingly smooth flight did little to jar him. He came awake periodically and drifted off again until he awoke and realized the big plane was starting its descent.

"I'm afraid it's time to become a stowaway, sir," said the first officer, emerging from the cockpit.

Blaine downed a mug of coffee and a roll first and then headed for the crate.

"It's eighty-five degrees and sunny outside," the first officer reported. "Great tanning weather."

"What about the time?"

"Four-thirty in the afternoon. Four hours until sunset."

"Thanks," Blaine told him, and together they moved toward the crate in the back of the cargo hold.

Under ten minutes later McCracken was settled between two heavy machine guns in his private tomb. The darkness was total and there was no way to be comfortable. Blaine stretched his limbs as best he could, fighting against spasm by rhythmically flexing his arms and legs. He felt he knew what it would be like now to be buried alive, and the jolts his body absorbed as the plane landed made matters worse. His head took a hefty measure of the blows, and he found himself powerless to shift his frame to a position that could spare any single part of him the pounding. He felt the brakes being applied, heard them squeak, and rejoiced as the plane taxied to a halt.

The most uncomfortable part of his journey, he hoped, was over.

Blaine heard the heavy cargo doors being opened and ramps wheeled into place. Next he heard footsteps, muffled and disjointed. Garbled orders were shouted. Each minute the footsteps and voices drew closer to his crate.

Finally he sensed motion. He felt his crate being dragged across the floor. There was a hard shove from the rear and a thud as it reached the ramp and began its slide down. At ground level impact with another crate made it sway and threatened to tip it over. Blaine grasped his pistol in the darkness. If he was exposed now, he meant to make a fight of it. But the crate came to a halt with no damage done. He heard trucks being backed up and forklifts motoring close by.

The heat inside the crate was stifling. He felt more cramped than ever and longed for more light to filter between the hairline cracks in the crate. His eyes would be his worst enemy if they were suddenly exposed to the blinding Caribbean sun. He would be unable to see and unable to fight. All he could do was hope it didn't come to that.

McCracken was shaken hard against the side of the crate as it was hoisted by forklift into the back of a truck. The meager light vanished, and darkness was total again. The minutes grew into an hour as the loading process continued. Blaine breathed his own sweat. The voices continued around him, sometimes laughing. A rumble sounded and he quickly realized it was the transport readying to lift off. There was another rumble, the engine of the truck he was stored in, and then Blaine was conscious of motion, slow at first but gradually picking up.

The road to the truck's destination was not smooth. Blaine was tossed against the crate's sides, doing the best he could to cushion the blows with his hands. He was jerked every way imaginable.

Blaine checked the luminous dial of his watch. Five forty-five, which left him three good hours of light to find what he was looking for. Fifteen minutes later the trucks came to a halt, the engines turned off, and the unloading process begun. McCracken could sense he was in a spacious building with a cool breeze soothing him from between the cracks of the crate. The unloading process went on and on. Blaine had only his watch to distract him from the monotony of his confinement. It wasn't until six-thirty that the voices disappeared and a heavy door slammed closed. Blaine waited another ten minutes just to be sure, then drew his feet up to his chest and aimed them for a thrust at the crate's removable panel. He kicked out hard.

The panel didn't give. Impact resounded in an echo he was certain would attract every guard in the compound.

He waited another two minutes before shifting his body from one end of his compartment to the other. Obviously he had tried the wrong side, the cost being near exposure and a painful repositioning within the crate. Finally he drew his knees up to his chest again and repeated the procedure.

The panel came away with surprising ease and fell to the floor.

McCracken became utterly rigid, daring barely to breathe, as if his silence might erase the noise already made. He took a deep breath and pushed himself from his prison.

His legs hit the cement floor and collapsed under him from the strain. He massaged them to get his circulation going, and pulled himself to his feet. His entire body felt compressed. He stretched his muscles and fought to loosen up. The pain was seething as his limbs expanded to normal size. Blaine's eyes began their work.

The room he was in was the size of a high school gymnasium with a high ceiling. Sun spilling in through the windows provided enough light to see that the floor was crammed with crates of all sizes. Blaine walked past them through dirt and dust, noting their contents. There were grenades, rifles, bazookas, and countless crates of ammunition. So far as he could tell no guard was prowling here, but he couldn't tell what might lay beyond the huge sliding door. He would have to make a careful check before even contemplating his exit.

A narrow ledge ran under the windows at the front of the building. Blaine leaned his shoulders against a crate and shoved it forward until it was almost touching the front wall. He pulled himself atop it and then, inhaling deeply, leaped for the ledge with his hands.

They grasped the edge, and his legs smacked up against the wall. Grimacing, he started to pull himself up. The process was slow and agonizing, and Blaine was constantly aware that the slightest slip would mean a twenty-foot drop to a hard surface.

Finally he was upright, wavering a little but maintaining his balance. Stealthily, he ducked down and gazed through the dust-coated window.

What he saw took his breath away.

The window looked out over an army base, on the perimeter of which lay a series of training fields, where dozens of men were drilling. Blaine saw target ranges, obstacle courses, hand-to-hand combat areas, war games props where two sides seemed to be engaging each other at that moment, one dressed in blue, the other in red. The target range was the farthest off and Blaine could barely make out the figures chewing up man-sized dummies with automatic weapons. The dummies danced mechanically across the field to give the shooters practice with moving targets.

All the training fields were too far away to make out anything clearly. He would have to get closer to do that. But getting closer without drawing attention would be difficult. All the men were wearing combat fatigues, and McCracken didn't have a pair handy. Besides, the soft scraping of boots beneath him indicated a guard was just outside this supply depot, not visible from his vantage point but nonetheless ruling out the possibility of Blaine escaping through the front. That left the back, where there was no door, and no convenient ledge below the windows. There were rafters, though, which ran beneath the whole ceiling. He would have to make use of them.

What Blaine really needed now was rope, but a quick inspection of the hangar yielded none. His best substitute was the twine wrapped tightly around a number of crates.

He yanked an all-purpose knife from his jacket pocket and set about cutting as much as he would need. It took another few minutes to fasten the twine strips together in knots learned long before in 'Nam.

Blaine pulled the different segments of the twine taut to check for weakness and then, satisfied, he tied one end to the knife and looped it over the lowest rafter. Then he twisted both ends together so the twine swirled upward like a single snake. He began to scale it, using both his arms and legs. The twine was sharp, and his hands quickly grew raw. He felt the sweat soaking his eyes when he finally grabbed hold of the rafter and pulled himself onto it.

He was in line with a window and he edged toward it. He reached for the latch. The window opened inward, allowing him ample passage out. Blaine felt for the twine behind him and passed its length out through the window. It came up three or four feet short of the ground, an easy drop at that point. Then he swung around so that he could pass his legs through the window first. Gripping the twine, he began to lower himself to ground level, where he landed firmly on his feet. He felt to make sure his knife and the Heckler and Koch were still in place. His next order of business was to obtain a uniform.

The guard at the front of the building would have to help him out.

Blaine moved to the side of the building and pressed himself against it, staying within its shadow. He crept along step by step until he was barely a yard from the corner. Then he kicked up dirt with his shoes. When that got no reaction, he dug deeper and rattled some pebbles.

The guard's boots pounded closer.

Blaine waited for him to round the corner before he moved. The man saw only a shape lunge from the shadows. By the time his mind had registered anything else, McCracken's blade had slid deep into his lower back. The guard stiffened and died without a sound. Blaine dragged him away from the corner farther into the shadows, then undressed him and pulled the guard's clothes over his own. His placement of the wound allowed him to tuck that part of the dead man's shirt into his pants. He noticed that the guard was white, which seemed peculiar, but there was no time to think about it.

It took no more than a minute for Blaine to put on the entire uniform of the dead guard, a poor fit, with the pants baggy and short and the shirt too loose. He pressed the man's corpse into a depression in the ground right against the building. Finally he stuck the Heckler and Koch into his belt, swung the guard's M-16 over his shoulder, and took up his position in front of the storage hangar.

From there he had a clear view of the various training stations, and inspection of them proved truly chilling. He recognized the methods of the same guerrilla training he had excelled in so many years ago. Several men at each station—the instructors, obviously—were dressed in darker uniforms topped with berets. Krayman was sparing no expense. He had probably hired the best paramilitary instructors available, men who had learned their trade in 'Nam or Korea. Most of the drills he knew well, others appeared to have been modified for an urban climate rather than a jungle one.

Blaine gazed to his right and saw rows of jeeps and troop carriers lined up in what must have been the motor pool. Beyond them lay a half dozen M60 tanks, scorched and scarred metal indicating they had seen battle at one time or another.

Blaine was wondering what possible use the PVR could have for tanks when something else occurred to him. The techniques the men in the training fields were practicing had nothing to do with what they would face on Christmas Eve. All the drills were based around coming up against similarly armed and prepared men. By rights, though, the PVR would be using a hit and run, total terror strategy, destruction of property their foremost aim. People would die, but most easily without a fight. The only resistance they might meet would be token police forces at Christmas Eve strength; most of the population would be home watching Jimmy Stewart in *It's a Wonderful Life*. Taking over major urban centers should prove effortless for such well-trained troops, but nothing they were practicing suggested that was what they expected.

Intrigued, Blaine watched the men in the fields more closely; not the men specifically but their actions and mannerisms. These did not appear to be radical amateurs turned into murderous pros in ten easy lessons. There was a swiftness to their movements, a sureness in their stride, professional sureness.

McCracken was still trying to reconcile this when a piercing siren went off. His heart leaped into his mouth and he felt panic rise with it. They knew security had been breached. The hundreds of soldiers off in the fields were sprinting closer to the main complex. Blaine held his ground and his breath.

From over a thin rise a pair of tanks followed by more heavy equipment appeared with men trotting in step behind the machines. So they were calling out the heavy stuff to bring him in. . . .

Then Blaine relaxed. The troops were just falling in, forming neat, precise rows on the edge of the cement area that contained the storage buildings and barracks. They were simply—

Blaine's mind stopped pondering. He squinted his eyes, then rubbed them. He could see the troops clearly now and what he saw was impossible.

It couldn't be. Yet it was.

Every single man was white.


McCracken's phone call from Paris had deeply disturbed Andrew Stimson. A Christmas Eve strike by a revolutionary black group was bad enough. But add the involvement of someone like Randall Krayman and obviously even more was going on.

McCracken claimed Krayman was financing the PVR's supply of weapons. Why? What could the mysterious billionaire possibly have to gain from such an association? Stimson knew little about the man and had put a team of researchers on to him immediately after Blaine's phone call. He would have stayed through the night himself, but fatigue finally consumed him. He had slept barely at all these past few days, and it was finally catching up with him. After he dozed off for the third time at his desk, Stimson figured it was time to call it quits for the day. He called his bodyguards and had his car brought to the front of Gap headquarters.

The procedure was standard these days for high-ranking government officials, even clandestine ones like Stimson. Two cars with two bodyguards in each, one behind and one in front. Usually he opted to drive his car himself because he enjoyed the solitude and loathed the helpless feeling of being driven around. Tonight he had almost called for a driver, then figured handling the chore himself would do him good.

Stimson climbed behind the wheel of his standard issue sedan and signaled his lead car to take off. The second one would hang back slightly, guarding against attack from the rear.

A freezing drizzle had begun earlier that evening, and by the time the procession hit the middle of a surprisingly barren expressway, a steady snow had started up and the roads were icy slick. Automatically, Stimson turned up his windshield wipers and switched the climate control to defrost. The wipers streaked unevenly across the icy glass, but Stimson barely noticed, too much else on his mind.

Obviously, Randall Krayman was using Sahhan because the Christmas Eve strike was part of a far more extensive plan. The implications promised to be catastrophic, with the PVR providing merely a spark.

Behind Stimson, the following car began to close the gap.

The Gap chief shuddered. Thank God for Blaine Mc-Cracken, he thought. No other agent confined by rules and regulations could have gotten this far. Stimson had been right in utilizing his skills.

The following car had moved still closer, not more than twenty yards back now.

Stimson checked the rearview mirror and felt something was wrong even before he realized one of the car's headlights was out. Both had been working when they passed onto the expressway. Something must have happened back there while his thoughts had been elsewhere. The cars had been switched, his bodyguards taken out, and now the enemy was close enough to spit on.

Stimson heard the roar of the engine as the car accelerated and drew up alongside him in the other lane. He floored his own pedal and started blasting the horn in the hope of attracting the attention of his men in the lead car.

Both windows on the strange car's passenger side slid open.

Stimson's throat clogged with panic, but he didn't give in to it, even as black barrels were being steadied on the sills. Part of him was still a field man. Part of him responded the only way possible.

Still holding the pedal to the floor and drawing closer to the lead car, Stimson veered sharply to the left, hoping to crunch the opposition's vehicle and thus buy enough time for the lead car to drift back.

It almost worked. Metal had just smacked against metal when the barrels blazed red and Stimson heard the glass around him shatter only after slivers of it had jammed into his flesh among the dozens of lead pellets stealing his life away. He tried to breathe, but his air was gone along with the steering wheel. He felt himself slumping, eyes locked painfully open, when another volley tore away his last grip on life. The trailing car slammed back into his and sent it careening madly for the guard rail, up and over the metal in a single leap down into a darkness that broke into flames on impact.

Then death.

# CHAPTER 18

THE ramifications of what he was seeing were lost only briefly on McCracken as the shock subsided.

*There were not one, but two armies! One white and the other black. And Randall Krayman was financing both!*

Blaine's mind could make no sense of it. There was too much happening too fast. He needed time to put things together.

If Sahhan's troops were being utilized on Christmas Eve, then where did these come in? As a supplement perhaps?

No, that didn't wash. The mix of the two armies would prove more volatile than their collective mission. Besides, these white troops were professional mercenaries. Compared to them, Sahhan's army of fanatics were rank amateurs whose greatest weapons would be shock and surprise. The men he was watching now lined up squarely in rows wouldn't need either. A similar number of these could—

Another siren wailed, breaking Blaine's train of thought. The men scattered in all directions, but mostly for the barracks. The leaders walked off together, leaving a small group of sentries to watch over the field and heavy equipment. Men were coming toward him from all angles and Blaine knew it wouldn't be long before the body of the real guard would be discovered.

He walked away from his post toward the fields, hidden by the similarly dressed men he passed among. He held

the M-16 across his shoulder a bit tighter and felt in the
gun belt for the exact location of its extra clips. For no
particular reason he headed toward the target range, where
mechanical dummies had made for realistic practice. Above
him loomed a guard tower with men manning binoculars
and a powerful machine gun. He did his best to appear to
be doing what he was supposed to, moving slowly at the
pace of an on-duty sentry.

His eyes turned back toward the storage hangar just before he reached the field. The commotion was obvious.
The men with berets were sprinting toward a large group
of soldiers in their practice fatigues. The guard's body had
been discovered. Blaine cursed the sun for not setting earlier in the damn Caribbean. Darkness would have shielded
the man's body indefinitely.

He reached the field, glad he had chosen it since it was
the farthest from the base complex and in the proper direction to reach the airstrip. Instinctively, he had begun to
contemplate escape. He had learned everything he was
going to here on San Melas and nothing he had been expecting. The puzzle merely had more pieces thrown in. He
would walk straight across the field, over the ridge, and
make his way to the airstrip. Sooner or later another craft
would take off and somehow he would have to make himself a passenger.

Blaine was halfway across the field, when one of the
mechanical dummies looked up at him. He froze in his
tracks and felt a tremor of shock pass through him.

The target wasn't a dummy.

It was a man. Shot full of holes and staring out through
sightless eyes.

The war games they were playing here were real, with
flesh and blood used in place of cardboard silhouettes. The
corpse's features were too bloodied to make out clearly.
Perhaps he was a recruit who hadn't been making it. The
law of San Melas might well be survival of the fittest. Only
the best were sent off the island to . . .

Where? Why?

"Hey, you there! You're off limits!"

Blaine hadn't heard the jeep squeeze to a halt. He turned slowly and faced two men with rifles at the ready.

"This is my area. I'm just on guard duty."

"Bullshit! I don't know you. I don't—"

McCracken acted before the sentence was complete. He felt the futility of his ruse, knew it would get him nowhere. He was going for the M-16 on his shoulder as he dove and found the trigger just as he struck the ground.

The two men were dropped immediately by his hail of fire, managing a harmless volley each. But the gunshots would certainly bring the force of hundreds descending upon the field. Outfighting or outrunning those numbers was impossible. Outwitting them was something else again.

Blaine fired a trio of bursts into the distance beyond the ridge. Then, faking panic, he grasped his rifle tight and sprinted back in the direction he had come from. A last-second thought made him dive to the ground near the two men he had shot. His hand found the wounds of one and came away thick with oozing blood. He smeared it over his forehead and half his face, then wiped the remainder on his green pants for still more effect.

He ran from the field, eyes gazing back with forced fear, one leg dragging theatrically behind him.

Floods of men were rushing toward him, led, as expected, by the bereted leaders.

"Help me! Help!"

Blaine struggled to reach them, eyes darting more feverishly than ever over his shoulder.

"Stay down!" he screamed in warning. "Stay down!"

Most of the charging men hit the turf and rolled. A few of the bereted leaders held their ground. Blaine collapsed at their feet. He was struggling for breath and made sure they saw the blood running down the side of his face.

"How many?" one of the men in a beret asked.

"I don't know," Blaine wheezed. "Six maybe. I couldn't tell. They took us by surprise from over the ridge. They seemed to be everywhere."

"How are they packed?"

"I don't know," Blaine huffed.

"How are they packed, I asked you? Get a hold of your-self, soldier!"

The bereted leader grabbed Blaine and shook him at the shoulders.

"I dunno, I dunno. . . ."

"I said, get a hold of yourself!"

Blaine gazed vacantly at him. "They're packed heavy. Automatic weapons."

"Get to sickbay," the bereted leader told him, and then signaled his men to move on.

McCracken hobbled off in the opposite direction. He had bought himself time, but that did nothing about an escape route. And now he was moving *away* from the airstrip. Wait! The motor pool where the heavy equipment had been stored! He could grab a jeep or truck from there and drive it to the airfield.

Blaine quickened his pace just a bit as more uniformed men streaked by him. Any moment now the leaders sur-veying the field might realize there had been no assault, that they had been fooled. He had to reach the motor pool before then.

He reached the macadam surface of the complex and straightened up. Suddenly his pace was that of a sprinter making fast for the motor pool. Shouts and screams started up behind him. He heard footsteps pounding the pavement and glanced back to see men rushing at him leveling their weapons.

Blaine turned all the way around and fired a spray to his rear which scattered most of the soldiers giving chase. Hundreds of others were rushing back from the target prac-tice field. His ruse was obviously up. A jeep would do him no good now, would only delay the inevitable. But a tank . . .

He lit out at top speed toward the neat row of tanks.

The machine gun in the guard tower opened fire, and Blaine dodged behind the side of a building to escape the bullets. The gun had him pinned, an easy target for the many troops sprinting back toward the complex. He had to move now.

In the amber light of the early evening Caribbean sun, Blaine focused on a tank at the end of the row. He had been in plenty of M60s over in 'Nam; they were powerful but cumbersome machines which took a minimum of three men to operate. Recently, though, many had been updated with computer technology, so it was possible for only one man to drive the tank and fire it. McCracken could only hope these M60s had been part of that lot. If not, the best he could hope for would be to do plenty of damage with its big gun until they got him.

Blaine sprinted out from his hiding place and dared the bullets to hit him. He ran in a zigzag to make it difficult for the tower machine gun to lock on to him. But now the troops were roaring back and fanning out in commando fashion to enclose him, not realizing yet what he was headed for.

Bullets chimed off the tank's steel flesh as he reached it with a final leap. He vaulted behind the gun turret for cover, popped open one of the hatches, and plunged in headfirst.

He landed hard and rose immediately to close the hatch and lock it down. Bullets continued to ricochet off the steel outside, some clanging harder than others. Blaine switched on the cabin's lights and moved to the dashboard. He blessed his luck; all the gauges were digital, indicating this was one of the updated tanks.

The control panel was on his right, and he hit the M60's master switch. Then he pressed the starter button and the diesel engine began to hum. The pedals beneath him were similar to those found in a car, the left being the brake and the right the accelerator. There was a T-bar located directly in front of him which took the place of a steering wheel. To his right and up a little was the weapons range and targeting indicator with readouts displayed on a miniature television screen. The digital counter above it read "3," meaning three rockets were stowed in the big gun. A button within reach of the T-bar would launch them, so he could drive and fire at the same time. The machine gun firing buttons were also within easy reach, and as he shifted the gear lever into low, Blaine couldn't help but be amazed by this wonder of modern ballistics.

Still, three rockets would be little more than a distraction. The chances of his getting off the island suddenly seemed extremely thin. The bullets chiming regularly off the tank's exterior reminded him he couldn't stay inside forever.

McCracken swung the T-bar hard to the right to make the M60 go left to clear the motor pool. He headed it straight toward the largest congestion of troops, going right into the teeth of their offensive. He pressed his eyes tighter against the rubber eye holes that functioned like a submarine's periscope. He saw the troops backing away unsurely, retreating under the onslaught of the monstrous vehicle. The M60's top speed was perhaps thirty miles per hour, but McCracken kept it slow for more maneuverability. An explosion to his right shook the tank, and Blaine adjusted his viewer to include a wider scale.

On the tower a man stood poised with a bazooka, a second behind him sliding in another shell. Blaine slowed the tank to a crawl and switched on the automatic targeting device.

A set of grids with numbers alongside appeared on the screen before his eyes. He kept adjusting until the guard tower was in the grid's center.

The man holding the bazooka went into his crouch.

Blaine pushed the red firing button.

Impact thrust him back against his seat and halted the tank's progress. Blaine watched through the viewer as a blur shot out toward the guard tower, turning it into an orange fireball spraying metal and wood everywhere.

The digital rocket counter clicked down to "2."

McCracken aimed the tank around to where most of the troops were dispersing. He dabbed at his brow and decided his next and last targets would be the greatest concentrations of men. Perhaps in the confusion he might slip away. Perhaps—

Wait! Confusion, that was it! The *ultimate* in confusion had to be created if he was to escape.

Blaine gave the accelerator pedal more pressure and reached over the T-bar for a pair of buttons. The tank's front-mounted, twin machine guns responded by cutting down those troops brave enough to chance a rush at the iron monster.

He swung the M60 to the left and angled it for the storage hangar he had come from originally. He had just come in line with the front of the building, when an armor-piercing shell ripped into the side of his tank, spraying dust and debris into the cabin. The smell of burnt metal and wires flooded his nostrils.

"Come on, baby," McCracken urged out loud. "Hold together for just a little longer. . . ."

The tank seemed to hear him and obey, limping forward with one tread crippled as more explosions outside battered Blaine's ears. He swung the turret in the direction they were coming from and fired the big gun quickly without taking proper aim. The shell landed short but bought him the last seconds he needed.

The counter clicked down to "1."

He crashed the M60 through the hangar's heavy doors, rolled right through them with the turret swinging back to the front. The T-bar shook in his hands and he had to twist it in crazed patterns to compensate for the crippled tread. The targeting scope was equipped with infrared, so even in the darkness he had no trouble locating the corner he remembered the crates of grenades had been stored in. With the tank struggling forward, knocking crates from its path, Blaine fired his last rocket.

The results were immediate. And spectacular.

That entire portion of the building went up in a blinding fireball, the intense heat and flames reaching out to consume box after box of other explosives and ammunition. Blaine was out of the M60's cabin an instant before the flames reached his area, and he rushed away as they licked at his back. An explosion catapulted him through the air and he felt himself strike the floor as another blast ripped out the wall before him. With the onrush of flames serving as his cover, Blaine crawled back outside.

On the base there was total havoc. Order had collapsed. Troops ran in every direction with no idea of what they should be doing in such a situation. The commando leaders were shouting commands, but it was useless. Explosions kept sounding in the storage hangar, which had become a formless mass of construction tumbling in upon itself to be swallowed by the raging flames.

McCracken's face was charred black and he was bleeding superficially in a number of areas. As he moved through the chaos, he saw many others who looked much the same, especially those who had followed orders to battle the fire with hoses bearing insufficient pressure. Then, above it all, a voice crackled over the loudspeaker.

"Attention all personnel! Attention all personnel! Prepare immediately for evacuation to Newport com-center. Repeat, prepare immediately for evacuation to Newport com-center. Trucks will begin leaving for the airfield in five minutes. Trucks will begin leaving for the airfield in five minutes."

They were abandoning ship, Blaine thought. I've accomplished that. And destroyed a prime weapons cache to boot. *Newport com-center* . . .

What in hell was that? No matter, McCracken figured, it's my chance for escape regardless.

He burst through a barracks door, where men were feverishly packing gear, and found an unoccupied bed and foot locker. In the near darkness and confusion no one took much notice of his features through the grime and blood that covered them. He would be fine so long as the bed's true occupant didn't make an untimely return.

Blaine redressed in shapeless green fatigues and rummaged around their owner's foot locker to find sufficient packing for a duffel bag as the others were doing. He would do everything just as the others did. They were his ticket off the island.

He moved from the barracks, duffel bag in hand, with the second rush of men through the door. The fire was now totally out of control. It had spread to neighboring structures in the face of facilities utterly inadequate to fight it.

Blaine ran toward the trucks near the motor pool and hurled himself into the back of one. Its darkness soothed him. Feeling cocky, he extended helping hands to the last of those who crowded in the back and shoved around to find seating space. A number gave up and settled on the floor. McCracken managed to find a spot on the bench way in the back near the truck's cab.

The truck rumbled to a start, lurched forward in one grinding lunge, and then another. The engine, not yet warm, resisted, but the driver pushed the machine until its gears ground in protest. Blaine followed the path they were taking as best he could through the open tailgate. It was smooth-going through the length of the complex until they reached the hardened dirt road that would lead them to the airfield. Blaine recognized its coarse feeling from the trip in and found it little more comfortable outside a crate than inside.

His fear of being recognized as an impostor had evaporated by the time the caravan of trucks reached the airstrip. Enough eyes had met his and turned away routinely to convince him that where the darkness and grime stopped being his ally, he was aided by the fact that these men had apparently remained strangers to each other through their training.

That led him to the conclusion that their training had not lasted long and to wonder how many had come before them.

*Newport com-center . . .*

What if this destination was one of many spots across the country Krayman's white mercenary troops had been airlifted to? Blaine had to assume that Sahhan's PVR cells were already in place in similarly strategic areas. Two separate armies, both prepared to strike, both financed by Randall Krayman. But where was the connection?

The questions and puzzles kept battering Blaine's mind as he sat in the crowded cargo hold of one of the transports streaking through the sky. He had overheard someone calling out the flight coordinates earlier and thus knew that the Newport of their destination was the one in Rhode Island—

quite fortunate since he had spent a month some years back resting and recuperating from an especially grueling mission on the prestigious community's famed beaches. He remembered the area well enough to suit his needs.

Blaine dozed a few times through the eight-hour flight, which ended harshly on an abandoned airfield at nearly three A.M. The troops stretched and shook themselves awake, trying to beat back the sluggishness the long trip had brought on. Once the plane came to a halt, the men closest to the doors slid them open and let down the ramps. Blaine walked out in the middle of the group and felt the cold air assault him on contact. Paris had been bearable and San Melas steaming, so a return to the unusually early winter cold was shocking. All the troops looked to be shivering. But the bereted leaders shouted at them and pointed them in the direction of a hangar which might have been a giant icebox.

After so long in darkness, even the temporary fluorescent lighting burned Blaine's eyes. He shielded them as he took his place in line, leaving his duffel bag by his feet and making sure his face was covered. The rows of men were neat and orderly. The troops stood halfway at attention in the cold. Beyond a window crusted with a combination of ice and dirt, Blaine noticed a few of the leaders conferring with a giant of a man wearing a civilian overcoat. Even from this distance, the big man did not look pleased. The men beyond the window dispersed, and moments later a raspy, slurred voice echoed through the hangar over a P.A.

"The unfortunate incidents on San Melas change nothing," the voice began. "You know what you have to do, where and when you have to meet up. Your weapons are ready for you, along with fresh clothes, cash, and additional paperwork where required. Everything becomes routine from here. Just stick to your orders as precisely outlined unless you hear differently from your station leader providing the proper access code. The abort and regroup signals are uniform nationwide to avoid confusion. Please follow your orders in the days ahead *exactly*. The time is almost upon us. Be ready and stay alert. That is all."

The troops swung toward the doors at the front of the hangar as if on cue, and Blaine swung with them. He was still digesting the shadowy speaker's words, when his row began to move in single file toward the exit. There was only this door to pass through and he would be free.

He was almost to it when a hand grasped his shoulder and shoved him around. He found himself looking up at the horribly mangled grin of a figure with only half a face and a gun in his hand.

"I've been expecting you, McCracken," said Wells.

# PART FOUR

# Newport

**Tuesday Morning to Wednesday Morning**

# CHAPTER 19

THE figure ran through the thickening snow, a furtive eye cast to his rear at regular intervals as if expecting a great beast to pounce upon him. He had run often since coming to these woods years before. His route was never the same, no concrete destination or purpose. He ran mostly when memories of the hellfire grew too near, ran as if to widen the gap separating him from them.

But today was different. Today he ran from a sense of wrongness, a feeling that something was out of balance. He was a huge man but his feet made only the slightest impression in the hard-packed Maine snow and his steps produced barely a sound. The old ones had taught him that anything was possible if one achieved balance, that of the spirit as important as that of the body and the world about. The three existed as one, none set into place unless all were. Today all were not.

Because something *was* coming. Not a great beast with dagger teeth and razor claws; something less defined but equally deadly. He could liken this feeling only to that which often preceded an ambush in the hellfire. He had survived on those occasions by heeding the sense of imbalance when it came, slight tremors which warned him when Charlie was about to spring from one of his innumerable tunnels.

But there was nothing slight about what he felt now.

It reached out for him from the shadows, only to dart back when he swung around. Soon, though, he knew it would show itself.

And he knew he would be there when it did.

"It's been a long time, Wells. Last time we met I think you had your whole face."

Wells shoved him hard and all at once a half-dozen men with rifles enclosed McCracken. A van skidded to a halt. One of the men threw open the back doors.

"Get in," Wells ordered.

Blaine started to, but then turned back to the guards. "Has Pretty Boy here led you on any massacres lately?"

It went back to 'Nam in 1969. Wells and McCracken had been in different divisions of the Special Forces. Blaine had known the war was unwinnable from his first month in. The Viet Cong had built tunnels under the whole country. Troops appeared out of nowhere and disappeared the same way. Traps, mines, ambushes—it was a guerrilla war, the Cong's war. But Blaine went about his business nonetheless with as much dignity and honor as the circumstances would allow.

His division had come upon the town of Bin Su in early March, and to this day the sight haunted him. The entire town—women and children included—had been slaughtered. Bodies and pieces of bodies lay everywhere, obviously there had been torture and, most hideous of all, a collection of heads had been staked to fence posts, where they had been used for target practice. Every code of ethics had been violated. Someone had to pay.

Blaine was warned to back off and told the adjutant to stick a Huey up his ass. The Cong was the enemy, but they were also people and there were rules in the field that had to be obeyed. Forget them and something far more important than this war would be lost. It took a month, and the help of a crazy lieutenant who happened to be an American Indian, but he tracked down the unit responsible for Bin Su. It was under the command of Vernon Wells.

Then Blaine made his only mistake. He should have

killed Wells instead of turning him in. Or have let the
lieutenant scalp him, as he had begged Blaine to let him
do. As it was, the whole incident was covered up. The
guilty unit was broken up, and Wells himself was dis-
charged to the States. The Indian had never let him live
that one down. Blaine seethed, but quietly. He had done
everything he could.

The van was moving. Wells handcuffed McCracken's
wrists and made sure all four guards held their weapons
trained on him. Light in the van was sparse, but occasionally a streetlamp would spill onto the big man's face and
illuminate the slight grin lurking beneath his twisted features.

"I always knew I'd get my shot at you," he taunted.

"Didn't I see you in *Phantom of the Opera*?"

Wells's grin faded. "Your impetuousness surprises even
me, McCracken. I told them all along that Scola couldn't
finish you. I knew she hadn't even when the reports said
otherwise. And when word came in about San Melas, I
knew you'd be on board that plane."

"I guess I should be flattered. When do I get to find out
where we're going?"

"We're almost there."

"You work for Randall Krayman, don't you, Wells? Or
is your hairdresser the only one who knows for sure?"

Wells's hand lashed out fast; not the one holding the
gun, but the other, appearing out of nowhere and knocking
Blaine to the carpeted floor of the van. The blow was barely
a graze, far more violence restrained than released, yet its
effect was dizzying and sharp.

"Can I take that as a yes?" Blaine asked.

Wells remained silent and expressionless.

"Isn't this when you're supposed to say I could make it
easy on myself by spilling my guts now?"

"Why should I bother?" Wells returned, words slurred
noticeably. "You won't talk now, and you probably won't
talk later. I know you well, McCracken, better than anyone
else does probably. We've had a half-dozen chances to kill
you that no other man could have slipped out of."

"Who's 'we'?"

Wells looked away as the van turned left and continued on for a mile or so, slowing up when it reached a spacious parking lot enclosing what looked to be a large Newport sports complex. Blaine made out tall, reflective letters on one of the buildings:

## JAI ALAI

"We going to the matches?" Blaine asked.

"They're out of season," Wells responded. "We've had to improvise."

"Save your money, friend," Blaine told him. Then, in a whisper, "The sport's rigged."

A demonic smile crossed the normal half of Wells's face. "It is tonight."

They pushed Blaine from the van and shoved him along toward the entrance to the fronton. A man inside the lobby was holding one of the doors open. Blaine was led through them, by a row of admission windows, through a set of turnstiles, and into the deserted and dimly lit betting area.

With Wells leading the way they moved into the lower tier of the most expensive seats and headed down the wide steps. Below, only the court lights were on, as if a heated match were going on, with many dollars riding on men with unpronounceable names. Blaine could almost imagine the cheers and boos. It would take an army the size of a capacity crowd to get him out of this now.

A few seconds later an arm at each of his elbows guided him onto the smooth court surface and steered him toward the green front wall. The wall was made of granite and showed thousands of white splotches from the constant impacts of the rock-hard ball. Tonight something else had been added to its starkness.

A pair of manacles.

Wells stood back on the court floor as the handcuffs were removed from Blaine's wrists and his arms shoved violently over his shoulders. The big man hung back as an unspoken warning: Subdue my men and you'll still have me to deal with. Blaine let himself be moved. They shoved him backward and his boots clanged against the waist-high metal covering that indicated low shots to the audience with a similar clang when jai alai was in season. Blaine's arms were stretched and his wrists locked in the manacles.

For the first time that night he felt totally defeated. He had no chance of escape now unless he was somehow able to squeeze his hands through the manacles at the right moment, tearing flesh along the way. But he doubted he'd ever get a chance even for this dubious pleasure; Wells didn't intend to take his eyes off him.

"Why does your boss need two armies?" Blaine asked as they faced each other from twenty yards apart. His voice echoed metallically.

"You have put the pieces together well," Wells told him, his face trying for a grin. "Now you will tell me who you have met along the way who has been of service to you."

"Why does your boss need two armies?" Blaine repeated.

"Tell me the trail you have followed."

"I work alone. You should remember that from 'Nam. Except for the Indian, of course."

Half of Wells's face reddened. "We know you were in Paris. Who else are you working with? Who else have you alerted?"

"You mentioned *abort* to the troops at the airfield tonight," Blaine persisted. "Abort what?"

"Why make things so difficult for yourself, McCracken?"

"Two armies, Wells. What does Krayman need two armies for? Sahhan's troops make perfect sense, though their connection with Krayman escapes me. But why the mercenaries? They don't fit."

The big man just looked at him.

"Unless the plan is to have them divide the country up equally, in which case—" Blaine suddenly realized the truth. "Krayman hired the mercenaries to destroy Sahhan's troops. That's it, isn't it?"

Wells's silence provided an acknowledgment.

"Why?" Blaine asked him.

"You tell me."

"Sahhan's people surprise the country with their Christmas Eve strike, wreaking chaos everywhere, financed by Krayman. Then the mercenaries move in to save the day and restore reasonable order, also financed by Krayman. It still doesn't make sense."

"Because there's something you're missing," Wells taunted him. "Something you'll die without knowing."

"Since I'm going to die anyway, why not tell me?"

"I've never gone in for melodrama and, besides, such important information would be wasted on a corpse." Wells paused. "I'll ask you one last time: where have you been and who have you seen since leaving the hospital?"

McCracken clenched his teeth and looked at him.

Wells turned away and nodded toward the players' entrance onto the court. A man wearing a black practice shirt strolled out and tied a wicker *cesta* basket around his hand as he twisted his shoulders to loosen up.

"Are you familiar at all with jai alai, McCracken?"

"I've lost my share of money."

"I was speaking of the physical aspects," Wells said. With that the player whipped his arm around and a white blur sped out from his *cesta*, smashing into the front wall with a crack ten feet to Blaine's right. "The ball is called a *pelota*. It's made of goatskin and has been known to travel at speeds exceeding one hundred eighty miles per hour." The player retrieved the ball and sent it whipping out again, this time smacking ten feet to Blaine's left. "This man's name is Arruzi," Wells continued. "He is known at the fronton not so much for speed as for accuracy."

Arruzi fired a shot from mid-court, scooped up the ball deftly on one bounce, and fired another. Both cracked home five feet from Blaine's head. His ears hurt from the sound. Arruzi was juggling the *pelota* about in his *cesta*.

"Impact from a rock-hard ball at that pace will crush bones beyond repair," Wells told him. "The pain, I'd imagine, would be extreme. Do you have any idea, Mc-

Cracken, how many different targets the human body can be made into?''

Arruzi fired again, low this time, a yard from Blaine's right leg. The ball banged against the metal.

''Tell me who you've reached, McCracken. Tell me who else knows anything about Christmas Eve, Sahhan, and San Melas.''

Blaine feigned deep thought. ''Key-wheel the seven in a trifecta and give me the four and one under it.''

Wells nodded to Arruzi. The player whipped the *pelota* out sidearm on the forehand side. It cracked into the wall no more than a foot over Blaine's head.

''Impact there would kill you,'' Wells reported. ''But we can't have that, can we? A few broken bones are in order first. After all the trouble you've caused us, you certainly deserve them.''

''All right,'' said Blaine, ''just give me the five on top in the Daily Double.''

Arruzi fired again, the white blur seeming to come straight at Blaine's eyes, only to curve away and smack the wall six inches under his right arm.

''My patience is growing thin, McCracken,'' said Wells. ''You are asking a lot of Arruzi's aim. He could make a misjudgment at any time and strike you before I am ready for him to.''

The *pelota* whirled at him again, this time under his left arm. Blaine flinched involuntarily and rose to his toes to stretch farther away from it. His heart thudded against his chest.

''Who have you reached, McCracken?''

''Okay, just give me a four-two quinella.''

''I think a sample is in order. . . .''

Arruzi unwound his arm more slowly. The *pelota* fluttered out, its motion clear instead of blurred, coming in low and straight. Blaine braced and squeezed his eyes closed.

Impact would have doubled him over to the floor if he'd been able to fall. The slow-moving ball smashed into his stomach with a force greater than any he'd ever felt. He'd been stabbed once in the abdomen and that was the only sensation he could liken it to. His breath escaped in a rush and his chest heaved. He tried to inhale, but there was no air to grab, just a raging pain in his stomach as if a burning football were wedged inside. He kept heaving.

The *pelota* rolled out between a pair of red lines used to denote legal serves, and Arruzi snatched it up in his *cesta*.

"That was perhaps forty miles per hour," Wells noted. "Impact against a rib even at that speed would lead to splintering, and perhaps a vital organ would be pierced. At a hundred and twenty miles per hour, well, the effects would be similar to jumping off a five-story building." Blaine could tell the big man was enjoying this. There had never been any expectation that he'd talk, or that he'd have anything meaningful to say even if he did. This whole scene was being played out just for Wells's sadistic pleasure. "Tell me about Paris, McCracken."

Blaine might have if he'd been able to find his breath. As it was, Arruzi's arm was coming forward again, the motion itself a blur, and Blaine turned his head away.

The *pelota* crashed between his spread legs, not six inches from his groin.

"He was just measuring off distance with that one," Wells explained. "Tell me who else knows about Christmas Eve."

Blaine caught his breath but didn't speak.

Arruzi twisted his *cesta* and whipped his arm forward again.

Blaine saw the blur of the *pelota* coming straight for his groin and acted when it seemed impact was unavoidable. Using all the muscles in his arms and shoulders to gain leverage, Blaine hoisted his legs high and straight like a gymnast. His boots pounded the wall well above his man-acled hands.

The *pelota* cracked into the precise spot previously occupied by his groin.

Blaine let his legs fall back down, his upper body a mass of fiery pain, ligaments and cartilage extended beyond their capacity.

"I think we'll go for your arm this time, McCracken," Wells taunted. "No way to move that now, is there?" He hesitated. "Tell me about Paris."

Blaine just looked at him again. He felt the sweat sting his eyes and the taste of it was heavy on his lips.

Wells nodded to Arruzi. The player went into his motion.

Suddenly the lights in the fronton died, plunging the entire place into total darkness. Arruzi's shot caromed into the side wall. Blaine felt the *pelota* whiz by him en route to the screen that protected fans from errant shots.

Wells was shouting orders, but the darkness had confused him as well and the words came out totally slurred, barely understandable. Blaine seized the chance to free his hands. He'd begun yanking his arms, steel ripping at his skin, when he felt a pair of strong hands steady him. A key was inserted into one manacle, then into the other. In the darkness all Blaine could see was the unusual blue glow of the man's luminous watch dial. His arms were pulled free of the unlocked slots.

"Get out of here," a voice whispered to him.

The only illumination in the fronton was coming from two exit signs, and Blaine dashed toward one. Motion flashed before him as he neared the heavy doors and he felt the heat of a body, heard rapid breathing. The man was probably fumbling for a gun, when Blaine crashed into him and followed up with a set of crunching fists that pummeled the man to the floor.

McCracken jumped over his downed body and crashed through the exit doors.

He knew the echoing rattle would give him away and didn't even bother to look back as he sped into the cold night with only his green fatigues and shirt to shield him against the bitterly frigid air. His stomach still ached horribly and felt like it was being kicked every time his right leg landed. He had emerged at the rear of the building and headed back toward the front, toward the main road on which he'd been brought in.

Doors slammed closed and orders were shouted behind

him. He'd been spotted, and the men from inside the fronton were giving chase.

Bullets sailed through the air from behind as the men rushed in his tracks. Hitting a moving target while moving yourself was virtually impossible even for the best shot, especially at night. This comforted Blaine, but he knew it was only a matter of time, and not much of it, before their superior numbers wore him down. Staying ahead of their bullets wasn't enough. He had to escape them altogether.

The gates leading into the fronton complex had been closed and chained. Blaine rushed at them and scaled the fence to the top. He pulled himself over as bullets whizzed through the air on all sides of him. His poor-fitting army boots would start slowing him down now, and that was the last thing he could afford. He ran up the road the van had come down and prayed for a vehicle with a sympathetic driver or an unsympathetic one he could overcome.

The sky was still pitch black with dawn more than an hour away. Good. Darkness was his ally. It significantly reduced the advantage of the opposition's superior numbers.

Blaine stayed off the road and ran along its bushy side. The darkness was even deeper here, unbroken by the spill of streetlamps. He'd be harder to spot. A car's headlights caught him briefly as it swung around a corner. Blaine raced to cut off its angle, flailing with his arms.

"Hey! Hey!"

The car swerved to avoid him and kept right on going. To his rear Blaine heard shouts and screams. He had been spotted by at least two of Wells's men. The advantage again swung to them.

He angled back into the brush by the roadside and kept following its course. So long as he stayed out of sight he had a chance. Another few hundred yards and he'd reach Route 114, a main road certain to be reasonably traveled even at this hour. One of the cars on it would provide his escape.

Forty yards up ahead McCracken caught the flash of movement on his side of the road. A gun barrel catching the spill of a streetlight. It came again and he stopped in his tracks, aware now of rustling sounds to his rear. They had him boxed in.

Blaine saw a car—no, a truck—bank into the curve before him. The truck was ablaze with lights and it was his last chance. He rushed into the street just as it swung over the slight rise and stood directly in its path. The screech of tires and squeal of brakes attracted Blaine's pursuers to his position, and they could see him in the truck's headlights. Their guns shattered the air and the truck swerved to avoid hitting Blaine.

"You crazy bastard!" the driver shouted as he skidded to a near halt by the shoulder.

Blaine *was* crazy, crazy enough to rush toward the pickup and grab hold of its side as the driver churned dust behind him. It was a few seconds after taking off again that the driver noticed Blaine's figure hanging at his side, feet dragging dangerously close to the road, and started to apply the brakes again.

The truck's progress still carried it well beyond Wells's men who were giving chase. They quickened their stride when they saw the pickup's brake lights flash once more.

"You fuckin' crazy bastard!" the hefty driver roared, and he lunged with a pipe wrench, intent on burying it in the bizarre hitchhiker's skull.

He never even got it started forward.

A stray bullet from one of the pursuer's guns caught him square in the chest and flattened him. Blaine went for the cab in a crouch with bullets ricocheting wildly around him, coughing up metallic splinters from the truck. He swung himself inside and was revving the engine even before the door closed behind him. A quick shift into first and he screeched away, leaving a cloud of dust in his wake to swallow his pursuers.

Blaine didn't have time to manage a 180, so he kept the pickup in the direction it was already headed—down the road past the fronton. Apparently, none of Wells's men had hung back and there were no barricades. Blaine started to relax.

Then, as he neared a point where the road forked, he saw two cars speeding from the right. Blaine swung the truck sharply to the left and watched the cars in his rearview mirror spin around to give chase.

Blaine gave the engine more gas and flew past a sign that said GOAT ISLAND. He followed the arrows and asked the pickup for still more speed. He had been on the exclusive Goat Island once years before for a social gathering. It was a small island, dominated by luxuriously expensive condominiums, harbors, and a well-known Sheraton booked several summers in advance. Hardly the ideal spot to hide out—no island was—but it was all he had. He streamed toward the causeway linking Goat Island with Newport, screeching into turns and corners, the engine screaming as he demanded more of it down the brief straightaways. Behind him the tailing cars held their positions, twin shadows in the night.

The causeway came up fast and McCracken's teeth clamped together as the pickup's tires thumped onto it. The cars followed him down it side by side. Blaine heard the loud blast of a shotgun and started swaying from side to side to make himself a more elusive target. Then the *stacatto song* of a machine gun found his ears an instant before the back window exploded, showering him with glass. A few ragged splinters found their way into his neck and scalp. He grimaced against the pain and straightened the pickup out, giving it all the gas it would take.

He saw the Sheraton clearly now, along with the large island marina virtually deserted for the winter. And there was something else.

A pair of cars were parked facing each other to block the end of the causeway. Men were positioned behind them, bracing weapons on roofs. A bright light caught McCracken's eyes and blinded him just before the fire began. He managed to duck low beneath the windshield, but in the process his foot momentarily lost the gas pedal. The tailing cars drew up on top of him and sprayed the cab with automatic fire. The bullets passed just over Blaine's head as he struggled to hold the wheel steady, his intention being to ram the pickup right through the makeshift barricade.

An extra loud blast assaulted his ears, followed by another similar one, and then the truck wavered out of his grasp.

*They had shot out the tires!*

Blaine struggled for control, but it was gone. The pickup squealed right, and then suddenly left, crashing over the right side rail just before the causeway's end.

McCracken braced for impact against the hard sea, but it came too fast for him and then the water was everywhere, drenching him with a black cold, the mouth of a great beast opened to swallow, sucking him down.

# CHAPTER 20

"**A**NYTHING?" Wells asked the man coordinating the search through the frigid waters.

"No sign of him," he reported, lowering his binoculars. "No one could have survived that crash. He's drowned."

The bright floodlights continued to sweep over the water and nearby shore.

"I want more men and a helicopter," Wells ordered. "And I want them now."

"That would attract even more attention than we have already," the man cautioned.

"I don't care. I want McCracken."

"He can't still be alive. Besides, it'll be dawn soon and—"

Wells's hand came out in a blur and locked onto the man's throat, shutting off his air. He lifted the figure up until his toes scraped against the causeway.

"I believe my orders were clear," Wells said coolly. "They do not need elaboration or comment. Am I correct?"

Blue-faced, the man nodded.

"Good." Wells lowered him back to the pavement. "Now, do it."

The man scampered away, hunched over.

Wells knew McCracken was out there, still in the water probably. Men like him didn't die easily. Others had failed in their assignments to eliminate him, and now Wells had failed too. He was not used to failure. If they had let him handle McCracken at the hospital instead of sending Scola, none of this would have been necessary. Now Wells felt the frustration gnawing at him as the floodlights continued to sweep the area around where the truck had crashed over the rail.

McCracken was still out there all right, and Wells meant to find him because now it was more personal than ever. He had destroyed his army career in 'Nam and embarrassed him tonight. There remained forty minutes until dawn's first light, and he meant to have the bastard dead or in tow by then.

Wells cursed the whole episode under his breath.

Blaine swam slowly. He stayed with the currents and kept below the surface as long as he could between breaths. Every ten yards or so his lungs would thirst for air and he would satisfy them with a quick poke above the surface. A few times he had been caught in the spill of the flood-lights and felt the panic swell within him, until he realized he hadn't been seen.

His plan was to swim out beyond reach of the lights and around the small island where it bent to the left. Then he could make his move toward shore. He had just a little more space to cover, but his strokes had grown stiffer. The cold bay waters were taking their toll. His lungs began craving air every other motion, and he did his best to appease them. His body had ceased its frantic shaking, but he knew this was only temporary. Once he reached the shore and was greeted by wind and temperatures not even half that of the water, hypothermia would be a definite possibility: frostbite, too, if he lived that long. He wondered how long he could move under those circumstances, wondered how effective he would be if Wells and his henchmen caught up with him again.

Not very, Blaine regretted. Still, he stroked.

At last the sweep of the floodlights failed to catch him. He had passed the end of the island and stroked to the left, making for shore in slow, even motions so as not to disturb the currents or risk a splash that might catch someone's attention. The shoreline of Goat Island was rocky, and his hands were scraped by the jagged rocks as he crawled onto land. A deep repose fell over him. He wanted just to lie there on the shore, to sleep for a brief period before forcing himself on.

No! The peace and sudden warmth were illusions cast by his exhaustion. If he slept now, it would mean death whether Wells caught up with him or not. Even if he kept active, though, the cold would kill him. He could feel it seeping through his flesh, turning his very bones brittle. He had to get a heavy jacket to ward off the chill.

Above him footsteps crunched snow. McCracken kept still and low as a flashlight swept over the general area. It made another pass, then the footsteps started up again. It had to be one of Wells's sentries, and the man was alone. Blaine crept down the narrow shore toward the flashlight's beam. As he neared it and made out the shape of its bearer not more than ten yards off, he climbed to the road and charged forward with caution thrown to the cold wind.

The sentry turned much too late and felt Blaine's fist hammer him before his eyes even had a chance to focus. Seconds later McCracken pulled his arms through the man's heavy coat. The warmth vanquished his chill almost immediately. The chattering of his teeth slowed, then vanished altogether as he started down the road, leery of more of Wells's guards appearing in his path.

Blaine tried to increase his pace, but his heart and lungs rebelled. Exhaustion swept over him. He felt cold again. The exertion from the chase and subsequent swim had proven even more a strain than he'd thought. The water on the legs of his fatigues had caked into ice, and he heard it crackling as he moved. Thank God for the coat. . . .

The Sheraton Islander loomed to his right and made a warm, inviting target. But that would be the first place Wells would expect him to go and there wouldn't be a chance of his even getting through the front door. His only alternative was to keep walking, playing the role of the guard whose coat he was wearing. There was no one around to question him. He kept his pace measured and gave the impression he was searching for someone. He was buying himself time, and with time came a chance.

He passed the causeway entrance cluttered with troops, his heart lunging against his rib cage. He kept walking through a parking lot into the marina complex where row after row of docks were reserved for summer boaters. None was present to offer him escape.

Except . . .

It was the yellow cover at the far edge of the docks that grabbed his attention first, and then the ramp angling up the water. He quickened his pace just a bit, eyes sharpening on his target. Almost there now.

His fingers scraped the sleek hull of a speedboat, a pair of potent engines peeking out from beneath the cover. No room for hesitation at this point.

In rapid fashion McCracken stripped off the yellow cover and unfastened the bolts that held the speedboat on the ramp. He noted it was called the *Sting* and gave it a little shove where the likeness of a bumblebee was painted to get it started down.

"Hey, what are you doing!" The shout came from the direction of the causeway and was followed by trampling feet.

Blaine vaulted over the boat's side and hit the cold, carpeted deck just as the *Sting* smacked the water.

"Over there! Over there!"

It drifted into the bay as bullets began streaking at him. They shattered the boat's windshield and covered Blaine with glass while he rested faceup under the dash toying with the starter wires. He twisted the proper two together and the boat coughed, then roared to life with the fury of a rocket ship. Blaine glanced behind him and saw why.

The *Sting* was equipped with twin 220 horsepower engines, which made for incredible power. Blaine gunned them for all they could give. The boat's nose lifted off the water, and it tore off into the bay like a horse free of the corral at long last. When he finally raised himself fully up,

satisfied that he was out of the bullets' range, the speed-
ometer was flirting with the seventy-mile-per-hour mark.
The din of enemy fire had all but subsided. The men would
be waiting for reinforcements. No matter. Unless they had
a boat to equal the *Sting*, Blaine had just bid them farewell.

He looked around to get his bearings. He knew this was
an inlet of Narragansett Bay, knew that reasonable civilization would be found by dawn by simply following it. For
the first time since landing in Newport, he relaxed. He was
still freezing, and his teeth chattered madly. The bay was
free of other boat traffic, but he did his best to avoid numerous floating ice chunks. Traveling at eighty now, he
neared the end of the inlet and switched on the *Sting*'s
running lights.

His ears registered the distant whirl and passed it off at
first to the racing of the *Sting*'s twin engines in the open
waters. When it intensified, his eyes swept about him just
as the spotlight caught his boat in its beam.

*A helicopter! A goddamn fucking helicopter!*

Good old Wells certainly didn't give up easy.

The helicopter raced over him with a man perched pre-
cariously on the edge firing down with a machine gun.
Blaine swung the *Sting* around in a narrow arc and headed
back for the inlet. The chopper compensated with a wider
swing and gave chase.

The boat's speed had topped ninety, when the helicopter
roared overhead again. Blaine swung the wheel hard to the
right to steer out of the inlet once more. The chopper lagged
a bit. It rose a little to aid its maneuverability, though this
would make it even harder for the machine gunner to find
his mark. But even if the helicopter did nothing more than
contain the *Sting*, that was good enough. Wells probably
had an entire army on the way.

The *Sting* leaped through the water, and Blaine had to
grip the wheel as tightly as he could just to control the
boat. The frigid wind whipped into his face, and when his
tongue tried to wet his lips, he realized he had lost feeling
in them as well.

The chopper's gunner sprayed the craft randomly, containment his goal, but his aim nonetheless right on the mark. The dashboard exploded in splinters and the *Sting* danced wildly for an instant when Blaine recoiled to avoid being hit by the pieces. Something sliced into his shoulder, a bullet graze or hunk of debris; he didn't know, and it didn't matter. The cold numbed it quickly, which made the warm flow of blood slipping out an even stranger sensation than at normal temperatures.

McCracken had turned the boat back into the inlet, when the chopper passed overhead again. The gunner's spray of bullets was a bit off this time, but one lucky burst found the fuel tanks and punctured them. The sharp smell of gasoline poured into Blaine's nostrils and he watched the yellowish liquid spill up to the deck from below. In seconds he'd be floating dead in the water, a sitting duck for the gunner in the helicopter. Another swim was unthinkable; he'd never survive it, especially now, with a wounded shoulder.

What did that leave him with?

The *Sting* still rode the waters gracefully, as if unaware of its mortal wound. The spill of the chopper's spotlight caught its shattered dashboard, and something red caught Blaine's eye. He grasped for it and touched metal under the steering wheel. He yanked it free and saw it was an emergency kit complete with flare gun. He undid the latch with one hand while he controlled the *Sting* with the other.

The flare gun fit neatly into its slot. Beneath it lay a single flare. Fired properly into a vulnerable area, it was as good as a hand grenade.

McCracken could take no chances. He pulled the flare from its slot and held it low on the deck to soak up some of the gasoline. This would increase its explosive properties.

The chopper roared overhead again, unleashing more rounds at the boat, which had begun to lose speed and sputter.

McCracken popped the flare gun open and slid the flare home, snapped it shut, and tested the trigger. He would get only one shot. It would have to be good.

The *Sting*'s engine sputtered, caught, then sputtered again. As its speed faded, Blaine aimed it toward the ice-crusted shore. The slowing boat made a more welcome target for the chopper, which came in slower, sensing the kill.

McCracken played with the wheel. He darted left and right to put up a good front, the flare gun grasped tightly in his right hand.

He didn't raise it until the machine-gun fire raged dangerously close and the helicopter loomed straight overhead. At that point it took barely a second for him to bring the gun up and aim it, even less for him to press the trigger.

The flare sped out toward the chopper with a pop.

The half-darkness of the approaching dawn was shattered by the fireball, a single orange sphere that belched black smoke and coughed steel. Only the *Sting*'s last burst of speed saved him from the killing shower of shrapnel and debris. The engine lasted until he was wading distance from shore and conked out at the same moment the chopper's smoking carcass hit the water to start its slow sink.

Blaine hurled himself over the *Sting*'s side and patted it like a loyal pet. He was in waist-deep water and moved toward the shore, above which stood a huge mansion converted into condo units. The climb up was steep, handholds available but difficult to manage with the ice.

Just as the sun's first light found the bay, McCracken pushed himself over the edge and found himself staring at a hot tub bubbling away with two couples starting the morning, or ending the night, inside.

Blaine started toward them, fatigues heavy with water already starting to freeze. He was shivering, but he knew a smile had forced itself out on the face he could barely feel.

"Care to join the party?" asked one of the women in the tub, obviously drunk. All the inhabitants had allowed their drinks to float away from them on the steaming water.

"Don't mind if I do," Blaine said, plunging in with all his clothes on.

"Were you in that plane that just crashed on the water?" one of the men asked.

"What plane?" McCracken returned, and then he tucked his head under the water.

The female occupants of the hot tub took turns telling Blaine where he had ended up. This was the Manor House, they explained, the most exclusive condo complex of the exclusive Bonniecrest Village. They had bought their unit for $200,000 and already it was worth twice that. Wasn't that something, they wanted to know.

Blaine said it was.

Time was foremost on his mind now, time and the fact that Wells wouldn't be giving up the chase for the loss of one helicopter. He might try to barricade the entire area to close in on his quarry once and for all. But it was morning now and residents of this Newport community would soon be on their way to work. Wells had his work cut out for him if he expected to find McCracken in all the activity.

After forty minutes in the hot tub to get his circulation going again, Blaine accepted a bathrobe and change of clothes. Before donning the undersized garments, he swabbed and bandaged his shoulder wound. It had proved to be merely a scratch. These people were being most hospitable and he made a mental note to return the favor someday. He could begin by leaving the condo as soon as possible. First, though, a phone call was necessary. He hadn't reported in for almost two days now. He had plenty to tell Stimson, enough for the Gap to move on Sahhan and Krayman, and to start looking for the mercenary troops scattered across the country.

Sahhan's troops would strike at the innocent and the mercenaries would strike at the troops with Krayman the force behind them both. The why of it all eluded Blaine, but he knew that was only because there was something he wasn't seeing yet. Krayman was a pragmatic man. This plan had been in the works for years at least. Nothing was being left to chance.

Blaine used the phone in a bedroom to dial Stimson's

private number. A beep sounded, followed by the whining
drone of a tape unspooling.

*"The number you have reached is not in service at this
time."*

Silence followed, replaced swiftly by a dial tone.

Blaine searched his memory. Could he have dialed the
wrong number? He tried again.

*"The number you have—"*

Blaine replaced the receiver. Stimson's private number
rang wherever he was: car, home, office, anywhere. Mc-
Cracken considered the worst ramification of the line's dis-
connection and dismissed it because it was the one thing
he could not afford. The idea of Stimson being dead was
unthinkable. Certainly there was another explanation.

Blaine dialed the normal Gap emergency exchange. Another tape-recorded voice greeted him.

"Please leave your number. Your call will be returned
immediately."

Blaine read the number listed on the white Princess phone
into the receiver. It rang not thirty seconds later.

"Your name," a dull voice requested.

"I need Stimson."

"Your name," the voice repeated.

"Look, you bastard, I'm not going to bother giving you
my name because I'm not on your active list. I'm sanc-
tioned by the chief directly and I've got to speak to him."

"Do you have an operative code or designation?"

"No, goddammit, it was cover clearance. Nine-zero
coding." Blaine slapped his forehead. "No, that's not what
you boys call it. I don't know what you call it."

"I'm going to terminate this line unless I receive a proper
designation immediately."

"All right. Just tell me if Stimson's still alive. I've got
to know."

The phone clicked off. Blaine dropped the receiver.

He was completely isolated. Stimson's plan had back-
fired. The unthinkable had happened. Someone had gotten
to the Gap chief and Blaine had no contact. Equally bad,
the call-back procedure he had followed would allow Gap

personnel to trace the unauthorized call into their most sterile of exchanges. They would investigate. A unit would be dispatched almost immediately, a unit that would see McCracken as an enemy.

He had to get out of here. But to where? Who could he take his story to?

*The CIA. He would have to make do with them. . . .*

The Company was still his official employer. And he could reach them because this time he would have the proper codes. He would give an alert signal and they would make arrangements to bring him in. Never mind the business with Chen and possible Company complicity in all this. The involvement of Krayman could account for everything he had previously blamed on his official employer. They were his best bet at this point, his only bet.

McCracken pounded out a new exchange.

"Box office," a voice greeted him without benefit of tape-recorded greeting.

"I've lost my ticket."

"Status?"

"Nine-zero coding."

"That is a discontinued exchange."

"Check my clearance, dammit! Gallahad, six-zero-niner."

"What is your designation?"

"Triple-X ultra."

A pause.

"I'm sorry, that file is no longer active."

The phone clicked off. Blaine slammed the receiver down.

*I'm sorry, that file is no longer active.*

How could he have been so damn stupid? Of course his file wasn't active anymore; the Company thought he was dead. Another element of Stimson's plan to seal his mission. Well, he was sealed now, all right, sealed off from every potential safe harbor in the government. A black revolutionary army and a mercenary resistance force were about to clash in the streets of American cities just for starters, and there was no one he could report it to. All the

emergency numbers stored in his head were of no use because each of the operators would request the same information and he could satisfy none of them enough to be
passed on to the next level. They regarded him as dead.
Because of that, ironically, he might soon be.

He had to get out of Newport immediately and buy himself some time elsewhere. Wells's men were no longer his
only concern. There were Gap and CIA teams to consider
as well, drawn to this area by an uncleared caller's breach
of sterile security lines.

Blaine's mind drifted back to the fronton, back to a fact
that had slipped away during the frantic chase that followed: someone had arranged for the lights to go out and
then freed him from Wells's manacles. For some reason
someone wanted him to stay alive.

But more people wanted him dead.

# CHAPTER 21

FRANCIS Dolorman's back was hurting so horribly Tuesday morning he could barely shift positions in his chair. Getting in and out of it was an agonizing experience for him, no less agonizing than the latest report from Wells.

"So McCracken is still alive after all," was his only comment to Verasco.

"Solely due to interference from the rebels this time," Verasco noted. "Wells had McCracken in Newport until one of them freed him."

"Not like Wells to let his own people be infiltrated."

"It may turn out to be a blessing," said Verasco. "One of his men, the rebel, we assume, has disappeared. Wells is in the process of retracing his movements, and undoubtedly the investigation will lead to his cohorts."

"Tell Wells to concentrate his energies fully in that direction. I'll handle McCracken."

"How?"

"Alone he can do us no harm. But if he were to reach receptive ears in Washington . . . We have the contacts in place to insure his continued isolation. They will be alerted. I want all these distractions cleared up before Omega is activated. Let's review the timetable."

Verasco opened a folder perched on his lap. "We will fly tomorrow to the airfield in Maine and make our way to Horse Neck Island for final preparations."

"All perfunctory at this stage, of course. And the mobilization of Sahhan's strike force?"

"Nine P.M. eastern standard time. That means six o'clock on the West Coast."

"Darkness in both instances."

"According to plan."

Dolorman nodded, obviously satisfied. "And when does phase two go into effect?"

"Exactly four hours after Sahhan's troops are mobilized. It will take sixteen minutes for our friend in the sky to pass from one coast to the other, insuring our goal of total paralysis at the optimum time. Phase three entry of mercenaries will begin twelve to sixteen hours later."

"I thought we had agreed on twenty-four."

"A slight alteration to obtain maximum visibility at the peak of panic. Their heroic response must appear irrefutable, but it must also seem vague. The rumors and obscure reports will work to our advantage."

"I assume the preparations for phase four are complete, then."

Verasco nodded. "All equipment is in place and functional on Horse Neck Island. Construction of all communications and broadcast facilities was completed yesterday. The testing has gone magnificently. Of course, the activation of phase four will be a give-and-take matter. We must be flexible. The timing will be difficult, public sentiment difficult to gauge."

"They will be our public by that time," Dolorman assured him. "They will feel what we want them to."

"But not until after Christmas Eve and your interview with Sandy Lister is scheduled for barely an hour from now."

"Your tone indicates you feel I should cancel it."

"I see no good it can do us so close to activation."

Dolorman eased himself forward. "She has seen people, talked to people. It would take only one receptive ear in the wrong place to do severe damage to Omega. By remaining cooperative with Miss Lister, we assure ourselves that she will have no reason to seek out this ear. We are fairly certain, based on her movements and correspondence, that she hasn't looked for this ear yet. But that says nothing for the others she has made contact with. One of them still might know the right numbers to call, in which case immediate action on our part would be called for.''

''You don't expect her to come out and tell you, of course.''

''Knowledge is her only weapon, so I expect her to reveal much of what she knows. The what will lead us to the who.''

Verasco looked unconvinced. ''She's a celebrity, Francis, a star in her own field. It's *her own* connections I'm most worried about.''

That drew a smile from Dolorman. ''But the most important ones have been severed. I think we can relax.''


Sandy Lister rested her shoulders against the elevator wall and tried to still her trembling. The doors slid closed and the compartment began its descent from Dolorman's office toward the lobby.

The interview was over.

And Dolorman had beaten her. She had not been up to the task. Desperation had worked against her, stealing her poise.

She had come straight to Houston from her meeting with Simon Terrell and arrived Sunday night. Monday morning first thing she dialed T. J. Brown's exchange at the network.

The voice that answered was not his.

''Who is this?'' she demanded.

''I'm sorry?''

''This is Sandy Lister. I'm calling for T. J. Brown.''

''Oh, Miss Lister,'' the strange voice responded, ''someone upstairs mentioned you might be calling. I just moved down from my office. Your assistant is on vacation.''

''He's what?''

''It came as a shock to me too. I just got the order to move—''

"Thank you," Sandy broke in, and abruptly hung up.

She grabbed for the receiver again and dialed T.J.'s home phone number. It rang and rang. No answer.

*Your assistant is on vacation. . . .*

Sandy felt a dread chill creep up her spine. With the receiver still in her hand, she dialed Stephen Shay's private number.

"Mr. Shay's office."

"Mr. Shay, please. Sandy Lister calling."

"I'm sorry, Miss Lister, I'm afraid he's not in."

"When will he be back?"

"Not for two weeks. He's gone to Europe for a special conference."

"Did he leave a forwarding? This is somewhat of an emergency."

"I'm afraid not," said the secretary, and Sandy hung up.

Because a man in Shay's position always left a forwarding address. Unless he had never left at all. Unless it was a front.

Everything was a front.

They had T.J. They had Shay.

Sandy spent the rest of Monday on the phone begging for appointments with a host of NASA officials. None would see her. With two she went so far as to mention *Pegasus* and received only curt denials. No one was talking. So there would be no help from NASA, not immediately, anyway, and immediately was all that mattered.

That left her only with Dolorman, and she had a strategy prepared. A small tape recorder hidden in her handbag would capture the entire interview. After it was over she would go to the FBI. She would tell them about the plagiarized Krayman Chip and the billionaire's obsession with controlling America. She would tell them about COM-U-TECH'S possession of *Adventurer*'s orbital flight plan and the thing Krayman had sent up into space in the guise of a satellite. When they asked for proof, she would hand them the tape recording of her interview with Dolorman. They could run it through their sophisticated machines to discover how many lies were told in response to her direct questions. Of course, that meant she would have to pose them, and that in itself was a grave risk.

Arriving at the Krayman Tower barely an hour before, she had been escorted up by a security guard in Dolorman's private elevator. Now the same guard was escorting her down and she felt for the reassuring bulge of the tape recorder in her handbag as she replayed the interview in her mind.

Dolorman's office was huge and plushly decorated. The wall paintings were originals and there were bookshelves filled with leather-bound editions lining one wall. Dolorman's desk, though, made the greatest impact on her. It was unquestionably the largest she had ever seen, neat and clean, without a trace of clutter.

"Please excuse me for not rising, Miss Lister," Dolorman said. "But my back has been a burden for several years now and is growing worse."

Sandy stepped forward and moved halfway between the door and his desk. "Yes, that turned up in my research."

They eyed each other briefly as the secretary closed the door behind her.

"Your research must have been quite exhaustive," Dolorman said.

"Just professional."

"Please, Miss Lister, sit down."

Sandy took the Chippendale chair a yard in front of the white-haired man's desk. As she reclined, her hand located the tape recorder through the fabric of her handbag and switched it on.

"You'll have to excuse my uneasiness," Dolorman continued. "I don't grant many interviews."

"The network and I both appreciate the exception."

"But the terms are understood, correct?"

Sandy nodded. "Nothing filmed goes on the air prior to your approval. I'll have the written agreements prepared before I return with a crew."

"Now it is I who appreciate the exception." Dolorman

leaned painfully forward. "It would help, though, if I understood what precisely the story is going to entail."

"It started out as a detailed profile of Randall Krayman, the richest man in the world. . . ."

"Many would dispute that."

"It doesn't matter. I found Krayman to be a fascinating individual, a man incredibly attuned to future trends, with the fortitude to throw vast sums into them. I felt there were a great many unanswered questions about this man whose power and influence touches so many lives. I set out to provide some of those answers in my profile."

"An ambitious pursuit indeed, since you were aware from the beginning that an interview with Mr. Krayman was out of the question."

"Actually, for a while I entertained hopes of at least arranging a telephone conversation with presubmitted questions if necessary. I thought I might be able to convince you to set it up for me."

Dolorman chuckled. "Miss Lister, you overestimate my influence with Randall Krayman."

"But you are the only man with direct access to him."

"That I have never denied. I am in constant contact with him, in fact, because he still maintains an active interest in the vast holdings he painstakingly built up by anticipating those future trends you spoke of."

"Then why did he withdraw?"

"Pressure, I suppose. Randall Krayman loved everything he did, but it reached a point where there was too much to love, too many decisions for any one man to make with the kind of attention and consideration Randall Krayman prided himself on. He just lost patience and wanted to be away from it all for a while."

"Does five years constitute a while, Mr. Dolorman?"

Dolorman's face turned contemplative. "Time is the one thing money can't buy, Miss Lister. I'm sorry if that sounds clichéd, but in Randall Krayman's case it was the truth. He had reached his forties and suddenly the things lacking in his life seemed greater than his awesome worth. There was never time for marriage or a family. Numerous mansions, resorts, estates, even private islands, but not one thing he could really consider his own.''

''When is a house not a home,'' Sandy murmured.

''Something like that, I suppose. And the problem in Randall Krayman's case is that he treated them more like hotels to pass through when it was convenient.''

''So this five-year sabbatical was taken so he could enjoy his property.''

''It's far more complicated than that. If it was possible for me to arrange the interview you seek, you'd understand. But Randall Krayman would never agree to it. He has come to loathe public attention. He prefers the status of enigma. I should think that would make profiling him quite a challenge, even for you.''

''I've had to proceed on the theory that a man is the sum of his deeds, Mr. Dolorman. And that led to a change in the story's focus.''

''Oh?''

''Someone I spoke with early in my research said you couldn't separate Randall Krayman from Krayman Industries, that they were synonymous,'' Sandy said, thinking of T.J., and with that a new flood of anger surged through her. ''Would you agree with that?''

''To a point I would have to.''

''So I changed the conceptual focus of the story from Krayman himself to his vast multinational holdings, especially those centered around COM-U-TECH.''

''Why COM-U-TECH?''

''Because it's the most current of his successful ventures. Today's television viewers don't want to hear about plastics or oil. They want to hear about computers and technology. *Telecommunications* is the great catchphrase these days, isn't it?''

Dolorman just looked at her.

''What kind of man would Randall Krayman be judged if that judgment were based on the sum of his deeds dealing with telecommunications, Mr. Dolorman?''

''If you're speaking of his holdings in cable television, his programming has opened up completely new avenues of broadcasting. It has shown that providing important public services can be accomplished while also turning a profit.''

Sandy felt her heart thumping against her chest. She couldn't back off now.

''I can't argue with that, Mr. Dolorman, but what about beyond cable television? What about commercial television stations, network affiliates?''

''Krayman Industries owns several.''

''How many?''

''I don't have the exact figures in front of me.''

''Just estimate.''

Now it was Dolorman's turn to square his jaw. ''Miss Lister, I know enough about reporters to be aware that they never ask a question they don't already have the answer to. Why don't you tell me?''

''My research has found twenty-seven individual franchises.''

''A clear violation of current laws. Obviously, the FCC disagrees with you.''

''Maybe they haven't looked as hard. I found the ownerships buried within a maze of Krayman holdings.''

Dolorman digested the information and wet his lips. ''Our unusual interests in the field of telecommunications have led to mergers and buyouts of other smaller companies with similar interests, though on a much smaller scale. When we absorbed them, it is quite possible a number of television stations strung along, but I assure you there is no pattern in what you have discovered. The action on our part was wholly inadvertent.''

''Would you be willing to say that on camera?''

''I don't see why not.''

''Because it might lead to questions concerning the Krayman Chip.''

Dolorman simply smiled, and the smile grew into a faint private laugh. ''I see the rumors have reached you. I suspected as much.''

''What rumors?'' Sandy asked, disappointed by the calm of his rejoinder.

"That we stole the chip from a man named Hollins and called it our own." Dolorman shook his head, still smiling. "Pure fabrication, I assure you."

"I suppose you can prove that," Sandy said lamely.

"We don't have to. Miss Lister, there are people who make their livings out of developing good cases for someone else's patented discovery being a ripoff of their own. They are more devious than clever. They know a long court fight would be far more costly than a modest settlement, and they are experts on gathering enough circumstantial evidence to insure that the fight will be a long one. This man Hollins was the foremost expert of them all."

"Except the case never went to court. Randall Krayman paid him sixty million dollars for what was then a worthless company, Mr. Dolorman."

"Then, yes, due almost entirely to Mr. Hollins's mismanagement and nothing else. Mr. Krayman doubled his initial investment in that company in the first two years, Miss Lister. And if you're really concerned about accuracy, it might interest you to know that the takeover bid began almost a year *before* the inception of the Krayman Chip. The whole incident was a ruse cooked up by Hollins to jack up the price of his company."

Sandy felt stymied. She could sit here and poke holes in Dolorman's answers all day long, but the fact of the matter was they were reasonable and would have stood up even on camera. His coolness under pressure surprised her. She had underestimated him and now she felt beaten. Frustrated, she felt her own strategy of patient prying beginning to waver.

"How many communications satellites does COM-U-TECH have in orbit?" she asked suddenly.

"Three, I believe."

"Three launched from Houston." And now the bluff. Sandy steeled her eyes. "And one from France."

Dolorman's eyebrows flickered. "Really? I'm afraid I have no knowledge of that."

"Do you have knowledge about one of your employees who was murdered in New York last week?"

The surprise on the man's face looked genuine. "I hadn't heard."

"His name was Benjamin Kelno, and he was a researcher at COM-U-TECH. He slipped a computer disk into my handbag before he died. The disk contained the orbital flight plan for the space shuttle *Adventurer*."

Dolorman's concern looked as genuine as his surprise. "Did you report this to the proper authorities?"

"Would you have wanted me to?"

"Miss Lister, if one of our employees is engaged in something illegal or unethical, I would report him or her myself."

"Why would COM-U-TECH need that program?"

"COM-U-TECH? I thought you said you received it from Kelno."

"I was just making an obvious connection."

"Not to me, it isn't. Krayman Industries employs almost one million people. We can't possibly be responsible for the actions of each one."

"How did you get the disk out of the network office?" Sandy demanded, frustration feeling like an acid pit in the core of her stomach.

"I don't know what you mean."

"It was stolen. You got it back."

"Miss Lister, your rudeness is—"

"Was Krayman Industries responsible for the destruction of the space shuttle?"

"*What?* No. Of course not."

"Does Krayman Industries control something in space *capable* of destroying the space shuttle?"

Dolorman's face was flushed red with anger. "Miss Lister," he began, struggling to restrain his voice, "this line of questioning has gone about as far as—"

"What did you do with T. J. Brown and Stephen Shay?"

"Who?"

"Two people I work with at the network who conveniently disappeared. Did Krayman Industries have anything to do with it?"

"I won't justify that with an an—"

"I think you should."

"Then the answer to all your questions is no. And let me spare you the trouble of posing any further ones by answering no to all of them now." Dolorman rose deliberately, the motion obviously causing him pain. "Miss Lister, I agreed to this interview in part due to your reputation for being fair, honest, and nonconfrontational. I don't know what you hope to gain from these wild accusations, but I will tell you now that no one in the employ of Krayman Industries will provide any assistance in completing this story of yours." He regarded her with a maliciously bent stare. "I would threaten you with damage to your career, but I won't because I'm sure you will do plenty of damage all by yourself before much longer. You have tarnished your own reputation this day, and the damage may well be irreparable."

"Mr. Dolorman—"

"Miss Lister," Dolorman interrupted louder, "our interview has come to a close. I am going to do you a great favor, though I can't say why. There is a button under my desk that goes direct to our security department. I am going to wait two minutes before pressing it. If you leave right now, that will give you time to exit the building without an embarrassing escort."

Sandy rose and started for the door.

"I suppose I owe you a debt of gratitude, Miss Lister," Dolorman called after her, the pain still etched on his features. "You have confirmed my reasons for never meeting with reporters."

Sandy left the office.

The elevator completed its slow descent, and the guard stepped out ahead of her, holding the doors. Sandy moved toward the exit and froze. Standing just outside the glass doors was a man in a cream-colored suit. He had been at the hotel that morning, in the lobby just before she left. She was sure of it. She hurried through the doors and hailed a cab, careful not to gaze in his direction.

The man in the cream-colored suit hailed one right after her.

Dolorman completed his report concerning the interview and switched the receiver from his right hand to his left.

"What she knows *can* hurt us, sir," he concluded to the man on the other end. "And she will find someone who'll listen, especially with the media at her disposal."

"Yes, that makes sense. But of course we can't allow it to happen. I trust you can handle things, Francis."

"I've sent for Wells."

"Good. Then I'll see you on the island tomorrow. Dress warmly. The forecast isn't promising."

"Good-bye, sir."

"Merry Christmas, Francis."

Wells had not slept in nearly two days. But his face showed more frustration than fatigue over losing McCracken in Newport. He accepted Dolorman's orders without expression. He had always liked military service because of its clarity. His work for Krayman Industries was no different.

"Wells, you must understand the risks involved here," Dolorman warned. "Sandy Lister is a celebrity. We can afford no martyrs now. It must look like an accident."

"It will."

"And the task must be completed by this evening."

The normal half of the big man's face rose into a smile.

Sandy arrived back at the Four Seasons Hotel and made straight for the elevator, not bothering to watch for the man in the cream-colored suit. So what if they were watching her? They knew she was here anyway, and later this afternoon she'd let them follow her right to the FBI.

She felt bad that Dolorman had outperformed her in the interview, but she had the tape and that was what mattered. She had managed enough direct questions, and he answered them with unhesitant lies. The tape would prove that once she got it to the FBI. They would take matters from there.

Sandy rewound the tape, pushed play, and waited as it rolled past the starting leader.

Silence followed. No sounds, not even static.

*The tape had been erased!*

Where? How?

Sandy felt her breath coming hard. Then she remembered. The guard who rode down with her in the elevator from Dolorman's office had brushed against her briefly as she stepped by him into the lobby. A sufficiently powerful magnet in his hand would have done the job nicely. Dolorman had considered everything.

There would be no trip to the FBI for her now, at least not yet. It would take hard evidence to make them move against Krayman Industries, evidence she no longer possessed. All she had were easily deniable accusations. Dolorman had proved that already.

But she wouldn't need hard evidence to take her story to the media. T. J. Brown and Stephen Shay had been eliminated, but that wouldn't silence her. There were other networks, newspapers, interview programs. People would listen to her because of who she was. At the very least, her exposure of Dolorman's plan might give the authorities the impetus they needed to learn the truth.

She felt alive again, even excited, the fear in her pushed back. She had to think, plan an exact agenda.

It took four rings of the telephone before she even noticed it.

"Yes," she said.

"Miss Lister?"

"Who is this?"

"I saw you at Krayman headquarters this morning," a male voice whispered. "I know what you're after and I've got it. The proof, I mean."

"Proof of what?"

"What Krayman's up to. The whole story."

"You've got to tell me who you are."

"It wouldn't matter. You don't know me. Kelno was a part of us."

"Us?"

"There are others. I can't talk anymore. We've got to meet."

"Wait a minute, how do I know you're not one of . . . them?"

"You don't. But it cuts both ways, doesn't it? There are risks involved, but if we don't take them, there'll be nothing left."

"What do you mean by nothing left?"

The man's voice became edged with panic. "They're watching me. I've got to get off this line. I can meet you in an hour. I'll lose them. You've got to come. Please!"

Proof, the man had said, what she needed most.

"Tell me where."

The man gave her the address. Sandy jotted it down.

The connection clicked and broke.

# CHAPTER 22

**M**cCRACKEN had anticipated leaving Newport would not be easy, and he was right. The town was part of an island with only three major routes of entry. Of course, Wells concentrated his forces on them, and his methods proved effective. Roadblocks were placed under the guise of construction work to slow traffic down for spotters. They seemed to be everywhere, at each corner and stoplight, their eyes peering in to inspect each car's occupants. If their quarry was spotted, a call would be made down the road and a reception committee would be waiting.

From the beginning, after his phone calls to useless emergency exchanges, Blaine had known that driving himself out of Newport was out of the question. Hiding in the trunk or the back of a truck was a possibility, but there was no one he trusted enough in this area to take the risk. The answer came to him with surprising ease.

He phoned for a cab, choosing a small private company. The driver turned out to be a young, bearded man. Blaine found it easy to strike a deal with him. For an agreed-on number of still drying bills, they would switch places. Blaine would drive the car with the cabbie as his backseat passenger. McCracken's only disguise would be a cap tucked low toward his eyebrows, though he expected that was all he would need. After all, even the best of spotters would not waste their time with a taxi driver. Only the passenger mattered to them, and in this case that passenger bore only the slightest resemblance to the man they sought.

Blaine followed the driver's directions exactly and ended up in the town of Bristol. His next order of business was to get somewhere where the resources he needed would be available, where he could learn what happened to Stimson. Trouble was, his lone wolf status on this mission had stripped him of backup, and his years abroad had evaporated any trusted contacts he might have had.

There was one, though, not in Washington, but in New York: Sal Belamo, who had saved his life twice already. He had Belamo's private number. Assuming Sal wasn't off on assignment, Blaine could use him to run interference and to arrange for someone to whom Blaine could take his story. Stimson's unavailability served as a warning for him not to come in on his own. People would be watching. Stimson's enemies were his as well.

Two phone calls later Blaine had determined his best route into New York City would be by train. It provided better cover than flying. A train was leaving from Providence just before noon, which gave him nearly an hour to reach the station.

Still using the cab, he got there five minutes prior to boarding and chose a seat in the no smoking section for the three-and-a-half-hour ride. The train proved more crowded than he'd expected, but the fact that there were only three stops between Providence and New York kept his most anxious moments to a minimum.

The train arrived on time, and Blaine had no trouble finding a cab outside Penn Station. He told the driver to head north. He had Belamo's number but not his address. Once he reached him, it would take the ex-boxer a few hours to obtain the information he sought. Blaine didn't fancy spending that period moving around, and a meal in a public place or even a drink in a bar were out of the question.

So when the cab swung past an apartment building with lots of lights out on East Fifty-sixth, Blaine instructed the driver to let him off. Getting past the doorman proved no trouble, and neither was finding an apartment left vacant for more than the afternoon. The slushy, snowy streets outside kept the standard issue welcome mats before each apartment constantly wet. Blaine had only to find a dry one that corresponded with darkened windows and he would have his temporary refuge.

He found one on the second floor overlooking the street. The lock was of the standard five-tumbler variety and thus easily picked in the time it would have taken to use a key. McCracken left the lights off as he dialed Sal Belamo's number.

"Yeah?" came Sal's raspy greeting.

"Do you recognize my voice?"

"If this is an obscene phone call, fuck you."

"It's not. Recognize it yet?"

"Keep talking. How 'bout a hint?"

"You saved my life twice last week."

"McCrackenballs! How they hangin'?"

"Not so good and don't use my name. I need your help."

"Why not go through Stimson, pal?"

"His phone's not working."

A pause. "You ask me, that's not good."

"I want you to check the front for me and find out what's happened. Then get a hold of General Pard Peacher or someone close to him. Find out if he's made any progress with his city inspections. I'll give you the details in a minute. Most important, I need a friendly party to bring me home."

"Take me a couple hours. Where are you?"

"I borrowed an apartment at One Forty East Fifty-sixth Street."

"I'll be outside with the limo at six P.M. on the nose. We'll talk as we ride. Nobody notices limos in New York."

"Don't bet on it."

True to his word, Sal Belamo pulled the black limousine up to the front of the apartment building at six o'clock sharp. Blaine watched him from the window and made no move to leave until Belamo stepped out and switched on the interior lights so he could see the limo was empty.

"Your car, sir," Belamo announced a minute later, holding the back door open.

"You own this tub?" McCracken asked when they were both inside.

"The Gap lets me keep it. Like I said, it makes good cover. You ask me, though, I don't look much like a chauffeur. Too pretty." He paused and looked at Blaine in the rearview mirror. "Look, excuse me for cuttin' out most of the small talk, but I wanna make this a quick ride."

"What'd you find out?"

"What do ya wanna hear first, the bad news or the bad news?"

"Let's start with Stimson."

Belamo swung onto Lexington Avenue. "Yeah, that's the bad news, all right. He's gone."

"Is he dead?"

"That's the indication, but nobody's confirming. I pulled out every stop I know of to reach him, and so did a few others. When he goes this long without answerin', pal, it's a pretty good bet he won't be answerin' again at all."

"Sounds like a cover-up."

"SOP at the Gap, pal. Our chain of command doesn't function like the three-letter boys'. We lose our top man and things get a bit interesting. You ask me, I'm glad all I do is sit and wait for phone calls. No complications that way." Another glance in the rearview mirror. "Until you called, that is."

"What about Peacher?"

"I got hold of his number-one man. We worked together a few times back in the old days. He didn't know what the hell I was talking about. Said they haven't heard from Stimson and none of those city inspections of yours have been taking place."

"Oh, Christ . . ."

"That's bad, ain't it?"

"Yeah. Peacher must be a part of all this. Maybe the

whole army is, at least at the top. It would explain a lot. What else have you got for me?"

Belamo took a left. "The best is yet to come, pal, the reason why this has gotta be a short ride. The real bad news is there's people lookin' for ya."

"Who?"

"Can't say for sure. After I finished with the Gap I called a buddy at the Company and mentioned your name. Your file's been pulled. You don't exist anymore."

"I'm supposed to be dead, remember."

"Sure, but your file wasn't pulled until this morning. Someone important wants to make the hoax real."

"Gap or Company?"

"Neither. Or both. The order was coded Blue. Don't see many of those. A joint effort you might call it and anybody with a gun's involved. Streets won't be safe tonight."

"Do they know I'm in New York?"

"Not specifically but, you ask me, it won't take them long." Belamo shook his head. "It's scary, pal, downright scary. Nobody's talking 'cause they don't know a thing. Everything's goin' down below the surface. The hired guns are being brought in. You can forget all about comin' home. I can't get you in, nobody can get you in. 'Less, of course, you don't mind arriving in pieces."

Silence filled the limo. Belamo started to speak a few times, only to stop.

"Look," he began finally, "you wanna lay low for a while, maybe I can set you up someplace. I got the right friends owe me favors. You ask me, that's your best bet."

McCracken shook his head. "Thanks anyway, Sal. Just get me to LaGuardia before the Blue Code reaches all levels."

"Where you headed?"

"Atlanta."

"What's in Atlanta, pal?"

"The headquarters of the PVR and Mohammed Sahhan."

* * *

The President leaned forward incredulously. "I think I need to hear that again, Bart," he said to CIA Director McCall.

"We have identified the caller to our box office positively as Blaine McCracken."

"How?"

"The coding and designation he gave. Each one's as individual as fingerprints, and even if they weren't, the voiceprint confirmed it was him."

"But McCracken's dead!"

"Only in Stimson's mind. It was a means to keep him active on this mission without us knowing."

"And the body at Roosevelt Hospital?"

"A John Doe. I just received a report from the team I dispatched up there this morning. Stimson filled all the holes in neatly. McCracken's still out there and the box office refused to validate his call because we deactivated his file upon termination."

"But we know he wasn't terminated. And right now he's the only man who can tell us what Andy was on to that led to his death."

"Finding him won't be easy," McCall said somberly. "He's too good, too professional. He's got no reason to trust us and he'll kill any man who gets too close. We'll just have to hope that he calls in again."

"What are the chances of that?"

"Slim. He knows he's alone and that's the way he'll plan to keep it now."

"Goddammit, Bart!" the President fumed. "I can't believe you're telling me all we can do with an entire intelligence network out there is to wait."

"And if he surfaces, hope we can move fast enough."

"To catch McCracken?" the President posed sarcastically. "Just make sure your boys have their running shoes on."

The address the caller told Sandy to meet him at was located in a rundown slum section of the steel and glass city known as the Fifth Ward, just past the University of

Houston. The population of the Fifth Ward was almost exclusively black, living in shanties and patchwork buildings, some dating back forty or more years. Scattered among them were numerous, more modern apartment buildings constructed at optimistic intervals by men who envisioned that Houston's great revitalization would stretch to here. It never did, of course, and the buildings had become tax write-offs left to their own fate.

It made no sense, Sandy thought as she gazed up at an abandoned six-story apartment building with boards nailed where most of the windows used to be. Why would the caller have chosen this place to meet?

Sandy had used a rear exit of the Four Seasons to avoid the man in the cream-colored suit or anyone else Dolorman may have had watching her. And now she started across the desolate street with her handbag clutched close, as if she expected someone at any moment to dash by and strip it from her grasp. The steps leading up to the building were still sturdy, and her high heels were grateful for that much. The door had splintered holes where locks had been ripped out. She guessed this building served now as a local youth hangout and perhaps as a temporary haven for squatters passing through the golden South.

The door creaked as she swung it open and the stench assaulted her immediately. It seemed a combination of dust, mold, sweat, and spoiled food. Inside the lobby Sandy noticed a series of steel mailboxes in the wall. They were missing their fronts, and the names of former residents were so dust-covered as to be unreadable. The stairway up lay right before her and her high heels clicked against the wood floor as she approached it.

The caller had instructed her to meet him in apartment 4C. Sandy started up the stairs and grasped for the bannister. The rotted wood wavered, the bannister's structure standing virtually free and unattached. The steps squeaked as she took them, and she hugged the wall close for support. Finally the first flight was behind her. She started up the second, a bit more confident now.

She was halfway up that one when a step gave out. Her

foot plunged right through the wood and most of her leg
followed. She groped for something to grab, but there was
nothing. Her fingernails scraped futilely at the wall, and
she had a vision of plunging all the way down into the
cellar and dying among the rats.

In the end she plunged down only up to her thigh. She
struggled to still her trembling and began to lift her leg
from the hole, careful not to tear any flesh on the ragged
splinters rimming the opening. She managed to save her
shoe, but her stocking was shredded. Sandy paused briefly
to steady herself, got her breath back, and started on again.

This time she was more careful with each step, testing
the wood before giving it all her weight. Clearly these steps
could take only the weight of the children who used the
abandoned building as a retreat. Evidence of their presence
in the form of ant-infested candy wrappers littered each
level. Nervously she reached the fourth floor, already
dreading the trip down.

There were six apartment units on each floor, and most
of the labels over the doors were long since missing. She
was looking for 4C and had to rely on impressions outlined
on the wood to tell which was which. Four C turned out
to be the last one down on the left, and the floor leading
down the corridor toward it seemed no more sturdy than
the stairs. She moved so tentatively that even the clicking
of her heels was stilled. She reached the door and knocked
lightly.

"Hello?"

No response from inside.

"Hello? It's Sandy Lister. . . ."

Still no response. Sandy knocked again.

The door swung open, and Sandy stepped into the mur-
kiness. Surprise clogged her throat. The apartment was actually furnished with several chairs and a couch. She saw
a desk, several lamps, and half-eaten boxes of Dunkin'
Donuts and Kentucky Fried Chicken strewn over the win-
dowsills. The lamps weren't on, so the only light came
courtesy of the afternoon sun. Its rays shone softly through

windows caked with dirt even a razor blade couldn't scrape off.

Sandy moved farther inside and switched on a lamp. Its light did little to change the room's dimness. But there was another room off to the right. She had started for it, when the door behind her closed softly. Sandy spun and saw three men coming toward her. A bald-headed man was one, a brawny hulk holding a huge pistol the second . . .

And Stephen Shay was the third. Stephen Shay, executive producer of the network news division and her boss at *Overview*, standing between two men with the promise of death in their eyes.

"I'm sorry, Sandy," was all he said.

# CHAPTER 23

"REALLY I am," Shay added calmly before she had found her breath again.

Sandy tried to ask a question, but there was only air. Her throat felt as if it had been stuffed with tissue paper.

"T.J.," she managed finally, and it took all the effort she could muster.

"He became a problem, I'm afraid," Shay told her matter-of-factly. "Too much of a risk that he'd contact the authorities before much longer. We couldn't have that."

"Who's we?"

"Does it matter?"

"You killed T.J., didn't you?"

Shay's silence answered her question.

"You've been a part of this all along," she charged. "A part of Krayman!"

Shay stepped farther into the apartment, the bald-headed man and the hulk staying in his shadow. He shook his head regretfully at Sandy.

"I never imagined you'd get this far," he said. "I underestimated your abilities and your persistence. Now both are going to cost you."

"You're going to kill me, too, is that it?" Sandy shot out at Shay, glad for the fury that distracted her from her terror.

Shay glanced away. His brown three-piece suit looked

246

totally out of place in the decaying building. Somehow he had made it up the stairs without gathering a single speck of dirt.

"I tried to convince them to let me reason with you," he said. "I told them I could explain the situation to you, make you join us."

Sandy knew she needed time if she was going to get out of this. "I'm listening."

Shay shook his head. "*They* didn't. Their orders were precise. You know too much, more than anyone else alive outside a small circle."

"About *what*, Stephen? That's the one thing I don't know, you see."

"It doesn't matter now."

"I think it does."

He regarded her impatiently. "You really don't know what you're dealing with here, do you? You really don't understand the scope of their influence."

"Influence that's just beginning to make itself felt. Right, Steve? It's got something to do with a few billion dollars worth of ultra-density microchips and a mechanical monster in outer space with the power to blow up space shuttles. Just tell me if I'm getting warm."

"This has gone far enough." Shay started forward. "This isn't easy for me, Sandy. Please believe that."

"Stow your bullshit somewhere else, boss." Sandy started backing up, searching for a means of escape, a weapon, anything. She had to keep Shay talking, had to buy herself as much time as he would sell.

"That's enough," Shay told her, and his two henchmen drew up even with him. The fat hulk holstered his pistol. "This has to look like an accident, Sandy. If you struggle, it will only prolong the pain."

"Does Krayman own the whole network? Or is it just you? How powerful is he, Steve? The only damn thing he doesn't own is the country, and that's what he's going after, isn't it?" Sandy had gone as far back as she could. Her shoulders rested against cracked and splintered windowpanes. Her hand grazed one and she felt a stinging prick from the daggerlike shard. "What's Krayman got in store for the good old U. S. of A., boss? What's he going to use his killer machine in the sky for?"

Shay gazed at her vacantly. He made no reply as the bald-headed man and the fat hulk advanced even closer to her.

*It has to look like an accident.*

They were going to throw her out the window! Famous reporter falls to her death while investigating story in rickety apartment building. . . .

Her fingers closed on the daggerlike shard of glass and snapped it free. She let the fear show on her features and begged the approaching pair off with her eyes.

"No, please, no." Then to Shay, "Make them stop, Steve, *please*," she pleaded, her voice strained with just enough desperation.

The bald-headed man came in first toward her left side, leaving the right for his lumbering fellow. For that instant Sandy's right hand was free, and an instant was all she needed.

She brought her glass dagger up in an ascending arc. There was no designed aim in the move. Impact anywhere would have satisfied her. She felt a thud and then the sensation of flesh giving way as the shard plunged inward. Sandy saw the thicker half protruding from the bald-headed man's throat as his eyes bulged and he began to retch. He stumbled into the hulk and Sandy darted past both. Stephen Shay moved to cut her off, but she crashed through him and bolted into the corridor.

She knew the advantage was hers. It was slim, though, and wouldn't last long if anything slowed her up. She reached the stairway and started down to the third level.

Footsteps pounded up the stairs from below. How could she have been so careless? Of course Shay would have left another man in the lobby to guard against possible intrusion. If she continued down, she would run straight into him. If she ventured back upstairs, Shay and the hulk would have her easily.

That left the third floor as her only option, and she swung down a corridor that was identical to the one on the fourth. She was sprinting now, oblivious to the precarious flooring and not caring that the loud clicking of her heels might give her away.

Voices mingled behind her, men meeting one another-and conferring desperately. Sandy started trying doors.

The first two were locked, but the third lacked a knob altogether. She hurried through it and crossed the living room floor to the window overlooking the street. This one was in far worse shape than the one she had grasped the shard from upstairs, and it resisted not at all when she hoisted it open to permit her access onto the fire escape.

She had them now. Three flights descent and she would be gone.

Sandy's heart sank as her eyes surveyed what would have been her route to the ground. A large section of steel stairs was missing between the first and second floors. Going down by this means was impossible. That left her only with up. Not bothering to consider the ramifications of her strategy further, Sandy squeezed out the window and started climbing the fire escape as quickly as her high heels would permit, cursing the shoes for restricting her.

The voices found her ears again when she passed outside the fifth story and headed toward the sixth and final one. She didn't look back, for a downward glance would only serve to slow her flight.

"No!" a voice she thought was Shay's screamed from a window beneath her. "No bullets, dammit!"

Her death still had to look like an accident. That meant she had a chance. She climbed from the fire escape onto the roof. She stumbled on the edge, fell to her face, and rose quickly to survey her next available move.

There weren't many choices. A jump to another building was her only chance, but of four possibilities, two were stories higher than this structure and one was far out of range. That left her with a building the same height as this one an alley's width away. Afraid that hesitation would

make her task impossible, Sandy kicked off her heels and
backed up to get a running start. The jump was eight feet,
possibly ten. She had to do it now.

Sandy threw herself into motion, dashing across the roof
with her eyes fixed on her target. During the instant she
was airborne, she resigned herself to not making it across
and tensed in anticipation of certain death.

Then she landed hard on the other side and tucked into
a roll at impact. Looking back over her shoulder, she saw
the fat hulk hesitate before following and heard Stephen
Shay's desperate orders as she located the rooftop door.
Her hands twisted the knob and found the door was open.
A bullet clanged against its outer frame as she slammed it
behind her. Obviously, Shay had abandoned his original
strategy of ''creating'' an accident. She had beaten him.

But there remained six flights of stairs to descend, and
Sandy took them quickly, without even bothering to consider use of another untested bannister. The first two flights
came easily.

Halfway down the third she felt her leg give out, then
realized fast it wasn't her leg at all, but an entire section
of the staircase. She grabbed on to the bannister as she
tumbled, but it gave way and she felt herself falling. She
tensed against the expected impact. It came quickly, but
Sandy found herself still in motion, toppling down the flight
of stairs she had landed on. She held tightly on to consciousness as she rolled to a stop and pushed herself tentatively to her feet. None of her wounds seemed serious,
but it was difficult to tell. She touched her fingers up to
her cheeks and they came away warm and wet, sticky with
blood from several small gashes. The areas where it came
from felt numb and swollen. She knew shock might overcome her and fought against it.

Her first step caused her right ankle to give out beneath
her. The injury might not be serious, but it was enough to
slow her down and that made it serious enough. She started
down the fourth staircase, relying on the bannister now,
though careful not to lean against it.

If Shay and the hulk had followed by way of the roof,

they would now have to negotiate past the hole left by her plunge through the staircase, and that would slow them down considerably. That thought fueled her resolve even as she heard the first sounds of footsteps from above. Sandy turned onto the third flight.

A burly monster reached out for her. One hand grasped her throat, and as the other joined it, Sandy realized she had forgotten about the man Shay had left in the lobby of the other building, a costly oversight, because now he had her.

Sandy used her nails as weapons, digging as deeply as she could into his eyes and flesh. The man screeched in pain but held tight and slammed her hard into a wall. She felt plaster crack behind her and tried to knock the man's hands aside, but he was too strong for her. Her legs would have made able weapons, except with one rendered useless it took all her strength just to keep the other from collapsing. She moved sideways across the wall, trying to keep the man's grip from shutting off her air totally. She went for his face again, but he extended her at arm's distance and she couldn't reach him.

His fingers closed tightly on her throat, his raw cheeks dripping blood. Sandy felt her breath choked off, felt the tremendous pressure in her head an instant before she began to grow numb. Her hands flailed frantically, finding nothing.

Sandy realized she was dying. Her eyes remained open, but her sight was dimming. Her ears heard only the raspy breathing of the man who was killing her.

Suddenly there was a crash and a scream from behind her. Distracted, her killer's grasp slackened. Sandy found the strength to struggle, swinging her entire body around to break free. She didn't understand what had happened, but she knew she had an opening, a chance to live, and she grabbed for it.

Sandy threw herself toward the staircase as the killer grasped for her again. When he shoved her toward the bannister, though, instead of resisting, Sandy just twisted into his motion so his force carried him by her. She pushed against him with all her strength while he was still off balance and heard his scream mix with the shattering of wood as he crashed through the railing and plunged three floors down.

She swung around and came face-to-face with the fat hulk's body impaled on some of the boards her fall had splintered. He had fallen through the same hole to his death. His limbs were twitching. Blood poured from his mouth.

That left only Stephen Shay between her and escape. She limped down to the next level. Just one more staircase to go and she was free. Suddenly she stopped.

The staircase leading to the lobby was totally rotted out. She swung as quickly as she dared and limped down the hallway, past doors splintered or missing. Her eyes and ears were alert for Shay's approach. She fought to imagine the layout of the building based on what she had seen of it. Part of the fire escape was still intact, accessible from rooms just a little farther on.

The floor gave way on her next step. She felt herself plunging downward and reached out with her hands, grabbing hold of what remained of the flooring. Her feet dangled in the black air beneath her. She looked down.

There was a wide, jagged hole below that went all the way to the cellar, a drop of almost thirty feet, with a pile of sharp, pointed wood and cement chunks waiting for her. Sandy felt panic seize her at the same time her grip on the rotting wood above began to slip. Somehow she had to find the strength to pull herself up with her throbbing fingers.

Sandy began to hoist herself upward, raising her upper body to take as much strain from her fingers as possible. It did little good. The pain was phenomenal and she had little power left in her arms and hands.

A shadow loomed above her. Sandy gazed up and saw Stephen Shay move emotionlessly to a position directly over her hands.

"Help me, Steve," she said softly, not pleading. "Help me."

His initial expression had given her hope, but it evaporated before her words were finished. Saying nothing, he brought the soles of his scuffed and dusty European loafers in line with her fingers and raised the tips. He would crush the fingers and she would plunge to her death, or to a crippled agony in which she would linger for hours before death claimed her. Resistance was futile. The end had come.

The tips of Shay's loafers had just reached her fingers when a muffled spit found Sandy's ears. Above her, Shay's face seemed to disintegrate into nothing as he rocked backward, freeing her fingers. One of her hands nonetheless lost its perch, and the second was sliding off, when a set of powerful hands locked onto her wrists and in one swift motion yanked her up through the cavern that had threatened to swallow her.

Breathless with relief, tears streaming down her cheeks to mix with the blood, Sandy found herself gazing at a man who looked somehow familiar. No, not the man, just his suit.

A cream-colored suit. It was the man who had followed her from the hotel!

He retrieved his silenced, still smoking pistol from the floor as he spoke.

"We've got to get out of here. More of them will be coming."

His words emerged with measured concern, not panic. His cream-colored suit showed barely a stain or tatter from the rotted building. His eyes swept the corridor like a lighthouse beam guiding ships through the night.

He holstered his gun. "You're hurt," he said, moving toward Sandy. "Here, lean on my shoulder. There's a fire escape that'll get us out of here just up ahead."

"Who are you?" she asked, finally finding her voice.

"Later," the man said, and he led her off.

# CHAPTER 24

**M**CCRACKEN headed the cleaning van through the Atlanta darkness toward the headquarters of the People's Voice of Revolution. Sahhan's nonprofit institution owned a modern ten-story office building located on the outskirts of the Fairlie-Poplar District in the shadow of the famed Peachtree Center. An hour before, the heavy security outside and in the building's lobby had convinced Blaine that Sahhan was inside. His problem then became how to gain access to the building.

The cleaning van had provided his answer. The real janitor was now unconscious in the back. His baggy overalls made a good enough fit on Blaine's frame.

He had been met at the airport by a man contacted by Sal Belamo. There was nothing official about the arrangement. Just an agreement between friends. The man would not provide backup, his job being only to deliver a gun to McCracken and then take him to Sahhan's headquarters.

Blaine swung the van around in a wide U-turn and brought it to a halt directly before the main entrance to the building.

"I'm new," he shouted to one of the guards. "Can you tell me where the service entrance is?"

"Around to the side that way," the guard shouted back, pointing.

"Thanks," Blaine said, and drove off again.

254

The service entrance was located just past a ramp that led into a private parking garage. Two guards stood on either side of the door. Blaine climbed out of the van and without acknowledging them moved to the rear doors and hoisted a floor polisher out. The real janitor's body lay under furniture covers.

"You got a pass, man?" one of the men asked.

Blaine fished in his pockets for the picture ID belonging to the real janitor. He had been hoping displaying it wouldn't be necessary to gain access into the building. He bore only a slim resemblance to the man he was impersonating.

The guard checked his face against the ID. "This don't look much like you, man."

"It's the beard. Didn't have it six months ago."

The guard was still looking.

"Hey, look," Blaine said suddenly, coolly, "you want me to leave, I get right in the van and head for home. Don't mean shit to me, boss. I got two guys out sick and I just as soon watch the Hawks game on TV. Up to you."

The guards exchanged glances, then shrugged.

"Keep the badge pinned on you anyway," the first one told him. "And wear this under it."

He handed Blaine a visitor's badge and Blaine immediately clipped it onto his pocket and started to back the floor polisher toward the door. One of the guards held it open. Then he was inside, the pounding in his chest starting to slow down. He wondered what might have happened if they had checked the machine before letting him enter. Would they have found the pistol he had wrapped inside the coils of the cord? No matter now. Blaine pulled it free and jammed it into one of his spacious pockets.

He dragged the floor polisher across the tile, his mind searching for a means to locate Sahhan and get in to see him. It seemed crazy, but back in New York Blaine had concluded that his best strategy now lay in convincing the black radical that he was being used, that he was merely a tool for a white billionaire. McCracken would offer his own knowledge of the plan as proof and hope Sahhan be-

lieved him. If he found Sahhan, he would have to find a
way to convince him. It was as simple as that. Tomorrow
was Christmas Eve.

Without realizing, Blaine had pushed the floor polisher
straight into the lobby, which was congested with guards.
Too late to turn around; that would draw even more attention to him. So he crossed the floor en route to the elevators.

A pair of Sahhan's guards appeared on both sides of
him. Blaine looked up briefly, then back at his polisher.
His heart was thudding against his chest again. He followed them into the elevator.

One of the men hit the button marked 10 for the top
floor. McCracken feigned pulling his hand back as if that
were his choice as well.

"Sorry, that floor will have to wait for tomorrow," an
icy voice informed him.

"I don't work Christmas Eve, boss," Blaine said.

The speaker just shook his head. "Not tonight."

Without protest, Blaine hit the 9. The tenth floor was
closed to him. He had found Sahhan. But which office?
Where on the tenth floor would he be? Each floor contained
yards and yards of corridors. There was no way he could
check the room arrangements on the tenth.

The elevator stopped on nine. Blaine backed out and
dragged his floor polisher after him. This level seemed deserted. All the doors along the corridor were closed, and
only the standard night lighting was in use. His quarry was
above him. Somewhere. Well guarded, too well guarded
to reach easily. There had to be a way.

McCracken started to unwind the polisher's cord, pretending to search for an outlet in case his actions were
being viewed on the building's closed circuit television
monitors. His mind kept working, though. He could take
the stairwell up but it, too, would be guarded and even if
he overcame the guards, there would still be too many
obstacles to surmount before he reached Sahhan. He needed
a direct route into the fanatic's office, but how?

His first thought was to make an approach from the outside by scaling the building. Its design, though, was quite modern, the side little more than a sheet of glass.

Blaine looked up at the ceiling and felt a thin smile cross his lips. If this was of the standard office building design, there would be an insulated crawlspace between each floor. The top floor, the tenth in this case, would have an attic over it containing duct work, wire conduits, and plenty of room to maneuver if he could get up there. Blaine logged the options through his mind. The stairwell was out, as was the elevator. . . .

Wait! The elevator! Certainly he couldn't use it in the traditional sense, but what if he improvised? With the polishing machine behind him, he moved to the elevator bank and pushed the down button.

The doors chimed open thirty seconds later and Blaine breathed easier at the sight of an empty compartment. He entered routinely, machine in tow. Once inside, he flipped the switch that would lock the doors open and, more important, hold the elevator in place.

McCracken's eyes focused on the trapdoor above him. There was no sense worrying about the possible discovery of the inoperative elevator on the ninth floor and the subsequent investigation. He would have to hope that with everything else on their minds, the security guards wouldn't notice until it was too late.

The trapdoor was well out of his reach, and Blaine did not want to venture into an office for a chair or something to provide a boost. Then he realized he already had just that in his faithful floor polisher. It was certainly heavy and sturdy enough to support his weight. With the base propped against the wall, it would do fine as a makeshift ladder.

Blaine had to get a yard off the floor and the polisher enabled him to do it. His hands pushed the trapdoor open and shoved it aside. Hanging tightly on to the edge of the opening, he pulled himself up into the shaft above the compartment, eyes widening to grow accustomed to the suddenly dim light. The smell of grease and oil flooded his nostrils as he climbed atop the elevator's roof and reached

out to test the cables. They were slippery but strong. His
eyes probed around him.

What he sought lay fifteen feet up, an opening in the
shaft half the size of a door. The opening would permit
him access to the attic that lay directly above the tenth
floor, thereby providing him with a direct route to Sahhan's
office from above. Blaine tested the cables one last time
and started to climb.

The going was extremely slow. The grease on the cables
coated his hands and made it hard to get a grip. Every time
he removed a hand from the cable, he had to lower it to
his white uniform and wipe it clean. Then he would pull
himself up a bit more and lower the other. He found a
twisted rhythm to the process and finally reached the doorway. It was latched but not locked. Blaine held tight with
his hands on to the cable as he thrust his legs out and forced
the door open.

He maneuvered his body through and crawled inside. In
the near darkness he made out miles and miles of wire
conduits and overlapping duct work, all in neat and orderly
patterns. The heat was stifling, adding sweat to the grease
coating his flesh, and Blaine started pulling himself along
on his stomach, skirting some obstacles and passing under
others. The tenth floor would be deserted except for Sahhan
and his guards. He needed to find a reasonable cluster of
activity, at least voices, to tell him he had found his mark.

He wanted to do his best to avoid the corridor. Guards
would be poised there, and they might be alerted by scraping noises coming from above. Stiff and cramped, the heat
cooking his flesh, McCracken crawled cautiously forward.
He stopped when he heard a voice beneath him, muffled
by the insulation, precise words indistinct. The words came
in spurts lined with pauses. Sometimes the spurts were
long, sometimes not. A phone conversation, Blaine realized. It had to be Sahhan, which meant he was directly
over the militant's office.

A few yards later, over what he judged to be the room
next to Sahhan's office, Blaine found a trapdoor which,
when opened, revealed the layers of fiber glass insulation

below. He stripped them away until the white drop ceiling panels were revealed and reached down to slide one back.

Beneath him was an empty room lit by a single lamp. He slid the panel back farther and lowered his head through to gain a better view.

It was a meeting room, dominated by a large conference table surrounded by chairs. McCracken's eyes, though, went straight to an inner door connecting this room with the one next to it: Sahhan's office. Blaine praised his luck.

He slid the ceiling panel all the way out and lowered himself softly onto the conference table below. He stepped down from it just as lightly. The carpet swallowed what little sound his stride made as he moved to the connecting door.

The knob gave enough to tell him it was open. He could hear Sahhan's voice clearly now coming from the other side.

Blaine fit the silencer onto the barrel of the automatic Belamo's contact had provided. He moved his shoulder against the door and grasped the knob tightly.

Then he burst into Sahhan's office.

# CHAPTER 25

**"P**UT it down. Slowly."

McCracken's rapid inspection of the dimly lit office showed no guards, only Sahhan seated behind his desk holding the telephone receiver tightly to his ear and wearing sunglasses as usual. Blaine stepped closer and made sure the fanatic saw his gun.

"Tell whoever you're talking to that something demands your immediate attention. Not a word different. Say one and I'll kill you now."

Shahhan obeyed the instructions exactly. Blaine could sense the fear in his eyes behind the dark lenses. The receiver clicked into its cradle.

"But you haven't come here to kill me, have you?" Sahhan asked.

"Not unless I have to."

The radical shook his head and turned his chair to better face McCracken. "No, if you had meant to kill me, you would have done so already. You're a professional. Professionals do not need to arouse their anger to motivate their kills."

"I'll take that as a compliment."

"I meant it as one." Sahhan leaned forward, his face screwed up into a tight ball. "Wait, I know you. You were at the reception a few days ago at George Washington. Mr. Goldberg, wasn't it?"

"It was Goldstein."

"And so, Mr., er, Goldstein, if you have not come here to kill me, what can I do for you? Surely you know that there are guards everywhere in this building, so you cannot possibly hope to get away with whatever it is you expect to." Sahhan moved his sunglasses lower on his nose, as if to get a better look at the man holding the gun on him. "But then, that wouldn't bother a man of your resources, would it? After all, you discovered a way in here. I'm sure you've devised a way out as well."

"You're going to escort me out yourself, Sahhan."

"Kidnapping?"

Blaine shook his head. "A decision you'll arrive at yourself after you've heard what I've come to say."

"If you plan to ask more challenging questions, I assure you that the answers will—"

"No questions this time. Just statements. I know about Christmas Eve."

Sahhan's expression didn't waver. "I suspected as much when you mentioned it at the reception. The proper people were alerted. Apparently they failed to eliminate you."

"You called Randall Krayman or one of his representatives, am I right?"

Sahhan's mouth dropped. Any words that might have been about to emerge were lost.

"Don't bother answering, Sahhan, I already know the truth. Krayman's financing your private army. He's bank-rolled this entire Christmas Eve rampage of yours and even set you up with Luther Krell to make sure your men were outfitted with the proper weapons."

Sahhan looked away. "Knowledge can be a dangerous weapon itself, sometimes a mortal one."

"So can guns. And in this case you know about only half of them." Blaine moved behind the desk until he was barely a yard from Sahhan. He could see the fanatic stiffen. "Listen closely, Sahhan, because here's where the fun begins. Krayman's been using you all along. You're part of a much greater plan. I've just come back from an island in the Caribbean called San Melas. Krayman owns it. He's

been training mercenaries there for God knows how many
months, training them to destroy your troops once they've
accomplished their purpose. I'm not talking about just your
troops either. You personally will pose too much of a threat
for him to leave around. Krayman's after some kind of
ultimate control. The PVR was important to him only because it would give him an excuse to mobilize his private
army into the nation's streets.''

Sahhan looked at him calmly. ''You have your facts
wrong, Mr. Goldstein. It is *I* who am using Krayman. This
entire affair was my idea.''

''No,'' Blaine insisted. ''Think back to your dealings
with Krayman and his people. Weren't they too neat, too
clean? How many ideas did they put into your mind, how
many words into your mouth? Where did you come up with
the logistics for this strike? This is a large-scale operation,
professional all the way. Krayman arranged consultations
for you. Advice was given, so subtly perhaps that later you
might have thought the ideas originated with you. There
are men who specialize in such areas. Believe me, I know.''

''You know nothing!'' Sahhan flared, his voice rising
slightly. ''You think I haven't considered everything you've
said? Krayman and I are working together to achieve mu-
tual goals, but when all this is over, only mine will be
achieved. There are fifteen thousand of my followers out
there waiting for Christmas Eve to come. But once they
begin to spread the justly deserved chaos throughout this
nation, hundreds of thousands more will join them. The
poor, the oppressed, the downtrodden, the frustrated—they
will rally together against their oppressors. Then whatever
else Krayman has planned won't matter because he won't
be able to accomplish it without me. The paralysis will be
total and only I will be in a position to lift it.''

''This is great,'' McCracken said in disbelief. ''He's got
a plan to double-cross you and you've got a plan to double-
cross him. Now, that's a match made in heaven if ever
I've heard one. You really want to beat Krayman? Then
call your troops in. Call off the Christmas Eve strike now.

His mercenaries will be frozen in place, unable to mobilize because there will be nothing to mobilize against.''

"Even if these mercenaries exist, they will play right into my hands," Sahhan returned, his eyes glowing. "Yes, their battles with my front-line troops will spur the rest of the oppressed into even faster action. I should have considered such a scenario myself." His stare sharpened. "Now, if you'll excuse me, my patience grows thin. . . .''

McCracken saw his finger move and lunged forward. Too late. The button beneath his desk had been pressed and the office door sprung open, a parade of guards charging through. Blaine grabbed Sahhan by the shoulder and jammed the silenced gun barrel against his temple. The guards froze, unsure, but held their own guns steady.

Then Sahhan broke the silence.

"Take him," he ordered his guards. "He won't kill me if it means he has to die himself." His eyes shifted briefly to McCracken. "I know his kind."

Blaine wanted to kill him just for that, but couldn't pull the trigger. Sahhan's guards approached slowly. McCracken turned his gun from the fanatic's head and raised his hands in the air.

A sea of huge arms were upon him, grips as sure as iron. They yanked Blaine viciously toward the door, and he didn't bother to protest, didn't bother with one last-ditch attempt to sway the radical fool who sat grinning behind his massive desk.

"Deal with him in the usual manner," Sahhan ordered his men. "But be especially careful. He may have friends watching him." He slid the sunglasses back to the bridge of his nose. "See that they don't have a chance to intervene. Now get him out of my sight."

McCracken let himself be swept into the corridor toward the elevator. Guns were poking into him. He was shoved up against the wall and his janitor's uniform searched as the compartment began to lower toward the garage level. Blaine's senses sharpened. He would try his escape once in the garage, probably when a number of the guards' hands were occupied with the doors of a car. If luck was on his side and the garage was dark enough, he might make it.

The compartment's doors slid open at the garage level. One of the blacks hung back by the elevator, while the others escorted Blaine forward through the dark underbelly of the PVR building. One of them moved beyond the pack to scout ahead. That left four—two on each side, all huge and well armed.

They reached a dark Oldsmobile sedan. Two of the men stayed with Blaine while two others went for the doors. If Blaine was going to move, this was the time.

At that instant the man on his right reeled backward, his chest spewing a fountain of red. A muffled sound like the echo of a single heel clicking against pavement found Blaine's ears as he plunged to the garage floor out of what he realized now was someone's line of fire. A second black collapsed near him, his face gone.

The remaining guards rushed around, screaming to each other, one struggling to free his walkie-talkie. A pair of long, silenced bursts came, followed by a shorter one. There was a pause, after which two more shorter bursts ensued. The last of the blacks crumpled to the floor near the elevator. Blaine heard the sound of shoes rushing in his direction and rolled closer to the body of the first guard who'd been downed. His gun was still clutched in his hand. McCracken was reaching for it just as a man dressed all in black and holding an Uzi huffed to a halt over him.

"We're on the same side!" the man screamed, but his words didn't convince Blaine as much as the fact that he let the Uzi dangle by his side.

Then McCracken saw his watch, its luminous face glowing a strange blue in the darkened corner. He recognized the glow from Newport. This was the man who had saved him there! He pulled his hand away from the dead guard's pistol.

"I've got a car waiting," the man said. "Come on!"

"Who are you?" Blaine managed as he rose to his feet.

"Everything will be explained to you in time. Right now we've got a plane to catch."

* * *

Francis Dolorman had been in his bedroom stuffing a large suitcase full of clothes when the call from Wells came.

"You're certain?" Dolorman asked after the big man had completed his report.

"Our rebels have grown desperate," Wells said, "and their desperation has led to their exposure. The evidence is irrefutable. Several are in custody and the rest are known to have gathered at the site in question."

"And our response?"

"Already in the works. Just a few more hours and we'll be ready. Dawn at the latest."

"None of them can be allowed to escape, Wells. Crush them all."

"Consider it done."

The long drive northwest toward Louisiana and Arkansas had proved an exercise in frustration for Sandy Lister. The late afternoon hours had grown into early evening, then night, and finally midnight had come and gone. She had tried questioning the man who had saved her life and was now driving without rest, but his answers were evasive when he bothered to respond at all. Finally he began ignoring her altogether. That had been at least five hours before, when they crossed into Louisiana. Sandy remembered specifically because that was when she had given up asking. She tried to sleep but came quickly awake each time. The drive with a mysterious stranger who had saved her life was too unsettling to close her eyes to.

The brush with death was bad enough, never mind that it had come at the hands of a man she trusted. But Stephen Shay had probably belonged to Krayman all along. When one of his people had stepped severely out of line, it had become Shay's responsibility to right matters. She felt little pity for his passing. No, what concerned her now was that somewhere an hour glass was emptying its sands, and when the last grain slithered down, an operation would begin that somehow involved a killer satellite in orbit around Earth.

Placed there by Randall Krayman, the man behind it all.

Since the driver in the cream-colored suit would not answer her questions, Sandy was forced to make assumptions. Obviously, he worked for some force opposing Krayman. She had felt from the start that Kelno was part of something bigger, and now she was about to learn precisely what that something was.

Sandy amused herself by mentally charting their journey toward Little Rock, a route purposely erratic so the driver could watch constantly for tails in the rearview mirror. They passed the outskirts of Little Rock just before four A.M. and continued north on Route 40 and later 65. Past Greenbier, they swung onto a desolate, unpaved road. Sandy leaned forward over the dashboard to see what must be their final destination.

It was an ancient abandoned airport, its few buildings left to the whims of the elements. . . .

No, wait. It wasn't abandoned. There were cars. And people. Specifically, men with guns watching from the shadows.

The driver drew the car to a halt apart from the others. Sandy climbed out and followed him forward. He waited for her to catch up and escorted her into a spacious lounge that was surprisingly well maintained. The man took his leave and closed the door behind him. Sandy heard something stirring and noticed a figure rising from a vinyl couch in the corner of the lounge.

"Welcome to the inner sanctum," the man said as he stretched his arms. He was dark and virile-looking, his face creased and bearded. His eyes were the darkest Sandy had ever seen.

"I'm Sandy Lister," she said.

"Blaine McCracken," the man replied. The woman looked familiar to him, but he wasn't sure from where. He had long before discarded the janitor's overalls, but the clothes he had worn beneath them still felt greasy and stiff with dried sweat. "You come here often?" he asked the woman.

"Only under escort . . . and duress."

"Yup. I know the feeling."

"Then I guess we have something in common."

"I'm beginning to think more than we realize. But, how was it put to me? 'It will all be explained soon.' "

"Sounds familiar," Sandy agreed.

The man moved closer to her. "Does the name Randall Krayman mean anything to you?" he asked suddenly.

Sandy felt her shoulders sag. "What made you—"

"Just testing." McCracken smiled, and was about to say more when a voice from the doorway caught his and Sandy's attention.

"The final exam is yet to come, unfortunately," the voice said.

And into the room stepped Simon Terrell.

# CHAPTER 26

M<small>CCRACKEN</small> could tell from the woman's face that she recognized the man who had just entered. The stranger stepped closer and extended his hand.

"The name's Simon Terrell. I won't bother introducing myself to Miss Lister, because we've met before."

Blaine took Terrell's hand. "I got your name. But *who* are you?"

Sandy answered before Terrell had a chance to. "Head of a rebel faction from deep within Krayman Industries, the common denominator in our individual pursuits."

"Miss Lister is not far off the mark," Terrell acknowledged. "We couldn't risk contacting either of you directly."

"So you waited for me to contact you," Sandy realized. "In Seminole."

"I had faith in your initiative, but I had a man prepared to aid you just in case. You bought him a beer at the bar and grill."

"Then when we met, why didn't you tell me more? The truth, for instance."

"Because your subsequent actions would have given me away. I knew then they were watching you. Seeking me out was a logical move on your part, and I had to make sure your moves continued to seem logical."

"They still tried to kill me."

"Your interview with Dolorman forced their hand. You

268

had become more than a simple aggravation for them."
Terrell paused. "But there is much more you need to know,
both of you. Between the two of you, you have almost all
the pieces of the puzzle. Perhaps we can all help each
other." Terrell's eyes focused on Sandy. "You first,
Sandy. Tell us all what you've discovered."

She had to think only briefly. "Basically that about ten
years ago Krayman Industries stole an ultra-density microchip apparently to provide them with control over the
telecommunications industry and later, somehow, the
country. They've also got something up in the sky dis-
guised as a satellite that destroyed the space shuttle *Adventurer* ten days ago."

"This feels like show-and-tell," Blaine quipped.

"Your turn, Mr. McCracken," Terrell told him.

"Krayman is financing two armies," Blaine started.
"One is a black radical group poised for a Christmas Eve
strike against major urban centers across the country. The
other is a mercenary group devoted to wiping out the rad-
icals once they've accomplished their task."

"Which is?"

"Causing disorder, chaos, 'total paralysis' as their leader
puts it."

"And could they accomplish all that?"

"By themselves, no. But they could come damn close,
kill an awful lot of people and terrify even more."

"But what would stop them from succeeding at creating
this total paralysis?"

"Channels of emergency response would be slower on
Christmas Eve, but eventually they'd call up retaliation
Sahhan and the PVR couldn't hope to contend with. The
army could mobilize a hundred thousand troops in a matter
of hours. It wouldn't be much of a fight. The country would
be aware of what was happening within an hour of its start.
People would know the situation was under control. That
would cut down the effects of the strike significantly."

Terrell was nodding now. "And if all the channels of
communication suddenly broke down . . . or were broken
down? What then, Mr. McCracken?"

Blaine felt stymied. "It's . . . hard to say."

"But unfortunately not so hard to bring about. Not any-more." Terrell paused and traded stares with each of them. As if on cue, all three sat down stiffly. "The two of you have just exchanged twin sides of a plot that aims to control America. I worked closely on it for the final two years I spent with Krayman Industries. It wasn't until four years after leaving that I realized the true scope of what I'd been involved in, so I went to the one man capable of stopping it: Randall Krayman. I made Randy realize that his dream had been perverted. He promised to put a stop to it."

"So they killed him," Blaine concluded.

Terrell nodded. "And concocted the entire ruse of his withdrawal from society. He had outlived his usefulness to them anyway, like so many others involved in Omega."

"Omega?"

"The name of the plot the two of you have uncovered. By five years ago, the time of Krayman's 'disappearance,' the wheels of Omega were already in motion." Terrell hes-itated and looked at Sandy. "You were right about why Krayman stole Hollins's discovery. He needed control of the ultra-density microchip."

"But why?" Sandy asked him.

Terrell's hand stroked his chin. "Have either of you ever heard of a computer virus?"

"Vaguely," McCracken responded. "Lab personnel can make themselves indispensable by putting bugs only they know about into programs."

"In a simplistic sense, you're not far off," Terrell con-firmed. "Let's say an employee is worried about being fired or laid off. He programs a virus into the computer that will become active only if his password is deleted from the system. Once the computer registers the deletion, the virus begins to infest every major program in the company's loop, deleting files, scrambling memory, and causing gen-eral havoc, possibly even including turning the entire sys-tem off."

"So obviously," McCracken noted, "this Omega involves Krayman Industries discovering a way of doing the same thing on a wider scale.''

"Much wider, Mr. McCracken,'' Terrell added. ''The whole country, to be exact.''

"How?'' Sandy asked.

"You've got to know more about computer viruses in general to understand the answer to that,'' Terrell told her. ''Basically, a computer virus is not unlike a biological virus. Both invade a host's body for the purpose of reproducing. Both are incredibly small at the time of initial entry: in the case of a computer virus, two hundred bytes of memory would be sufficient to get the process rolling. And both spread remarkably fast. A computer virus could infest every program in a major system in a matter of weeks by transmitting itself from program to program—from host to host. But the virus would be undetectable during this, its incubation period. Then when certain preprogrammed conditions are met, like the deletion of a password in the case of that disgruntled employee, the virus is released to attack the system with all its power, creating a kind of epidemic. By the time desperate programmers find the virus in their system, it will in effect *be* the system. The attack takes over the machine as easily as a biological virus makes its host sick.''

Terrell leaned forward. ''There are two ways to create a computer virus. Either you program it into a chip already in place . . . or you make it part of that chip even before it's installed into the computer.''

"Oh, my God,'' Sandy moaned, goosebumps prickling her flesh. ''The Krayman Chip . . .''

Terrell's eyes confirmed she was right. ''In Seminole, Sandy, I told you Krayman abandoned the direct-appeal approach for gaining control over the nation in favor of a technological one. The type of computer virus his scientists discovered provided this means. Keep in mind now that the key to any computer virus is a preprogrammed set of conditions stored inside a chip. The computer is waiting for something to happen or not to happen, depending on the individual programmer. Krayman scientists discovered a way to build a shutdown response into a memory chip. A billion microchips all waiting for the same signal which would cause them all to shut down their respective systems—that's the essence of Omega. The only thing Krayman lacked then was the chip itself and, more, total control over the production market. He needed both if Omega was going to succeed.''

"Spud Hollins," Sandy muttered.

"Exactly." Terrell nodded. "There's a saying in the computer industry that if you can't come up with your own idea, steal someone else's. Well, COM-U-TECH not only stole Hollins's chip, they marketed it at a cost so low that they effectively became the sole supplier of this particular chip.''

"Used exclusively in telecommunications?" Blaine asked.

"And its various offshoots, yes. You're starting to catch on to the scope of this plot, the utter monstrousness of it. So now we have a billion microchips in place all over the country in everything related to data transmissions, from television, to telephone, to commercial air travel. The chips are in place in all the machines, doing what they're supposed to do, all the time waiting for the signal to come instructing them to shut down their systems."

"And I suppose Krayman recruited a hundred thousand computer programmers to push the right button at the right time," Blaine said incredulously.

"Not quite. It would take only one man with one button.''

"How?"

"Why don't you tell me?"

It was Sandy who spoke, though. "COM-U-TECH's satellite that destroyed *Adventurer*. The signal to all those microchips is going to come from space.''

Terrell nodded deliberately. "It takes the satellite approximately sixteen minutes to cover the entire continental United States. During that time it will send a high frequency beam signal the chips are keyed into. When they receive it, all television and radio stations will cease broadcasting. The telephone will become useless and you can forget all about most business dealings, especially in the area of banking. Banks won't have access to their computer logs, which means customers won't have access to their money.''

"My God," muttered Blaine. "The whole country will be—''

"Paralyzed, Mr. McCracken? You were fond of using that word before. You believed that Sahhan couldn't accomplish the paralysis on his own. Probably not. But along with Omega, paralysis will be the inevitable result.''

"So the power gets knocked out—''

"Not the power," Terrell corrected him. "Telecommunications and data transmissions in general. And those transmissions, records such as bank accounts, won't be erased, they'll just be frozen, rendered inaccessible.''

"Then what?'' Blaine asked anxiously.

"Your timing is a bit off. As I understand it, the Omega phase of the operation is not scheduled to go into effect until several hours after Sahhan's troops begin their simultaneous assault on urban centers at nine P.M. eastern standard time''—Terrell watched the sun rising beyond the windows—"this evening. Christmas Eve. The communications channels will be cut off just as the true panic begins, say, by midnight, after the shooting is well under way and the country has had an opportunity to be informed of it. Even a simple call to a police department or check of the television news will be impossible. The panic will escalate, feed off itself. All systems of control will break down.''

"And then Krayman's mercenaries ride in like the cavalry to the rescue . . . unless the army beats them to it, of course. They're set up for the kind of emergency you're describing—civil defense in the event of nuclear war and all that. They've got backup communication facilities. No way to stop them from talking to one another.''

"Yes, there is," Terrell said simply. "Communication backup facilities are useless if no one plans to issue any orders over them. Omega goes much deeper than machines. There are men who've been involved in it from the start who believe the time has come for a more central and enduring leadership for the country.''

"Peacher," Blaine muttered. "Christ, it all fits. . . .''

"The military's been infested at the highest levels," Terrell continued, "levels that can effectively shut down the whole apparatus. The same holds true for your own intelligence community. It was Dolorman who isolated you and ordered your elimination. Only a few Krayman people have reached directory positions, but they are high enough to assume control while the chaos is proceeding and the various branches of the government are cut off from one another. Don't you see? Through it all, Krayman people will be the only ones who will know precisely what's going on. Everyone else will fall prey to whatever illusion is forced upon them.''

Something clicked in Blaine's mind. "The mercenaries . . . The people will think they're part of the real army, which has been paralyzed.''

Terrell nodded. "Exactly. And the mercenaries won't just obliterate Sahhan's troops, they'll also complete their work by eliminating those who stand in Dolorman's way, clearing a path for Krayman Industry plants to assume control. They'll appear to be the good guys, which will make their job all the easier. Assassination, execution—in all the confusion who's to know or judge? Without the media to turn to, the people will see only what's directly before them: the army riding in to save the day against a vast insurrection and proclaiming martial law.''

"While the real insurrection is actually taking place," Blaine concluded. Then he shook his head. "But I still don't buy the army sitting on the sidelines while all this is going on. Your point about communications breakdown is well taken, but there's still the chain of command to consider. They're poised to function in an emergency, and Krayman Industries can't possibly control all the levels.''

Terrell shrugged. "I've thought of that too. Obviously there's something we're not aware of. Dolorman's got another way to neutralize the army for as long as he needs to and we've just got to accept that no help will be coming from that quarter.''

"You're allowed to miss one thing," Blaine told him. "Dolorman's plan is brilliant. He hasn't given you much."

"That's the *second* thing I may be missing," Terrell said. "I've spent five years of my life organizing and controlling every move we've made. I've studied Dolorman. He's a tremendous businessman, ruthless and cunning, but not very creative. I can't believe this whole plan is really his."

"So you think he's fronting for someone?"

"But if not Krayman, then who?"

It was Sandy who broke the ensuing silence, changing the subject. "Why did you send Kelno to me, Simon?"

"Because our first hope was to use you to expose Omega after we learned you were planning a story on Krayman. But after Kelno was killed, you became only a distraction to draw Dolorman's attention away from us. We continued to watch you and provide help when it was needed on the chance that you might still be of use to us eventually."

"Did you know that Stephen Shay was one of them?"

"All the networks are infested with Krayman people who are poised to take control during the course of Omega. When the telecommunications system is switched back on, new men will be at the controls. In fact, that's the essence of Omega. Control telecommunications and you control the nation. People will be allowed to see only what Dolorman wants them to see. He'll be able to paint any picture he desires, stalling the ultimate return of all communications apparatus until the first line of his private sector and government forces are firmly in place."

"You can't tell me people aren't going to question," Blaine argued.

"Some will, but to what end? There'll be no way to spread their views or link up with others who feel as they do, at least not soon enough."

"And where does the destruction of the space shuttle come in?" Sandy asked.

"For its signal to be effective in reaching the billions of

infected microchips,'' Terrell replied, ''COM-U-TECH's satellite has to broadcast from approximately one hundred eighty miles above the earth's surface. Although the satellite is invisible to ground station radar thanks to a sophisticated jamming apparatus, *Adventurer*'s orbit would have brought it into visual contact. Dolorman couldn't have that. Originally, his satellite was armed to protect it from asteroids and space debris. But when *Adventurer*'s orbital flight plan showed a direct approach line, the satellite was programmed to attack. The damn thing's invulnerable.''

''What about *Pegasus*?'' Sandy reminded him. ''You said it was armed, too, and it's scheduled to go up—''

''The day after Christmas with a dry run on Christmas Day,'' Terrell said. ''It's all very hush-hush and it doesn't matter, because *Pegasus* will never get off the ground. Cape Canaveral and NASA are infested with Krayman Chips. Omega will make the launch impossible.''

''Which reminds me,'' Blaine began, ''while the whole country lies in the communication dark, what stops the Russians from blasting the hell out of us?''

''Very simply, the fact that missile defenses have received a different kind of Krayman Chip,'' Terrell explained somberly. ''Love for America was where this plot started and that same love prevented carrying out anything that would place the United States in a vulnerable position. NORAD, SAC, and all missile silos will continue to function, obviously under statuses of increased alert.''

''Dolorman seems to have thought of everything,'' Sandy said softly.

''Maybe not,'' Terrell said, and turned all his attention to McCracken. ''We learned of your involvement through a source in Krayman security when your death was originally ordered. He was one of the men on the team that captured you in Newport.''

''The one who saved my life in Atlanta . . . and at the fronton.''

''We would have preferred to have picked you up there, but circumstances, of course, made that impossible. You see, Mr. McCracken, by then we had come to the conclusion that we needed you.''

"Somehow I don't think I'm going to like this. . . ."

"I know your file, Blaine," Terrell said, a bit uncomfortable using his first name. "I know about your somewhat checkered past. I know about McCrackenballs and all that goes with it. But I also know that you're an expert in infiltration. It was your specialty in Vietnam, as I recall."

"And after."

"Good, because it's needed now. COM-U-TECH's killer satellite can be disabled only one way: by destroying the computer that controls it. This computer happens to be located on an island off the coast of Maine, also owned by Krayman, and protected by a formidable series of natural defenses."

"Don't tell me, let me guess." Blaine stroked his chin dramatically. "You want me to get onto this island and pull the plug."

Terrell nodded slowly. "I'm afraid so. The entire base of operations for Omega is centered there. But knock out the computer, and the satellite never turns the machines off, so the paralysis we've spoken of won't have a chance to take hold."

Blaine settled back. "Sounds simple enough. We get ourselves a plane, a few bombs, and knock the hell out of the island."

"It's not that simple," Terrell interrupted. "It's not enough to just take the island out. Beleive me, we've considered that plenty of times ourselves. We wouldn't need you for that. The problem is there's still Sahhan's troops to consider. The satellite's destruction will not stop them from claiming thousands of lives, many of the designated victims being crucial to governing the country. Sahhan's people are just as fanatical as he is. They've probably whipped themselves into a frenzy by now. There's no telling what they might do, how many people they might kill for no reason. Tonight."

Blaine thought quickly. "Then there must be some sort

of abort signal for the troops in the event a change in plans."

Terrell's face showed frustration for the first time. "Of course. But there's a complication."

"Connected with the island in Maine no doubt," Blaine said knowingly.

"Indeed. The abort signal is also programmed into the computer controlling the killer satellite. So destroying the island will also destroy our only chance of recalling Sahhan's troops."

"Is there any way we can duplicate the signal?"

Terrell shook his head. "Impossible. The abort signal will be a temporary activation of Omega's effect on telecommunications between seven and eight P.M. tonight eastern standard time. If the radios or televisions Sahhan's men are tuned to go dead for a five-second period during that time, they will know their Christmas Eve revolution is temporarily off."

"So let me get this straight," said Blaine, putting things together for himself as he spoke. "I have to get into this island headquarters, make sure the computer broadcasts the abort signal, and then destroy it. No problem. Piece of cake."

"There's more," Terrell added tentatively. "We'll need a printout of all Krayman Industries' agents in place so we can give them to the proper authorities once Omega is exposed."

"Just put it on my bill. . . ."

"You'll have help, Blaine—every man here today, including myself."

"You're not a soldier, Terrell, and it's gonna take some awfully good ones to pull this thing off."

"Some of the others are soldiers. And damn good ones too."

Blaine nodded. "Tell me about this island."

"It's called Horse Neck because of its irregular shape. The coastline is jagged, a natural defense that makes night approach virtually suicidal."

"And we'll be going in at night, right?"

"There's no other way, believe me." Terrell began probing through his pockets. "Let me show you a map. . . ."

Something caught Blaine's ear, a familiar sound that set his heat beating faster. Overhead a mechanical whine grew gradually into a roar.

"Jesus Christ," he muttered.

"What's wrong? What is it?" Sandy asked.

McCracken swung toward Terrell. "We've got to get out of here! Come on, hurry!"

Terrell rose but didn't move. "What are—"

"Planes, Terrell, coming in fast and probably ready to blow us to fuckin' hell. They're—"

The rest of Blaine's words were drowned out. Fucking jet fighters!

He was trying to scream a warning when the first blast shook the building. Splinters of window glass exploded inward, becoming deadly projectiles. Instinctively, Blaine dove on top of Sandy, because she was closest to him and took her to the floor.

The glass sheared Terrell's body like a hundred knives, mostly above the waist. His head was held in place only by a few sinews of stray skin. His body shook and writhed horribly.

More blasts came, every second it seemed, and the screams of dying men were all that could be heard through the blasts and the jets' roar. More rubble showered down as Blaine left Sandy pinned to the floor and crawled over to Terrell's corpse. He grasped a large piece of paper folded into quarters from the dead man's pocket. The upper portion was bloodied, but the paper, Terrell's map of Horse Neck Island, was still whole.

Away from him Sandy was starting to rise, gasping, fighting for a scream. Blaine lunged and tackled her. He brought her back down hard and covered her mouth with his hand to block out her sobs. More bits of the ceiling covered them, the entire structure collapsing a section at a time.

"Listen to me," Blaine said into her ear. "Keep quiet

and keep down. It's our only chance to get out of this. Do
you understand me?''

Sandy made no motion to indicate that she did. Instead,
she kept squirming.

''Listen!'' he commanded, and tightened his grip on her.
''If they land at all, it won't be for long. The won't check
all the buildings. They won't be sure how many people
were supposed to be here, so we've got a chance. If you
want to live, don't make a sound or a move. Keep struggling and I'll kill you myself!''

Sandy stopped squirming. She looked into McCracken's
eyes and saw he was as scared as she was, while more of
the ceiling crumbled above them.


En route to the airport the limousine made its last stop—
Francis Dolorman's home. It was seven A.M. sharp on
Christmas Eve morning. The chauffeur gathered his bags
and stowed them in the trunk while Dolorman climbed gingerly into the back. Verasco and Wells were already inside.

''Their base was located in central Arkansas,'' Wells
reported. ''It's been leveled.''

''Splendid,'' Dolorman said, suppressing a grimace of
pain. ''And what of the man in Sahhan's office who bore
an uncanny resemblance to Blaine McCracken?''

Wells knew the remark was meant as an insult, but he
shrugged it off. ''We've got good reason to believe he was
at the base in Arkansas.''

''So have we finally eliminated him this time?''

''With McCracken there are no guarantees. But even if
he did manage to survive, there is nothing he can do that
can possibly hurt us now. Without the rest of the rebels,
he is alone.''

''He has been alone from the beginning, Wells.''

''Now, though, he is up against our island fortress, assuming he's even aware of it. An army couldn't penetrate
its walls.''

Dolorman's eyes dug into Wells's single good one.
''Your men checked this base in Arkansas thoroughly?''

''Enough to find no survivors.''

Dolorman turned to Verasco. "And everything is arranged at the airport?"

"I've bumped the schedule up a bit," Verasco reported. "It seems Maine is going to be blessed with a white Christmas. There's a blizzard in the forecast."

The figure sat in the grove as the wind whipped snow from the sagging branches above him. He dropped a huge hand into a pouch worn on his belt and came out with a fistful of feed. He waited. Barely a minute later the first of the winter birds dropped down, followed swiftly by a pair of others. As always, they moved toward him tentatively, at last settling just close enough to peck the feed from his outstretched palm.

Birds had always been able to tell him much. On the day he had stepped into his greatest personal horror of the hellfire, they had shown him the fruitless agony of death without reason, of women and children staggering with their insides sliding through hands cupped at their midsections and of men continuing to fire just for pleasure. He had not rested until those responsible were found. The birds would not have forgiven him otherwise, nor the souls of the tortured dead he had happened upon first. Discovering them made the souls his responsibility and the balance would be forever off if he failed them.

Today, though, the birds told him nothing. What was coming was beyond them, beyond all perhaps, its shape great enough to envelop everything at once so that even the birds wouldn't feel the change. But nothing was ever shown to him without reason. He understood now that it would be left to another to lead him to the source of the shape. The past and present were swirling together, intermixing until the lines of distinction he had come here to forge became lost. He smiled, certain now who the other would be.

The birds emptied his hand without breaking flesh and the figure reached into his pouch for a fresh batch.

# PART FIVE

# Horse Neck
# Island

**Christmas Eve and Christmas**

# CHAPTER 27

"**Y**OU'RE fuckin' nuts, pal!" the pilot screamed again. "You know that?"

"I've been accused of it before," McCracken told him. "I want one more look at that island, a closer one."

"The winds over that water will rip us apart. No way. Not for all the money you can whip out of that pocket of yours."

"Just make one more run up the shoreline. For an extra hundred."

The pilot hesitated only briefly. "This is the last one." And the small plane banked again.

Blaine sat in the copilot's seat. Sandy huddled in a third chair with her arms wrapped tightly over herself. The temperature was barely out of single digits and the storm had started to intensify savagely when they neared the coast. The snow was piling up in huge drifts. The water stood out dark against the whiteness.

"Satisfied?" the pilot asked.

Blaine looked away from Horse Neck Island and nodded. "There's a small airfield about twenty-five miles north of here near a town called Stickney Corner. I want you to put down there."

"No fuckin' way, pal! This has gone far enough. I'm bringing this junk heap down at home in Portsmouth and putting her to bed. And I don't care what you say or—"

McCracken didn't say a word, didn't even bother tempting the pilot with more money. He just froze him with a stare colder than the air outside the windshield.

"You'll have to direct me," the pilot relented.

"No problem."

The plane headed north.

Blaine had pulled Sandy from the rubble of Terrell's Arkansas headquarters a little before six that morning. Over two hours of walking and hitchhiking had brought them to Little Rock Airport, where they were able to book a non-stop to Boston. Blaine used his government issued credit card to get plenty of cash from an automatic dispenser in Logan Airport. It was typical, he reflected, that the CIA should wipe his existence off the books but forget to cancel his credit card. With some of the cash he bought winter coats and a change of clothes for himself and Sandy in airport shops, where he also learned that the entire New England coast had been put under a winter storm watch.

It was all rain when they left Boston, a drenching winter downpour. Blaine rented a car and started northward with a still-shaken Sandy in the passenger seat. By northern Massachusetts the rain had frozen to sleet, and before they reached the New Hampshire border, snow had taken over. There were already two inches on the ground, with the intensity increasing by the minute. Road crews struggled to keep up with the mess, but it was rapidly becoming too much for them. Blaine was forced to cut his speed back to forty-five, then forty, hands twitching nervously on the wheel. At this rate they might never reach the Muscongus Bay area in time to pull off what he was planning.

He had spent the flight east going over the bloodied map lifted from Terrell's pocket. Horse Neck Island was located in the bay due east of Port Clyde. It was a small island close to an isolated peninsula that jutted out into the water. The island's shape was indeed erratic and its coastline looked to be a dangerous mix of crags and crosscurrents. Even during daylight and in the best of weather, approach would be difficult. And Blaine would be going in at night into the teeth of a killer blizzard.

In the sketch the island was dominated by the fortress Terrell had spoken of. It was a spacious mansion built with its back to a steep, low mountain and its other three sides enclosed by a high stucco wall. A courtyard lay between the wall and the mansion, lots of ground to cover in an open assault. In this weather, and given the limitations of time, approach over the mountain was not feasible. That left getting into the complex over the wall. There would be lots of guards beyond the wall, on it, and within the courtyard itself. If even one of them saw him or suspected something and contacted the people inside the mansion, Blaine's plan would be destroyed. Luckily, though, the weather would keep patrol boats from the shoreline and that should assure him a free approach.

If he made it safely past the rocks.

If he found a boat to begin with.

Blaine and Sandy had arrived at the private airstrip in Portsmouth, New Hampshire, to find their pilot closing up shop. An absurd sum of money waved in his face led to his acceptance of the risk involved in making a run up the Maine coastline, specifically to an area twenty miles northeast of Boothbay Harbor. The pilot started complaining as soon as they were airborne, and Blaine was forced to raise his fee at regular intervals just to keep him quiet.

Now he would drop them at a small airfield near Stickney Corner, because getting there was the key element of Blaine's plan. He could not possibly hope to take Horse Neck Island alone. He needed help.

There was help available in the woods around Stickney Corner.

Blaine had exchanged few words with Sandy Lister through the duration of the trip. She seemed tense around him, uneasy, not very trusting in spite of the fact that he had saved her life.

"I've got to ask you something," she had said during the drive north.

"Go ahead."

"Back in Arkansas you said that if I didn't keep still, you'd kill me. Did you mean it?"

Blaine didn't hesitate. "Absolutely not. But I had to get you quiet. It worked, didn't it?" he added with a wink.

"You've killed before, though. I can tell that much."

"It's my job, lady. And mostly I do it better and cleaner than anyone else."

"Cleaner?"

"No one innocent gets caught in the middle. I can't stomach that. Unlike some of my colleagues, I don't regard dead bystanders as acceptable losses."

"My God, what kind of world do you live in?"

"The same one you do, lady, only I see it more for what it really is. You've seen enough these past few days to understand what I mean. They tried to kill you, didn't they? And you killed to save your own life. It didn't feel good, but you did it and I'd bet you didn't feel any guilt afterward."

"The difference is, you enjoy it."

"You really think that?" Blaine asked in disbelief. "Let me tell you, lady, I do what I believe I have to because believing is all I've got. There are things greater than you, or me, or all the people I've killed."

"Like the country, for instance, right?"

"As a matter of fact, yes. Sounds trite, doesn't it? Well, maybe it is. The United States has a lot more enemies out there than she's got friends. Somebody's got to do something about the balance."

A few long minutes passed before Sandy spoke again.

"You said we were meeting someone in Maine. Who is it?"

"Wareagle."

"Not *where*, who?"

"Wareagle is a who, Johnny Wareagle. A bad-ass Indian who makes me look like a Sunday school preacher. We worked together in 'Nam for a while. Johnny did four tours, got himself decorated three times, and won two Purple Hearts. Came back home and life just fucked him sideways. When it got too bad, he pulled out altogether and went to live in the woods. Took a few of his Indian soldier friends with him. They live off the land. No power, no telephone. A kind of reservation for battered Vietnam vets.''

''And you think they'll help us?''

''They might, if they don't kill us first. Johnny and his boys aren't too fond of outsiders. I was up here last about eight years ago. Wareagle barely recognized me. He was too busy quoting his Indian philosophy to remember old times. But he's almost seven feet tall and, between you and me, he's the only man I ever met who scares me shit-less. The guys with him aren't much different. If anyone can get us onto Horse Neck Island and into that fortress, it's them.''

''That's the airfield down there,'' Blaine said, directing the pilot with a thrust of his finger.

''It's not even plowed, goddammit!'' the pilot protested. ''You're crazy if you think I'm settin' this junk heap down on that.''

''We've already established the fact that I'm crazy, so don't push it. Do as I say or your tip will be a bullet in the head.''

The pilot gulped hard and swung into his descent. ''I might not be able to make it back up again,'' he persisted.

''Then we'll cover your plane and wait till spring, when the thaw comes. Understand?''

''Asshole,'' the pilot muttered under his breath.

The landing came with surprising softness, the plane cushioned by the thickening blanket of snow. The only uneasy time was when application of the brakes caused a skid. The pilot fought with the wheel and managed to keep the plane from pitching off the narrow airstrip into the woods. Blaine checked his watch. It was just after four o'clock; five hours until Sahhan's troops would begin their assault and less than four to send out the abort signal.

The pilot kept the engine running as Blaine helped Sandy down from the cabin.

''Next time you're in Portsmouth, don't look me up,'' he called out.

Blaine flipped him an extra pair of hundred-dollar bills.

"Buy yourself a new personality." Then he led Sandy off the snow-covered field into the woods.

"I hope you know where you're going," she sighed a few hundred yards of heavy walking later.

"It's been a while," Blaine told her, "but things in these parts don't change much."

"What about people? Johnny Wareagle could have moved on for greener pastures."

"He was determined to be buried in these woods last time I saw him. The Indian spirits foresaw it, and he didn't want to insult their vision. Be a while before it happens, though. This bastard is indestructible. Even the spirits are probably scared of him."

Another hundred yards passed and the woods thinned out a bit. Trees were missing, cut to their stumps, the work obviously done by man. Sandy caught the bubbling sound of a fast brook and was searching for it when McCracken grasped her arm to restrain her. She looked up at him and saw a finger pressed over his lips to indicate quiet. His eyes glanced up and to the right, and Sandy looked in the same direction.

Creeping slowly up the trail toward a small wooded clearing was the biggest man she'd ever seen. Wareagle's bulging, bronzed arms were exposed through an animalskin vest, and his long black hair was tied off at the forehead by a colorfully designed bandanna. Sandy noticed his hair was worn in a traditional Indian ponytail. He approached the clearing and suddenly Sandy saw his target.

A deer, a young buck with a season's growth of antlers, was picking over the ground for food, it haunches hollowed by the thin winter supply.

Wareagle crept closer. The buck raised its head and sniffed the air, as if aware of a presence it couldn't quite grasp and didn't feel threatened by.

Wareagle held his ground until the buck returned to the thin patch of frozen grass it had found. Then he started moving again, so slowly and steadily that his progress was virtually undetectable within the falling snow.

Sandy had to fight down the scream of warning that rose

in her throat as the huge Indian drew to within arm's distance. Her heart was thudding hard, the sight in the clearing held her mesmerized.

Wareagle's hand came up suddenly. Sandy saw it was covered with a leather half-glove which left the fingers exposed. It looked like a club as it came down suddenly, hand slapping on the buck's hindquarters and startling him into a mad dash forward from the clearing, legs into the snow up to his knee joints.

"It's called thumping," Blaine explained softly.

"Huh?" Sandy managed, lifted from her trance.

"An ancient Indian ritual meant to symbolize the unity of strength and stealth. Boys do it to challenge manhood and men do it to challenge themselves. Johnny tried to teach it to me once without much success. I guess it must be in the blood."

Wareagle had knelt down in the very spot where the buck had been standing, as if to absorb whatever aura the majestic beast had left behind. His huge back was to them, but Sandy could tell that his hands were perched nimbly on his knees and he seemed to be meditating as flakes of snow collected on his hair.

Blaine held a hand up to indicate Sandy should stay where she was, and then he approached the small clearing. He stopped two yards from Wareagle, respecting the giant Indian's privacy.

"Hello, Blainey," Johnny said without turning.

"How'd you know it was me, Indian?"

"I felt you approaching from the woods. Your aura is distinct," Johnny explained, still turned away, hands remaining poised on his knees. "And the spirits have warned me of your coming. They've carried your name on the wind."

"It's been a long time, Indian. Many moons, as you guys say."

"And should have been many more." Wareagle turned his upper body and faced him. "You bring blood in your shadow, Blainey. Your spirit disrupts the peace of the woods."

"I need your help, Johnny."

"You must learn to quell your violence, Blainey. The strongest bow does not have to fire an arrow to prove its strength."

"You didn't talk that way when you were saving me from a Cong ambush."

"Karma, Blainey. A month before that you carried me through a mine field."

"All three hundred goddamn pounds of you. I think the mines shrank away in fear."

Wareagle smiled and rose to his feet. He stepped forward and grasped McCracken at the shoulders.

"It darkens my spirit to remember those times, Blainey, but I do seek not to forget them. We were many things back then, but mostly we were alive. Survival gave us purpose. Life was simple, so free of the complications that soil the spirit." He backed off, his expression stiffening again. "I came here to escape those complications, Blainey. You are nothing but a reflection, a trick of the falling snow."

"How many men have you got with you, Johnny?"

"Six souls in search of peace."

"Are they good?"

"They are good at breathing, drinking the fresh water that runs clean through these hills, and smelling the air."

" 'Nam?"

Wareagle nodded. "The spirits from those days still haunt their sleep."

"Mine too."

"Why the questions, Blainey?"

"Because there's another war on right now, Indian. The front's about thirty miles from here, and it's up to us to fight. Again."

Wareagle nodded again, not seeming surprised. Fresh snowflakes danced around his face. "The spirits warned me of this, even before they warned me of your coming. They spoke of an evil that knows no rival set loose in the world and about to make its mark."

"That's as good a way of describing the opposition as any. . . ."

"They spoke of men who thirst for the blood of power, men who wish to drink it until their bellies burst and then drink some more. Their evil has reached even these woods. I can feel it falling with the snow, scorching the ground."

McCracken moved closer and brushed the snow from his brow. "The people I'm after—Wells is one of them. He's on Horse Neck Island."

The Indian was quiet for a long time and his eyes bore through Blaine's, as if seeing not Blaine but the massacre at Bin Su and the man who directed it. When Blaine finally broke the silence, his words were barely a whisper. "Will you help me, Johnny?"

Wareagle's eyes glanced far away. "My spirit died over there in the hellfire, Blainey. I came here to the woods to forge a new one. I was crippled inside, hurting, and the spirits said this was the place to seek healing. So I came. And the healing commenced. Spiritless, without existence, I began the forging process. I reshaped my soul. I kept forging and forging, a new man each day emerging, not better, but different. Then one day not far from this, the stream waters ran still and the spirits let me glimpse the new aura I had forged." Wareagle paused, face challenging the wind. "It held the same shape as the old, Blainey. The spirits had taught me a valuable lesson: a man cannot change what a man is. One's manitou is one's manitou. Refined perhaps, but never altered, refined through the many tests the spirits place in our path."

"This mission is the ultimate test."

"*Life* is the ultimate test. 'Nam, Laos, Cambodia—just minor progressions along the way."

"And now Maine, Indian."

# CHAPTER 28

"WHO is the woman, Blainey?" Wareagle asked as they started toward Sandy, who stood restlessly beneath a tree that partially shielded her from the snow.

"Someone who's been involved in this for as long as I have."

Wareagle nodded understandingly. "Her spirit is disjointed, split apart by fear. She treads in new waters and does not fully control her strokes in even the calmest currents. Be patient with her."

McCracken started a shrug which gave way to a smile. "I gotta tell ya, Indian, once in a while you really scare me. These words the spirits whisper to you are pretty close to the truth. Someday I'd like to learn how to hear those words. I'd be better at it than I was at thumping. Promise."

Wareagle stared somberly at McCracken and stopped suddenly. "To hear, Blainey, first you have to listen. And then your manitou must act as a sponge and absorb all the meaning of the words. But your manitou is unyielding. It permits no challenge to the narrow scope it accepts." The Indian looked far into the distance, beyond the white-frosted branches that crisscrossed the air. "That is how you have been able to stay out there for so long. I envy you for it in a way, for it allows you to endure life without questions. You accept, Blainey, and that is a greater gift than you can possibly know."

They started walking again.

"Wells," Wareagle said, as if the name tasted like dirt on his tongue. "His manitou was black and soiled. He had lost that which provides balance."

"Well, since then he's lost half his face too. He'll be in charge of the enemy forces and, balanced or not, he's a hell of a soldier. That doesn't help our odds."

"Odds mean nothing to the spirits, Blainey."

When they reached Sandy, rapid greetings were exchanged. The giant Indian obviously made her even more uneasy, and Wareagle had been out of civilization too long to feel comfortable around strangers. They walked north about two hundred yards and Sandy caught the smell of a campfire. The Indian led the way into a clearing lined with seven small cabins.

In the center of the clearing another Indian stood tending a fire, spreading the kindling with a stick as he prepared to stack on larger pieces. Something seemed wrong about him, and as they drew closer to the small canopy under which he was sheltered, Sandy saw what it was.

The Indian was missing a hand.

He looked up, noticed Wareagle and the approaching strangers, and stiffened. Johnny moved on ahead and spoke briefly. The smaller Indian nodded and sped off.

"Running Deer will fetch the others," Wareagle told McCracken. "They are spread through the woods. It will take time."

Blaine frowned. "If they're all missing pieces of themselves, Johnny, you might as well tell him not to bother."

"We are all missing pieces of ourselves," Wareagle said calmly. "Inside or out. Losses cripple us only if we let them. In the case of Running Deer, his remaining hand is quite good at throwing tomahawks. The spirits have compensated him well."

"They'll have to do more for us in the weapons department if we're going to succeed," Blaine said.

"Here, as in olden times, Blainey, each man is a master with his chosen tool of death. The ancient weapons are just as effective as the modern ones we left behind us in the hellfire.''

''We're going up against an army, Indian.''

''Then stealth and silent kills are needed more. Besides,'' Wareagle added with a faint smile, ''not all of the modern weapons were abandoned.''

He led Blaine into one of the cabins, Sandy following to get out of the cold as much as for curiosity. Once inside, Wareagle slid an army foot locker from beneath a single cot and threw it open. McCracken's eyes gleamed at the contents.

''Not bad, Johnny,'' he said, gazing down on a pair of M-16s, one equipped with a grenade launcher attached to its underside. There were several sidearms as well, along with plenty of ammunition and some thermolite explosive charges; demolitions had been one of Wareagle's specialties in 'Nam. ''Think you still remember how to use all this stuff?''

''Knowledge is like the sun, Blainey: it sets only to rise once more. While the guns might help us, though, I must warn you that most of my men will want nothing to do with them. The spirits have been stricter with them than they have with me.''

''We can't let them go into this empty-handed, Indian.''

''We won't. Each embodies the spirit of his weapon. Their prowess will surprise you.''

''Just so long as it keeps us alive. . . .''

''You must share the details with me now, Blainey.''

McCracken pulled Terrell's map from his pocket and spread it out on the Indian's bed. ''This is Horse Neck Island in Muscongus Bay. The island's our target, and we've got to reach it no later than seven-thirty tonight.''

Wareagle glanced out the window and inspected the little remaining light. ''Just two and a half hours away. A difficult task even if the spirits are with us.''

''You know the area in question?''

Wareagle nodded. ''The shorelines of all the islands in these parts are treacherous. But before we can reach that obstacle, there remains a difficult drive ahead of us and an impossible journey across the waters.''

"Impossible?''

"The storm will have forced all worthy boatmen off the docks; their crafts will be worthless to us.''

"Not if we can steal one.''

"Only a seaman familiar with those waters would stand a chance of eluding the rocks in such weather. A boat by itself is useless.''

"Your spirits taking Christmas Eve off, Indian?''

"They advise, Blainey. They do not work miracles.''

"Then let me tell you something. It might take a miracle for us to pull this off. And there's plenty more at stake than just our lives; it's the whole goddamn country we fought for in that godforsaken pit and the enemy on Horse Neck Island is worse than any we faced over there.''

Wareagle was nodding, expressionless as always. The snow on his hair had melted to shiny wetness.

"We will get to the docks, Blainey,'' he said, "and the spirits will find us a way across the water. They would not have guided you here to me if that wasn't their plan.''

"So all we need now is one of our own.''

Wareagle began pointing to spots on Terrell's scale drawing where guards were sure to be posted.

"The problem, Blainey, is that we must approach in a boat. Even the spirits will not be able to hide that from the island lookouts.''

A howling wind whipped through the trees. Blaine's eyes strayed out the window. "But the blizzard will.''

"Only from a distance. Once we cross the rocks and approach this single dock here, the flakes will no longer shield us.''

"Then we'll have to think of something.''

A knock came on Wareagle's cabin door. The big Indian opened it to find Running Deer standing outside, slightly out of breath. Quiet words were exchanged. Wareagle turned to Blaine and then briefly to Sandy.

"My men are waiting for us outside. I think you should meet them.''

There were six of them including Running Deer. They stood in a single row, the light of the fire dancing off their faces.

"They know what's happening, don't they?" Blaine asked Wareagle in a whisper as they approached the men.

Johnny nodded. "The spirits have much to say in these parts, Blainey, for all who listen."

Sandy stopped halfway between the men and Wareagle's cabin. Something about the group chilled her. Their faces were fearfully stark and barren, eyes darker than the night and shining like a cat's. Their potential for violence was held in those eyes, a violence they had come here to escape but that once again had sought them out. Only one of them besides Running Deer was physically handicapped. Instead of a hand he was missing a leg and wore a wooden replacement.

"We're moving out," was all Wareagle told them. "Ten minutes. Prepare your weapons."

The six Indians moved away quickly but not in a rush. The one with the wooden leg hobbled to keep up.

"I think we can leave Tiny Tim behind," Blaine suggested.

"Nightbird was a sharpshooter in the hellfire, Blainey. He will be of great help to us."

"There's only two rifles, Indian, one for you and one for me."

They were walking back toward his cabin. Wareagle shook his head. "For you and Nightbird, Blainey. The bow is much more to my liking these days."

When they were inside again, Blaine finally looked at Sandy.

"You'll stay here."

"Not on your life!" she replied sharply. "I don't even know where the hell I am. If you guys don't make it back, I'll be stuck here for the winter."

"Then we'll drop you off along the way."

Sandy glared at him with both shock and anger. "Maybe you've forgotten that they tried to kill me too. You really think I'd be any safer making my way through Maine alone than I would going to the island with you? Let's face it, if you screw up, I'm as good as dead anyway.''

McCracken looked at Wareagle, who nodded. "Can you fire a gun?" Blaine asked Sandy.

"I can learn."

McCracken gave her a .45, which she stuck uncomfortably in her belt and also made her responsible for toting two green canvas knapsacks full of extra ammo. The big Indian carried the most potent explosives. Blaine slung the M-16 with the grenade launcher over his shoulder and issued the standard version to the sharpshooter Nightbird. Running Deer boasted an assortment of handmade tomahawks suspended from his belt. Of the other men, one carried a crossbow, another an assortment of throwing knives; a third preferred a long ball and chain, while the fourth opted for a bow and arrow just as Wareagle had.

Ten minutes after the men had separated, two four-wheel-drive, enclosed jeeps pulled up to a halt. The snow was thick on them everywhere but their front windshields and rear windows. The wipers did their best to keep up with the snow still pouring down.

"The spirits cosign the financing for these babies, Johnny?" Blaine asked.

As always, Wareagle ignored his attempt at humor. "Withdrawal from society does not mean an abandonment of reality, Blainey. Emergencies come up. Supplies are needed. Besides, it was not machines that were responsible for the struggles within our souls.''

Sandy and Blaine rode in one jeep with Wareagle and a driver, while the other five Indians crowded into the second. They headed down a snow-covered road that seemed to have been cleared by nothing more elaborate than machetes. Collapsing branches scraped at them as they passed; with the snow intensifying, the visibility was reduced to near zero. Standing still in the woods, they had not realized how savage the storm had become. Johnny guessed ten inches had fallen already with another one likely before they reached the dock on Horse Neck Island.

It was an agonizing ten minutes before they turned east onto Route 17. The driving, even for the four-wheel-drive jeeps, was treacherous. Occasionally a drift appeared nearly as high as the jeeps themselves, and only the nimble reflexes of the drivers saved the vehicles from becoming hopelessly stuck.

They saw not a single other car or snow plow on the road, and the closer they drew to what should have been civilization, the worse the road became. The jeeps' lights were useless. Sandy had no idea how their driver could possibly anticipate the corners and obstacles, but somehow he did. The journey was maddening, and she could not stop her heart from lunging toward her mouth around each blind curve. The snow lashed against the windshield, sometimes coating it with a thick blanket which temporarily stopped the wipers. They struggled hard, managing to win, but each instance seemed to take more out of them as the snow grew still thicker.

*"I'm dreaming of a white Christmas,"* Blaine sang in his best Bing Crosby impersonation when they had turned onto Route 1. *"Just like the ones I used to know. . . ."*

Sandy wanted to tell him to shut up, then smiled in spite of herself and noticed that even Wareagle had cracked a slight grin. Of all McCracken's features, it was his sense of humor that confused her the most. It seemed so out of place in the world of violence and death he had been immersed in for so long. Then something occurred to her: perhaps that was how he had survived and kept his sanity at the same time. She recalled the horror she had experienced in Houston of having to become a killer to avoid being killed. It still lingered, and she knew it would haunt her sleep for as long as she lived. Blaine McCracken had lived with such experiences for most of his life. He was cynical and sarcastic, and maybe that kept him going. His sense of humor, she supposed, was a kind of weapon to be used like any other.

Route 1 was no better than 17. Plows had obviously been over the road once earlier in the storm and had produced a thin coat of ice beneath the snow piling up again.

The jeeps lunged drunkenly down the road, brakes now as useless as lights. If there were road signs, the snow had long since obscured them. The Indian driver had studied the map to Muscongus Bay and Horse Neck Island only once that Sandy could remember. He took his eyes off the snow-blown road only to check the rearview mirror to make sure the second jeep was still in his tracks.

The jeep slowed finally and Sandy thought she saw water to their right, distinguishable by its dark surface. They had turned off Route 1 some minutes before and seemed to be passing through a small village. Her eyes found few lights and these were dim, behind drawn blinds, as though the village's residents were hiding from the raging storm outside.

The jeep continued through the town, and Sandy could hear the sounds of waves thrusting violently on a nearby shore. Another few hundred yards later Wareagle signaled the jeep's driver to stop.

"It's almost seven o'clock," McCracken announced. "There's not much time left."

"The spirits guiding us do not go by minutes, Blainey. Their view is eternal. The time they provide us with will be enough."

Blaine just shrugged and climbed out, bearing his personal arsenal. Sandy followed and stood to his rear as Wareagle and the other Indians approached. In the distance across the bay she could make out the dark shape of Horse Neck Island. It lay like a great serpent writhing on the water—an illusion provided by the blowing snow.

"Over there." Wareagle motioned.

Blaine followed the line of Johnny's finger to a small, rickety pier extending from the farthest jagged edge of the shoreline. From this distance all was pale except for a trace of darker motion bobbing in rhythm with the wind.

It was a boat, a fishing boat.

"Looks like those spirits of yours are taking care of us after all, Indian," Blaine said, feeling hopeful again.

Wareagle shook his head. "We'd never make it, Blainey. In calm waters we'd have a chance. But now, tonight, the rocks will feed us to the icy seas. The boat is useless to us. Only a man whose manitou knows these waters by heart could make it.''

"We've got to try, Johnny," Blaine insisted. "Even if we have to swim across the bay, we've got to try."

"Maybe we won't have to," Sandy said suddenly, noticing the small clouds of gray wood-smoke billowing from the chimney of a shack just off the pier. A light flickered in the window. "There's someone in that shack."

McCracken turned to Wareagle. "The boat's owner?"

"If the spirits are with us, anything is possible."

"Then let's go see if we can hire ourselves a driver."

# CHAPTER 29

MᴄCʀᴀᴄᴋᴇɴ rapped on the door five times hard before he heard a knob being turned on the inside. The windows were so caked with ice that inspection of the shack's interior was impossible from the outside. There was a dim light glowing within, but until the knob began to squeak, he had no way of knowing if someone was inside.

"What do ya want?" the boatman asked, opening the door just a crack.

"We need your help," Blaine told him as the wind blew fresh snow through the narrow opening. He could feel the heat of a warm fire from the inside now, could smell the pine-scented relief it promised from the cold.

"Ayuh," the boatman drawled in a raspy, weather-scorched drawl. "You fellas best come out of the storm 'fore it freezes ya dead."

"We haven't got time."

"You got time enough to freeze, and that's just what you'll do 'less you listen up to me."

Blaine gave in and entered, followed by Sandy and then Wareagle, who elicited a sharp look from the boatman.

"There's more of ya out there," he said. "I heard 'em."

"If they come in, the cold will only seem crueler when they must go out again," Wareagle explained. "It was their choice."

"Ayuh. This night'll kill what it can. You fellas . . .

and lady . . . are white-faced. You been out in it for a while. I can tell.''

"We need your boat," Blaine started.

"My boat ain't for rent, friend."

"What about charter? We also need you to drive it."

"Better men 'an me been lost in coastal blows, friend. Better boats too."

Blaine followed the boatman closer to a single kerosene lamp, which gave him his first good look at the man's face. It was a formless face, neither young nor old, features hidden by beard stubble and dull eyes held low beneath a nest of graying hair.

"Money's no problem," he offered.

"You're right, it ain't," the boatman snapped, " 'cause money can't buy nobody a new life."

"A new boat, though."

"I'm happy with the one I got now," the boatman insisted. "She's got some life left in her." He paused. " 'Sides, where you boys gotta get to so fast in this kind of blow?"

"Horse Neck Island." Blaine checked his watch. "We've got to hurry."

McCracken briefly considered using his gun as impetus and the boatman must have read his mind, for his dull eyes turned to the M-16 slung over his shoulder.

"You boys fixin' to fight a war or somethin'?" he asked, scratching at his beard stubble.

"Something," Blaine replied anxiously.

The boatman nodded. "I know these waters better than any, mister. But this storm's a killer. It might take us 'fore the rocks even get a chance to."

"We're willing to take that risk."

"How many are you?"

"Nine," Blaine replied, not bothering to leave Sandy out.

"The boat'll be weighted down, friend. She'll be ridin' awful heavy, low in the water. With the waves out there now, that ain't hardly advisable."

"But you'll do it," Blaine said, and for some reason he

knew this ragged man living in a shack stinking of stale
sweat and cheap whiskey would.

"Just let me get my gear, friend."


Wells had spent most of the afternoon in the surveillance
room with the closed-circuit television monitors and communications equipment that linked him to his guards scattered across the island. The blizzard had become a blessing
for it totally precluded attack by air. Since approach by
water was impossible in this weather even before night had
fallen, he should have felt at ease.

But he didn't. Something was nagging at him. The
storm's lashing snows had rendered the closed circuit cameras virtually useless for nighttime monitoring, which left
Wells totally dependent on his guards. Several times he had
ventured out beyond the fortress's walls to check the island
himself, searching the swelling waters through a pair of
binoculars as if he expected visitors.

Now, though, seven-thirty was fast approaching. In little
more than half an hour the computer would exclude the
possibility of aborting the mission and Omega would be
inevitable. Wells relaxed a bit at that reassuring thought,
but only when the moment had come to pass would he be
totally at ease. He left the communications room and
headed up to the fourth floor command center, where two
armed guards stood poised before the door. Wells inserted
his ID card into a slot, which caused the door to swing
open.

"Ah, Wells," greeted Verasco from behind a computer
console. "I was just running some final checks. Our satellite is operating without a single malfunction."

The command center had six computer terminals on one
side and on the opposite side a large aerial map of the
world that constantly displayed the location of the Krayman
satellite. At present the white blip representing it was flashing over central Europe. Two men stood before the map,
jotting notes onto their clipboards. The terminal operators
behind them were responsible for monitoring all vital readouts from the satellite. The room's single set of double

windows looked out toward the mountain. Snow and ice had caked up on them, giving the command center the feel of a tomb.

"Where's Mr. Dolorman?" Wells asked.

Verasco's round head tilted toward a heavy door across from the map display. "Making the final preparations."

As if on cue, the heavy door opened and Dolorman walked gingerly out. "Anything to report, Wells?"

"All stations report no intruders."

"You still sound worried."

"Just concerned."

"About McCracken?"

"McCracken's dead. There may be others."

Dolorman smiled up at him. "Save your nerves the bother. Thirty-six minutes from now, nothing anyone can do will be able to change what will commence at nine o'clock." Then, to Verasco, "Are our communications people prepared to receive reports from the spotters?"

Verasco nodded. "They're in place now."

"Then nothing can stop us."

A phone buzzed on Verasco's desk. He lifted it to his ear and listened briefly, then turned quickly toward Dolorman.

"He wants you back inside."

Dolorman moved to the heavy door again, gazing up at the wall clock before he entered. "Thirty-five minutes, gentlemen."

The boatman's craft rode the waves sluggishly from the extra weight. The currents battered her sides and spilled cold seawater onto the deck. Blaine and Johnny Wareagle remained on deck, while Sandy and the other Indians huddled in the small cabin. They were two-thirds across the inlet to Horse Neck now, and they could see the island gaining substance up ahead. It looked ominous.

"How long before the men on shore spot us?" Blaine asked the boatman, who stood rigidly behind the wheel, eyebrows and beard stubble speckled with ice crystals.

"Soon as we cross the rocks, I'd figure. Ayuh, that's when the storm'll stop covering us."

"Any ideas?" Blaine asked Wareagle.

"If they see us, they'll blow us out of the water . . . unless they see no reason to."

"What do you mean?"

"No one shoots down a horse without a rider. That must be the way we make it seem with our boat. If the spirits are with us, it might work."

"And if they aren't?"

"Then we would have been dead already—a long time ago, Blainey, in the hellfire."

McCracken turned to the boatman. "After we cross the rocks, would it be possible to drift toward the island's dock?"

"With the currents, you mean, friend? Hard to figure them on a night like this. Storm winds blow the waters all different ways. But with a little luck, ayuh, I think I could manage it."

"We've got my friend's spirits with us," Blaine said with an eye on Wareagle. "That should take care of the luck department."

A minute later, with the island's erratic shape now clearly in view, they reached the rocks. The boatman's eyes were locked forward, though they were virtually useless to him when it came to seeing the deadly obstacles reaching up to tear the bottom from his boat. Instead, he focused on the island's shoreline. He could then chart the murderous rock formations from memory and steer the boat accordingly. Although he had eased the throttle down almost entirely, the craft was still at the mercy of the lashing waves and was shoved from side to side against the boatman's concerted efforts to hold the wheel steady.

In the cabin below, Sandy could feel rocks scraping at the hull. She could hear the horrible scraping rasp on the wooden bottom and wondered how long it would be until saltwater began to leak in.

Above, the boatman continued to throw all his energies into avoiding the most dangerous formations and risking abuse from the smaller ones. Occasionally the craft would slow with a grinding snarl to the point where it seemed they were scraping bottom and could go no farther. But always the boatman would twist the wheel just enough for the currents to free the craft so it might continue on its deliberate passage. Blaine felt his heart pounding and knew even Wareagle was fighting to retain his calm. The snow was vicious so close to the island, and they could look into it only for brief periods before the stinging on their faces became too much and they had to turn away.

Suddenly the boat's progress was arrested, as if a giant hand had clamped onto its hull from beneath the water. The boatman advanced the engine patiently and eased the wheel to the right. The sound below was ear-wrenching, fingernails on a chalkboard, but the craft shifted free of the rock formation into the surging black sea. They had escaped the rocks.

In the cabin below, Sandy felt the cold soak of seawater through her gloves. It wasn't coming from a central leak, but from many smaller ones. Soon she felt it rushing around her legs. A tremor of fear shook her as the engines switched off and the horrible anticipation of drowning made her breath come fast. Then the cabin door eased quietly open and Wareagle lowered himself in, followed by McCracken. While the giant Indian explained the next phase of the plan to his men, Blaine took Sandy aside and went over her role. She accepted it willingly, glad to have something to take her mind from the panic.

Blaine led her onto the deck, where they covered themselves with a single tarpaulin. She could not find the boatman and realized he, too, had covered himself up somewhere, leaving the craft to the whims of the water. Blaine had positioned them so he could follow their progress through a crack in the tarp, and Sandy was able to steal a few glances herself. They were heading erratically for a white dock that jutted out into the black water. At first it seemed certain they would overshoot it, but the boatman had calculated the currents well and from twenty yards away their route was straight on.

Blaine noticed the single man on the dock, glad he was alone but unhappy that he held his rifle poised. The man's job was to watch for approaching craft but this one, obviously deserted, must have been stripped away from its mooring and been propelled here by the wind. Miraculously it had escaped the fury of the jagged rocks. There was nothing to report to headquarters until he had inspected the craft more closely. He expected to find nothing but held his gun steady just in case.

Ten yards later the cabin door opened just a crack, enough for Windsplitter, Wareagle's knife-wielding man, to make a passage for one of his blades. Blaine stilled his breathing and pulled the tarp farther over him and Sandy. He was totally vulnerable from this position, but there was no alternative. If the dock guard noticed anything that made him shoot or contact his base, their mission was forfeit.

The man watched the abandoned craft pick up pace as it neared the dock. It slammed hard against a piling, and the guard noticed it was riding low, its deck sloshed with seawater. The boat was obviously sinking. He would have to contact headquarters for further instructions. His hand started for the walkie-talkie pinned to his belt.

Windsplitter hurled his knife through the crack in the cabin door.

The blade split the guard's chest up to the hilt. He stood transfixed for an instant before tumbling down onto the deck.

Blaine stripped the tarp away. Immediately Windsplitter yanked the blade from the guard's chest and returned it to the sheath on his belt. Then Blaine undid the buttons and snaps on the dead man's heavy winter coat. If the guard's killing had been witnessed by any of his fellows, the area would be crawling in seconds with Wells's men. If not, and if they worked fast enough, Blaine's plan might work.

He finally managed to tear the bulky jacket from the corpse and held it open for Sandy. She slid her arms through it and let him buckle it up for her. The final touch was to fasten the hood tightly in place, so from a distance in the blizzard she would appear to be the guard on duty on the dock. Less than a minute after Windsplitter's blade had jammed home, she was standing on the snow-covered dock with a heavy rifle in her gloved hands, glancing down with a shudder at the dark splotch on her chest.

"All you have to do is stand here," Blaine told her. "If they call you on the walkie-talkie, don't answer. Better yet, talk with your hand over the mouthpiece and say you can't hear them."

The boatman would remain behind as well to make whatever repairs were needed to keep the craft seaworthy. The one-legged Nightbird, meanwhile, would take up a position away from the dock to cover their return from the fortress after completing their mission. Blaine knew the Indian would have fared much better in the guard's role than Sandy, but his handicap would make the substitution too obvious. He gazed around. The pier jutted out twenty yards from the shore into the water. After that came thirty yards of snow-covered beach and then the woods that would take them to the fortress.

"Let's go," said Blaine.

With Wareagle in the lead, they moved quickly away from the waterfront and found a trail at the entrance to the woods.

"You figure there'll be any electronic traps?" Blaine whispered to Wareagle. "Trip wires or something?"

"Doubtful, Blainey. Too many small animals around to trigger false alarms."

A few silent minutes later the small group reached a clearing and stopped at its edge. From where they stood, the mansion was visible through the falling snow, along with a number of guards perched atop the tall stucco wall enclosing it.

"They're going to be a problem," Blaine said softly. "More than we expected. I count seven."

"Eight," said Wareagle.

A branch snapped not far off, forcing them to silent stillness. A pair of boots approached, crunching snow and closing on their position. Wareagle motioned to Thunder Cloud, the Indian whose specialty was a long chain with a steel ball attached to its end, a variation on the ancient bolo. Thunder Cloud freed his weapon from his belt and quickly unwound it as he glided to the front of the clearing.

The approaching guard was still six feet away when Thunder Cloud crouched and whipped his bolo forward. It swished through the air and twisted around the man's throat, the chain propelled by the heavy ball, until it shut off his air. His hands groped desperately for the chain, his frame reeling backward as Thunder Cloud took up the slack and the gnarled steel tore through the flesh of his throat. The scream he was forming died in the blood and pain. Thunder Cloud yanked his writhing body into the clearing as he started to fall.

"There will be others patrolling the immediate grounds," Wareagle cautioned. "The spirits tell me six, perhaps seven between us and the wall." He nodded to Running Deer, Windsplitter, and Thunder Cloud, who had just finished untangling his weapon from the dead guard's throat. Together the three Indians fanned out ready, with their silent weapons of death, to clear their approach to the mansion's wall.

"There are still the wall guards to worry about," Blaine reminded Wareagle. "We'll have to scale the wall to get to the mansion."

He stripped the M-16 rifle and rocket launcher from his shoulder. Wareagle grabbed its barrel and held it.

"Bullets bring with them a noisy message, Blainey. There is another way."

And McCracken watched the giant Indian and his two remaining soldiers, Swift Colt and Cold Eyes, lift their bows nimbly from their backs and ready their arrows.

In the woods beyond, soft sounds reached them through the storm. A grunt, a groan, a whistle through the air, a thud—all of these were repeated several times and each indicated to Wareagle that another of the enemy had fallen at the hands of his troops. But there was no time to relish the success of his tactics. The dead guards would have reports to make and checkpoints to pass. Soon too much would seem wrong to the men on duty inside the mansion.

''We must move now, Blainey,'' Wareagle whispered.
''The spirits command it.''

Blaine nodded and followed Johnny from the clearing.
Cold Eyes and Swift Colt were right behind with bows
ready.

Inside the mansion Wells had returned to his perch in
the communications room. The closed circuit monitors had
him totally frustrated, and squinting his good eye to make
sense of their pictures had done him no good at all. Wells
stripped back the shades from the windows overlooking the
courtyard, but he could make out only the closest shapes
at their posts.

The nagging feeling in his gut increased, the icy fingers
of foreboding tightening their grasp. Nothing could possibly be wrong. And yet he felt something was. There had
been no reports of anything strange or suspicious from his
patrols beyond the walls, and surely no assault could come
without at least some of them being alerted.

Wells was nonetheless restless. None of the logical as-
surances could override his feeling of dread. His nerves
were getting to him. Maybe his repeated failure to eliminate McCracken had something to do with it. Failure was
something Wells seldom experienced. But McCracken had
finally been killed in Arkansas. If there was someone here
on the island, it wasn't McCracken.

''Get me the guard on duty at the dock,'' he called to
the man monitoring the communications console.

Wareagle stopped.

''What's wrong?'' Blaine whispered.

''More men inside the courtyard,'' Johnny told him. ''If
we shoot down the wall guards but do nothing about the
men in the courtyard, our presence will be given away to
those inside.''

''The element of surprise is all we have. We can't lose
that.'' McCracken thought quickly. ''We've got to attack
the men inside the courtyard at the same time we take out
the guards patrolling the wall.''

The three Indians Wareagle had dispatched arrived within

seconds of one another. Blaine didn't bother asking how they had located their leader. They behaved like homing pigeons.

*Pigeons . . . Trees . . .*

Blaine glanced up through the falling snow. Trees surrounded the wall, some of them hanging over or close to it. The right men up there with the right weapons could take care of the courtyard *and* the wall. He explained the plan briefly to Wareagle.

"Can your boys get up in those without being seen, Indian?" he asked finally.

"They can get anywhere without being seen, Blainey, until circumstances force them to appear. Once in the courtyard, their presence will not be secret long from those inside the mansion."

"Just get me to the front door, Indian," Blaine told him. "I'll take care of the rest."

Sandy heard her walkie-talkie squawk and nearly jumped out of shock. She hesitated, hoping the call was meant for someone else.

"Water guard one, do you read me," the voice repeated.

She lifted the walkie-talkie from her belt and covered the plastic mouthpiece with her gloved hand just as Blaine had instructed. Taking a deep breath, she began to speak in a deepened voice.

"I can . . . hardly . . . hear . . . you."

"Say again, water guard one."

"You're broken up. I can't hear you clearly."

A different voice came on. "Water guard one, you missed your last report. Is everything all right?"

"Yes. I tried to report but I couldn't make this thing work." Sandy tightened a portion of her glove over the mouthpiece. "Could you send someone with a replacement?"

"No need, water guard one," said the second voice. "Just stay alert."

Wells yanked the headpiece from his ears and turned to a befuddled communications officer.

"What was that about, sir? Water guard one wasn't scheduled to make a report."

"I know," said Wells. "Now get me one of the field guards on the radio immediately."

"Which one?"

"Any! All! It doesn't matter!"

The radioman made the call, waited, then repeated it. After the third repetition he turned back to Wells.

"They're not . . . responding, sir."

Wells was already moving fast for the door. "Signal an alert!"

The radioman hit the red button on his console.

# CHAPTER 30

IT was twenty-two minutes to eight when Wareagle's men had finally achieved their positions in the trees. Windsplitter and his knives were in one, Running Deer and his tomahawks in another, and Cold Eyes with his crossbow in a third. Blaine gazed up at the trees and honestly couldn't see them, so complete was their camouflage. They had scaled the branches so adroitly that they barely disturbed the pilings of snow.

Johnny had kept Swift Colt, wielder of the second long bow, with him, and now they separated to find clearer sightlines to their designated targets on the wall. Blaine went with Thunder Cloud to the base of the wall and watched him fasten gnarled lengths of chain to the ends of a pair of ropes. There was a ridge protruding close to the top of the wall, and assuming there was a similar ridge on the inner side, the gnarled chain once tossed over would hook on it. The Indian handed one of the completed climbing ropes to Blaine and kept the other for himself. They'd climb the wall together and drop into the courtyard, with Wareagle and Swift Colt soon to follow if all went according to plan. The others would drop down from their tree perches a bit later. Taking the courtyard guards by surprise should overcome the advantage of their superior weapons.

The sound of an owl hooting came. It was time.

Wareagle and Swift Colt shot the guards closest to them

on the wall and had their second arrows loaded before the
next closest pair had even noticed their two fellows plunging to the ground. There were six guards patrolling the
inner courtyard, and before they could respond, a series of
weapons hurtled on target toward their chests or heads. A
pair of Windsplitter's knives found their marks neatly,
along with one of Running Deer's tomahawks and three
whistling crossbow arrows courtesy of Cold Eyes.

Blaine and Thunder Cloud had reached the top of the
wall just as the last of the guards atop it fell to Wareagle's
and Swift Colt's arrows. They had just dropped into the
courtyard when the alarm bell sounded.

Suddenly the courtyard was ablaze with light that made
the snowflakes seem to dance in its beams. The front doors
of the mansion crashed open and a horde of men surged
out, machine guns already flashing.

McCracken rolled and fired a burst, taking out a few
men of the first rush, and then slid back the catch on his
grenade launcher. He pulled the secondary trigger and felt
the recoil slam him backward. The grenade blasted into the
front of the mansion and sent rocks and wood splinters
flying everywhere. Running Deer and Windsplitter dropped
into the courtyard, Cold Eyes staying at his perch to provide cover with his crossbow.

McCracken ran along the far edge of the wall, firing at
the guards rushing forward and trying to angle himself for
a dash into the mansion. Wareagle and Swift Colt, still on
top of the wall, released a constant barrage of arrows at
the troops charging from the hole blasted in the front of
the mansion. The one-handed Running Deer managed to
take out two others who'd escaped the arrows. Then, down
to his last tomahawk, he raised it wildly over his head and
hooted a war cry as he charged into a pack of Krayman's
men. He killed a final one before a bullet spilled his blood
onto the snow.

Blaine kept firing until his clip was exhausted, then
ducked behind the cover of a Land-Rover to snap a new
one home. Krayman's men controlled the courtyard now.
There seemed to be hundreds of them, though dozens would

have been enough and was probably more accurate. He felt for the thermolite charges in his pocket and wondered if the time had come to make use of them.

He had just fitted his second clip in when one of Krayman's guards lunged behind the Land-Rover and aimed down at him with a rifle. Blaine started to spin away, aware it was too late, when a whistle split the air and Thunder Cloud's ball and chain wrapped around the man's throat. The Indian yanked viciously back, and blood spurted from the guard's throat as a spray of machine-gun fire cut Thunder Cloud's torso in half. He fell to the snow with a silent scream drawn over his lips.

McCracken grabbed the dead guard's automatic rifle and tossed it up to Wareagle, who had just exhausted his supply of arrows.

"Cover me!" Blaine screamed, ripping a pair of thermolite bombs from his jacket and tearing the ring from one. Still running, he hurled it at the largest cluster of Krayman's men. It had barely landed, when he tossed the second toward another group. The blasts came almost together, coughing up hundreds of pounds of blood-drenched snow into the air. Dashing through the white tunnel of his own creation, McCracken readied a third bomb.

He reached the front steps as the firing began again, and more troops charged through the entrance only to be met by fire from his M-16. They sought refuge down a hallway, and Blaine hurled his third bomb in their direction. A spray of fire from the opposite side stung him with its closeness, and he turned the grenade launcher that way and fired. The thermolite explosion had already sounded, shaking the walls, and with the grenade blast the whole structure seemed to tremble.

Blaine sprinted toward the main stairway. Johnny had three men left and alone they couldn't hope to overcome all of Krayman's guards. The best Blaine could hope for was a distraction that would give him enough time to reach the computer that controlled Omega. He stole a glance at his watch. Barely sixteen minutes to get the job done.

He started running up the stairs, taking them two and three at a time.

Wells sealed the steel-reinforced door to the command center behind him. The eyes of all the men at their stations turned toward him, the room silent save for a few beeps coming from computer terminals. Verasco waved a hand, signaling them to return to their work. On the monitor board, the satellite was just reaching Asia.

"What's going on out there?" Dolorman demanded, his face a mask.

"We're under attack," the scarred man reported breathlessly. "I don't know how many men there are, but they're damned good." Wells paused. "It's McCracken. I can feel it. . . ."

Dolorman's eyes shifted to the heavy door Wells had just closed behind him. "For God's sake, Wells, find him!"

Outside, the firing seemed to be letting up.

"I'll find him," Wells said.

McCracken dashed down the second floor hallway. The desperate pounding of feet above and below made it impossible to tell if anyone was giving chase. He assumed he had been seen entering the mansion and could only hope that confusion would remain his ally long enough for him to avoid capture. He didn't know exactly what he was looking for, only that he would know when he found it. He opened four doors on the floor and found nothing.

The fifth door was the entrance to a nightmare.

Inside was a perfect replica of the Oval Office. Krayman's operation was sparing nothing. Terrell had said the illusion of control would be maintained through whatever means were available, and he had been right. With the presidential insignia behind him, broadcast over every television station in the country, any man could command attention, the efficacy of his position apparently confirmed by an illusion. It was incredible. But it was about to happen, and only activation of the abort signal within fifteen minutes could stop it.

Blaine quickly searched the rest of the second floor and hurried to the third. The door-opening process and the succession of reconstructed offices continued. The White House pressroom was re-created in one room, a replica of the State Department briefing room in another. In still others sat VCRs with tapes already loaded into huge broadcast consoles containing whatever messages . . . or illusions . . . Dolorman and company had prepared.

From within these walls all of America could be controlled. Sahhan's troops would begin their rampage, the killer satellite would shut down all telecommunications, and then the mercenaries would move in. The rest of Dolorman's plan would be achieved subtly, the changes all but unnoticeable as his people rose to levels of control. The country would be in the hands of Krayman Industries.

Blaine realized the firing had stopped outside the mansion. Wareagle's resistance had ended, meaning the troops would be free to concentrate their efforts back inside.

Blaine started up the third stairway. He kept his back pinned to the wall and his M-16 at the ready. He was out of grenades but had a full clip of cartridges.

The fourth floor seemed as quiet as the last two. A low water table would have prevented Dolorman from risking placement of his command center in the more defensible cellar. Nor would he have expected an attack in the first place. So the command center had to be up here somewhere.

Blaine crept forward.

The long corridor was almost totally black when he reached it. The only light came from beneath a door at the very end. The sound of his footsteps swallowed by the thick carpeting, McCracken started to approach. If that was the command center up ahead, there should have been guards everywhere. It made no sense.

Blaine was halfway between the stairway and the lit room when the doors lining the hallway opened simultaneously and men lunged out in all directions, covering him with weapons, the corridor suddenly awash with light. Blaine glanced down at his M-16 and let it slide gently to the carpet.

A path opened amid the guards fronting him, and Wells stepped through it.

"It's over, McCracken," the scarred man spit at him, coming closer. "You lose."

"The odds weren't exactly in my favor, pretty boy," Blaine taunted. "Now, if it had been just you against me, then—"

Blaine never saw the kick that smashed into his stomach and doubled him over.

"That Indian band of yours is all dead and I've got men sweeping the island to see if any more are waiting in the wings." Wells grasped his shoulder and pulled him effortlessly upright. "Come on. Mr. Dolorman would like to meet the man who has caused him all this trouble."

They moved to the door at the end of the corridor which Wells opened by inserting a card into a slot. The steel-coated door swung open.

There were computer consoles everywhere, all of them manned by individuals carefully monitoring the readouts on their screens. Here obviously was the central command point for the satellite about to shut off every television, radio, and telephone across the country. Blaine had finally reached it, for all the good it would do him. He noticed a white blip flashing toward the Pacific Ocean on a giant display of the world. He noted the only means of escape from the room other than the entrance was a single ice-crusted window. Not much good from four stories up. There was also a heavy door in the wall opposite the world display, beyond which Blaine assumed lay still more equipment.

A digital clock on the wall read 7:48.

A white-haired man eased himself slowly from a high-back chair in the room's farthest corner.

"Blaine McCracken," began Dolorman, a slight smile crossing his lips. "I wanted Wells to deliver you to me alive so you might witness the moment of your failure before he kills you. The eight o'clock abort signal is now an impossible dream. Despite your heroic efforts, you have failed, and I wanted you to experience the pain of that before your death."

"And now I say, you're mad. You won't get away with this."

"Spoken halfheartedly because you know it not to be the truth. In point of fact, we have *already* gotten away with it. Nothing you or anyone else could do can possibly stop us now."

Blaine gauged his options and found none existed. "So your satellite plunges America into communications darkness while Sahhan's puppet troops begin a revolution your own mercenaries will swiftly squash. What then, Mr. Dolorman?"

"Quite simply, Mr. McCracken, we take over."

"Using a fake Oval Office? Somehow I figured you for better."

"That's only part of the plan, I assure you. It's all laid out. The country will see what we want it to see, believe what we want it to believe. There are still a few things you're not aware of. Come, there's someone else who wants to meet you. . . ."

Blaine recalled Terrell's theory that someone above Dolorman was actually directing the Omega operation. "Yes," he said, "take me to your leader."

Blaine felt Wells's powerful arms grasp him at the elbows and aim him forward toward the heavy inner door. Dolorman twisted the knob and eased the door open.

"This way, Mr. McCracken."

With Wells still holding tight, Blaine followed Dolorman into a dimly lit room filled with luminous diodes, digital readouts, high speed printers, and CRT monitors. Empty chairs sat before a host of computer terminals—all empty except one, that is. Wells closed the door behind them and McCracken's eyes locked on the man seated with his back to them.

"He's here, sir," Dolorman announced.

The man swung round and stood up, silver-haired and rugged-looking.

"Randall Krayman," Blaine said, confident he had figured everything out.

"Sorry to disappoint you, son," the man said, striding over. "But the name's Alex Hollins." He stuck out his hand. "My friends call me Spud."

# CHAPTER 31

SANDY tensed when she heard the rapid footsteps pounding through the snow. Men were rushing toward the shore. What was she to do? Many men, dozens of them. McCracken had said nothing about this.

The footsteps sounded closer. Still she stayed rigid. She thought of the Indian sharpshooter, Nightbird, waiting, rifle in hand, nearby. Would he take action? No, his orders had been to provide cover for Wareagle and company's return. He could not risk betraying his presence now. The decision of what to do was left to her. But she couldn't make it.

Suddenly an arm wrapped itself around her shoulder. She turned and found the ragged boatman by her side, his face and hands smeared with grease.

"We'd be best off to hide, miss," he whispered, tugging at her. "Ayuh, they'll shoot us down for sure if they find us here."

He started to lead her from the dock.

"What about the boat?" Sandy asked.

"They won't pay it no heed," he told her. "They might not even see it. It's not what they're looking for. We'd best hurry."

"But how can we hide? They'll look everywhere."

"There's a way," the boatman assured her as their legs sank into the foot-deep snow beyond the dock.

* * *

McCracken was still staring. "Sandy Lister interviewed you."

Spud Hollins jammed his thumbs into the pockets of his faded jeans. "Yup. I guess you see why I had to mislead her a bit. My down-home country boy act never fails."

"This has been your operation all along," Blaine surmised. "The satellite, Sahhan, the mercenaries—everything about Omega."

Hollins nodded. "I always believe in taking credit where it's due, son, but plenty of it belongs to Mr. Dolorman over there. I went to him with the beginnings of the idea and he fine-tuned it a mite."

"The Krayman Chip . . . No one stole it, you gave it to them."

"Absolutely. It was the key to this whole damned business. But I couldn't even come close to matching the distribution Krayman Industries offered. The chip gave us control of the telecommunications business. The rest fell into place naturally."

Blaine looked over Hollins's shoulder at the giant computer. "Like the satellite up there your mechanical monster is obviously controlling."

"As you've no doubt discovered, that satellite is the key to this entire operation. A few hours from now it's gonna issue the last command our nation's computers receive before we take over. The Omega command, son."

"But Omega didn't start with a machine, Spud. It started with you. Why?"

"Because I, like Randall Krayman, believed America was being beaten into the ground by shortsighted men who were mismanaging it. We were losing our edge almost everywhere and the few advantages we had left—high tech, agriculture—were starting to decline. Just as bad, we were losing our pride. Something had to be done, something drastic. Krayman had the resources, the facilities, but he didn't have the guts."

Blaine's eyes left Hollins's for the various consoles built

directly into the mammoth computer. Somewhere was the abort mechanism he had to find. It was 7:51.

"So you went to Dolorman and concocted the whole ruse surrounding the Krayman Chip, right? Dolorman sold Krayman on the story so you could get the production and distribution end going, and with that completed you killed him."

Hollins nodded. "It was five years ago. The car he was riding in was wired with a bomb and he and his driver were both killed. It was around Christmas time, too, as I recall. We arranged the hoax of his withdrawal so Francis could take over the company without question."

"With you whispering in his ear. You sold out to Krayman because you knew before long you'd be running his consortium. Then you moved out to that ranch in Hicksville so everyone would forget you."

Hollins winked. "Worked pretty good, didn't it? I needed room to move around, freedom to arrange all the things that needed to be arranged."

"Except none of it's going to work. You can dress up your mercenaries like soldiers, but that's not gonna make the regular army sit back and watch, no matter how much of the upper echelon you guys control."

"Who said anything about sitting and watching? They're going to be mobilized almost from the beginning."

"What?"

"Oh, not in any way that disrupts the role of the mercenaries, I assure you. Their orders will be confusing. They'll be serving as perimeter defense in areas away from the real action. And they'll have no reason to question that assignment since—"

"They'll think the mercenaries are crack troops sent in to engage the insurgents directly," Blaine completed.

"Then," Hollins picked up, "we'll move the army in to restore and maintain order. Enforce control—our control. Everything they do will be by the same book you're quoting from, McCracken. They won't suspect a damn thing has happened besides the quelling of a violent revolution. By then, after the Omega command is issued, this computer will control every bit of communications and data transmission in the country. Without the communications network, every sphere of American life will have come to a dead stop. When things start moving again, son, it will be as we direct. Our people will be in place or moving into place.''

''You say you're doing this for the country, Hollins. So what about all the people that are going to die starting tonight, *innocent* people? Or don't they count for anything?''

Hollins shrugged his broad shoulders. ''If there was another way, believe me, son, I would have chosen it.''

The clock read 7:54.

''Now, McCracken, I'm gonna have to ask Mr. Wells to take you back into the control room, while I issue our satellite its final instructions. You go too, Francis.''

Dolorman nodded subserviently.

Wells shoved Blaine brutally toward the door as a twisted smile rose to his lips. ''You're mine,'' he said softly. ''When this is over, you're mine.''

Dolorman closed the computer room door behind them. Wells reached into his pocket and came out with a pair of handcuffs, yanking Blaine's wrists toward him. If he was going to move, it had to be now.

The blip was just a few flashes away from reaching the West Coast. The abort system had to be triggered before it got there.

Blaine was about to pull away from Wells and go for one of the guards' rifles, when the ice-crusted window at the end of the room exploded. A horrible wailing cry filled his ears and his eyes locked on the most beautiful sight he had ever seen.

Johnny Wareagle dropped into the control room through the shattered glass, machine guns blasting in both hands, slicing up everything that moved. Johnny focused on the armed guards first, so by the time his legs were steady, there was no one left to provide real resistance. A few scampered about, only to be stopped by rapid bursts from Johnny's guns. Dolorman was struggling toward the computer room door, when a burst made a bloody line up the back that had pained him for so long. He slumped to the floor.

Wells was the only one who responded quickly enough to take evasive action as he went for his gun. But Blaine lunged upon him, pinning him to the floor and grabbing a brass paperweight from a nearby desk. He pummeled the big man's face again and again, reducing everything he struck to pulp until Wells struggled no more.

Blaine looked up to find Wareagle rushing for the door, machine-gun barrels still smoking.

There was activity coming from outside in the hallway, men battling with the entry system.

Wareagle shot out the plate holding the wires and fuses. The door was sealed.

"The computer's in there!" Blaine shouted, and rushed for the door that sheltered Hollins. "The abort mechanism, satellite control, everything!"

Blaine twisted the knob. It wouldn't give. The door had been bolted from the inside!

"Johnny!" he screamed, intent clear.

It was 7:56.

The Indian was breathing hard. Blood dripped from the exposed areas of his neck, face, and arms. Cold wind and snow blew into the control room through the window he had left shattered. In the corridor men were pounding on the entrance to the command center.

Wareagle stripped a green thermolite charge from his belt and tossed it at the computer room door. He hit the floor right next to Blaine.

The door exploded inward, smoke and splinters surrounded them. Together they regained their feet and rushed into automatic fire, obviously from Hollins.

"Don't kill him!" Blaine screamed to Wareagle. "Don't kill him!"

Johnny had already made the connection. His knife split the air and lodged in the fleshy part of the shooter's wrist. Hollins screamed in agony and let the gun slide to the floor. The knife was buried in his flesh up to the hilt, the blade

poking out the other side of his wrist, and blood spreading
down the sleeve of his denim shirt.

An instant later Wareagle was holding another knife
against the soft flesh of his jugular.

"The abort signal!" Blaine demanded. "Where is it?"

Hollins said nothing.

"You haven't got the guts to die, Hollins," Blaine shot
out at him. "Tell me or the Indian rips your throat out."

Hollins's breathing came fast and hard. His eyes fought
to see the blade perched on his throat.

"The abort signal!" Blaine repeated. "Now!"

The clock turned to 7:59.

"There's a key beneath the center console," Hollins
wheezed. "Turn it."

Blaine rushed to the center console and followed his instructions. A red button popped up on the console.

"Press it and you'll activate the abort sequence," Hollins explained between labored breaths.

Blaine depressed the red button. The console seemed to
swallow it.

*"Abort system triggered,"* a mechanical male voice announced. *"Contingency plan now in effect. . . ."*

Blaine and Johnny looked at each other. The clock
clicked to 8:00.

*"Repeat, contingency sequence now in effect. . . ."*

Blaine yanked Hollins free of Johnny's grasp and shook
him hard. "What just happened? What did I just do?"

Hollins looked up at him with strange calm, quivering
from the pain in his wrist. "You can't win, son. You never
could. You haven't aborted Omega, you've merely post-
poned it. Even now, our satellite has begun shutting down
all telecommunications for just a few seconds as a signal
to Sahhan's troops *not* to abandon their mission, but to *wait*
twenty-four hours till when the communications are shut
down again—for good this time. That will be the signal for
them to launch their strike. Everything will proceed as
planned. Only the sequence will have been affected."

"But the abort sys—"

"There never was any abort system, son. Terrell's people learned of it because we wanted them to. Disinformation, you might call it, developed as a final security precaution against a successful penetration of our defenses. Did you really think we'd be foolish enough to leave such a hole in our operation?''

"There's got to be a way to stop it, Hollins, there's got to be!''

"Then try to make the computer work.''

Blaine touched one of the console keys. His hand was jolted by a surge of electricity.

"Pressing the abort switch automatically shut down the computer once it had issued its final instructions,'' Hollins explained triumphantly. "It will accept no more instructions for thirty-six hours and has been programmed, like our satellite, to defend itself against penetration. It has already beamed a signal to the satellite telling it to activate the complete stage of Omega beginning at eight o'clock tomorrow night, eastern standard time. There's nothing you can do to stop that now. Not even the computer can stop it. The satellite is on its own. You've triggered the Omega command, son.''

"Then I'll blow your fucking computer up!''

And Blaine grasped the machine gun still lying on the floor.

"Go ahead,'' Hollins taunted. "Destroy the computer, and the effects of Omega will become irreversible. There will be no way of telling the satellite to reactivate communications once it has shut them down.''

Blaine let the machine gun slide from his hands. "You bastard! There's got to be a way!''

"There isn't. It's over. You've lost, son. The satellite is operating on its own, prepared to trigger the entire operation tomorrow night, and it's beyond even your reach.''

Blaine's eyes were still locked on the computer, searching for the impossible. The calm certainty of Hollins's words lulled his attention away from him long enough for Hollins's good hand to creep from his pocket holding a small pistol. Blaine saw it and saw Wareagle start in motion from the other side of the room. But he knew the

Indian could never reach Hollins in time to prevent him from firing, and neither could he.

Blaine's hands locked on the rolling desk chair in front of one of the computer terminals. In one sudden, swift action he propelled the chair forward as Hollins's arm came up to aim.

The chair crashed into him. His legs were yanked from under him and he reeled backward.

Hollins struck the computer with enough force to send 30,000 volts charging through his body, frying him as he stood. His flesh turned purple, and his eyes bulged to twice their normal size, jeans and denim shirt smoking. His mouth dropped for a scream which lasted barely a second before death swallowed it, though the current kept him pinned there, writhing, his entire frame a mass of jittery convulsions.

"The main door, Blainey! They're almost through it!"

That lifted McCracken from his trance and he rushed with Wareagle into the control room toward the shattered window. A series of ropes ran from the roof to six feet above ground level. Obviously, Wareagle had escaped the battle in the courtyard by way of the roof and then had climbed down the top portion of the rope to gain entry into the command center.

They slid down the rope quickly, hands burned raw from the coat of ice on its strands. When they let go, the cushiony snow broke their falls, and Johnny shot the rope down with a single burst from a machine pistol to prevent the guards from imitating their rapid plunge.

They ran together through the woods toward the dock. Wareagle's instinctive sense of direction gave him the lead, and before the exertion stole too much of Blaine's breath away, he was able to think out loud.

"The satellite! It's the key now. If we destroy it, we destroy Omega!"

"The spirits do not roam the skies, Blainey. We must seek help elsewhere."

"There's no time! Who would believe us?"

''We must try,'' Wareagle shouted as he ran. ''No other choice.''

Suddenly Blaine realized there was. ''Florida,'' he muttered. ''We've got to get to Florida. Canaveral.''

That was the last of the conversation between them. They drew closer to the general area of the shoreline, where the boat was docked. Johnny gave his hoot-owl signal. Nightbird would be expecting them now.

They could hear the pounding of boots, everywhere, it seemed, all around them. Both freed their machine guns from their shoulders and ran with the barrels poised and ready. The shoreline was just up ahead, under its thick blanket of snow. The storm showed no signs of letup. If anything, the snow was coming down harder than ever. Blaine and Johnny lunged into a clearing.

Forty yards ahead was the pier. Both strained their eyes. Incredibly, the boatman's craft was still tied up in place.

Suddenly men dashed in front of them and opened fire. Blaine took a few out with a single spurt, but his position was now forfeit and the shore was clearly held by Wells's troops. Wells might be lying back in the command center with a pulverized face, but he wasn't finished with them yet.

From his position of cover in the snow, Blaine could see the troops fanning out between him and the pier. No wonder they had left the boat intact. It was the bait for a trap he and Wareagle had stumbled right into. But what of Sandy, the boatman, and Nightbird?

Then he made out rapid footsteps, crushing the snow well behind him, evidence that more of the troops were giving chase from the mansion. He and Wareagle were surrounded, or would be shortly. There was barely enough time to act.

''Any explosives left?'' Blaine whispered to Johnny as machine-gun fire whizzed over their heads.

''Two thermolites.''

''Give me one. You take the right. I'll take the left. We've got to reach that boat.''

Wareagle nodded his acknowledgment. More machine-gun fire coughed up snow into their faces. The pounding steps behind them sounded closer.

"Go!" Blaine signaled.

And in unison they rose and sprinted parallel to the shore in opposite directions. Snow spit everywhere around him as Blaine ran. The storm and the darkness were confusing the troops' aim, but they were sure to lock on to him before long. Blaine estimated there were at least fifteen soldiers facing him, perhaps as many as twenty, most concentrated in the area fronting the pier. He ripped the tab from his thermolite bomb and hurled it at them. Wareagle did the same on his side.

Blaine then circled back for the boat and timed his entry into the open for the moment the explosives would ignite on the beach. His blast came an instant prior to Wareagle's, and, again, as if on cue, they started moving inward in an attempt to catch as many of the now defensive troops in their crossfire. He rushed right at them, machine-gun hot in his hands.

Then it jammed and he knew he was dead. But he caught the flash of motion at the far edge of the dock, coming from behind the enemy troops' line. As if in answer to a prayer, a figure covered with snow rose from the white blanket with a rifle in his hands, cutting Wells's men down as if they were bowling pins falling to a perfect strike. A few turned to offer resistance, but Wareagle, coming fast from the right, used his final burst to kill them. In seconds the bodies were strewn everywhere, warm blood cutting scars in the deep snow.

Blaine discarded his jammed gun and sprinted toward the snowcrusted wielder of the rifle, fully expecting it to be the sharpshooter Nightbird, but this figure looked taller, and as Blaine got closer he saw why.

It was the boatman!

"Never did fancy these things much," he said, and tossed the rifle to the snow. "If I was you, friend, I'd want to make it off this island real fast."

The snow stirred below him and Sandy Lister rose to her feet, brushing the white powder from her clothes and

coughing it free of her mouth. She was about to speak,
when more shots split the air, coming from the woods.

"Get to the boat!" Blaine shouted.

Wareagle was already halfway there, the boatman well
on his way. Sandy stumbled and Blaine reached to aid her.
Together they started to cover the twenty yards of beach
and pier that separated them from the small craft.

"Hurry, Blainey!" Wareagle called out as he untied the
ropes from the pilings.

McCracken trudged faster through the thick snow. Sandy
slipped and he yanked her back to her feet. Behind him a
new series of bullets had begun to sound, smooth and even.
The last of the enemy troops had finally come within
Nightbird's patient range and were paying for it. But even
Nightbird couldn't shoot down all of Wells's men. A stray
bullet caught Sandy in the leg and pitched her forward.
Blaine knelt to pick up her unconscious frame.

The black shape hurled itself at him through the darkness. A scream punctured the night and Blaine knew before
a set of massive hands had closed around him that it was
Wells, far from dead, with fury lending him more strength
than ever. They rolled in the snow, the scarred man's hands
searching for a grip on his throat. The good side of his face
was bruised and bloodied, but his remaining eye still focused well enough to land a fist against Blaine's jaw, stun-
ning him.

They rolled again, and McCracken ended up on top,
cracking the scarred man's teeth with an elbow and then
struggling to regain his feet. Wells reached out when he
had almost made it and tripped him up.

A knife flashed in the scarred man's hand.

It came down swift and sure, and only Blaine's sudden
move to the right stopped it from splitting his throat in two.
Wells slashed again, and this time McCracken dodged to
the left, at the same time jamming a hand up under the
scarred man's chin.

Wells seemed not to feel it. He plunged the knife down
a third time and McCracken caught his wrist early and
high, pinning it in the air. Wells's teeth bared like an an-

imal's, and he screamed again as his free hand shot down for Blaine's throat.

McCracken felt the fingers digging into his flesh, trying to tear through. His eyes bulged with fear. He fought futilely to pry the fingers off, the last of his breath choked off and his strength starting to give.

Wells tensed suddenly. The hand locked on Blaine's throat spasmed, then let go. Wells spilled over backward, an arrow embedded a third of the way up its shaft through his good eye.

Dead this time.

Blaine looked up to see Wareagle kneeling on the dock above the boat, sliding another arrow into place to deal with a guard rushing from the woods, gun clacking. More men followed behind him.

"Come on!" Johnny shouted.

Blaine picked up the unconscious Sandy and ran toward the boat with bullets scorching the air around him. He kept his frame as low as he could and lowered Sandy's body to Johnny as soon as he reached the boat. The boatman had begun to inch it away from the dock and Blaine jumped to the deck. The bullets followed them from the shore but they kept low and soon gained the full protection of darkness and snow.

"The souls of Bin Su can rest now, Blainey," Wareagle said softly.

"Twenty years too late," McCracken replied.

"How is she?" Blaine asked Johnny after the boatman had steered them safely through the rocks.

"The bullet passed through," the Indian reported. "The spirits deflected it. The woman was not meant to die tonight, Blainey. She is strong, just as I told you this afternoon."

"She'll need a doctor."

"Nightbird will arrange for one."

"Nightbird's still on the island."

"With the spirits guiding his bullets. He will stop them from pursuing us in boats and then he will steal a boat for himself and return to the dock where we started." Wareagle's eyes looked up at the boatman. "She will be safe with him until Nightbird returns."

Blaine accepted because he had to. "I'm sorry about your men, Indian," he offered lamely.

"They have made their peace with the spirits, Blainey. They are better off than you and I." He paused. "The spirits laughed when you spoke of going to Florida. I heard them. We must not tempt their good graces. They have helped us get this far. To ask for more would be to mock that favor. Ask for too much and you receive nothing."

"Then we'll have to help ourselves, Indian. Cape Canaveral's our next stop, and we've got to get there by late tomorrow morning."

"What lies there for us, Blainey?"

"Our only remaining means to stop that satellite from activating Omega: an armed space shuttle called *Pegasus*. It's scheduled to launch on Friday with a practice runthrough tomorrow. We're going to pay the shuttle a Christmas visit, Johnny."

"To help it on its way?"

"To hijack it."

# CHAPTER 32

For Nathan Jamrock, it had already been a ten-Rolaids day, and he had stored an extra pack in his pocket in anticipation of things getting even worse.

"Say again, Paul," he said into his headset from his position in the control room of the Johnson Space Center in Houston.

"I said, screw all the other preparations tests," came back the voice of *Pegasus* commander Paul Petersen from the cabin of the shuttle seven hundred miles away in Florida. "Just make sure you get the crappers workin' this time. Plumbers charge a hell of a price for a house call in outer space." Petersen was a cornbread southerner from Alabama who'd dreamed of being an astronaut ever since John Glenn orbited the Earth in *Friendship 7*. Taking care of bodily needs and functions in outer space hadn't occurred to him much in those days.

Jamrock popped another pair of Rolaids into his mouth. "The commodes check out fine, Paul."

"Sheeeee-it, that's what you said last time and I nearly died of spontaneous combustion when I had to hold my crap in for two days."

"We got the problem fixed."

"I'm fixin' on bringing ya back a shoe box full if you're wrong, boss."

In spite of himself, Jamrock smiled. Petersen was the

right man for this mission. No question about it. Career air force and a military man all the way and this was, after all, a military mission. It was also the most important mission Jamrock had ever been associated with. *Pegasus* had to go up tomorrow. It was as simple as that. Before that could happen, though, almost a thousand tests had to be successfully completed. After *Challenger,* NASA could not afford to submit itself to second-guessing. And yet, if *Pegasus* couldn't make it up . . . Jamrock chose not to complete the thought. He'd give himself another ten minutes and then chew two more Rolaids.

"Commander, this is Jamrock, do you read?"

"Dirty books, boss, read 'em all the time. What can I do for ya?"

Jamrock consulted a clipboard his assistant had just handed him. "We have clearance on all primary boosters, fuel flows, and jettisoning outlets."

"Gonna get to work on the crappers now, boss?"

"Launch countdown stands at T-minus twenty-four hours, thirty-one minutes, Paul. We'll be ready to start your lift-off run-through anytime you're ready."

"Me and Bob would be more than happy to oblige ya, but the weapons officer ain't made it here yet."

"Where the hell is he?"

"Since this is a precise run-through, he's probably taking a crap like he will before lift-off tomorrow. I'll tell ya, boss, we should be carryin' diapers up this time just in case."

"Get back to me when the weapons man is on board, Paul."

Jamrock stripped off his headset and massaged his temples. He hated run-throughs even more than he hated launches, because although he was in charge, he wasn't in control. From seven hundred miles away from the launch pad, all he had to rely on were faceless voices and endless dials, gauges, and computer overviews. Once *Pegasus* was in the air, it was his baby, but until then too many things could go wrong. Not that the situation would be any different once this particular shuttle reached outer space.

Commander Paul Petersen was worried about taking a crap once they achieved orbit.

Jamrock was worried about what *Pegasus* might find up there.

Forgetting his ten-minute time limit, he chewed two more Rolaids.

Two hours earlier a car holding two NASA inspectors from Houston passed through the high security gate of Cape Canaveral on its way to the Kennedy Space Center. The car's occupants made their way immediately into the preparations area, where astronauts were given their final tests and meals prior to boarding. Since their passes allowed open access, no one challenged the inspectors. And since their home base was Houston, no one expected to know them, though a seven-foot man with Indian features would certainly make for conversation later.

The route Blaine McCracken and Johnny Wareaeagle had taken from Horse Neck Island to Florida had been long and arduous. The boatman promised to watch over Sandy Lister until Nightbird arrived and agreed to take care of the medical arrangements himself if the sharpshooter failed to make it off the island. Wareagle gave him the name and address of a doctor his people used in emergencies.

"He doesn't ask questions," Johnny explained.

The pounding storm ruled out Portland Airport, necessitating a drive to Boston to reach the nearest functioning airport. Before setting out in one of the jeeps, McCracken called a number in New York. He had already catalogued what he would need for Christmas and he knew of only one man who could come up with the goods.

"Wow!" Sal Belamo exclaimed when McCracken had completed his list. "What you fixin' to do?"

"Long story, Sal."

"You ask me, cut it short. I think those balls of yours have gone to your head."

"Can you pull it off?"

"No sweat with the clothes and ID badges. I'll take a

box of Crayolas over to a friend of mine. As for the other stuff . . .''

"I need it, Sal. I wouldn't ask if it wasn't crucial."

"It ain't easy to come by, pal, especially on Christmas Eve.''

"I've got faith in you. I'll call from LaGuardia in about six hours. We'll drink a Christmas toast.''

"I'll bring the star from the top of my tree. You ask me, you're gonna need some magic to pull off whatever you got planned.''

Blaine and Johnny made the long drive south to Boston. The snow had given way to rain when they boarded the shuttle to New York. Their clothes were damp and filthy, but there was no chance of changing until they met up with Belamo. Blaine called him as promised and thirty minutes later they met in a LaGuardia Airport bar. Sal said *all* the requested merchandise was outside in the trunk of his car. It hadn't been easy to obtain, he reiterated, and guzzled the rest of his drink.

At four A.M. a suitcase filled with clothes concealing various other items Blaine had requested was loaded onto a plane bound for Miami. McCracken and Wareagle booked separate seats so each could watch for suspicious activity around the other. They rested in prearranged shifts until the plane landed in Miami ninety minutes past sunrise. They booked a room at a roadside motel, showered, and changed into another set of the clothes Belamo had obtained for them. Wareagle's were a poor fit, but they'd do. All that really mattered were the badges they'd wear pinned to their lapels, and those badges were perfect, a fact later borne out by their swift, unchallenged entry onto the grounds of Cape Canaveral and the Kennedy Space Center.

They made themselves scarce until eleven A.M., playing the role of simple observers who checked procedures and jotted down notes. They spoke with few others and did nothing to attract undue attention.

Just before eleven the shuttle commander and first officer, in full gear, made their way to the launching pad with a heavy security escort. Since this was a dress rehearsal for tomorrow's launch, every step was identical to those to be followed tomorrow.

But tomorrow was too late. By tomorrow Hollins's killer satellite would have shut down NASA along with the rest of the country.

There were three crew members assigned to *Pegasus*'s maiden flight. The remaining one—the flight engineer, a cover in this case for weapons officer—was having some trouble with his equipment back upstairs in the preparations building. This was his first flight and he was experiencing the usual jitters. Blaine and Wareagle rode the elevator up to the floor on which he was dressing. The area was under heavy security, and only their badges permitted them access. They were directed to the weapons officer's dressing room and knocked, then entered without waiting for a reply. The security men in the corridor were told not to interrupt. This was official NASA business. Don't expect the flight engineer for another twenty minutes, the guards were told.

It was actually almost a half hour later when the helmeted flight engineer emerged from the room toting his air conditioner. The Indian had subdued the weapons officer quietly and applied an ancient hold that would keep him unconscious for hours. They had swiftly loaded the contents of Wareagle's briefcase into the air conditioner and Johnny, calling upon his expertise in demolitions, made the proper connections while Blaine stripped the space suit off the man whose place he would take. The suit felt heavy and restricting on Blaine, and without Wareagle's help, he would never have gotten himself into it.

"See you tomorrow morning, Blainey," Wareagle said fondly before snapping McCracken's helmet into place.

"Hopefully."

"Hope has nothing to do with it. Just give yourself up to the spirits. They'll take care of the rest."

"I thought you said they don't roam the skies."

"The skies will be new for them . . . as they will for you."

Blaine shrugged.

He kept his eyes away from those leading him from the preparations building toward the shuttle van that would take him to the launching pad. Wearing a helmet at this point was not an unheard-of practice but not the expected one either. The guards and technicians, though, didn't seem to be paying much attention. This was, after all, just a dry run. The real thing was tomorrow and they were saving their enthusiasm and emotion for then. Today being Christmas was a blessing as well, an added preoccupation for workers forced to be away from their families.

Wareagle's mission, meanwhile, was to remain in the preparations building and keep anyone from entering the room in which the real weapons officer lay unconscious until Blaine was safely on board *Pegasus.*

McCracken was helped into the waiting van that drove across the black tar toward the shuttle. The gantry still rested near it, to be removed as soon as *Pegasus*'s final crew member was deposited inside. Blaine breathed easier. Besides the driver, only two men had accompanied him in the van, and neither spoke.

Blaine, though, was boiling inside his suit and the confinement of it was nearly unbearable. Never mind the fact that he was about to suffer a launch into deep space with no training or preparation whatsoever. Worrying about that would do him no good at this point. The fact was he would soon be on board *Pegasus,* leading it on an intercept course with the killer satellite that would begin its deadly pass at eight P.M. that evening.

The two men who had accompanied him helped Blaine down out of the van and joined him in a small elevator that was open in the front. The ride up the gantry to the shuttle's hatchway seemed interminable. Blaine passed through it uneasily with the men's assistance and then climbed upward to the front cabin dragging his air conditioner along. As he drew nearer the cockpit, an impatient voice laced with a southern accent found his ears.

"I don't know where he is, I tell ya. They told me he's on his way, boss. . . . Yeah, I know. But I'm just saying that if I get up in space and can't take a shit, I might open a window and let it fall right on your lap.'' The speaker, the commander obviously, turned toward Blaine as he made his way through the doorway into the cockpit, holding tight to the handgrips. ''It's about time, Gus.'' Then, back into his headset, ''He's here, boss. We're ready to begin the launch sequence.''

By the time the captain turned toward him again, McCracken had his helmet off and a nine-millimeter pistol in his hand.

Captain Paul Petersen did a double take, eyes bulging. ''What the blue blazin' fuck is—''

Blaine cut him off with his best rendition of a Spanish accent. ''Take thees plane to Cuba, mahn.''

''You're being *what*?'' Nathan Jamrock emptied a pile of Rolaids onto his desk.

''Hijacked,'' came Petersen's monotonal reply.

''You can't hijack a space shuttle!'' Jamrock shrieked. ''The flight's not even scheduled until tomorrow.''

''We're bumping things up a bit,'' a new voice said.

''Who is this?''

''Santa Claus. I left my sleigh in a tow zone last night and I've got to get back to the North Pole pronto. The wife, you know.''

''*What?*''

''Mr. Jamrock,'' Blaine continued in a more serious tone, ''I have a bomb on board this shuttle wired to go off with a simple touch of my finger. Twenty pounds of potent plastic explosives. Captain Petersen will confirm all this later. For now, just consider what would happen if *Pegasus*'s multi-ton fuel tanks went up. Remember *Challenger*? I've heard the effects on ground level would not be unlike a minor nuclear explosion of over three kilotons. Lots of damage. Kiss Cape Canaveral good-bye.''

Jamrock popped four Rolaids into his mouth. The man knew what he was talking about. How he had gotten on board the shuttle was something else again. But he had done the impossible and thus must be assumed capable of anything.

"Okay," he relented, "how much do you want?"

"Money? None. I want the shuttle. It launches within one hour or I push the button."

"*What?* That's . . . impossible!"

"A dry run is close enough to the real thing to make the necessary changes, Mr. Jamrock."

"No, we can't work that way. The program's different since reactivation. We can't take chances. Lives are at stake."

"My point exactly. One hour."

Jamrock searched for a way out, couldn't find one. "Why?" he managed. "Why are you doing this?"

"Is this communication line open?"

"What do you mean?"

"Can anyone else hear what we're saying, dammit?"

"A few," Jamrock admitted. "I put out the emergency signal."

"Well, I hope they've got top security clearances," Blaine said into his mouthpiece, gun still held on the pilot and copilot. "This isn't a random act, Mr. Jamrock, nor is it political. I know the basis of *Pegasus*'s mission tomorrow. Only tomorrow will be too late."

"What are you talking about?"

"*Adventurer* was destroyed by something in space and you're sending *Pegasus* up to return the favor. This shuttle's armed with laser cannons that may or may not be a match for what it's going to be taking on upstairs."

"How do you—"

"It doesn't matter. I know what we're fighting here. I know what it's capable of and I know who put it up there. And I know what's going to happen at eight o'clock tonight if it isn't destroyed. But most of all I know the damn thing's coordinates so you brains down here can plot an intercept course heading."

"You're not making any sense," Jamrock gasped, realizing he was.

"You've got to trust me."

"How can I trust someone who's trying to hijack a space shuttle?"

"I'm not trying, Jamrock. I've already done it. And don't even bother considering anything melodramatic like a commando raid because it won't work and a lot of innocent people would get blown up for the effort."

Jamrock hesitated. He needed to stall while security got a fix on what was going on. The FBI was already on the way.

"I need specifics. Names, dates, explanations of who's behind these . . . things you allege."

"There's no time. If you haven't called the President yet, you're about to. Let me speak to him." Blaine smiled faintly. "Tell him it's McCrackenballs, and I'm ready to bust some more nuts."

# CHAPTER 33

THE cubicle containing the direct line to the White House was hot and stuffy, suffering from poor ventilation. Jamrock completed a summary of what had just happened.

"Did the shuttle commander confirm the existence of these explosives?" the President asked at the end.

"He's no expert but he said they've got the potential to cause a big bang. Security's already issued me a report on how they could take the shuttle back. We've got contingencies for this sort of—"

"No!" the President ordered. "Under no circumstances will you do anything of the kind. You don't know who we're dealing with here. Just trust me."

"That's what McCracken said."

"Well, maybe we should."

"Sir?"

"Patch a line through to him for me, Nate. Let's hear what he's got to say."

"We tried to locate you after you called in from Newport," the President told Blaine minutes later. "Stimson's death knocked us for a loop. We didn't realize it was you he was still running."

"Somebody made it hard for me to drop by. As they say, there's a price on my head."

"Placed by whom?"

"It's a long story."

"We've still got fifty-one minutes until your launch."

And Blaine highlighted as best he could the events of the last ten days from Easton's discovery and subsequent murder, to its connection with Sahhan and the PVR; from the shootout at Madame Rosa's, to his trip to Paris which led him to San Melas and Krayman Industries' second army. Here he switched tracks to the discoveries made by Sandy Lister, confirmed and elaborated on by Simon Terrell. Finally, Blaine related the events on Horse Neck Island and his subsequent trip to Florida. In all, the story took twenty minutes to tell, a labyrinth journey of death and violence leading, perhaps irrevocably, to a new system of order in the United States.

"And you say these Krayman people are everywhere?" the President asked.

"They're Hollins people now but, yes, everywhere it matters. They're poised to take control. No one's above suspicion. You've got to be as careful as I do."

"What can I do?"

"Order the shuttle to launch, Mr. President," McCracken told him. "We've got to intercept that satellite before it begins transmitting its signal."

"And Sahhan's troops?"

"According to the contingency plan, they won't mobilize until the satellite does its part. Without the satellite they'll be neutralized and so will the mercenaries."

"You make it sound simple."

"I don't mean to. It's anything but. Just because *Pegasus* goes up doesn't necessarily mean it's going to succeed. If it doesn't, you'll have to stop Sahhan with more conventional methods. I'd recommend putting some contingency wheels of our own in motion now, like preparing the army to mobilize into all major cities. Otherwise lots of people might not be opening their Christmas presents next year."

"Right," the President said. Then after a pause he spoke again. "I'm going to order Jamrock to get the shuttle up as soon as he can. I don't suppose there's any way of persuading you to vacate the cockpit."

"Absolutely not."

"Then have a nice flight."


"You don't mind, fella, I'd appreciate you puttin' that thing down now," Captain Petersen requested, his eyes on Blaine's pistol.

"I feel better with it in my hand."

"Look, I'm on your side. If you can help us find the damn thing we're supposed to shoot down, I say fuck the rest of 'em. But have you ever been up in a space ship before?"

"I was always good on roller coasters."

"Yeah, well, multiply that feeling by about five and you've got yourself three Gs, which is what we'll be facing at takeoff. Better men than you have passed out from the pressure."

"I brought my Dramamine."


*"We are at T-minus twenty-two minutes to lift-off."*

Activity at both the Johnson Space Center in Houston and Kennedy Space Center in Florida became frantic with the announcement that the dry run had become the real thing. Personnel scurried about, the most practical ones stealing a few minutes to toss plastic covers over their cars to prevent damage from the hot dust the launch would scatter over a quarter-mile radius.

*"We are at T-minus twenty minutes. . . ."*

The emergency alarm had shrilled through the base for a full minute after the launch order was received from the White House.

*"This is not a drill. Repeat, this is not a drill. Emergency launch procedures now in effect. Emergency launch procedures now in effect."*

Since the run-through included all the procedures of the actual launch, the *Pegasus* crews in both Houston and Florida were able to pick up where the drill left off, albeit with a faster stride and more resolute approach. The only prob-

lem encountered thus far had been a burned-out motor in
the gantry which had to be moved from the launching pad
before *Pegasus* could take off. The Florida ground crew
ended up towing it out of the way with the help of two
bulldozers.

*"We are at T-minus twelve minutes. . . ."*

*"All systems are go. All light are green."*

On board *Pegasus* Captain Petersen was helping Blaine
strap himself into takeoff position, with the gun still making him nervous as he tightened the straps around Mc-
Cracken's waist and chest.

"I hope you plan on puttin' that thing away before we
take off, fella."

"Just as soon as you're strapped in too, Commander,"
Blaine told him, his eyes on the ever-silent copilot as well.

"Yeah, well, since you don't trust me, you should keep
in mind that if I wanted to make this the shortest flight you
ever took, all I'd have to do would be to leave one of your
straps unfastened. The G-forces at lift-off would send you
bouncin' 'round the cabin wall to wall. But don't worry,
fella, I fastened them all 'cause I believe ya and I know
you're the best chance we got once we hit the sky."

Blaine flicked his pistol's safety on and wedged it beneath his seat.

"That's better," sighed a relieved Petersen. "Now we
can get the final check under way. . . ."

*"We are at T-minus four minutes. . . ."*

When the final check was complete, with all systems
operating satisfactorily, Petersen turned back to McCrack-
en.

"You wanna hear the flight plan?"

Blaine found he was squeezing the arms of the seat
through his thick gloves. "I've got nothing else to do at
the moment."

Petersen smiled. "Two minutes after lift-off, the SRBs—
that's the solid rocket boosters—will be automatically
ejected. The main engines—SSME system—will continue
blasting us toward orbit for another seven minutes or so.

Once they cut off, that monster of a propellant tank will jettison and we'll enter a low, oval orbit.''

*"We are at T-minus sixty seconds to launch. . . . Fifty-five . . ."*

"I'll fill you in on the rest later," Petersen said, and turned back to his three monitors flashing a constantly changing display of data.

*"Fifty . . ."*

There was really nothing for Petersen to do at this point. Everything connected with launch procedures was handled by computer from Houston. He felt more like a passenger than a pilot.

*"We are at T-minus thirty seconds. Twenty-nine, twenty-eight, twenty-seven . . ."*

Blaine felt his teeth chattering. A horrible sensation of dread filled him. He fought down the urge to tear his straps away and pop the escape hatch to flee this nightmare. He closed his eyes and steadied himself. His whole frame had begun to twitch.

"Good luck," said Nathan Jamrock into his mouthpiece.

*"T-minus twenty seconds and counting. T-minus fifteen, fourteen, thirteen . . . T-minus ten . . ."*

The monstrous lift-off rockets beneath *Pegasus* had begun to fire. The spacecraft rumbled and seemed to tremble in eager anticipation of its launch.

*"T-minus five . . . We have gone for main engine start. . . ."*

A thunderous roar found Blaine's ears. Those in the observation area saw a blinding spout of orange and yellow flames burst out from the shuttle's base, intermixed with a rush of erupting steam.

"Main engines and solid rocket boosters firing!" a voice said inside Blaine's helmet.

The ground shook and threatened to break open. A quake of heat rolled across the miles of empty land surrounding the launch pad.

"We have lift-off!" a voice bellowed.

*Pegasus* rose patiently into the air, seemingly unburdened by all the frantic activity that had preceded her rise.

The majesty and glamour of the event was totally lost on McCracken. His entire frame felt as if it had been squeezed into a crate a third its size. There was pressure from both above and below, seeming to compress his head closer and closer to his toes. He tried to scream, but he couldn't find his voice. He knew he was breathing, but the action felt separate from himself. He was convinced he was choking to death, and he would have groped for his throat had he been able to free his arms from the rests. Finally he gave up and forced his shoulders back against his suit as far as they would go. He was vaguely conscious of a slight smoothing of *Pegasus*'s track and of words being exchanged rapidly in his headset.

"*Pegasus,* this is Houston Cap-Com," came the voice of NASA's capsule communicator. "You're flying a few degrees higher than your planned trajectory. Should be no problem, but expect a slightly higher release altitude for SRBs and SSMEs."

"Roger, Houston," said Petersen.

A little over two minutes later Blaine heard the Houston Cap-Com announce that the SRBs had been released from the shuttle. This left *Pegasus* to be carried up by the thrust of its three main engines. McCracken was more relaxed now, breathing easier, but still he felt disjointed, as if he were riding some dizzying amusement ride he couldn't get off. Three minutes into the flight, *Pegasus* was traveling at 6,200 feet per second. At six minutes that pace had more than doubled. McCracken's heart was pounding at twice its normal rate. Through a side window he watched the earth shrinking away.

Less than a minute later the shuttle's nose angled down to increase velocity. When its tip came up again, its speed had risen to more than 16,000 feet per second.

It was nine minutes into the flight when Blaine felt something buckle, as if someone had applied the brakes briefly.

"Houston, we have main engine cutoff," Petersen reported.

Blaine felt his stomach make a determined leap for his

throat, until a sudden shift in the shuttle's trajectory forced it to drop for his feet.

"*Pegasus*, this is Houston. Propellant tank is away. Good work with the wheel, Captain."

"That's a roger, Houston. Thanks for your help."

The sensation Blaine had felt had been an evasive maneuver enacted by the flight computers to steer *Pegasus* away from the free-falling tank.

He could have used some Dramamine after all.

"What is your altitude, *Pegasus*?"

"Houston, we read altitude at one oh five miles and climbing. Twin orbital maneuvering engines burning now. Climbing toward one seven five nautical-mile orbit."

"Roger, *Pegasus*. We show all systems go. You'll be passing out of range of our Bermuda tracking station in seconds. We'll catch up with you over Madrid."

"*Si, señor,*" said Petersen.

"What's happening now?" Blaine asked the commander a few minutes later.

"To begin with, we've achieved initial orbit. But we're still climbing and the orbit will change slightly as we do. Eventually it'll become elliptical for maximum maneuverability once we reach our cruising altitude and proceed on our intercept heading." Petersen adjusted his headset. "Here's the strategy. We're going to assume the same orbit *Adventurer* did when it ran into this thing. Since we've got the advantage of knowing exactly where it's gonna be at eight o'clock, thanks to you, the flight computers will time our course to insure that we meet up with the bastard somewhere over the Pacific before it begins its pass over the country. Things happen pretty fast at seventeen thousand miles per hour, but we've got a few minutes to play with."

McCracken's eyes wandered over the endless rows of gauges, dials, and cathode-ray tube displays on the cockpit's front and sides. "Yeah, but how well can you control this bus once the time comes?"

"You mean in manual?" When Blaine nodded, Petersen

went on. "I'll spare you the details, but because of its military nature, *Pegasus* was built to handle like a god-damn Ferrari."

"So you'll be able to maneuver once we meet up with our friend."

"I'll be able to take you wherever you want to go."

"You already are, Captain."

# CHAPTER 34

THE minutes passed into agonizingly long hours. Cabin pressure had stabilized, allowing Blaine to remove his confining helmet long before. Still, comfort was a thing not to be found. His motions felt slow and elongated, the fun of being able to float buoyantly at whim totally lost upon him. He had to admit, though, that the view was spectacular. Petersen acted as tour guide for much of the trip's duration by pointing out various countries and bodies of water as *Pegasus* passed above them.

They were into their fifth orbit, cruising comfortably toward the mid-Pacific, when Captain Petersen steadied his headset.

"Houston, this is *Pegasus*. We have reached our cruising altitude of one seventy-five nautical miles and are proceeding on intercept course with Comet X-ray. Final engine burns complete. Cap-Com, she's riding smooth."

"Roger, *Pegasus*."

"Houston, we should be in the vicinity of Comet X-ray in minutes now. Do your instruments show anything?"

"Negative, *Pegasus*. All boards and monitoring stations look clear. The sky's all yours."

"That's a roger."

Because the transmission was open, the true purpose of the shuttle's mission was being cloaked in seemingly mundane talk. Comet X-ray was their private name for the intruder satellite they were seeking. Petersen held no illusions about Houston's response to his query, though. He had read all the reports on *Adventurer*'s destruction in detail and memorized the final transmissions. There had been no warning in that case either. The killer machine had appeared out of nowhere.

"Houston, we will maintain present heading in attempt to sight Comet X-Ray. We will check in every minute. Repeat, every minute."

"Roger, *Pegasus*."

"Give us a buzz if you catch wind of anything down there, Cap-Com."

It was 7:50 eastern standard time when *Pegasus* passed over Wake Island. Petersen was steering manually now, simply holding the shuttle on its preprogrammed heading.

"Houston," said Petersen, "this is *Pegasus*. I'm going to raise us a mite higher to slow our orbit and give Comet X-ray a fair chance to catch up."

"Roger, *Pegasus*."

Petersen turned to McCracken. "If we do find this thing, Blaine," he said somberly, "it's gonna be your job to blast it. I'll fill you in." He shifted in his seat to allow Blaine to creep up closer. Then he pointed to a center panel within easy reach of his right hand. The panel was dominated by a monitoring screen and a twin pair of joysticks. "This thing may look like a video game, but it's the firing mechanism for the laser cannons."

"Where do I insert the quarter?"

"In Jamrock's toilet to the rear of the shuttle. Anyway, when the system's activated, this is what you get."

Petersen flipped a switch and the viewing screen came to life with a series of three-dimensional angular shapes merging into a single square sliced up into individual boxes.

"Okay," he continued, "we've got two cannons, one inside each side of the front. For security reasons, since no one's supposed to know we're armed, the lasers are hidden behind heat shield panels that slide away upon activation. See that green light in the right corner of the panel?"

"Sure."

"That indicates the panels are open and the cannons are operable. The fail-safe mechanism makes it impossible to fire them if the panels are still closed. Anyway, the cannons' angle of fire can be changed by manipulating the joystick controls. They're tied into the same circuit, so moving one is the same thing as moving both." Petersen's hand moved onto the screen. "Now, here's the most important thing. Once we find this satellite of yours, you've got to adjust the joysticks so that it fills out the center of the box on the viewing screen. The closer we get and the bigger it is, the more individual cubes it will take up. And, remember, up here it doesn't take long to cover lots of ground. But the thing's still gotta be centered in the square to be sure of a hit. Savvy?"

Blaine shrugged. "It would seem a lot safer for you to do the shootin', Sheriff."

"I've got to drive this baby."

"What about your deputy over there?" Blaine asked, head tilting toward the copilot.

"He's gotta track the damn thing and adjust sensor and deflector shield levels."

"Deflector shields? What is this, another of the continuing voyages of the starship *Enterprise*?"

"We're well on the way to that, Blaine, but don't be too impressed. The deflector shields are just a new toy that work on reverse polarity and it's not quite perfected yet. We'd be best off not to rely on them."

"Let's hope we don't have to."

It was 7:52. The Philippines were drawing slowly closer. From this altitude the Pacific looked like a beautiful blue blanket.

Blaine's chair was set back from the pilot's and copilot's, and the weapons mechanism was built into what might have been a sloping desk within easy reach. He shifted about uncomfortably, growing eager for the confrontation that was about to come. His eyes looked out through the shuttle's elaborate windshield, searching for something, anything. In the profound darkness of space objects not producing their own light were virtually invisible. If the killer satellite were painted black, it could be almost on top of them and they wouldn't be able to see it.

"I'd better check in with Houston," Petersen announced.

McCracken's fingers flirted with the joysticks.

"Houston, this is *Pegasus*. We're just reaching the Philippines now. I'm gonna fire the maneuvering rockets, bring her around, and hold steady as she goes."

"*Pegasus*, this is Houston. We read you but you're a bit garbled. Could you repeat your last sentence?"

"I said I'm gonna bring her around and—"

At the command center in Houston static drowned out the final part of Petersen's sentence. The interference was getting stronger now. All eyes rose from their terminals and gazed up at the world's most sophisticated radar board responsible for monitoring the shuttle and anything near it. At present it showed only a single blue blip to indicate *Pegasus*.

"*Pegasus*, does your board show anything?"

"Say again, Houston," requested Petersen through static.

"Is there anything on your board?"

The copilot shook his head. Petersen gave the response. "Negative, Houston. Nothing." His last word was indistinguishable to the men on Earth.

"*Pegasus*, you're breaking up. We've lost your television transmission. Repeat, your television transmission is scrambled. . . . What's going on up there? *Pegasus*, please acknowledge."

Static was the only response.

"*Pegasus*, please acknowledge."

More static. The shuttle's existence was reduced to a tiny blue blip on a huge screen. Every eye in mission control was locked on it, searching for reassurance, fighting against the panic each felt.

"Oh, my God," Nathan Jamrock said out loud. A handful of Rolaids slipped to the floor. "It's happening again."

* * *

"Houston do you read me? This is *Pegasus*. . . . Come in, Houston." Petersen finished bringing the shuttle around in a 180-degree turn, so it was now moving backward in its orbit, and looked at McCracken grimly. "We've lost them."

"What happens now?"

Blaine could see Petersen swallow hard. "We hold our course as best we can. The thing should be here any second."

A red light started flashing on the copilot's warning board, and a beep started sounding.

"Captain," the copilot called, "sensors have locked on to something."

"Where?"

"Twenty thousand meters behind, in front now, and closing."

"Switch on front deflector shields." Then, to Blaine, "Looks like the fucker's about to show itself." And he pressed a button that activated the weapons system.

The copilot hit four switches, lighting a green signal under each.

"Shields in place, Captain."

Petersen's eyes strained out the viewing panels. "Come on out, you bastard," he urged the thing.

"Fifteen thousand meters, Captain."

"What's its heading?"

The copilot hesitated. "Direct intercept."

Petersen raised his eyebrows. "Looks like it's gonna be eyeball to eyeball, Blaine. Flip your visor down and get ready on those guns."

Blaine grabbed the joysticks between warm, sweat-soaked hands and locked his eyes on the now functioning targeting screen. Something had started to fill in the squares.

"Range ten thousand meters," said the copilot. "Still closing. Should be in view any— Oh my Christ . . ."

The three men gazed out the shuttle's windshield and saw it together. The killer satellite looked like a giant bullet rotating in the sky, at least as tall as *Pegasus* was long.

Starting about two thirds of the way down its sleek, dark structure were thick legs like landing nodules linked together in a maze of wire and steel. Its lower third appeared to be wider than the top.

"Looks like somebody fired it out of a fuckin' giant cannon," muttered Petersen.

"Range seventy-five hundred meters . . ."

McCracken was working the joysticks feverishly now, trying to capture the killer satellite in the center of the square. It kept eluding him, changing direction to match *Pegasus*'s orbit, these slight alterations throwing the weapons' sensors off.

"I can't get a fix!" he complained into his helmet, licking the sweat from his upper lip.

"Range five thousand meters and . . . slowing." The copilot swung toward Petersen. "The damn thing's slowing, Captain."

"Get your fix, Blaine!" Petersen ordered. "For God's sake, shoot the fucker out of the sky!"

Before McCracken could fire, the thing came to almost a complete stop relative to them in space. Cylindrical attachments popped free of its sides and spread like a fan. The attachments were reflective. The center base rotated, its blackness abandoned for the same shiny surface its extended sides were composed of.

"Jesus Christ," muttered Petersen.

McCracken gained a brief fix on the satellite and hit both joystick buttons. A pair of ice-blue rays shot out from either side of the shuttle, angling toward intercept right smack in the center of the adversary. Blaine could feel his smile forming.

But not for long. The lasers' rays bounced off the reflective surface like light off a mirror and cascaded through space.

"Aim higher!" Petersen ordered. "We got to find a weakness in— What the . . ."

McCracken saw the flash coming from the satellite what felt like a second before it impacted. His face shield went opaque for an instant, saving him from blindness, while

*Pegasus* shook violently. Pieces of white surface material flew off, soaring past the viewing windows.

"We're breaking up!" Blaine screamed.

"It's the heat shield," Petersen corrected him as he struggled to maintain the shuttle's balance. "Pieces of it anyway. Not enough to do us much harm."

"Jesus . . ."

"Deflector shields?" Petersen asked the copilot.

"Still holding. I've got four green lights."

The killer satellite sent out another charge, catching *Pegasus* just as Petersen lowered her into an evasive dip. Impact rocked her hard and Blaine's head snapped back in a whiplash. Vibrations rattled through the shuttle, forcing his teeth to clamp together.

"We've lost a deflector shield!" the copilot reported, his eyes on a red light that had joined the three green ones.

"I'm gonna rotate the ship to protect the side with the lost shield," Petersen said, starting the maneuver.

The killer satellite angled itself for another attack. Its shape flirted with the targeting grid square on Blaine's screen but never quite locked in. He fired on timing and again a pair of ice-blue rays shot out, joining up on one of the thing's winglike extensions. Once more a dazzling display of white light exploded outward, individual streams crossing and converging into the blackness of space.

"Range thirty-five hundred meters . . ."

The satellite fired another of what Petersen could only identify as some kind of energy torpedo. Again their visors turned opaque, saving them from the bright flash which seemed everywhere at once, enveloping all of *Pegasus* in its white-hot aura. The shuttle shook the hardest it had yet, and felt as if it were stumbling in space. The cabin lights flickered, faded, came back on.

"Main battery's shorted out!" the copilot screeched. "We're running on emergency power. Second deflector shield's gone and a third's weakening!"

"Don't tell me," Blaine interrupted, "we can't take an-other hit like that one. Scotty, where are you when we need you? Beam us the hell out of here." Then something occurred to him. "Get me closer to it," he told Petersen.

"You crazy?"

"Absolutely. Give me a shot at a closer hit."

Petersen pulled back to minimum speed as his wounded bird continued to float backward in orbit. "Just so you remember it'll have a closer shot at us too. . . ."

"Range twenty-five hundred meters," the copilot reported. "It's gaining. Two thousand . . ."

Blaine caught the satellite within his square and fired both cannons. The lasers blasted into the metallic skin, the resulting parade of shooting lights brighter and eerier since *Pegasus* was closer to them. A few seemed to pass right by the viewing panels, looking like the tails of an all-white fireworks display.

A blinding flash erupted from the satellite's center. Blaine involuntarily raised his hand to his eyes to shield them. He had barely gotten it up, when the blast came. The copilot's head slammed against the instrument panel, opening up an ugly gash on his forehead. Once again the cockpit lighting faded and came back on dimmer.

"Range seventeen hundred fifty meters," the copilot muttered.

"I'm gettin' us the hell outta here!" shouted Petersen.

"The energy torpedo, did you see where it came from?" Blaine asked rapidly.

"What?" the captain returned as he began to roll the shuttle.

"There was a black spot in the middle of all those reflectors. It's gotta be a door in the base the thing has to open to fire at us. I saw it!"

"That doesn't mean you can hit it," Petersen pointed out.

"But if I can, it'll mean a direct shot to the guts and kiss that thing good-bye."

"Terrific," Petersen moaned.

*Pegasus* had come all the way around now and was fleeing at top acceleration toward the sharpening California coast.

"Range fifteen hundred meters," said the copilot. "Auxilliary power's just about had it. We've lost the left laser cannon and can only generate a few more bursts from the right. . . . Range seventeen hundred fifty." Then, to Petersen, "We're pulling away."

"Only until the gas runs out. . . "

"That's it!" Blaine screamed. "Turn this thing around!"

"Huh?"

"Turn it around and kill all the thrust and defensive systems. Just leave me a final burst from the laser cannon."

"Have you gone fuckin' nuts?" Petersen challenged.

"No! Think! The thing moved right on top of *Adventurer* before it fired because she couldn't defend herself. The satellite sensed that. It doesn't think, it just responds. We've got to make it respond the way it did with *Adventurer.*"

"Range twenty-five hundred," from the copilot.

"Captain!"

Petersen squeezed his lips together and fired the maneuvering jets to roll *Pegasus* around toward the satellite once more. When the maneuver was complete, he killed the main batteries to the shields and cut back to standard computer orbit.

"Range two thousand and closing," announced the copilot. "Fifteen hundred and closing. . . "

Blaine locked the thing into the center of his firing grid. He had to be sure, had to make his last burst count. His hands felt stiff as boards, but they'd do the job well enough.

The satellite kept coming at them, growing into more of the individual cubes of the grid as it approached.

"Range one thousand and closing . . . "

"What the hell are you waiting for?" Petersen shrieked. *"Kill the fucker!"*

The killer satellite loomed near them like a giant hawk spreading its wings over its prey, the steel support legs looking like talons.

Blaine raised the joysticks so the center of the firing grid was in line with the area of the satellite where the door had opened to release its last energy torpedo.

"Range seven hundred fifty meters . . . ."

Blaine saw a black area in the shape of a square appear amid the thing's reflective surface, indicating the door had opened again. He closed his eyes and squeezed both red firing buttons.

There is no sound in outer space, but there is vibration, and the one that came when the last burst of *Pegasus*'s laser cannon pierced the guts of the killer satellite shook McCracken's stomach up to his mouth. His teeth snapped together and he felt himself slammed backward against his seat. His eyes closed for an instant, and when they opened, he wanted to hoot and holler for joy and would have if he could have found his breath.

Because the viewing windows were filled with a beautiful circle of silent orange which absorbed the remains of the killer satellite into oblivion. What few particles remained showered harmlessly toward the ridge of the Earth's atmosphere.

"*Heeeeeeeee-yahhhhhhhhh!*" Petersen shouted, one hand struggling to control *Pegasus* from the shock waves and the other slapping Blaine on the shoulder. "We did it! We fuckin' did it!"

And *Pegasus* passed over the California coast.

The expiration of the blue light on the main monitoring board in Houston had sent most of the mission control personnel to their chairs with heads bowed, weeping silent tears. Nathan Jamrock sat stone-faced amid it all. He held the direct line to the President in his hand and wished there was something encouraging he could say.

Then all at once a voice split through the thick silence and tension in the room, seeming to come from heaven or somewhere almost as high.

"Houston, this is *Pegasus*. Sorry you boys missed all the fun. . . ."

Petersen said more, but nobody could hear him through all the shouting and screaming.

"The heat shield's my biggest worry," Petersen repeated at the close of his report. "We can get all other necessary functions patched up good enough, but we've lost a lot of tiles, maybe as many as a third from the nose area."

Nathan Jamrock swallowed four more Rolaids. The knots in his stomach didn't loosen. "What about the bottom?" he asked, aware that the heat shield on the shuttle's underside was the most crucial.

"Tiles ninety-five percent accounted for, but I can't tell what reentry might do to them after what this tub's been through."

"They'll hold tight, Paul. I glued them myself. But things will get a little hot."

"We'll wear our summer clothes, Nate. Oh, and there's something else. The shitters sustained some real bad damage. Looks like you guys got an excuse for them not working this time around."

"I'll take the responsibility."

"How's the weather at Edwards?"

"Clear, calm, and sunny by dawn. That's 6:03."

"We'll set down by seven."

"I'll have the band waiting."

"And a bathroom."

"A slight change of plans, Paul," Blaine said softly after they had completed seven hours of grueling repairs that included Petersen having to spend some tedious moments on the outside of the craft to realign *Pegasus*'s navigational beacons.

"Uh-oh . . ."

"See, Paul, any way you cut it, I'm still a wanted man. There are still too many people working for the guys who put that thing up in space, and I'm a threat to them. Getting a medal from the President would be nice, but staying alive'll do just fine for now."

Petersen shrugged. "I guess you know these people pretty well."

"Too well. Omega's not over. It won't be until all the people in positions of control are exposed. They'll be waiting for me, if not at Edwards, then somewhere else down the road."

"I understand. What do you want me to do?"

Blaine told him.


*Pegasus* reentered the atmosphere right on schedule. The loss of so many heat shield tiles forced the cabin temperature up over 110 degrees, uncomfortable but not life-threatening, and most important the underside shield worked magnificently. The retrieval crew on the ground at Edwards Air Force Base in California broke into spontaneous applause when it was announced that the shuttle was on its way.

In Houston Nathan Jamrock had sworn off Rolaids once again and returned to cigars, which seemed to have an infinitely superior effect at settling the stomach. On the main board, the blue blip represent *Pegasus* came lower and lower. Then came a three-minute radar lapse before ground spotters at Edwards and the surrounding area would make their first visual sightings.

"You see her yet?" he asked his direct link on the scene in California.

"Is she off your screen?"

"What are you talking about?" Jamrock demanded, tossing his cigar aside. "She's been off my screen for over three minutes now."

"There's no sign of her here, sir."

Another phone rang on Jamrock's raised terminal. He picked it up and told his man in California to hold on.

"Houston, this is California tracking. We just picked up your returning shuttle on our screen."

"Where the hell is it?"

"As near as we can tell, making a descent into the Utah salt flats. . . ."

Jamrock started grasping for some stray Rolaids tablets.

* * *

"Thanks for the lift," McCracken said as he walked down the steps of the space shuttle *Pegasus*.

"The pleasure was all ours," Petersen answered from the doorway. "You can fly with us anytime."

Blaine begged off. "Once is enough for one lifetime."

"Suit yourself."

A Land-Rover driven by Johnny Wareagle raced down the barren flats toward the shuttle's position. Blaine waved to him.

"Sorry I had to make you miss the reception party at Edwards," he apologized to Petersen.

The captain winked. "I hate parties."

They smiled at each other and Blaine walked off. The Land-Rover pulled to a stop and he climbed into the passenger seat next to Wareagle.

"The spirits were with you up there, Blainey."

"They made pretty damn good astronauts, Indian."

# EPILOGUE

"THERE'S just one thing I don't understand about all this," Sandy Lister said after McCracken had completed his account of the events since he and Wareagle had left Maine. She lay propped up on pillows in a room in the discreet doctor's office. A hospital had been out of the question under the circumstances, and she was making a fine recovery from her wound here. The damage to her leg would not be permanent. "If Hollins was behind the plot from the start, why'd he agree to let me interview him?"

"Because he didn't plan to tell you anything some good investigative work couldn't have told you anyway. And he was afraid that if he turned you down, you might have dug deeper and come up with something about his link to Krayman Industries he couldn't let be uncovered."

"Makes sense. So it's over then." When Blaine didn't respond, Sandy's face grew concerned. "It *is* over, isn't it?"

"I don't think so," he said finally. "I mean in the minds of Washington it is, and that's the problem. There are hundreds of people out there, maybe thousands, who owe their positions to Krayman Industries. Sahhan's troops are still out there, too, along with the mercenaries. And don't forget the billions of Krayman Chips in place all over the country. So it wouldn't take much for a smart man in the Krayman hierarchy to pick up right where Hollins and Dolorman left off. With a few modifications, the Omega command could still be given."

"Are you telling me the government would allow that to happen with everything they know?"

"They don't know a damn thing. All they have to go on is what I told them from the space shuttle, and I was vague. They can't move because they've got nothing to move on."

"What about Terrell's suggestion to get the names of Krayman Industry plants from the computer on Horse Neck Island?"

"Without the specific access codes, we wouldn't have a chance."

"Then you'll have to go in and tell them everything."

"How far do you think I'd get? Do you think Hollins's people will simply stop gunning for me? I don't. The kill order stands. I trust the President well enough, but that's as far as it goes."

"What if I tried my network, or a different one?"

"Try anything, lady, but don't expect to get very far. We've got no proof, and without it anyone who takes this on camera would look like a damn fool. Besides, you think that boss of yours was the only one in television Krayman Industries had in its pockets?"

"So you're saying Washington will do nothing if left to itself?"

"By doing nothing, they're accomplishing something—saving their asses. The people at the top fear embarrassment more than assassination. They can't risk exposure of how close they came to losing control. It makes them look ineffective, which is just what they are, but so long as the illusion holds up, who's to know? Even if I got by Krayman's people, I'm not sure I'd be able to find anyone in the capital to listen to me. Remember what Terrell said about everything coming down to one group seizing control from a weaker one? Well, if everything about Omega comes out, that might just happen—quite legitimately—on Election Day. They can't take that chance."

"So the bad guys want us dead and the good guys want us quiet," Sandy concluded grimly.

"There are no good guys, just levels of bad."

Sandy raised herself up more. "Then why don't you just walk away from it all, find yourself your own private island in the Caribbean?"

Blaine shook his head. "No, I can't. The job's not finished and if it stays that way, the country just might be. I still believe, Sandy. When you come right down to it, that's all I've got."

They looked at each other for a long moment. Sandy tightened her features. "You could have sent flowers and a card, Blaine, but instead you came in person. This is all leading somewhere, isn't it?"

"Yes, but I'm not sure where myself. All I know is that you're right about exposure being our best, our *only* chance to stay alive and end this for certain."

"But how?"

"I've got this crazy feeling, but before I can pursue it I've got to ask you some questions."

"You gonna tell me what this feeling is?"

"Not until I'm sure. When I am, you'll be the second to know. Let's just say there's only one way to expose Omega irrefutably and only one man who can help us do it. It's a long shot, but it's all we've got."

"Ask away," Sandy told him.


Christmas had brought with it forty-degree temperatures and the beginnings of an early thaw. The boatman had spent his holiday with his whiskey. Between swallows he had started repairs on his battered craft. The island was quiet now, less ominous, sulking in the shadows across the bay like a beaten bully. The boatman was finally alone, which was just the way he wanted it.

The sloshing of shoes through the slush made him poke his head through the opening in the boat's engine compartment. A big, bearded man was approaching, better groomed and less anxious than the last time the boatman had seen him.

"Good afternoon," said McCracken.

"Seems to be," returned the boatman as he climbed back

upon his craft's deck. "If you come to bring me a Christmas present, friend, you're a day late. And if you're after my boat again, you might notice she ain't exactly seaworthy."

"It's not the boat I'm after, it's you."

"Don't think I caught that, friend."

"I think you did . . . Mr. Krayman."

The boatman's face lost all its color. He pulled his frame to the dock and sat down on the edge.

"How'd you know?" was all he said.

"I didn't. At least, I wasn't sure. But I did a little research on the car crash that supposedly took your life five years ago in New York. Fire made identifying the bodies impossible, and one was actually unaccounted for."

Randall Krayman's gaze grew distant. "They came out in a helicopter to make sure they'd finished the job."

"Dolorman's men?"

"Or Hollins's. It didn't much matter."

"And you hid from them by burying yourself in the snow just like you did two nights ago on the island, correct?"

Krayman nodded.

"That woman with us Christmas Eve was a reporter," Blaine said by way of explanation. "She's been researching you for months. She told me about your brave enlistment in the army and subsequent training in which you learned how to use an M-16. You saved our lives by emptying a clip into Wells's men. That was obviously no fluke."

"Ayuh," acknowledged Krayman softly. "I enjoyed it too."

"Revenge, Mr. Krayman?"

"Justice, friend, something you should know about better than most if I read you right."

"I wasn't criticizing."

"What else did that reporter lady tell you 'bout me?"

"General features like height, the color of your eyes, and, of course, the fact that you were born in Maine. You came back here to hide from them, but you wanted to watch, to monitor their actions. An inlet across from Horse Neck Island couldn't have been a random choice.''

Krayman's blank expression confirmed all of Blaine's words. "At first all I wanted was to stay dead. I thought maybe Dolorman and Hollins had done me a favor. I didn't know about Hollins at first, but I had my suspicions and over the years, well, I had plenty of time to figure everything out. Thing of it was, here I sat with everything behind me. . . ." Suddenly his eyes sharpened. "But I couldn't let go, friend, not then.''

"And what about now?''

"You want me to go back to civilization with you?''

Blaine nodded. "You're the only man who can expose Omega's existence once and for all and begin the process of destroying its remnants. You're the only man no one can argue with on the subject . . . since the operation was yours originally.''

"Not the way Dolorman and Hollins envisioned it. I realized that in time. But they decided to get me out of the way 'fore I could do anything about it.''

"Dolorman's dead. Hollins too.''

"So am I, friend, and that's still the way I want to keep it. Don't you think I coulda gone back and told the world the truth if I'd wanted? Well, I didn't. I just wanted to stay dead. I'd had enough.'' A pause. "I still have.''

"I'm not going to argue the merits of society with you, Mr. Krayman. I've seen enough to know that your position is justified. But speaking of the world, it would be a hell of a lot worse off with Omega still threatening it.''

"Do you really believe that, friend?''

"Absolutely. The world's not perfect and neither is the country. As a matter of fact, lots of it stinks. But we can't let the Dolormans and the Hollinses feed off the rot.''

"I guess you'll expose me if I don't turn myself in,'' Krayman said, scratching at his beard stubble.

Blaine shook his head. "No, Mr. Krayman, the decision's yours. You saved my life and I owe you for that.''

"Lord in heaven, an honorable man. . . . Where were you fifteen years ago?''

"Killing people somewhere in Indochina. Things haven't changed much since."

"No," Krayman said reflectively, "I suppose they haven't. You've been fighting a lot of wars, friend."

"No, just one big one. A lot of people say it's futile. I say, what isn't? The world's a lousy place by nature, but things tend to get even worse when men like Hollins gain control. It's out there for them to grab and there aren't many of us left to keep their fingers off it."

Randall Krayman slapped his thighs and stood up. He gazed at the sun, treating his leathery flesh to its warmth.

"You got a car, friend?"

"Gassed up and ready."

"You think I oughta shave?"

McCracken shook his head slowly. "The stubble becomes you."

"Well," said Randall Krayman, "just give me a few minutes to pack my things." Then, with his stare fixed on nothing in particular, "I don't suppose I'll be coming back here again." They started walking toward the shack. The snow on the roof was beginning to melt. "Tell me, friend, what have I missed these past five years?"

"Not much," Blaine smiled, "not much at all."

# About the Author

Jon Land, twenty-nine, is the author of four previous novels: THE DOOMSDAY SPIRAL, THE LUCIFER DIRECTIVE, VORTEX, and LABYRINTH. He lives in Providence, Rhode Island, where he is currently at work on his next book.

# Chilling Thrillers!

## FAWCETT FICTION BY
# DAVID MORRELL